Also by Julia Brannan

The Jacobite Chronicles

Book Two: The Mask Revealed

Book Three: The Gathering Storm

Book Four: The Storm Breaks

Book Five: Pursuit of Princes (Summer 2017)

CONTEMPORARY FICTION

A Seventy-Five Percent Solution (Early 2017)

Mask of Duplicity

The Jacobite Chronicles,
Book One

Julia Brannan

DISCLAIMER

This novel is a work of fiction, and except in the case of historical fact, any resemblance to actual persons, living or dead, is purely coincidental

Formatting by Polgarus Studio

Cover by Quirky Bird. http://quirky-bird.com

In memory of Lynette Evans, a wonderful friend and an inspiration. I miss you very much.

ACKNOWLEDGEMENTS

First of all, I would like to thank my good friend Mary Brady, who painstakingly read and reread every chapter as I wrote, spending hours on the phone with me, giving me encouragement, and valuable suggestions as to how to improve the book. I owe her an enormous debt of gratitude.

I also want to thank my wonderful and talented partner Jason Gardiner, who put up with me living in the eighteenth century for over two years while I wrote the first four books in the series, and listened to me while I rambled on incessantly about fascinating historical facts that no one else cared about. You are lovely!

Thanks also to all the friends who have read my books and encouraged me to publish them, including Alyson Cairns and Mandy Condon, who has already determined the cast list for the film of the books, and to the other successful authors who have so generously given me their time, advice and encouragement, including Kym Grosso, N M Silber, Ellena Jennings, MJ Harty and Michelle Gent.

Thanks also have to go to the long-suffering staff of Ystradgynlais library, who hunted down obscure research books for me, and put up with my endless requests for strange information.

If I've forgotten anyone, please remind me and I will grovel and apologise profusely, and include you in the acknowledgements in my next book!

HISTORICAL BACKGROUND NOTE

Although this series starts in 1742 and deals with the Jacobite Rebellion of 1745, the events that culminated in this uprising started a long time before, in 1685, in fact. This was when King Charles II died without leaving an heir, and the throne passed to his Roman Catholic younger brother James, who then became James II of England and Wales, and VII of Scotland. His attempts to promote toleration of Roman Catholics and Presbyterians did not meet with approval from the Anglican establishment, but he was generally tolerated because he was in his 50s, and his daughters, who would succeed him, were committed Protestants. But in 1688 James' second wife gave birth to a son, also named James, who was christened Roman Catholic. It now seemed certain that Catholics would return to the throne long-term, which was anathema to Protestants.

Consequently James' daughter Mary and her husband William of Orange were invited to jointly rule in James' place, and James was deposed, finally leaving for France in 1689. However, many Catholics, Episcopalians and Tory royalists still considered James to be the legitimate monarch.

The first Jacobite rebellion, led by Viscount Dundee in April 1689, routed King William's force at the Battle of Killikrankie, but unfortunately Dundee himself was killed, leaving the Jacobite forces leaderless, and in May 1690 they suffered a heavy defeat. King William offered all the Highland clans a pardon if they would take an oath of allegiance in front of a magistrate before 1st January 1692. Due to the weather and a general reluctance, some clans failed to make it to the places appointed for the oath to be taken, resulting in the infamous Glencoe Massacre of Clan MacDonald in February 1692. By spring all the clans had taken the oath, and it seemed that the Stuart cause was dead.

However, a series of economic and political disasters by William and his government left many people dissatisfied with his reign, and a number of these flocked to the Jacobite cause. In

1707, the Act of Union between Scotland and England, one of the intentions of which was to put an end to hopes of a Stuart restoration to the throne, was deeply unpopular with most Scots, as it delivered no benefits to the majority of the Scottish population.

Following the deaths of William and Mary, Mary's sister Anne became Queen, dying without leaving an heir in 1714, after which George I of Hanover took the throne. This raised the question of the succession again, and in 1715 a number of Scottish nobles and Tories took up arms against the Hanoverian monarch.

The rebellion was led by the Earl of Mar, but he was not a great military leader and the Jacobite army suffered a series of defeats, finally disbanding completely when six thousand Dutch troops landed in support of Hanover. Following this, the Highlands of Scotland were garrisoned and hundreds of miles of new roads were built, in an attempt to thwart any further risings in favour of the Stuarts.

By the early 1740s, this operation was scaled back when it seemed unlikely that the aging James Stuart, 'the Old Pretender,' would spearhead another attempt to take the throne. However, the hopes of those who wanted to dissolve the Union and return the Stuarts to their rightful place were centring not on James, but on his young, handsome and charismatic son Charles Edward Stuart, as yet something of an unknown quantity.

STUART/HANOVER FAMILY TREE

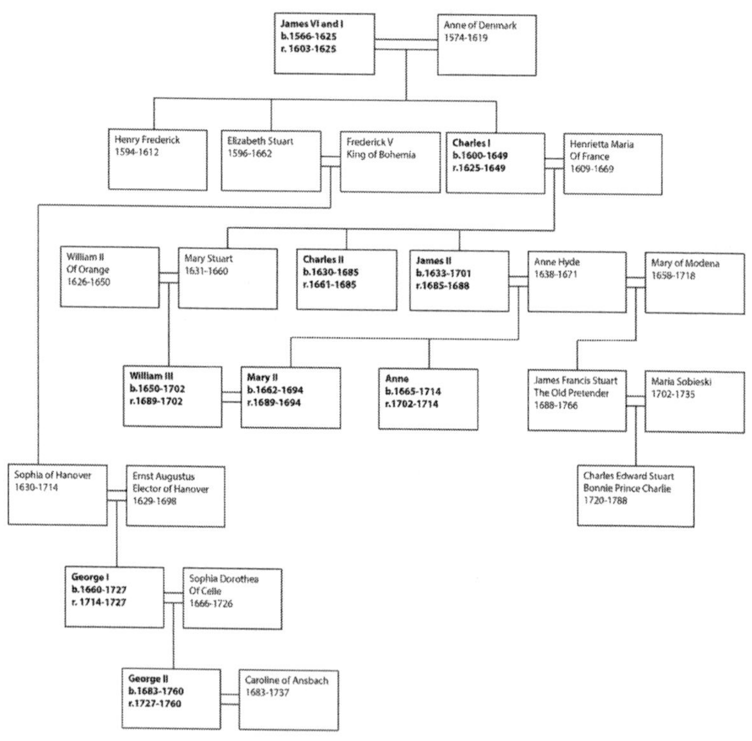

LIST OF CHARACTERS

Elizabeth (Beth) Cunningham, a young lady, recently orphaned.
Richard Cunningham, Beth's brother, a sergeant in the dragoons.
John Betts, Beth's stable boy.
Thomas Fletcher, Beth's steward.
Jane Fletcher, wife to Thomas, and Beth's cook.
Graeme Elliot, Beth's gardener.
Ben, a young servant to Beth.
Edward Cox, Beth's solicitor.
Martha Smith, Beth's maid.
Anne Smith, Martha's daughter.
Grace Miller, lady's maid to Beth.
Mary Williamson, a childhood friend of Beth's.
Sarah Browne, a maid hired by Richard.
Mary Swales, Beth's scullery maid.

Lord Edward Cunningham, cousin to Beth and Richard
Isabella Cunningham, eldest sister of Lord Edward.
Clarissa Cunningham, middle sister of Lord Edward.
Charlotte Stanton, a widow and youngest sister of Lord Edward.
Samuel, footman to Lord Edward.
Tom, coachman to Lord Edward.

Sir Anthony Peters, a gentleman of fashion.
John, coachman to Sir Anthony.
Edwin Harlow, a member of Parliament, and friend of Sir Anthony.
Caroline Harlow, Edwin's wife.

Alexander (Alex) MacGregor, a Highlander.
Duncan MacGregor, a Highlander, brother to Alex.
Angus MacGregor, a Highlander, youngest brother of Alex and Duncan.
Jack Holker, an English Jacobite.
Dougal MacGregor, a Highlander, clansman to Alex.

Jamie MacGregor, a Highlander, clansman to Alex.
Iain Gordon, a Highlander, clansman to Alex.

Lord Daniel Barrington, a young nobleman.
Joshua White, a smuggler.
Gabriel Foley, leader of a smuggling gang.
Lord Bartholomew Winter.
Lady Wilhelmina Winter, his wife.
Anne Maynard, an impoverished relative of Lord Winter.
Lydia Fortesque, a young lady.
Jeremiah Johnson, a puritanical gentleman.
King George II, King of Great Britain and Ireland, Elector of Hanover.
Prince William Augustus, Duke of Cumberland, second son of King George.

Prologue

Scotland, September 1741

The young Highlander strolled aimlessly across the plateau, his feet negotiating the uneven terrain automatically, his mind totally occupied with the new life he was about to embark on. He was a tall, well-proportioned young man with the muscular build of the accomplished warrior and the light, graceful walk of one accustomed to moving silently and stealthily through nature, by day or night.

He was not, however, accustomed to the life he was about to embrace, and had no wish to be. In fact, he dreaded it. Idly, he wondered how long he might survive. Not long, probably, when the slightest error could cost him his life. But then, that had always been the case, for him and all who shared his surname. In the past the rewards had never consisted of any more than a full belly and a safe place to sleep for a few days, or weeks. Now, though, although the risk was greater, and the dangers very different to any he had faced in his life up to now, the rewards, if he was successful, would be enormous. Even so, he was finding it extremely difficult to maintain a southerly direction, his heart already yearning for home. The knowledge that unless he was very careful he might never see it again, weighed heavily on him. That was why he had taken the opportunity to be alone for a short time, to say farewell to his beloved country. His brothers understood and had gone on ahead, knowing he would catch them up when he was ready.

Totally absorbed in his own gloomy thoughts, he only became aware of the group of soldiers as they appeared over the ridge ahead of him, whereas if he'd been on full alert as he should have been, he would have heard their approach long before they came within sight. He froze instantly, made a lightning assessment of his options, and then dropped like a stone to the ground. He wriggled along carefully on his belly, coming to rest finally in a waterlogged depression in the soil, surrounded by a thick patch of heather. He was dressed in kilt and plaid in shades of green and brown, which blended well with his surroundings, and his hair was dark, which was a blessing. Quickly he splashed the muddy water over his bare legs in an attempt to camouflage them, and then the men were upon him and he froze in place, aware that his hiding place was far from ideal, and that any more than a cursory examination of the territory would reveal him. Any other passing Highlander would have seen him immediately. But the men who were now within feet of him were not Highlanders, not even Scots, but English redcoat soldiers of King George's army, unused to the Scottish terrain and the ways of its indigenous people.

The young man knew that even though his right hand was still in plain view to anyone who cared to look down, any movement he made at this point would attract the notice of even an untrained eye, so he left it where it was, nestling in a clump of heather. His heart was banging hard against his ribs, but he forced his breathing to slow, his chest hardly moving.

The redcoats were chatting as they approached, clearly in high good humour. There were four, no, five distinct voices. Too many for him to take on, fully armed as they would be, unless he was discovered, in which case he would run, or kill as many as he could before they finished him off.

"Bloody hell, how anyone can live in this godforsaken hole is beyond me," one man was saying. "The sooner we're called back to England the better."

"We'll be lucky if we're recalled before spring, now," came a younger, higher-pitched voice. "We'll be at Inversnaid till April at least, unless the Frenchies attack."

"No chance of that, not this year," replied the first man. They were right next to him now, no more than two feet from where he was lying, and had paused for a moment. Why had they stopped? There was nothing here to divert them; the top of the hill where they were consisted of a fairly level stretch of uninteresting scrub, followed by a reasonably steep descent to the valley below. The hill was not even high enough for there to be an interesting view from the top. Perhaps they had seen him. He felt the adrenaline roar through his blood, listened for the sound of swords being drawn, felt his body tense ready for action.

"There's still some fun to be had, though," another voice said. This man was older, with the flat vowels of the northern Englishman. "Less chance of getting the pox than with the city whores, too." The tone was relaxed. They had still not noticed him, then.

The feet moved closer, a pair of muddy black leather boots coming into the view of the hidden man, whose face was turned slightly to the side.

"I still think we should have buried her, though, afterwards," said the young soldier.

"Why? Do you think her ghost'll come back to haunt you?" the older man teased.

"No, course not, it's just...well, it seemed wrong to just leave her there, for the animals and crows to have a go at."

"Suffering from a guilty conscience now, are you? Still took your turn, though," another voice said, laughing. Six of them, then, at least. "I'm sure her husband'll find her when he gets back from whatever thieving he was up to. He'll bury her. Save us the trouble."

"Are you coming, then, or are you staying to admire the scenery all day?" the first man said.

The other voices were receding, but the northerner was still standing next to the prostrate Highlander. He spoke again now.

"No, I need a piss. You go on, I'll catch up in a minute." The soldier stepped forward, onto the hidden man's hand, the heel of his boot grinding into the fingers. The Scot caught his breath, commanded his brain to ignore the excruciating pain, forced his body to remain still. He listened, hard. The other men were moving on, eastwards, their voices growing fainter. In less than a minute they would be negotiating the descent, out of sight of the man now fumbling with his breeches. He was clearly having some trouble. Was he drunk? His voice had been steady enough, but that did not necessarily signify much, if he was a regular tippler.

After a time there came the sound of water pattering on the earth, and then the Scot felt the stream of urine hit his back, soaking warmly through his plaid and shirt, in contrast to the icy water beneath him. He gritted his teeth and counted silently and slowly to thirty. The soldiers' voices could not be heard at all now. Enough time had passed for them to be well out of sight.

The soldier grunted, and although he could still see no more than the black leather boots, the young man knew the redcoat was shaking the last drops of urine off before tucking himself away. As he started to button his fly, he took a step back, releasing the Highlander's hand. That was the moment he had been waiting for.

Exploding from the heather and drawing his dirk left-handed as he rose, he drove the razor-sharp blade up under the redcoat's chin, through his tongue and on into his brain. The force of his attack carried them both over onto the grass and as they hit the ground the Scotsman felt the tip of his dirk strike the inside of the man's skull. The redcoat, although mortally wounded and unable to cry out for help, was not yet dead and flailed weakly at the attacker now straddling him, his hands pushing against the big man's chest. The Highlander twisted the blade viciously, watching with satisfaction as the soldier's eyes widened, then slowly glazed over. Carefully he withdrew the dirk, wiping it on the scarlet coat before sheathing it. He rose to his feet, looking around him, preparing to flee if the others doubled back, but there was no sound other than the wind murmuring gently through the heather and sparse grass. With his foot, he rolled the body roughly into the depression from which he had just so spectacularly materialised, and then cleared his throat, spitting accurately and copiously onto the corpse's back.

"Ye'll no' be murdering any more women, ye bastard," he said softly.

He examined his injured right hand, watching the scar that bisected the back of it from wrist to knuckle writhe snakelike as he flexed his fingers. Nothing broken, only bruises, although it hurt like hell.

He splashed some mud over the bright coat of the soldier, and then began to move rapidly southward, where his brothers would be waiting for him. In a while the redcoat's companions would come looking for the northerner no doubt, but the Highlander would be well away by then. His nose wrinkled in disgust at the acrid smell of urine emanating from him. He would rinse his shirt and plaid in the river before rejoining his brothers. He'd never live it down if they found out he'd been pissed on by a redcoat. He grinned to himself, then jogged south across the plateau and down the rocky slope, his long legs eating up the distance effortlessly.

By the time he neared his companions, he'd changed his mind, decided to tell them what had happened after all. He could take a joke, and they needed cheering up. They had no more desire than he did to undertake this new venture. Its failure would result in torture and the worst death imaginable. But its success would result in the freedom, after a hundred and forty years, for his clan to use their own name again, and for him to legally carry the weapon he had just employed so effectively. Their stolen lands would be restored to them, and they would no longer be known as 'Children of the Mist,' an appellation that sounded romantic, but was only really another term for outlaw. Yes, the risk was worth taking. Well worth it.

He waved to his brothers as he came in sight of them, and paused for a moment, turning his face eastward, towards France and Italy, where lay salvation.

He would come, with an army, when the time was right. Until then, all the Highlander could do was use his particular and remarkable skills to the best effect, and then, once fully prepared, be patient, and wait.

For a man of action, waiting would be the hardest part. The rest would be easy, by comparison. At least, that was what he prayed.

Chapter One

Didsbury, near Manchester, October 1742

The stables were immaculate. Fresh straw had been laid, and the soiled straw was in a neat pile outside. The two people responsible for this order were now engaged in friendly dispute. The young woman held the bridle of a black mare loosely in one hand, and absently stroked the horse's long nose with the other. The young man, who was really hardly more than a boy, thin and coltish, but with the promise of bulk to come in his wide shoulders, stood at the stable door, peering up dubiously at the cloud-covered sky with troubled brown eyes.

"I don't think it's such a good idea," he observed sensibly. "It looks like rain."

The young woman was in no mood to hear sense, however, and letting go of the bridle, moved across to stand beside him in the doorway.

"Nonsense!" she snorted. She had just spent two hours mucking out the stables, and now she wanted a little fun, by way of a reward. "Come on, John, let yourself go for once. It's not as though there's anyone here to see, after all."

There was a fair on in the nearby town of Manchester, and all the servants had been allowed the day off to go to it. Only John, who preferred the company of animals to people, and detested crowds, had opted to stay, along with Beth, who hated dressing formally and relished the rare peace of being alone in the house. She had spent the morning slouching around in a dressing gown reading a book, and then, finally tired of sitting still, had gone to help John at his work.

"Besides," she added persuasively, "there isn't another person in the county who can ride as well as you – except for me, of course. Go on, just up to the top field and back. We'll only be half an hour at the most. It won't rain in that time."

"You want to race cross-country? Bareback? No, it's too dangerous, Beth."

"Oh, pooh!" she replied. "Riding bareback is more interesting. Besides, by the time we've saddled the horses up, it probably *will* be raining. And where's the fun in racing along the road? And if I'm going to fall off – which I won't," she added, blithely tempting fate, "I'd rather do it on soft grass than on the hard roadway. Anyway, there's more chance of someone seeing us if we're on the road rather than in the fields." She impatiently brushed a tendril of yellow hair off her face, tucking it back under her kerchief, and inadvertently leaving a streak of dirt on her forehead, transferred from her none-too-clean hands.

"I don't know…" John's voice was still uncertain, but she detected the wavering in it and pounced.

"Very well, if you won't come with me, I'll go on my own, although it'll hardly be a race then."

That decided him, and two minutes later they galloped out of the yard, Beth astride the black, and John on a chestnut gelding. Once mounted, he lost all his inhibitions, and they charged across the field side by side as though all the devils of hell were after them, their shouts of youthful laughter carried back on the sudden breeze, heavy with the scent of the rain soon to come.

* * *

The man cantered along the lane, turning left into the cobbled driveway and gradually slowing as the house came into view through the trees, until by the time he arrived in front of it his horse was travelling at no more than a sedate walk. He came to a halt and looked up at the house with a mixture of eagerness and apprehension. It was much as he remembered it; a compact three-storey red brick Palladian cube, with square-paned sash windows. Two stone columns flanked the front door, which was reached by mounting four stone steps. Although small, it was still impressive, except that now the whole effect was somewhat dilapidated, as if reflecting the gradual decline of its previous owner's health and fortune. One of the small panes of glass in an upstairs window was broken and had not been replaced, he noticed; instead the hole had been patched with a piece of wood. The green paint on the front door was flaking, as was the cream paint on the window frames, and grass was growing between the cobbles of the drive in places.

The man's forehead creased with impatience. He had expected that someone would come out immediately to find out who this stranger was, but there was no sign of any interest from the occupants. He was reluctant to dismount at this stage. He knew what a fine figure he cut when mounted and in the splendid uniform of his dragoon regiment. His scarlet coat with its decoration of white lace at lapel, sleeves and pockets was a bright splash of colour against the greys and browns of the dull English day, and his black boots were polished to a mirrored shine below immaculate buff breeches. He was of athletic build, although his legs bowed slightly, and he was only of average height. But these deficiencies were not apparent when he was astride a horse.

"Hallo, the house!" he called, hoping that someone would now appear and call out the rest of the household to view this fine stranger astride the magnificent grey stallion. From his elevated position he could then identify himself as the master of the house, come to claim his inheritance.

No response came from the building.

Surely the whole household could not be out, even if the mistress was not at home? He rode around the side of the house. Perhaps the servants were all at the back. He remembered that the kitchen and laundry were in an annexe built on to the back, and it was possible they had not heard him call out. His attention was caught by the open door of the stable, which was moving slightly in the wind. Surely no one would go out for the day without closing the door behind them? The stable was clean but bare; clearly the mistress was not at home. The man was disappointed at the failure of his plan for a grand entrance. Nevertheless, he would get some satisfaction out of rousing the obviously lazy servants from their stupor, and by the time the lady of the house returned he would be well ensconced in his new position as master.

He had just released his feet from the stirrups, preparing to dismount, when the two riders tore into the yard, the woman slightly ahead of the man, and looking back as she skidded to a halt with a most unfeminine yodel of triumph at her victory. Although John rode in behind her, he was the first to see the stranger, who was now struggling to bring his startled horse under control without the aid of stirrups. By the time he had done, he was incensed.

He glared at the young woman, who was still mounted and was watching him through cornflower-blue eyes whose expression registered a mixture of curiosity and amusement at his undignified efforts. Even through his anger he could not fail to recognise that she was beautiful. His eyes travelled up her body, taking in her small feet, her well-shaped legs, exposed almost to the knee due to her position astride the horse, and her delicate, slender figure. Her kerchief had disappeared somewhere in the fields and her hair hung in untidy straggles around her face, but nevertheless it was the most beautiful shade of pale gold.

Yes, he thought appreciatively, *she will be well worth a tumble later.*

However, at the moment he had his dignity to preserve, and this strumpet was eyeing him as though she were his equal.

"I presume your mount belongs to the mistress of the house. Am I correct?" he said imperiously.

"Yes, you are," replied the young woman, clearly unabashed.

"And where is the rest of the household?"

"They have all been given the day off, to attend the fair in Manchester," she answered coolly. A suspicion was forming in her brain as to the identity of the visitor, but she did not say anything. Depending on the purpose of his visit, it could be better not to identify herself as yet.

"And do you," the dragoon said, his eyes flickering briefly to the boy hovering uncertainly in the background, then back to lock on the woman, "think that lady would countenance what I presume to be her scullery maid haring around the countryside on her horse, in a state of the most improper undress?" His voice rose as he spoke, and ended almost on a squeak.

She knew without doubt who he was now. Ever since his voice had broken at the age of twelve he had been unable to control its pitch when he was in a temper.

"No, I am sure Miss Elizabeth would be extremely angry if she were to find out that the scullery maid had been riding her horse," Beth replied, trying to sound humble and afraid. She would indeed be angry; the scullery maid was ten years old and had never been on a horse in her life.

The soldier now realised that he had this lovely girl under his power, which would render her suitably compliant to his wishes that evening.

"Well, we will speak of this later. But now you will conduct me to your mistress, if she is at home." He would leave her to stew for a while. Later she would certainly be willing to do anything he wished, to avoid being dismissed or beaten. Maybe he would beat her anyway. He smiled in anticipation, but Beth, who was dismounting smoothly, didn't see.

"If you will follow me, I will show you to the drawing room, and tell Miss Elizabeth you are here," she said, her voice shaking slightly with repressed laughter, which she hoped he would interpret as fear.

He dismounted, and handing the reins to John, followed Beth round to the front of the house. The front door was unlocked, and opened onto a narrow wood-panelled hall, which ran the length of the house and which opened out two-thirds of the way down to accommodate a carved wooden staircase. Several doors led off the hall to the ground floor rooms, and it was to the second of these that she now led him, opening the door onto a comfortably furnished, if somewhat old-fashioned room, two of whose walls were lined from floor to ceiling with shelves of books. A coal fire burned in the grate, and a chair was drawn up to it. A volume lay open on a small table next to the chair. Clearly the mistress had been relaxing here earlier in the day, he thought.

"May I tell Miss Elizabeth who is calling?" she said softly, eyes downcast so he wouldn't see the merriment in them.

"You may tell her that her brother Sergeant Richard Cunningham, of his Majesty's Dragoons has come home, and it seems, not before time," he said imperiously.

She bobbed a little curtsey and left the room, closing the door quietly behind her, before tearing up the stairs as fast as she could.

Fifteen minutes later a young lady walked gracefully down the stairs, dressed in a pale blue satin dress, its voluminous skirts draped over a hooped petticoat to form a bell shape. Her elbow-length sleeves ended in frills of lace. She had washed her hands and face and brushed her hair back, securing it with a ribbon. More than that she could not achieve without a lot more time. The main thing, Beth thought as she smoothed her skirts outside the library door, was to be presentable and as Richard would expect the lady of a small country house to look.

She opened the door and sailed in.

He was standing by the hearth, his hands clasped behind his back, examining a picture of their father, painted several years ago. The similarity between the portrait and the man standing beneath it was remarkable. In looks if not in temperament he was his father's son to a T; just as Beth was her mother's daughter.

"Good afternoon, Richard," she said politely, and he turned to look at her.

She watched with amusement as his face first drained of colour and then flushed to a deep unbecoming red as he realised that he had been made a fool of.

"Ah…I…em…" he stuttered. She decided to be merciful and give him a chance to compose himself.

"It is wonderful to see you, Richard," she said, wondering if it was, "although you really should have written in advance to tell me you were coming. I would have had everything prepared for you. As it is, I cannot even send for refreshments, although if we go over to the kitchen I am sure there will be something cold in the larder. As I said, everyone is in town and I do not expect them back for at least a couple of hours." His colour had faded back to its normal sallow shade now, so she stopped talking.

"That was most unfair of you, Beth, to play such a trick on me," he said grumpily, a frown creasing his brow. "You have made me look ridiculous. And in front of the stable boy, too. I assume he *is* the stable boy, and not some visiting dignitary?"

In anyone else this last statement would have shown that the victim had seen the humour in the joke, but Richard's tone was formal, and she realised with a sigh that the young boy she had last seen when he was sixteen might have grown up, but he had not learned to take himself any less seriously.

"Yes, John is the stable-boy," she answered. "I'm sorry, I had no intention of making you look ridiculous." *You did that by yourself, with your pompous manner,* she thought. "But when I realised you hadn't recognised me, I couldn't resist playing a little joke. Forgive me," she added, going for the conciliatory approach. "Let's start again. Shall I run down to the kitchen and see what I can find to eat? I'm sure you must be hungry."

He agreed, but by the time she returned, carefully balancing several plates of cold meat and cakes in her hands, his mood had not improved; one glance at his face told her that.

"Here we are," she said gaily, ignoring his brooding look and setting the plates on the table. "There's a bottle of claret in the cupboard here." She bustled about gathering all the necessary things together, before throwing herself down in a chair, careless of her fine satin dress. He sat down more carefully opposite her and helped himself to a glass of wine.

"I've been expecting you to come for three months," she said. "Didn't you receive my letter?"

"Yes, I did," he said. "It reached me too late for Father's funeral, but I did receive it eventually. I couldn't take leave from my regiment at that time, though. We have gone into barracks for the winter now. This was the first chance I have had to come."

"I see," Beth replied thoughtfully. "Have you been in the Low Countries then?" The war of the Austrian succession had broken out the previous year and many European countries were becoming involved, including England's traditional enemy, France. A large force of British troops, amongst others, had been sent abroad and was now awaiting action. If Richard had been amongst them, it was quite understandable that he would not have been able to get leave, although he should at least have been able to write, which he had also not done. However, if he had been stationed in England all that time, she thought it unlikely that any commander would deny a soldier bereavement leave.

"No," Richard answered, confirming Beth's suspicions that he had stayed away voluntarily. "But I am here now, and I see there is a lot to be done. You have let things slip, Beth. The house is not in a fit state to receive visitors."

Beth's conciliatory mood evaporated instantly.

"Have you read Father's will?" she asked.

Richard nodded, and opened his mouth, but Beth continued before he could speak.

"Then you will know that he left everything to you, except for the sum he set aside for my dowry, which is considerable, I admit, but also inaccessible unless I marry or reach the age of thirty, neither of which I have yet done. Father was ill for some years before he died," she explained, her voice catching a little, "and he was not able to keep up with repairs."

"I didn't know that," Richard said testily.

"No, well, you wouldn't, would you? You have had no contact with the family at all since you disappeared into thin air thirteen years ago. The only reason we knew you were in the army was because Sam the farrier saw you and told us. Mother and Father were beside themselves with worry until then. They thought you'd been murdered or had met with a terrible accident. You could at least have let them know you were safe. You must have known how distressed they'd be."

"How would I know that?" Richard replied hotly. "Father never took any notice of me at all after he married your mother. How long was it before he noticed I'd actually left?"

"Of course he took notice of you!" she said. "He loved you. You were his son."

"I might have been his son, but he never loved me. Not after the lovely Ann came into his life. All he could see after that was her. You weren't there, you don't know what it was like. And after you were born, the only time he spoke to me at all was to tell me why he was about to beat me!" The venom and distress in his voice shocked Beth out of her temper. Was that really the way he'd seen their father?

"I was nine when you left, Richard," she replied quietly. "I remember a lot of things. I remember Mother always tried to be nice to you. You wouldn't let her love you."

"She wasn't *my* mother. *My* mother loved me. And until she died, I thought he loved me too. But I was wrong. He never loved me, he hated me, just like he hated Mama." Richard's voice was harsh and petulant, and she was reminded again of the saturnine young boy who had skulked in corners with a permanent frown on his face. She had caught him by the pond once, when she was no more than five years old, pulling the legs off a frog, smiling cruelly as it struggled feebly in his grip. She had crept away quietly before he had seen her. After that she had been a little afraid of him and had kept out of his way as much as possible. Father had seemed to beat him a lot, that was true, but never without good cause. He was always naughty. Beth had been relieved when he left.

She looked across at the man sitting opposite her. Pain was etched on his face, and his eyes were deep pools of despair. Clearly he was also reliving some distressing event from the past. She had never realised how rejected he had felt. In her memory it had been him doing the rejecting. Richard had never accepted his father's second wife, Beth's mother, in spite of all her attempts to reconcile him to the marriage.

Richard saw the sympathy in Beth's face and froze. His face closed, his mouth became a thin hard line, and he looked at her with open dislike. God, she looked exactly like that beautiful slut who had stolen his father's love. How could he not have recognised her in the yard earlier?

"Anyway, that's all in the past, and over," he said, his tone telling her that it wasn't over at all. "But the house is in need of some work before we can accept visitors."

"We never have any visitors," Beth replied practically, welcoming the change of subject; the previous one had been far too deep for a first meeting after thirteen years.

"You mean you are never invited to call at any of the local houses?" Richard sounded incredulous. Clearly his memory of the past was not perfect, then.

"No, Richard. You must remember that after Father married Mot…my mother, the family rejected him." The well-to-do Cunninghams had been appalled that a member of their noble family should stoop so low as to marry a penniless Scottish seamstress, and had virtually cut him off from their society. Initially upset, he had soon resigned himself to his eldest brother Lord William's rejection, and had retired to the country to live happily with the woman he loved.

"Yes, but she died years ago," Richard countered. "Do you mean to say that they still aren't speaking to you?" He was worried. He was banking on using his family connections, coupled with his inheritance, to achieve promotion and launch himself into society. If they still held a grudge, it would be a serious blow to his ambitions.

Beth sighed. This conversation was a far cry from the joyous reunion she had envisaged, where they caught up with events, brought together by their shared loss of a father, regaling each other with tales of the lost years. Instead of which they had not yet exchanged two truly civil words.

"It's true that after Mother died some of them did contact him. I remember going with father to see Cousin Edward once, about four years ago. It didn't work out very well." Her brow furrowed as she remembered sitting stiffly on the edge of her seat in a hideously uncomfortable formal gown. The conversation had dried up after ten minutes, becoming increasingly stilted, and she had sat politely, listening to the pendulum of the drawing-room clock tick away the silent minutes until they could leave. They had not returned, nor had they been invited to while her father was alive. "Cousin Isabella came to Father's funeral," Beth added. "She apologised for Lord Edward, who was out of the country, it seems. Anyway, she said I could go to visit them any time I wanted."

"And did you?" Richard asked.

"No. I never wanted to. I have nothing in common with them, Richard. I enjoy the simple country life."

"Nonsense." The imperious tone returned. "We will write to them at once and tell them we would be delighted to call. Of course we must make the necessary repairs to the house so that we can return the invitation."

"Do you have the money?" she asked.

Richard looked perplexed. "Surely there is money in the accounts?" he said. "Father had a lot of investments."

"That was thirteen years ago, Richard," Beth pointed out patiently. "As I told you earlier, after Mother died, Father became ill and didn't have the energy to manage his investments properly. We're only just making ends meet. There is a little in Father's bank account, but only you can access that. Otherwise he owned the house and all the furniture outright. He left no debt, but he left no great amount of money either."

Richard clearly did not believe her.

"I haven't been able to pay the servants since he died three months ago, Richard. That's why I allowed them all to go to Manchester today, as a reward for their loyalty. We certainly can't afford to entertain."

"But I thought…he left such a generous dowry for you… surely he wouldn't have done that unless he had plenty of money?"

"The will was made ten years ago, when he did have enough money to leave me such a dowry. He never got round to changing it." She didn't add that if he had changed it recently, he would most certainly not have left his whole estate to a son who had persistently failed to contact his family. As it was, she was now fully dependent financially on a brother with whom she was already suspecting she would not get on. However, she would try. They had got off on the wrong foot, and she had to admit that was partly her fault. She had forgotten that he had no sense of humour.

"Anyway," she said. "The fact is that we are left in the position where the only decent sum of money available to us cannot be touched unless I marry, and even then it will go to my husband, not me, so it's pretty useless really."

Richard looked like a child who'd just been allowed into the toyshop after years of standing outside, only to find the shelves bare.

"It's not that bad," she continued cheerfully. "You have your career, after all. If you employ someone to look after the investments, or even better, someone who can teach me how to do it, I'll be quite happy where I am. I can keep the house ready for whenever you want to come home, and I don't need much to live on, so I'm sure there will be sufficient extra income from the investment interest for you to enjoy some luxuries. I'm not interested in clothes and jewellery, so you don't need to be worried that I'll fritter your money away if you entrust me with the charge of it. The only luxury I allow myself is books."

This was supposed to be reassuring, Richard realised that. He decided to accept the olive branch his sister was offering, as a delaying tactic. He was a plodder by nature, not liking to make speedy decisions, preferring to weigh up all the possibilities before deciding on a course of action that would be to his advantage. Where possible he would delegate responsibility to others, especially if he could then take the credit for any success, while avoiding the blame for any failure.

He had envisaged coming home to a bereft and helpless sister surrounded by luxury, and had planned to get her out of the way by marrying her off as soon as possible, then buy himself a commission with his father's money and install a housekeeper and steward to maintain the house for when he came home on leave, or wished to entertain his officer friends. He had no intention of letting Beth take control of his business and house, but as he didn't know what he was going to do now, he said nothing.

The return of the excited servants from their day out saved him from having to comment on Beth's proposal. She heard them, and suggested that she go out first to tell them of Richard's arrival and arrange them in a line to be presented formally to him. He agreed to this, and observed discreetly from behind the curtain as Beth went out to meet the staff. He saw with distaste how they crowded round her in a far too familiar way, laughing as they shared their tales of the day's exploits with her. Beth was holding a child in her arms, its grubby face sticky with sweets. *Who did the child belong to?* he thought. Married servants with children usually lived outside the household, somewhere nearby. And what was the mistress of the house doing allowing a grubby urchin to tangle its filthy hands in her hair, laughing as a young dark-haired woman, presumably the mother, came to her rescue? Clearly they had been allowed far too much licence. He also saw that some of the people were giving Beth small presents; a ribbon, a cake, even a book, which she exclaimed over. How could they afford to buy gifts, if they had not been paid? Either his sister was exaggerating the financial situation, or she paid the servants far too much, if they could save enough to buy fripperies after receiving no wages for three months.

As he went out to introduce himself to the staff, his mind was seething with all the new information he had to process. He had made no decision as yet, but one thing was certain. Things would have to change. He was the master now, and soon everyone would know it.

* * *

Richard spent the first couple of days settling in. His luggage arrived, and Beth, in conciliatory mood, moved out of the front bedroom with its view across the lane to the nearby church and village green, helping the maids to prepare it for him. She moved into a slightly smaller bedroom at the back of the house which overlooked the stables and yard, and spent a lot of time cleaning, hanging pictures in an attempt to cover up the faded wallpaper, and generally making it her own. This also gave her an excuse to keep out of her brother's way for a while, which she hoped would have the dual purpose of giving him time to forget the bad start they'd made, and also to become accustomed to his new role as master of the house without her interference.

She only interfered once, and he would never know about that. After she had arranged the servants in a line in the yard on their return from the fair, Richard had stalked out to advise them all peremptorily that he was the master now, that he expected unquestioning obedience from them, and that he would tolerate no impertinence. With that he had marched off, leaving all the staff deeply concerned and not a little hostile. Beth had been aware that he was probably covering up his nerves with brusqueness, and knowing the personalities of her staff, decided to try to smooth his way a little.

To that end she gathered all the servants together in the kitchen for a secret meeting on the first night, after her brother had retired to bed. She then tried to reassure them that Richard's bark was certain to be worse than his bite.

"He's used to dealing with rough soldiers," she said to the sea of sceptical faces. "No doubt they require very strong discipline. He's not accustomed to being the master of a household, and feels it better to appear very firm at first, but I'm confident he will relax once he has established his authority and feels a little more secure. After all, he doesn't know you all as I do, but he'll soon come to appreciate how loyal and trustworthy you all are."

She was not flattering them. They were not a large household, and had diminished along with her father's money, but every one of the servants had been there for years. Some of them, like John Betts the stable boy, had lived in the house since they were small children. They were like a family to her and she loved and valued them all. She was certain that when Richard got to know them he would feel the same way. Beth had seen an inkling of his desperate need to be loved earlier, and had already resolved to do her utmost to make him a full member of this group of people who had kept her sane throughout her father's terrible deterioration into depression and terminal illness.

“Well, I hope you’re right, Beth, but he made a very bad start, and he didn’t look insecure to me,” Thomas Fletcher said. He, along with his wife Jane, the cook, ran the house. As with all of the servants in this eccentric household, he had more than one job. He oversaw the work of the others, but also acted as handyman, and had kept the house in good repair until the master had died and Beth’s small supply of cash had run out. Beth herself acted as housekeeper, ordering food and other essentials and dealing with the very rare disputes that arose.

“No, but then he’s used to wielding authority,” Beth reasoned. “He needs to adjust the way he wields it to suit civilians. I’m sure he will.”

“I’m not so sure,” put in Graeme, the gardener. “I remember him when he was a boy, and he was a nasty piece of work then. It doesn’t seem to me as he’s changed overmuch, except that the master isn’t here any more to give him a good whipping when he oversteps the mark. Begging your pardon, Beth, I know he’s your brother, but none of us missed him when he left. And none of us are particularly happy to see him come back.” There was a general murmur of agreement at his comment.

“I’m not asking you to love him, Graeme, I’m asking you all to give him a chance. Yes, I admit he wasn’t always a nice child, but that was a long time ago. He’s a man now; he’s bound to have changed.”

“‘Give me the child until he is seven, and I shall give you the man,’” quoted Graeme. “His mother ruined him with her mindless devotion. And in all fairness, Beth, your father let her, rather than suffer her hysterical tantrums. Richard was allowed to do whatever he wanted. And all he wanted to do was be vicious and mean. He almost lost me my job through his spite.”

“Oh Graeme, don’t you think you’re being a bit unfair? After all, he was only small when his mother died. He can’t have been that bad,” Beth replied.

“With all due respect, you weren’t born then. He was only six when he got his mother to dismiss me because I caught him trying to hang the cat from the barn door and stopped him. If your father hadn’t finally put his foot down and refused to let me go, I’d not be here now. And there was hell to pay for weeks afterward. You were only young, Tom, but you must remember that, surely?”

"I do. We all had to keep our heads down, the mistress was in such a foul temper," Thomas said.

"After the mistress died, your father did his best to bring the boy into line," Graeme continued. "But it was too late by then. He seemed to delight in causing trouble. Sometimes I used to think he enjoyed being beaten."

Maybe that was it, Beth thought. Maybe he'd been so desperate for attention from his father that even a beating was better than nothing at all.

"Why didn't you tell me this before?" she asked.

"It was a long time ago, and we thought he was gone for good. The subject never came up," Graeme said simply. "But surely you remember what he was like yourself, Beth? After all, you were nine when he left, and he was all but uncontrollable by then."

Beth put her head in her hands. Rather than smooth the way for Richard to take over the house, she seemed to have made things worse. All the servants who had not known Richard as a child now looked more alarmed than they had when she'd called the meeting. She tried again.

"Well, I acknowledge he was probably wild, but he was only sixteen when he left. He's been in the army for thirteen years. I'm sure it's made a man of him, taught him honour and respect. He couldn't have got to be a sergeant otherwise."

"I don't know about that. I've not such a high opinion of the Elector's army myself," said John wryly.

His comment reminded Beth of something else she had to address before the evening was over.

"The fact is," she said practically, "he has come back, and he is the master now, although he's bound to ask my advice. I'm sure I will have influence and I'm hoping to persuade him to let me continue to run the household, which it's customary for the mistress to do. In the meantime all we can do is to make him feel welcome, and put the past behind us. I suggest that you obey all his orders until he's more secure. It will probably be better to be more formal with him than you are with me, call him Sir rather than Richard, that sort of thing. And don't offer him any advice or suggestions as to how things could be done. I welcome them, but I don't think he will – at the moment."

The look on everyone's faces said that they doubted he would ever appreciate servants telling him how things should be done, but they all agreed to give him a chance. John, and Ben, the boy of all work, whose job it was to clean shoes, light fires and fetch water amongst other things, now got up to leave, but Beth stopped them.

"Wait a minute, there's one more thing, which may be obvious to you all, but I need to say it anyway. I think we'll have to stop our weekly discussions about the news, for now."

Everyone moaned in protest. When Beth's father had fallen ill three years before, she had taken to reading the newspapers to him in an attempt to get him to renew his interest in life and current affairs. She had then extended this practice to the servants, and every week an evening was set aside, when Beth would come down to the kitchen with the newspapers and topical issues would be discussed.

Everybody including Beth looked forward to this, she particularly so in the last months of her father's life, when he had refused to leave his bedroom at all and had insisted that the shutters be kept permanently closed. Much as Beth had loved her father, it had been a great relief to escape from the stuffy dark confines of the sickroom to the airy kitchen, with its stone flagged floor and light, whitewashed walls. A fire burned constantly in the wrought iron grate, which was used for cooking and for heating water. Rows of gleaming copper pots and utensils hung on the walls, warmly reflecting the firelight. The room always smelt welcoming, a combination of freshly baked bread, roasting meat, and the delicate fragrance of the bunches of drying herbs which hung from the ceiling.

The servants all assembled here at mealtimes, sitting on benches around the scrubbed wooden table to eat and discuss the events of the day. On Wednesday evenings Beth would eat with them, and once the meal was over and Jane, having finished her work, could sit with them, they would attack the newspapers with relish. Their debates were lively, to say the least. This was partly because Henry Cunningham had given his staff access to an education. They could all read well, and both Thomas and Jane could write a fair hand, too. They had also been encouraged to think for themselves and take an interest in the outside world. Whilst remaining the best of friends, the servants were divided in their political sympathies, reflecting their former master and mistress's loyalties.

Henry Cunningham had come from a staunch Anglican and Hanoverian family, who had thoroughly approved of the exile of the Catholic King James II in 1688, and his replacement by William of Orange, later succeeded by the Elector of Hanover, who became George I. Henry himself had been rather less vigorously approving than his Whiggish older brother Lord William, but had nevertheless supported the Hanoverian succession, as had his first wife, Arabella, Richard's mother. His second wife Ann could not have been more different. They had married for love, not convenience, and Henry had not cared at all that his wife was a dyed-in-the-wool Jacobite, who longed for the return of 'the king over the water,' as the late King James II's son, now James III or the Pretender, depending on where your sympathies lay, was called. Beth had been brought up with a keen interest in politics from an early age, and had loved listening to the discussions between her father and mother, eventually developing her own strong views.

"I'm as sorry as you," Beth said. "I assume Richard's sympathies lie with King George. Until I know how open minded he is, and what he feels about Jacobites, I think we'd better keep our political sympathies to ourselves. I think it'll be better if you stop calling King George 'the Elector,' for a while, John."

"I'll be damned if I'll call him the king!" John growled. Graeme nodded agreement.

"I don't expect you to do that. Don't call him anything at all, just be discreet," Beth suggested.

She looked at the sea of dismayed faces.

"It's not all bad," she said unconvincingly. "Now Richard's here, he'll be able to access the accounts and pay you all what you're owed."

There was no change of expression from the others.

"And if the worst comes to the worst," she said desperately, "he'll have to rejoin his unit in April. How much damage can he do in six months?"

* * *

Judging by the amount he managed to achieve over the next ten days, a great deal, Beth thought sourly as she went down to dinner the following week. She had done her absolute best to welcome him to the house, taking pains to find out what his favourite foods were, ensuring his linen was washed and ironed and his coat brushed. John had been instructed to take special care of Richard's horse, although they could ill afford the extra hay to feed it, and Beth had attended her brother at every meal, asking after his welfare and trying to engage him in conversation, to little avail. He was a taciturn man, and after two evenings of monosyllabic answers to her queries about his adventures during the intervening years since she had last seen him, she had given up and had taken to eating mainly in silence, after a few polite comments, and retiring to the parlour with a book as soon as she had finished her meal.

The only thing approaching a conversation they had had was three days after his arrival, when he had expressed an intention to dismiss John. When she had asked why, he had told her that he found the boy insolent and over-familiar. Beth had informed him patiently that he was used to being treated as part of the family, as were all the servants, but that she was certain he would adjust. When Richard had still seemed inclined to get rid of the stable boy, she had not argued with him, but had pointed out that John single-handedly took care of every aspect of the stables, and also helped out with other heavy chores in the house and garden, when needed. She suggested sweetly that Richard wait until he could find someone else who would take on such a workload for the salary John received, before dismissing him. Richard had not argued, to her surprise, and as far as she was concerned that was the end of the matter.

She had been impressed by her brother's reasonable attitude, and thought it boded well for the future, although he had been no more garrulous since then.

When she entered the room that evening he was poring over some paperwork, the carefully laid dinner service pushed to one side and a candle pulled close to the papers. As she went to her place, he looked up at her, his brow furrowed. He had been to see the solicitor that morning and was still wearing his uniform, although he had removed his wig. His red coat suited his sallow complexion and dark hair, she thought, and was on the point of telling him, hoping he would appreciate the compliment, when to her surprise he spoke to her first.

"We have to find a way to challenge the will, Beth," he said. "There must be something we can do. It's absurd that we should be left in this ridiculous position."

Beth had already discussed this possibility with Edward Cox the solicitor, who was also a family friend. She took her place and sat down.

"Did Mr Cox have any suggestions?" she said.

Richard shook his head. "No, he said the will is watertight, and although he's sure Father would have changed it had he known how badly his investments were performing, the fact is he didn't. So now we're in the ridiculous position of having to live on two hundred a year, while your dowry of twenty thousand pounds is held in trust and accumulating interest at three per cent a year." He swept the papers impatiently to one side, overturning the candle in the process. With a soldier's quick reflex, he caught it as it fell, and a little spilt wax on the tablecloth was the only damage.

"Did you find out how much ready cash we have available at the moment?" Beth queried.

Richard started to retrieve his cutlery and glassware, and looked toward the door impatiently. Martha was late with the soup.

"Yes," he said. "The interest is paid quarterly, and the last quarter's had not been touched, so there was six months' worth of interest in the account."

Beth did a quick mental calculation.

"Well, that's not too bad," she said. "By the time…"

"Damn it to hell, Beth! How can you say it's not bad?!" Richard shouted suddenly, smashing his fist onto the table so hard the cutlery leapt in the air. Beth jumped, and Martha, who had just opened the door and was entering with the soup, almost dropped it. She hovered uncertainly in the doorway, clearly unwilling to approach her master in his current mood. Beth beckoned her in with what she hoped was a reassuring gesture. Neither of them spoke further until the maid had served them both and disappeared, which she did as quickly as possible.

Beth took a spoonful of the thick vegetable broth.

"It really isn't too bad," she ventured again, ignoring her brother's glowering countenance. "Even after we've paid the servants what we owe them, and the butcher…oh and I owe Sam for a new horseshoe as well…we'll still have enough to get by on if we're careful. We've got enough hay for the horses, and plenty of flour, apples and potatoes. Once the pig…" Richard shot her a look of such venom, she stopped mid-sentence.

"You don't understand, do you?" he said slowly, as though speaking to a small child. Beth gritted her teeth, but waited for him to continue. "I am only earning a sergeant's pay. We cannot live any sort of decent lifestyle on what we have. I will never get promotion unless I can buy a commission. Do you really want to live the rest of your life counting every penny?"

Beth was about to say she had spent the last three years doing just that and was quite happy with the life she had, but realised it would probably not be prudent, seeing as he was so clearly not content with his life.

"I don't see what alternative we have, Richard," she said patiently. Normally forthright and honest, she was already getting sick of pussyfooting around her brother. How she was going to cope with six months of this, she had no idea.

The second course arrived. Beth looked at the roast beef and gravy on her plate with distaste. She didn't know how she was going to cope with the new menu for six months either. Richard was an advocate of 'good plain English food', which consisted of roast meat, gravy, a few overcooked vegetables on the side which he usually ignored, and stodgy suet-based puddings. All this was washed down with copious quantities of beer. Before Richard's arrival, Beth had procured a French cookery book and had spent many a happy hour in the kitchen with Jane, translating the recipes and experimenting with different ingredients to create unusual dishes that were often delicious and at the very least varied.

She pushed the food around her plate with her fork. Richard was building up to saying something, so she kept quiet. At least it would be a change for him to fill the silence instead of her.

"There is an alternative," he said at last, round a mouthful of beef. He swallowed, and took a swig of beer. "We can write to our cousins and renew our acquaintance with them."

"We don't have an acquaintance with them to renew," Beth pointed out. "You haven't seen them since you were a small child, and I had one dreadful afternoon there years ago. That hardly constitutes an acquaintance. They disowned us, Richard. I'm not going begging to them now."

"Lord Edward didn't disown us, it was his father who did that," Richard retorted. "And even he didn't disown *us*. It was your mother he really objected to. It's about time we put the past behind us."

"If you want to put the past behind you, go ahead," Beth answered, still in a reasonable tone. "I have no intention of doing so. Uncle William hurt Mama dreadfully with his pompous condescending attitude, and from what I saw of his son on my brief visit, he's an exact copy of his father."

Richard stared at his sister in exasperation. He had thought about this for days, and had formulated a plan. But it required Beth's co-operation. If he outlined it to her, she was bound to understand the logic behind it.

"Beth, I cannot do this on my own. It's you who has the huge dowry. If we renew our acquaintance with Lord Edward, it will give us contacts with society. We will maybe be able to go to London for the season, who knows, maybe even to Court." Richard smiled, as he imagined the dashing sergeant and his extraordinarily beautiful sister taking the capital by storm. "You're beautiful, you must know that, Beth. You will have no shortage of wealthy bachelors proposing to you. It will be the making of us." There, he had said it. She would be bound to agree.

"You have forgotten one or two crucial things," Beth said coolly. "Firstly, as you so rightly pointed out, we have little money. Certainly we don't have the money to buy the clothes and other ridiculous fripperies we would need to cut a figure in society. And secondly, even if we miraculously came by such a sum and I was proposed to by someone I loved enough to marry, it would be he who got my dowry. You and I would be no richer for it."

Richard sighed. He had had little experience with women, whores and camp followers excepted, but had thought they would have *some* capacity for reason.

"I'm sure that our cousins would be happy to help. Lord Edward's sisters are dried-up old prunes with more money than sense. I'm certain that it would give them great pleasure to launch their cousin into society. And we wouldn't be looking for a love match, Beth, but someone who would be willing to buy me a cornet's commission, and who could keep you in luxury. Just think," he concluded enthusiastically, "you could say goodbye to this place for ever!" He smiled broadly at her.

He looked almost handsome when he smiled, she thought, and realised it was the first time he *had* smiled since returning home. Reluctant as she was to destroy his jovial mood, she had no intention of co-operating with his plan.

"You ask too much of me," she said after a moment. "Not only do you want me to be disloyal to my mother by cultivating a friendship with people who rejected her for no good reason, but you also want me to go cap in hand, begging for favours from them. Then you want me to sell myself into slavery to some court fop so that you can get promotion." She threw her napkin down on the table and stood up, her meal untouched. "If you want promotion you will have to concoct another plan. You go and beg to them if you want. Maybe you can bag yourself a wealthy heiress."

She made her way towards the door, which started to open as she reached it. In a flash Richard leapt from his seat and reached the door before her, slamming it shut in the startled Martha's face and standing with his back to it.

"Let me past," she said coldly. When he didn't move, she reached past him towards the doorknob, certain he would stand aside when he realised she had no intention of staying to listen to any more of this rubbish.

Instead he reached out and gripped her by both arms, pulling her round to face him. Startled, she pulled against his grip, but he squeezed tighter. His mouth twisted.

"Do you know nothing of society life, you little fool?" he said, shaking her. "It is not possible for a sergeant in the dragoons to marry a wealthy heiress, even if I were the most handsome man in Christendom. Beautiful women on the other hand, marry above themselves all the time. Particularly when they have a huge dowry!" His voice rose almost to a shout on the last sentence.

"I am not like you, Richard," she replied, struggling to break his grip. "I'm quite happy living here. I have no great ambitions, and even if I did, I would not demean myself to achieve them." She kicked out at him, but to little effect, hampered as she was by her skirts. "Let me go, Richard, you're hurting me!" she shouted, enraged.

Instead of complying with her wish, he dug his fingers deeper into her biceps, smiling as she cried out. A muscle twitched in his cheek, and she realised with horror that he was actually enjoying her pain. Then he released her suddenly with a push, and she staggered backwards. He opened the door and turned back to her.

"Take a little time to think about it," he said. "It's the only reasonable solution."

"I don't need any time," she retorted coldly. "I will not change my mind."

She moved forward again to pass him and he pushed the door closed slightly, impeding her exit, although he made no attempt to seize her again.

"Oh, you will, sister," he said quietly. "You will." He opened the door wider and she took the opportunity to escape, making herself walk slowly, and not run as she wanted to. She was uncomfortably aware of his eyes following her as she mounted the stairs, and she reached her room with a feeling of the utmost relief.

It was the first time her brother had touched her, and was a far cry from the fraternal embrace she had hoped for when he had first arrived. Normally inclined to look for the best in anyone, she began to suspect that Graeme had been more accurate in his assessment of Richard than she had thought, and prayed that her suspicions were wrong.

Chapter Two

She expected him to badger her day and night to accede to his plan, but to her surprise he did not. Instead he was almost affable over the next two days, which although probably intended to reassure her, had the opposite effect. When she told him of her intention to visit a friend, Mary, who lived in the nearby village of Withington, he didn't demur at all, but expressed the wish that she have a pleasant time. She would have thought that he had resigned himself to their financial circumstances, had it not been for the fact that she was not stupid, and that the attitude of the servants continued to deteriorate. They no longer spoke to her in the familiar relaxed manner she was used to, and called her 'Miss Elizabeth' as Richard had commanded, rather than 'Beth' as she preferred. They seemed to be constantly hurrying from one place to another, with no time to stop for a chat, and there was a general hunted look about all of them except Graeme, Thomas and Jane, who were too old to be so easily cowed, although even they were growing more reserved with each passing day. Beth made a resolution to arrange a meeting with them all as soon as possible in order to find out exactly what was going on. She had seen no signs that Richard was actually abusing them, although he was, as she had feared, very strict and demanding. She still had hopes that he would relax with them in time, as he now seemed to be doing with her.

It was a great relief to be out of the house for a while, and Beth's mood brightened considerably as she rode to the neighbouring village of Withington to meet Mary. Mary Williamson's mother Sarah had been a close friend of Beth's mother, and they had worked together as seamstresses before Ann was lucky enough to marry

Henry Cunningham. In spite of the social differences now between them, the two women had remained close friends for the rest of their lives. Their daughters used to play together as children while their mothers talked, and had also become good friends. Mary was now employed as an embroiderer, but today was her half-day off, and Beth settled down happily in Mary's small but pleasantly furnished room for an afternoon of relaxed chatting.

Mary was excited for two reasons; firstly because her employer had very generously provided her with a small quantity of the fashionable and expensive beverage tea, and had even loaned her a tea service so that she could really play the lady. The second reason, as she explained to Beth once they were sipping the fragrant brew, was that she had met a young man and was now courting seriously.

"He's working in Manchester for Mr Thwaite, the gentleman's tailor, but he'll have the opportunity to become a partner in the firm once he's of age. We're saving every penny we can at the moment towards it. Once he's a partner, we are going to be married. Oh, I don't know how I'm going to wait two whole years! It is so difficult to say goodbye to him at the end of the day."

She was really smitten. Beth smiled.

"As long as he feels the same way about you, I'm sure he'll be willing to wait for you. Why do you have to wait until he's a partner, though? With both your wages you should be able to rent a room together and live passably well."

"Yes, we could. But then we wouldn't be able to save anything. And Joseph has to buy his way into the firm. Mr Thwaite is being very generous, especially because Joseph's a Catholic, and Mr Thwaite is Anglican. He only wants fifty pounds, but that's a lot to us. And then Joseph's father insists that we wait. He wants us to have a good start in life. He said he will give us twenty pounds at the end of the year. He's right. After all, if we were to marry now, and then a baby came along straight away, we'd be trapped." Mary had certainly thought it through.

"Will Father Kendall marry you or are you going to have a civil ceremony?" Beth asked.

"Father Kendall will marry us. We may have a civil ceremony as well, but as long as we're married in the eyes of God, I couldn't give a fig for the authorities. But when are you going to find a nice young man, Beth? Wouldn't it be lovely if we could be married together?" Mary's face creased as she saw Beth's despondent look. "What have I said wrong?"

"That's what my brother is asking," Beth said sourly. "Although he'd have an apoplexy if I married a Catholic. He wants me to make a great match to get us out of our financial difficulties." She went on to give an outline of Richard's plan and her rejection of it, although she did not mention his manhandling her.

"Well, it would be one way of getting away from your brother, if he's as horrible as he appears to be," Mary said practically.

Beth let the conversation move on to lighter topics. She had come to see Mary to escape from her problems for a while, not to dwell on them.

It was early evening before they finished their visit, ending as was customary to them with a toast to the exiled Stuart King James, and Beth rode back with a light heart. She was truly happy for her friend. It seemed she had found a good and devout man, and someone who shared her Jacobite sympathies. Although that was not difficult in Manchester, which had a high proportion of supporters for the 'king over the water,' many of whom were particularly vociferous in their wishes for the current king, George II, to be sent packing back to Hanover where he belonged.

For the first time in her life she approached her home with a sinking heart. *This is ridiculous,* she thought. *I'm allowing Richard's mood to affect me.*

She made a conscious effort to cheer up, and entered the house with a bounce in her step. Richard was coming down the stairs, and actually smiled when he saw her. He had a scratch and a bruise on his left cheek.

"Did you have a pleasant day?" he asked jovially. Beth told herself she was being uncharitable for feeling suspicious at this uncharacteristic behaviour.

"Yes, thank you," she replied carefully.

"I have just called for some light refreshment to be served in the library. Would you care to join me for a glass of wine?"

Beth accepted the olive branch, and after taking off her riding coat and hat, went into the library, where Grace was arranging a tray of cold meats and bread on a small table. Richard was already sitting down in a chair by the fire, and motioned Beth to the seat opposite him. Unusually he was not dressed in his uniform, but casually, in a pair of brown woollen breeches and a linen shirt. The room was warm, the rich golden wood panelling and shelves of books lending a cosy glow. Candles were burning in the wall sconces, and their father gazed down benignly at them from his portrait over the fire. It was a picture of domestic bliss, and Beth welcomed it with all her heart. She sank into her seat.

"What have you done to your face, Richard?" she asked, although she didn't really care. "Have you been fighting?" There was an air of suppressed excitement about him.

He raised one hand to his cheek, as if he had only now become aware of his injury.

"Ah. No, I fell off my horse while riding through the woods. A branch caught me in the face. It was my own fault, I wasn't concentrating on where I was going."

"Is that why you're not wearing your uniform?" she said. "Is it damaged?"

"No, just a little muddy," he replied, smiling. "It needs cleaning, that's all."

There was a short silence while Beth tried to think of something else to say.

"Why are you serving, Grace?" she asked the chambermaid as she finished arranging the food. "Is Martha ill?"

Grace cast a wary look at Richard, who was sitting back in his chair in a relaxed pose, one ankle resting on the opposite knee.

"She's left, Miss Elizabeth," Grace said carefully, bobbing a curtsey.

The picture of domestic bliss shattered into a thousand pieces and tinkled to the floor.

"She's left?" Beth echoed incredulously. "Why?"

Grace looked nervously at Richard again, who still didn't respond.

"I don't know, Miss," she ventured after a pause. "She didn't say." Her eyes were huge, pleading silently with Beth not to pursue the matter.

"Thank you, Grace," she said formally. "That will be all." Grace left the room as hastily as she could without running. The moment the door had closed, Beth rounded on her brother.

"What have you done?" she asked. Richard regarded her over his glass of wine.

"Me?" he said. "I have done nothing. It is hardly my fault if a maid chooses to leave of her own accord."

"Martha would not choose to just leave of her own accord," Beth said. "Of all the servants in this household, she is the last one who would leave. Something has happened. What is it?"

"I have no idea, "Richard replied carelessly. "The steward fellow, Thomas, is it, came up earlier today to tell me that Martha had decided to leave, and requested that I pay her wages up to date."

"And did you?" Beth asked.

"Of course I did. What do you take me for?"

"Did you give her a character? Where has she gone?"

"No, in answer to your first question, I do not consider someone who abandons their post on a whim to be deserving of a character. And as for where she has gone, well, that is no concern of ours. She has left the household. It is most tedious. I will look for a replacement for her tomorrow. Now can we enjoy our evening?"

"No," said Beth flatly. "Do you know what you've done? Martha has little chance of obtaining another job, even with a good reference. She has none at all without one."

"Ah, you mean because of the brat. I must confess I was a little surprised that you employed such an immoral woman. She's no better than she should be, and a bad example to the others. Maybe it's a blessing that she has decided to leave." He was enjoying himself, and Beth knew she should let the matter go, but couldn't.

"There is nothing wrong with Martha's morals, Richard. She made a mistake, that's all, and has paid dearly for it. She has also learnt from it."

"She's a slut, in my opinion," Richard said, his voice rising slightly.

"How many women have you bedded, Richard?" Beth asked suddenly.

His colour rose slightly, but he maintained his casual demeanour.

"Very many, over the years," he replied. "But I don't see what…"

"And any one of those women could have gone on to have your child, and presumably become a slut as a result," Beth interrupted, her voice laced with sarcasm. "Whereas you, no doubt, have become a great lover and a dashing man about town."

"That is the way of the world, dear sister," he replied coolly.

"It is not the way of *my* world. In my world a woman is not to be condemned for one mistake, nor to be branded a harlot for committing the same action that a man is commended for!"

"Your moral attitude disturbs me, Beth," Richard replied, his voice suddenly stern. "But we can address that another time. For now I would remind you that this house is no longer your world, but mine. If you wish to have your own household, I suggest you comply with my suggestion of the other night. I am sure that you will have no difficulty in procuring a doting husband who will allow you to populate your house with whores from top to bottom."

So that was it, Beth thought as she paced her bedroom later, too angry to think of sleeping. He was going to slowly erode her whole way of life, driving away as many of her servants as he could until she was completely isolated, in an attempt to wear down her resolve. He would not do it, she was determined.

She had taken some consolation from the staff. As soon as she had left her brother she had run to the kitchen, where Thomas, Jane and Graeme were enjoying supper. To her surprise they also had no idea why Martha had left. It seemed she had just appeared in the kitchen with her bag packed, holding the child Ann by the hand, and had announced her decision to leave immediately. Thomas had insisted she wait while he got the wages she was due, and whilst he was upstairs the others had questioned her as to why she was leaving and what she would do. Her eyes had been red and she was obviously upset, but she would not be drawn, saying only that she was leaving of her own accord, that she would stay with a friend for a few days and would contact them soon.

In common with Beth, they were certain Richard had had a hand in the matter, but there was no proof, and all Beth could do was promise to write a good character for Martha, in the hopes that she would get in touch as she had promised. She had expressed her concern that they would all leave, one by one, and Thomas and Graeme both pointed out that they, along with Jane and John would be very difficult to replace and therefore were unlikely to be dismissed, and would not leave under any other circumstances while their mistress still needed them. Their loyalty had reduced Beth to tears and determined her to fight her brother all the way, if she could not bring him round by reasonable means, which seemed increasingly unlikely.

* * *

She avoided him as much as possible over the next few days. He had settled into a habit of incarcerating himself in the library during the evening with a bottle of claret, and sleeping late in the mornings as a consequence. Being an early riser by nature, this meant that Beth had breakfasted before her brother even woke, and consequently the only shared time they had was at dinner, which she had no way of getting out of except by being rude. Once a week she would visit Mary, and when the weather permitted, it now being late October, she would go for long rides through the fields and woods behind the house. When the weather was inclement, she would stay in the parlour, or retire to her bedroom to read or sew. Richard had taken over the household accounts and would sit for hours poring over the complex figures. He was obviously not particularly numerate, but Beth did not volunteer to assist him and he would not request her help.

Two days after Martha left, Richard announced at dinner that he had found a replacement, who would start the next day. Beth eyed the new girl with some concern. Although she was dressed respectably enough, her apron clean and her brown hair neatly braided and covered by a kerchief, there was something slatternly about her, and she had a sly smile that Beth found irritating. She told herself she was being unfair to the girl and did her best to make Sarah feel at home, until she went up to her room one day and found the kitchen maid at her writing desk, in the act of opening one of the little drawers where Beth kept her paper and spare quills.

"What are you doing?" Beth asked. Sarah jumped as though she'd been shot and slammed the drawer shut.

"I was just doing a bit of cleaning, Miss Elizabeth," she replied after a pause.

Beth looked at her sceptically. She had no cleaning implements with her at all.

"It seems my brother has not explained your duties to you,

Sarah," Beth said icily. "Your job is to assist Mrs Fletcher in the kitchen and to wait on table. You have no duties in any other rooms in the house."

The maid sketched the briefest curtsey propriety allowed, and without answering, walked towards the door, smiling slightly as she passed Beth. Beth threw her leg back and kicked the door shut. Sarah stopped, momentarily confused.

"Listen to me," Beth said in a commanding tone. "I have no idea where my brother got you from, but if I see you in my room again you will be going straight back there, do you understand?"

Sarah smiled. "The master told me that only he could dismiss me, Miss," she said smugly.

Beth fought the urge to knock the smugness off the maid's face with her fist, and instead smiled herself, so coldly that Sarah's own grin faltered.

"It is true my brother is the master here," she said icily. "But believe me, if I wish to, I can make your life a living hell. If I see you anywhere near my room, or if you speak to me in a disrespectful way again, I will do just that, with the greatest pleasure. You will beg my brother to let you leave before I have finished with you. Do you understand?"

Sarah's recent years had been spent in the lowest echelons of society, and she had been stunned when the sergeant, after paying for her services, had asked her if she fancied leaving the streets and acting as a kitchen maid, with a few other services thrown in, for which she would receive extra remuneration. She had jumped at the chance. From what he had said, his sister was weak, had no influence at all, and was all bluster. He had instructed the maid to take no notice of Beth and to obey only him.

She stood now eye to eye with her adversary, assessing her. Beth was a good few inches shorter than her, and several pounds lighter. It was true that she had higher birth on her side, but it was not that that caused Sarah to lower her eyes after a moment. She had been in many fights in her short life and could now calculate her chances of victory before a blow was exchanged. She was under no illusions that Beth would carry out her threat if necessary, and would not scruple as to the means by which she achieved her ends. Clearly the master had underestimated his sister, but Sarah was taking no chances.

From that day on Sarah gave Beth a wide berth. Beth took to locking her room when she wasn't in it, and thought longingly of the happy and relaxed atmosphere which had filled the house only a month ago, but which now seemed so distant.

In spite of Beth's attempts to put on a cheerful face, the general mood of the household did not improve, even though the staff had received their wages. They were now very aware that there was an interloper in their midst who was probably reporting back to Richard, and this prevented them from openly airing their views and grievances in the kitchen.

Therefore when she went downstairs early one morning to find her brother had already breakfasted, having the intention of visiting some friends in town and not returning until dinner, she was ecstatic. His horse had hardly clattered out of the yard before she summoned Sarah to her room, telling her that the master had told her she could have the day off, and had instructed Beth to give her a shilling to go into Manchester and spend. If Sarah was suspicious, she was not about to give up the chance of a day off and money to spend, and having changed into her best dress, she left the house half an hour later.

Beth flew downstairs to inform the staff of this delightful turn of events, and within twenty minutes they were all sitting around the kitchen table enjoying a couple of bottles of Richard's claret and chatting, their duties postponed for a while. Grace, as usual, sat separately by the fire, darning stockings. She had been brought up in a devoutly Presbyterian family, whose policy was that a woman's hands should always be occupied, and that it was not seemly for them to engage in masculine topics of conversation or express opinions. In spite of Beth's efforts to liberate her maid's mind, Grace remained quietly resolute. Absolutely trustworthy and loyal she was, but she would not join in, and the others had come to respect that.

Determined not to spend the precious time discussing Richard's devastating influence on the house, Beth repaired to the library to retrieve the week's papers and they settled down to discuss the topical events.

Inevitably the conversation turned to politics, the ongoing War of the Austrian Succession, and the replacement earlier in the year of Sir Robert Walpole as Prime Minister by Lord Cartaret.

"If it wasn't for Walpole's pacifist policies, we wouldn't be on the point of going to war now," commented Thomas. "He allowed France and Spain to become strong. We should have crushed them in the war over the Polish succession ten years ago, and then they wouldn't be threatening Austria now. By not getting involved, we looked weak and lost a lot of our credibility as a nation."

"Yes, but that war had nothing to do with us, and he did have a point when he said that 'if there is a war, the king's crown will be fought for on this land'," Jane quoted. "The king wasn't as secure on the throne as he is now, and if we'd gone to war ten years ago France surely would have encouraged the supporters of the Pretender in Britain to rise. Could King George have survived a war abroad and a civil war in his own country at the same time? By avoiding war Walpole allowed the king to establish himself. He'll be much harder to uproot now."

"I'm not so sure of that," Thomas countered. "France managed to take Lorraine and strengthen its connections with other countries. If it succeeds in conquering Austria, it will be well on the way to taking control of the whole of Europe. If Walpole was still the minister, we'd no doubt be abandoning Marie Theresa to her fate in the interests of peace."

Everyone had sympathy for the young Marie Theresa, who, on the death of her father Charles VI, had succeeded to the dominions of Austria. The powers of Europe, recognising her helplessness, had been overwhelmed with greed, and King Frederick of Prussia with France's support had invaded the Austrian province of Silesia. Walpole had attempted to reconcile Austria and Prussia, to no effect, and King George II, eager for war, had promised help to the beleaguered young Empress.

"Yes, but why is George promising help to Marie Theresa? Because his beloved Hanover is threatened, that's why. He's never liked Britain, and nor did his father before him. He only took the throne because he thought it would help his electorate," Graeme put in. "All we are to him is a source of revenue and troops."

"That's right. The sooner we have a king who cares about the country, the better, I say," John said. "I've no great love for France but if they help us get the Stuarts back on the throne where they belong, good luck to them."

Beth had remained quiet up to now, enjoying the animated expressions on the others' faces. Ben and Mary, as yet too young to participate in the debate, were listening attentively. Beth sincerely hoped that however their political views developed, they would always be able to have differences of opinions with their friends without making enemies of them.

"Who knows what will happen while the Elector is away fighting his war? It's a prime opportunity for Prince Charles to invade, if he can persuade the French to help him," Beth said wistfully.

Jane shuddered at the thought of a Catholic monarch regaining the throne and the persecution that Protestants could then expect to suffer.

"Yes, but there's no proof that Charles is as fanatical a Catholic as his grandfather was," Beth countered when Jane expressed her views. "I'm sure he will have learned from James's mistakes. He would hardly want to alienate most of his people, if he succeeded in regaining the throne for his father."

"Yes, but that's the problem, Beth," Thomas said, automatically abandoning the formal 'Miss Elizabeth' now that Richard was absent. "Charles may be liberal. But the old Pretender is certainly not, and it's he who will be king if his son succeeds in a rebellion."

"I think he'll abdicate in favour of Prince Charles, if it comes to it," said John.

No one had thought of this, but it certainly made sense. James III, or the Old Pretender as his enemies called him, seemed to have now accepted his exile following his abortive attempt at an invasion over twenty years ago. His fiery eldest son, Charles Edward, was a completely different matter.

"It's true James isn't as young as he was," Graeme said after a minute. "But at least he tried to get his throne back, which is more than his father did. Oh, those were good days, when we marched on Lancaster. You should have heard the pipes and seen the men, thousands of them, singing as they went and proclaiming King James all the way." His eyes misted over as he remembered the '15, as it was now called, when he had left his home in Kendal as a young man to join the Jacobite forces invading England to regain the throne for James.

"King James wasn't there though, was he?" Thomas replied dryly. "By the time he landed in Scotland the rebellion was all but over."

"That's true. But it was no fault of his that he was late arriving," Graeme countered hotly. "The weather was awful. He was a brave man, and his son's of the same blood, thank God. If another chance comes, we'll not waste it this time."

"We certainly won't," said John. "The day that King James or his son lands on British soil is the day you'll be looking for another stable hand, Beth." His voice was particularly vehement, and everyone looked at him in surprise. Whilst he was a confirmed Jacobite, John was also renowned for his gentleness and dislike of violence in any form.

"I thought you would be the last person to fight, John," said Beth, puzzled. He was not insulted; she was not doubting his bravery, and he knew that.

"Yes, well, I've changed my mind. I've grown up a lot recently," he said, with a distinct tone of bitterness in his voice. The others exchanged puzzled glances, but he would not be drawn any further, and to fill the awkward silence Graeme continued to talk about the glorious days of the '15, the drawn swords glinting in the sun, the rapturous welcome given the rebels by the Jacobite sections of the towns, the camaraderie of the soldiers.

The children, Ben and Mary, were gazing in awe at the seemingly ancient figure of the gardener, his brown hair now liberally sprinkled with grey, his joints slowly starting to succumb to rheumatism due to the long hours spent outside in all weathers. They were clearly trying to imagine him as a young man in armour brandishing his sword, and failing.

Beth intercepted their look.

"Graeme has been alive for ever, and remembers everything," she said, winking at them. "He'll tell you of the time he met Oliver Cromwell, if you ask nicely," she added. The children giggled.

Graeme regarded her with mock severity, his bushy eyebrows bristling over grey eyes brimming with humour.

"Take no notice of your mistress. I'll tell you no such thing. Old Ironsides died over thirty years before I saw the light of day, and I'll thank you for less of your cheek, madam. You should be setting a good example to your servants by showing respect for your elders."

Beth laughed, and opened her mouth to retort.

"I have to go," John said suddenly, standing up. He seemed a little stiff when he moved, and Beth wondered what additional chores Richard had assigned to him to make him so.

"Whatever for?" said Beth. "The discussion's only just started. And so has the wine!" Everyone laughed and motioned him to sit down, but he remained standing.

"The master has told me I need to polish all the harness before he comes back, and that he'll inspect it as soon as he returns. If I'm to do it, I'll have to start now." John began to move towards the door.

"To hell with the master," said Beth, reaching over for the wine bottle and filling John's glass to the brim. "He won't be back for hours. I'll come and help you later."

John hesitated.

"For God's sake, lad, we'll all come and help, if we need to," Thomas said, exasperated. "Sit down. The Jacobite cause needs all the help it can get, and these two," waving a hand at Beth and Graeme, "have no chance against us, without you to help out."

There were good-humoured protestations at this and John gave in, and sitting down, continued the discussion by raising his brimming glass in a toast to King James. There was a rush for the wine bottle by Thomas and Jane to counter with a toast to King George, after which the debate continued until lunchtime.

Beth ended the merry meeting with a toast to free speech and an end to tyranny, which all of those assembled drank to, knowing that the tyrant she referred to was neither King George nor King James, but someone much closer to home.

The others were as good as their word, and all assisted John in polishing the harness and cleaning out the stables. Even Richard would be able to find no fault with his work. Then they all went merrily off to their own chores. Everyone was in good spirits, in spite of the looming threat of Richard's return, and Beth hoped sincerely that his friends, whoever they were, would demand a lot more of his time in the future.

John and Beth repaired to the barn after the others had dispersed. He had been learning the art of knife-throwing in his spare time and Beth now offered to give him a lesson. John ran off to fetch his knife from his room, returning moments later, and Beth hitched up her skirts and seated herself on a barrel outside the barn to observe him. He stood facing the barn door, and then took several steps backwards.

"Just another couple of steps back, John," Beth advised.

John readied himself. He held the knife about half way along the blade and after a moment's preparation, threw it at the door. The blade nosedived into the ground a few feet in front of him.

Beth went to retrieve the knife. "You're flicking your wrist as you throw. Keep it straight. Try again," she said, passing it to him.

He held the blade as she had just demonstrated.

"Don't curl your finger round the blade, John, or you'll cut yourself." He readjusted his grip, then turned to her, a puzzled look on his face.

"But I've watched you, lots of times. You hold the knife with the edge toward the ground. And you flick your wrist. And the knife always lands in the target."

"Yes, but I've been doing this for a long time," she said.

He still looked doubtful.

"But I used to watch when your mother was teaching you, and she always held the knife with the edge toward the ground too." He regretted the words as soon as they were uttered, and looked at her nervously.

"You never told me that you used to watch us," Beth said, feeling disgruntled. She treasured her memories of the knife-throwing lessons with her mother. They had been private, intimate moments, when Ann, in between correcting her daughter's fumbling attempts to avoid amputating her own fingers, had told her stories of her wild youth in the Highlands. Beth had been unaware that they had been observed, and irrationally, even after all this time, resented it.

John blushed.

"Yes, well, I hadn't been here long, then. I didn't know you very well. I didn't like to intrude." He shifted his weight uncomfortably from foot to foot, wishing he hadn't said anything. He had watched the mother and her smaller replica in fascination, mesmerised not just by the mistress's skill with weapons, but also by the relaxed and easy intimacy between them, of the casual loving gestures which Beth had taken for granted, and which he, having never known his mother, had longed for. "She loved you very much," he murmured, half to himself, and the longing in his voice drove Beth's resentment away. She sat down on the barrel, turning the knife over in her hands.

"Yes," she said. "I was very lucky, I know that."

"I spent months trying to pluck up the courage to ask her to teach me to throw a knife," John admitted.

"Why didn't you?" Beth said. "She probably would have said yes. Although she'd have made you wait until you were older," she added thoughtfully. Beth had been ten when her mother had deemed her old enough to start learning to defend herself. John would have only been six or seven then.

"I wanted to, but I asked Jane how to go about it, and she forbade me to even mention it. I was too frightened of her to disobey her. I thought she might fire me. Jane never approved of your mother teaching you 'manly skills', as she put it."

Beth laughed.

"I know," she said. Jane had worshipped Ann Macdonald, but had not approved of either her Jacobite convictions or her thoughts on the necessary skills a young lady should learn. "But my mother was brought up very differently to Jane. Her family suffered very badly in the massacre in 1692. My grandfather was imprisoned and died of typhus after the massacre when mother was only two, and my grandmother was beside herself with grief, apparently, and vowed vengeance on the Campbells. She was arrested for killing a Campbell Dragoon a few years later and died in prison. My mother was brought up by her aunt and uncle. And then in the '15 the MacDonalds came out for King James and a lot of the clansmen died in battle, including her uncle. She told me that the clanswomen had to learn to fight, because they never knew when they would have to. If the men were away fighting another clan, it was up to the women to hunt for food, and to defend themselves if necessary against any other clans that sought to take advantage of the fact that their menfolk were away to raid the village. She had a very hard life, John, and if it hadn't been for her skills with a knife, she'd not have survived to move down to England and meet my father. Some of the stories she told me would make your blood curdle."

John waited for a moment, hoping that Beth would regale him

with one of these blood-curdling tales, but after a short silence she shook her head, as though to drive away some unpleasant thought.

"Anyway," she continued. "She was of the opinion that every woman should be able to defend herself against attack, especially as women are not as strong as men. It would be nice to think that most men are too courteous to hurt a member of the weaker sex, but it's not true, unfortunately. She held the view that you never knew when your circumstances might change. Even the most privileged might be brought down by a stroke of fate, and it was as well to know how to survive, just in case. So she taught me how to throw knives, and how to kill too, if necessary. And I'm very glad she did, although I hope I'll never have to do it."

"You must miss her a lot," John said.

Beth looked up at him, her eyes brimming with tears.

"I think of her, and of Father every day," she said, smiling sadly. Then she swiped at her eyes impatiently with her hand and jumped down off the barrel, handing the knife back to John. "But if we carry on talking, Richard will be home before you've had a chance to throw the knife at all. Come on, let's get on. Remember what I told you, and try again."

He moved into position, and took aim carefully. This time the knife hit the door, although it didn't penetrate the wood.

"That was better. Your wrist was straight. But you're twisting your body. You must stand square on to the target. The only part of your body that moves is your arm."

She came up behind him as he aimed the knife for another throw and gripped his shoulders, intending to hold him in position as he threw. To her surprise he cried out in pain and leapt away from her, the knife landing on the floor at his feet.

"What on earth's the matter, John?" Beth asked. His face had drained of all colour, and as she made to move towards him, he put his hand up to ward her off.

"It's nothing," he said. "I fell and bruised myself, that's all. I'll be fine in a day or so."

He was not a good liar. Beth did not try to approach him further, but her face was determined.

"You're lying, John, and you never lie to me. What's really happened?"

"Please, Beth, it's none of your concern." The colour was returning to his face now, but he still looked sick. A nasty suspicion crossed her mind.

"It's Richard, isn't it? What has he done to you?" she asked.

"Nothing!" he retorted, too quickly.

She stooped, and picked the knife up off the floor, sliding it into its sheath and putting it in her pocket.

"Very well," she said. "If you won't tell me, I'll ask Richard myself as soon as he comes home. If he has hurt you, it is my concern, John, whatever you may think." She made to turn away, but John's anguished cry stopped her.

"Don't, please, you'll only make things worse," he pleaded.

"Take off your shirt," she replied. "I want to see what's wrong."

He shrank away from her, moving backward into the barn, and her heart contracted. They had been friends since they were children, had argued and fought like brother and sister. Never in his life had he shrank from her. And never in her life had she used her superior status against him, as she now did. She followed him and stood in the doorway, hands on her hips.

"If you don't do as I ask, I will go and ask Richard. I will not have my friends and employees abused by him behind my back. Take off your shirt."

He did, reluctantly, and stood facing her, shivering slightly for a moment before turning round so she could see his back. She gasped in horror, her face paling to almost the same shade as his.

"My God, John," she breathed. "What has he done to you?"

The young man's back was a mass of red welts, which spanned from his shoulders to his waist. Some of the stripes were partially healed, others were still fresh. Where she had gripped his shoulders she had scraped some of the scabs off, and a thin trickle of blood ran down his back.

"I…he…he was not pleased with my work," John said, lamely.

"What did he beat you with? His riding crop?"

"No, he had a switch. He…"

Now the initial shock of seeing his injuries was over, Beth had moved into the barn, closer to him, and was examining the wounds in more detail. They were not the result of one beating, but at least two, maybe more. This had been going on for some time.

"I will not tolerate this," Beth said, very quietly. "Why did you not tell me?"

John turned to face her, but did not answer. She made a decision, and swirled away.

"What are you going to do?" John cried.

"Firstly I'm going to destroy that switch of his. Then I'm going to wait for him to come home. I cannot let this go, John. I'm sorry."

In desperation John stepped forward and grabbed her arm to stop her leaving. He swung her round to face him.

"No! He said that if I told you, he would kill me. I believe him, Beth," John said, his voice desperate.

The sunlight coming through the open door suddenly diminished.

"And so you should, boy," a cold voice came from behind Beth. John let go of her arm as though it had burnt him and backed off into the shadows. Beth spun round to see her brother in the doorway of the barn, leaning nonchalantly on the doorpost.

"I'm sorry," he said. "Did I disturb your little tryst by my early return? Although it's as well I did. After all, you would be no use to me if you were ruined. I presume even you will now agree to the boy's dismissal, after he has tried to seduce you."

Beth's hand went instinctively to the knife concealed in her pocket and stayed there.

"He has done no such thing, and well you know it. Why are you victimising him, Richard? Or are all my staff wearing a uniform of stripes?" Beth fought to control her temper, to remain rational.

Richard moved away from the post and took a step into the barn.

"May I remind you that they are *my* staff now," he said acidly. "Many of them deserve chastisement, yes, for their lack of respect. But they show signs of coming round without it. This," he waved his hand in the direction of John, who was cowering in the shadows, "persists in his impertinence. I see now that he will not learn his place, no matter what I do."

"You can stop this ridiculous pretence now, Richard," Beth said, her voice shaking with rage. "You tried to dismiss him once, and I stopped you. You have decided to drive him away with violence instead. I know what this is about. You are trying to get rid of him because he saw you make a fool of yourself the day you arrived. That is the real reason, is it not?" She saw his mouth twist, and knew she had hit on the truth.

"I will not discuss this here. John, you are dismissed." Richard turned to leave, with a contemptuous gesture.

The knife thudded into the doorpost no more than an inch from his head, and stuck there, quivering. Richard leapt instinctively to one side, then whirled to face his sister, who was standing rigidly before him, her fists clenched at her side. He looked from her to the knife in disbelief.

"I have not finished yet," she shouted. "You are very free with your whip with those who cannot fight back, you coward!"

Richard's face reddened, and he took a step toward her.

"No one calls me coward, sister, not even my family," he growled.

"Family!" Beth cried. "You call yourself my family! My staff are far more family to me than you will ever be! I am ashamed to own you as my brother. You make me sick!"

He saw red. Lunging forward, he swung his fist, catching her squarely on the side of the head before she could move and sending her sprawling into the hay, where she lay as though dead. Richard bent over her, his fist still clenched

"No!" John cried. He moved forward out of the shadows, brandishing a pitchfork threateningly. Richard straightened slowly, and turned on the balls of his feet to face his attacker, drawing his sword smoothly from the scabbard at the same time. He quickly gauged the situation. The boy facing him was white and his eyes had widened at the sight of the sword, but he did not back off. Concern for his mistress overrode his fear, and Richard felt a momentary flicker of admiration for the boy's courage, before his anger at the insult to him overrode any finer emotions.

"Stand away from Beth," John commanded, his voice trembling.

That was good. He was terrified, and more likely to make a mistake. Richard was not overly worried. He was an expert swordsman, and contrary to what his sister believed, for all his faults, he was no coward. However, the boy was young and strong, and very competent with a pitchfork. Richard's instinct was to make a fight of it, and kill the boy, but if he did, there would be sure to be an enquiry, at which his sister would no doubt speak against him. Richard knew he would not be convicted, but he could do without the inconvenience at a time when he was hoping for promotion.

"Well, boy," he said quietly. "It seems we have a situation. Why don't you put down that ridiculous thing and we can talk about it?"

"I said stand away from Beth," the boy repeated. Richard moved away, two steps, then another. "You will not hurt her any more. She was trying to help me," John said.

"I had no intention of hurting her. I was trying to see if she was all right," Richard replied truthfully. He had hit her harder than he intended and was a little worried by her stillness. But at the moment he was more concerned for his own safety. The pitchfork shook in the stable boy's hands, and Richard smiled.

"Come, see sense," he said reasonably. "You are brave, but I am a soldier, trained in arms. You cannot beat me. You must know that. Put the pitchfork down. I promise not to hurt your mistress, you have my word as a gentleman."

John still hesitated, and Richard fought to quell the rage that rose in him. How dare this puppy doubt his word as a gentleman!

"Put down the pitchfork," he said, "And you may leave."

John wavered for an instant, and Richard pounced. With one sweep of his sword he sent the pitchfork flying from John's grasp, then drove his fist into the boy's stomach. He doubled up with a strangled gasp, winded, and Richard seized him by the hair, pushing him back into the wall. He writhed in the older man's grasp, fighting for breath, until Richard placed the sword across his neck.

John froze, although his throat still worked convulsively as he managed to draw a trickle of air into his lungs. Richard pressed slightly, and a thread of red appeared along the line of the blade.

"You have five minutes to pack your things and be gone," he said coldly. "In six minutes I will come looking for you. If I find you, I will kill you. Is that clear?" John's eyes flickered over his assailant's shoulder, but there was nothing more he could do for Beth. He nodded. Blood trickled down the blade of the sword.

Richard released John so quickly he staggered. Then regaining his balance, he ran out of the barn.

The soldier went to where the youth's shirt still lay discarded on the floor. Picking it up he wiped his sword carefully before replacing it in the scabbard. Then he moved to where Beth still lay immobile in the hay. He placed two fingers at her throat, and felt the pulse, strong and steady. He slapped her cheek lightly, and she sighed softly, then was still again.

Satisfied that she was not in any danger of expiring, he left the barn. He would not go looking for John in six minutes. The boy would be gone. He had dealt with enough subordinates to know when he had broken a man, and it always gave him a thrill of satisfaction to do it. He whistled softly as he ran lightly up the steps and into the house to change for dinner.

* * *

When Graeme found her she was on the point of recovering consciousness, and moaned slightly as he carefully gathered her up in his arms. Jane had first expressed concern as to the whereabouts of the mistress after she had failed to arrive in the dining room. Richard had told her to go ahead with the meal, saying that it was his sister's own fault if she could not tell the time. Jane had duly served the first course of mutton broth, but something in his voice worried her, and she had voiced her concerns to Graeme, who had been the first of the senior servants to appear in the kitchen. Having discovered from Grace that Beth was not in her room, Graeme had gone across the yard to the stables, where she had last been seen, expecting to find John at least, who would no doubt be able to tell him where she was. But the stables were empty, and what was more alarming, Richard's horse was in its stall, but untended. There was clearly something wrong.

On his way back out he had met Ben, who told him he had seen John running from the barn some time earlier. On hearing this, Graeme had made that his next port of call, and now carried his mistress across the yard to the house, his face set and grim.

The first sense to recover was her hearing, and Beth listened hazily to the concerned murmurs going on around her. Her limbs felt heavy as though they did not belong to her, and she was pleasantly drowsy. Then she felt something cool and soothing on her head, and her mind cleared.

"John…" she cried, although her voice came out as no more than a whisper, and she struggled to pull herself upright. Pain exploded in her head and stars danced across her vision. She slumped back against Graeme's arm. She closed her eyes, and dimly through the banging in her head was aware of something being held to her lips.

"Here, drink this." Jane's voice came from a distance. "It will help to ease the pain."

Beth swallowed painfully, then lay still, waiting for the pain to subside a little before attempting to move again. She was aware now that she was on Graeme's lap, his arm supporting her in a half-sitting position. Her face was turned towards his chest, her cheek resting against his worn leather waistcoat. She inhaled the scent of leather mixed with freshly turned soil and the sweet smell of growing green things that emanated from him, and was transported momentarily back to her childhood, when she would curl up on his knee like a kitten and listen to the conversation of the adults, only half comprehending what they were talking about, but enjoying the sound of their voices. Sometimes he would tell her stories of the great deeds of the '15 and his exploits during his brief period as a rebel. Sometimes she would doze off, and he would carry her gently up to bed, or to her mother.

But the voices around her now were not engaged in pleasant conversation, and she was no longer a child. She fought the impulse to drift off into the welcome oblivion of sleep. She moved slowly this time, managing to achieve a more upright position without too much pain.

"John," she said again, her voice audible this time. "Where is he?"

Thomas and Jane looked at each other. Jane nodded.

"It seems he's gone. At least we can't find him anywhere, although his shirt was in the barn. There was blood on it." Thomas hesitated, but he had to ask the question. "Did he do this to you, Beth?"

"John? No! Of course not!" she cried, outraged that Thomas could even think such a thing.

"I'm sorry, Beth, but I had to ask. After all, we found you unconscious in the barn, and Ben saw John running away half naked…"

She saw now how it must have looked, and how Richard could make it look if he chose to. She beckoned for another drink, and took a deep swallow. She felt a bit better now. The room was no longer tilting and her limbs were recovering their life.

Sarah walked in.

"The master is ready for dessert…" Her voice faltered as she took in the sight that presented itself to her; the mistress sitting on the gardener's knee, white-faced, the other servants around the table, their faces full of concern. Jane jumped to her feet and cut a large slice from the suet pudding which was steaming on the stove. Slopping it carelessly into a dish, she ladled a generous helping of cream on to it, then turned to the maid.

"You may take the rest of the evening off, and go to your room, Sarah," Jane said.

The maid hesitated. "But the master…"

"I will take his dessert to him. Go to your room. I will see you in the morning."

"But…"

Thomas stood up.

"Are you offering to disobey my wife, girl?" he roared, his hand raised ominously. Sarah fled, and Thomas sat down again.

Beth waited until Jane had returned from the dining room and then told them what had happened that afternoon, leaving nothing out. When she had finished, there was a short silence, then Thomas got slowly to his feet.

"Where are you going?" Jane and Beth asked together.

"To the dining room. I've put up with insults, ridiculous orders and contempt from that jumped-up puppy, but I'll be damned if I'll stand by while he beats women, and flogs young boys for no reason." His handsome face was grim, but his green eyes flashed fire.

Graeme shifted in his seat, and put his arm under Beth's knees to lift her off his lap.

"I'll come with you," he said.

Beth leapt from Graeme's knee and stood, chalk-white and swaying slightly.

"No!" she cried. "You cannot reason with him, Thomas."

"I wasn't thinking of having a conversation with the man," Thomas replied coldly. Jane's face paled as well now, and Beth braced her arms on the table to keep herself upright.

"Thomas," she said determinedly. "If you do this, you'll be playing into his hands. He's a soldier. If he doesn't kill you himself, he will certainly call the authorities to you, and will derive the greatest pleasure from doing so. What help will you be to Jane or to me if you're rotting in prison or transported to the colonies?"

Thomas rubbed his hand across his face in vexation.

"Well, then call the law in yourself, Beth. We'll all stand witness for you. He has no right to treat you this way. You're his sister, not his wife."

"I know, Thomas, but what would I tell the magistrate? I threw a knife at him and called him a coward. He could argue that he hit me in self-defence."

"And did he?" Jane asked.

"No," Beth admitted. "But he'll likely be believed if he does. He accused John of trying to seduce me. If he tells the magistrate that he caught his sister in the arms of the stable boy, after which she attacked him, he'll be commended for saving me from ruin."

Thomas sank down on to the bench opposite Beth again, to both women's relief. Beth also sank down gratefully next to Graeme.

"And if we do nothing, what then?" Thomas asked. "Which one of us will be beaten next? And how long will it be before he hits you again?"

"Richard wanted rid of John, because he made a fool of himself in front of him. As for Martha, he didn't approve of her morals."

Jane snorted derisively. "I don't see him having any problems with that slut who warms his bed every night," she said, referring to Sarah. "I've no doubt he tried to have his way with Martha and she told him where to go." That Sarah was Richard's bedmate was news to Beth, although she didn't comment on it.

"Even so, he's got rid of the two people he disapproves of. I don't think he'll take such extreme measures against any more of you. As for me, I will not antagonise him again. But that doesn't mean I will do nothing."

The next morning Beth was up, dressed and riding for Manchester by daybreak. When Edward Cox arrived at his office in

Deansgate, he found her waiting for him.

"Miss Cunningham!" he exclaimed, when he had identified her through the veil which covered her forehead and eyes. "What a pleasure to see you."

"I am sorry to disturb you at such an early hour, but I hoped that you could spare me a few minutes of your time."

Within twenty minutes she was sitting in his office sipping chocolate, while he regarded her across his desk.

"I really don't see what I can do to help you," he said. "I can only tell you the same as I told your brother yesterday. The dowry can only be released to your husband, or to yourself if you attain the age of thirty unmarried. If you die before either of those events takes place – which I am sure you will not, my dear – then the money goes to build a hospital for foundling children. Your father made it quite clear what his wishes were."

"My brother was here yesterday?" Beth asked.

"Why, of course. I thought you knew…"

"And did he ask you specifically about what would happen to the dowry were I to die?"

"Well, he asked a lot of questions. But that was one of them, yes. I thought he was speaking on behalf of both of you. But I see now that I was misled." Mr Cox was not impressed. He had given Richard the benefit of his advice in good faith, but was now feeling distinctly uneasy about the man's motives.

"And you are certain there is no way we can challenge this in the court?" Beth asked.

"Well, of course you can make a challenge, but it would be expensive, and even if you were to agree to your dowry being made over to Sergeant Cunningham, which of course you wouldn't, it could still…"

"I would," interrupted Beth.

"You would what?" Mr Cox asked.

"I would do anything to get my brother out of my life. If giving him my dowry will achieve that, I will do it."

Edward Cox was dumbfounded.

"You cannot be serious, my dear," he said after a moment. "That would leave you penniless. And as I was about to say, a challenge might take several years to be ruled on and could fail even then."

"I will be frank with you, Mr Cox. My brother is hungry for promotion, and wants an officer's commission. He also wants to make an entrance into society. In our current financial situation, that is impossible. He feels that the only solution is for me to go begging to my father's noble family in the hopes that they will assist me in finding a wealthy and influential husband who can help Richard achieve his aims."

"Your brother does have a point, my dear. You are quite amazingly beautiful. It is one answer to your problems."

Beth put her cup down on the table with a crash that threatened to shatter the delicate porcelain.

"I am sick of people telling me that I am beautiful and that he may have a point! Why can nobody understand that I have too much self-respect to sell myself to the highest bidder to satisfy my brother's ambition?"

"It is the way things are done in society," Mr Cox pointed out gently. "Few nobles marry for love."

"But I am not noble, nor do I wish to be. I just wish to live a quiet peaceful life in the country, and be left alone."

The lawyer looked incredulous. He had known Beth since she was a child, and although he could not see her fitting into the strict etiquette of society life, no more could he see her living peacefully and uneventfully in the country. She had always been full of life and mischief and showed no signs of mellowing as she matured.

"Is there any way we can release enough money to at least buy Richard his commission?" she pleaded.

"I will look into it," Mr Cox said doubtfully. "But if not, your brother can surely wait? If you agree to buy him a commission when you marry or reach thirty… at the most he will have to wait seven years. He is a young man and has achieved the rank of sergeant on his own merit. He may go higher without having to purchase his rank."

Beth removed her hat.

"My brother grows impatient for me to comply with his wishes," she said. "I doubt I will survive another seven years of his impatience."

Edward Cox eyed the livid black bruise which coloured her right temple and cheek with horror.

"You must go to the authorities," he said, aghast.

"I don't think they will be sympathetic." She sat down and smiled sadly. "Just before he did this I threw a knife at him and called him a coward for brutally flogging my stable boy without cause." She leaned her elbows on the table and looked at the elderly lawyer.

"May God forgive me, but I am fast growing to hate Richard," she said earnestly. "He is making my life, and the lives of my servants unbearable. We cannot continue like this. Please, you must help me."

Edward Cox bit his lip. He did not have the money to loan her the sum she needed, or he would have done. He looked down at the Cunningham papers, which sat on the table between them.

"I cannot promise anything," he said. "But I will do everything I can to find a loophole in the law. I don't hold out much hope, but if there is a way I will find it. Come back to me in a week."

"Thank you." She stood to leave, and he got up to assist her to the door. When she offered her hand he took it and pressed it gently, then retaining his grip, looked at her with concern.

"Is there no one you could go and stay with?" he asked.

She shook her head.

"I will not leave him alone with my servants. But I won't throw any more knives at him, either," she smiled. "I will give him a very wide berth and will see you next week."

Chapter Three

Two days of staying mainly in her room to keep out of Richard's way drove the normally active Beth to distraction. She had written a letter to her friend Mary, had re-read Robinson Crusoe, and on the evening of the second day had started to write references for her servants, which she determined to give to all of them, so that in the event they were to be obliged to leave quickly as John and Martha had, at least they would have a good chance of obtaining employment elsewhere.

In the whole two days Richard had not budged from the house either, to Beth's annoyance. No doubt this was partially due to the heavy rain that slanted down almost continuously from a leaden sky. Looking out of her window intermittently during the day, she had seen Ben and Graeme splashing to and from the stables. They had now temporarily taken over John's tasks, until a new stable hand could be found. The rest of the servants had kept indoors as much as possible, and the general atmosphere of depression inside the house matched the grey gloom of the wintry weather outside.

As a result of this adverse weather Beth had used more candles than usual, and it was late in the evening of the second day, when she was just putting the finishing touches to Grace's reference before going to bed, that her candle suddenly flared, then started to gutter. A quick look in the drawer revealed to her that this was the last of her supply, and unwilling to abandon her task when it was so nearly completed she quickly wrapped a shawl around her shoulders, being dressed otherwise only in her shift. Taking the guttering candle with her, shielding the flame from the draught with her hand, she ran quickly and silently downstairs to get some more from the cupboard under the stairs, automatically avoiding the third step from the bottom, which creaked loudly when weight was put on it. The house appeared deserted. The servants would already be in bed but she had expected Richard to be ensconced in the library. But the library door was open, and no light or noise came from within. Either the hour was later than she had thought, or he had decided to have an early night. She lit a fresh candle from the stub of the first, then decided to take advantage of Richard's absence to get another book.

She chose a volume quickly, and was on her way out when the person she had been hoping to avoid suddenly appeared in the doorway. In one hand he held a candle and in the other a bottle of brandy. He smiled when he saw her.

"Well, sister, this is an unexpected surprise!" he said warmly. "I must confess, I had thought you were avoiding me." He surveyed her lazily, his eyes moving slowly upward from her bare toes to her face. She drew the shawl closer around her. His gaze made her feel as though she was standing naked in front of him, which was ridiculous.

"I came to get another candle, and a book," she explained. "Now I'm going to bed."

She had no choice but to move forward to pass him, and expected him to step away from the door. Instead he remained in the doorway, moving to one side so that she had barely enough room to get past. She shrank back against the doorpost as she left the room to avoid coming into contact with him, and interpreting her repugnance as fear he chuckled, although he showed no inclination to lay hands on her.

"Goodnight, Beth," he said softly and mockingly as she achieved the comparative safety of the hall.

She did not answer, but walked away as fast as decency would allow. He stepped out into the hall to watch her, his gaze following her up the stairs until she turned the bend of the landing and was gone from sight. Then he uncorked the bottle of brandy with his teeth and moved into the library, kicking the door shut behind him.

The reply to the letter he had written a week before arrived the next morning, and if Beth had been present when he received it, Richard would probably have read it out to her immediately. But she had taken advantage of the break in the rain and had gone riding, not returning until halfway through dinner, which she then ate in the kitchen with the servants, although she knew he disapproved of such familiarity.

On reflection, he thought as he re-read the letter over a glass of brandy that evening, it was a good thing that she had not been there this morning. It had given him time to think about the best way to reveal its contents to her. He reached over to replenish his glass, and noticed to his surprise that the bottle, started only last night, was almost empty. He did not recall having drunk that much the previous evening, yet must have, unless the servants were stealing it. He doubted they would be that stupid. They were well and truly under his control now.

It seemed his sister was also learning to respect him, which was good. He thought back with pleasure to the previous evening, when she had shrunk away from him. That, coupled with her general avoidance of him over the last two days, made him wonder why he hadn't hit her weeks ago. Clearly the realisation that he was willing to punish her physically if necessary had been all that was needed to bring her into line. He was certain now that she would acquiesce to his proposal. He would show her the letter first thing in the morning. It was a little late to do so now. She would no doubt already be asleep. He toyed with the idea of fetching another bottle of brandy from the cellar, then decided against it. He wanted to be clear-headed when he faced his sister in the morning. He would have an early night instead.

Once in his room, he undressed down to his shirt and then sat on the edge of the bed. He wasn't at all tired, he realised, and excitement at the thought that all his plans were about to be put into action rendered even the idea of sleep impossible. He turned the letter over in his hands, and then, suddenly decided, stood.

Outside Beth's room he hesitated, his hand raised to knock, then thought better of it. Instead he turned the handle carefully and opened the door slowly. If she was asleep, he would go away, he thought.

He was so quiet that she did not hear him at first. She had her back to the door, and was bending down to retrieve her shoes and place them under the bed. He was greeted with the sight of her long legs and buttocks, outlined perfectly by the thin cotton of her nightgown, back-lit as she was by the candle on the writing table in front of the window.

He drew in his breath sharply at the unexpected sight, and she whirled round, holding her shoes in one hand. Her eyes opened wide when she saw him standing clad only in his shirt, which reached almost to his knees. His hair was unbound and hung straight and loose to his shoulders. With his dark colouring he looked distinctly gypsyish, and she moved back a step.

"What are you doing here?" she said shortly. Her hair was also loose, and rippled down her back in thick silver-blonde waves, almost to her hips. Her shift was open at the throat, revealing a tantalising glimpse of creamy white breast. He stared at her, mesmerised. He had never seen her like this before and felt an involuntary stirring in his loins. To cover his confusion, he waved the paper in his hand at her.

"I…I received this letter today," he stuttered. His mouth was dry, and he licked his lips to wet them.

She made no move to take the letter from him, instead crossing her arms over her chest to shield it from his gaze.

"Put it on the table, if you want me to read it," she said, indicating the small table at the side of the bed, "then leave." It was a command, and he felt the anger rise in him, pushing aside the uncertainty of a moment ago.

"It's from Cousin Isabella," he elaborated, his voice steadier now. "I wrote to her last week, telling her that we are interested in renewing our relationship. She is delighted, and says that the whole family would be happy to see us at any time we choose to call. We will call next week, but I'll leave it to you to choose the day." There. He had established his authority, and in view of recent events was certain of her capitulation. He could allow her the small concession of choosing the day. He placed the letter on the table and started to turn away.

"You may choose any day you wish, Richard," Beth's voice came coolly from behind him. "I will not be accompanying you."

He turned back, hardly able to believe what he had heard. He had been sure she was cowed. But there she stood brazenly facing him, her head thrown back defiantly. He felt his rage rise, fired by the brandy he had consumed that evening.

"Read the letter," he said curtly. "We will discuss it in the morning."

He was halfway through the door when he felt the touch on his back. He looked back at her. She had reached across to the table and now held the letter in her hand. She had touched him with it to attract his attention, and she now held it out to him.

"I don't need to read the letter, Richard," she said, her voice soft, although her eyes still flashed. "I cannot come with you. But I've been to see Mr Cox, and he has assured me that..."

Richard slammed the door shut. The blood roared in his ears, blocking out her last words. All he knew was that she was still intent on defying him, and that she had had the temerity to go to the lawyer and discuss his financial affairs without asking his permission. By God, he would not tolerate this from a woman! On impulse he reached forward and gripped her round the waist with both hands, lifting her bodily off the floor and throwing her backwards.

She landed in the middle of the bed in a tangle of arms and legs, and before she could recover he had leapt on top of her, grasping her wrists and forcing them above her head. He leaned up, supporting his upper body on his arms, pushing hers into the mattress and making her cry out in pain as the fragile bones of her wrists took his weight. He adjusted his position so that he was sitting astride her, her lower body pinioned by his, one heavily muscled thigh on each side of her legs, crushing them together.

He was as surprised as she was by his reaction. When he had gripped her waist, he had intended to strike her, but was now glad he hadn't. He was enjoying the feel of her slender body struggling futilely beneath his, her eyes wide, pupils dilated with fear and pain, a great improvement on the defiance of moments ago. He felt the rush of adrenaline that always coursed through him when he inflicted pain combining with the alcohol, and he smiled.

Beth sensed his pleasure, and stopped struggling. She fought to bring her ragged breathing under control, but her chest heaved, drawing his attention. He looked down at her breasts, the nipples clearly visible through the thin cotton, and felt her arms tense as she instinctively tried to bring them down to cover herself.

"Richard," she started, then hesitated, having no idea how she was going to appease him, apart from promising to visit Isabella. "You are drunk," she said, smelling the brandy fumes on his breath. "Let me go, and we will talk about this in the morning, as you suggested."

"No," he said firmly. "We will talk about it now. I have been giving some thought to your curious reluctance to see sense. My plan is the only sensible course of action open to us if we're to avoid a life of penury. And yet in spite of all my persuasion you will not see reason. I begin to wonder if there is not another cause for your obstinacy."

What on earth was he talking about? She looked up at him, puzzled. She tugged experimentally at her wrists, to no avail.

"I have told you why I won't visit them," she said. "I have asked Mr Cox if he can find a way to release the money you need to purchase the officer's commission you want. He's promised to do his best."

Richard snorted dismissively.

"I have already discussed that with him. There is little hope. And even if he did find a way to get me my commission, I would still have to try to live, and keep you, on two hundred pounds a year, which is not enough. The life of an officer is not cheap, if he wishes to participate fully in the society of his fellow gentlemen. No, like it or not, sister, you are going to swallow your pride."

"You cannot ask this of me, Richard, it is too much," she said, looking up at him desperately.

"Are you virgin, sister?" he asked suddenly, startling her.

"What?" she gasped.

"Only it seems to me that you must have more reason than pure pride for being so recalcitrant. Your behaviour since I arrived has left me in grave doubts as to your purity."

"How dare you question my virtue?" she shouted, outraged. She pulled with all her might to free her hands from his grasp, but he took no notice of her struggles.

"I think I have every reason to question your virtue," he replied conversationally, sitting back on his haunches and lifting her arms from the bed. Deftly he transferred both her wrists to one hand and forced them back to the mattress above her head. "After all, when I first saw you, you were riding around the countryside in a state of considerable disarray. Then I come home unexpectedly and catch you with a half-naked stable boy." She opened her mouth to protest, but he put one finger warningly on her lips. "Then last night I find you wandering around the house in your shift. Who were you going to meet?"

"I told you what I was doing," she said icily. "My virtue is intact, and you know it."

"No, I don't," he replied. "But I am about to find out."

He shifted his weight suddenly, driving his knees between hers and using his free hand to pull her shift up to her waist. He forced her legs apart and then angled his legs so that one knee was across each of her thighs, splaying her legs outwards. He sat back and she cried out in pain as his knees dug into the soft flesh of her inner thighs.

He looked down at her most intimate parts deliciously exposed to his view, and drew in a sharp breath. She writhed in panic, tearing at her wrists, thrashing her head from side to side on the mattress. Lust coursed through his blood and he stiffened, his erect penis pushing against the linen of his shirt. He reached up impulsively and pulled hard at the top of her shift. The worn fabric gave way, and he folded back the edges to expose her perfect breasts.

"Oh God," he breathed in awe. He traced the curve of her breast with one finger, trying to hold on to the fact that she was his sister, which the lust threatened to drive from his mind. He pulled his thoughts with difficulty back to what he intended to do. He did genuinely have doubts as to her virginity, although they were not as strong as he made out. But now he had her at his mercy, he might as well find out for certain.

He moved his hand back down her body, and gently stroked at the soft golden curls. Then slowly, carefully, he slid one questing finger between her legs.

She arched from the bed, writhing and struggling like one possessed, almost succeeding in freeing her arms in her desperation. He tightened his grip on her wrists and felt the bones grind together. Then he withdrew his finger, and reaching up, gripped hold of one nipple hard between his thumb and index finger and twisted it viciously. She screamed in agony, and he let go, clapping his hand over her mouth to stifle the cry.

"Be still!" he commanded, and for the first time in her life she obeyed him instantly, to his immense satisfaction. "I wish only to discover for myself if you are pure. If you struggle like that, you are in danger of taking your own virginity." He removed his hand from her mouth, and she remained silent and rigid, as he carefully inserted one finger, slowly moving deeper, until he felt the delicate obstruction that told him all his hopes were still intact. He withdrew a little, feeling the slight rush of moisture as her body prepared itself automatically to receive him. He met her desperate, pleading gaze, saw the tears trickling down the side of her face into her hair, and was lost.

She saw his control snap, his eyes glaze with lust, and for the first time was truly terrified of him. She realised with horrifying clarity that she was about to be raped by her own brother, and that unless a miracle happened she was helpless to stop him.

All he was aware of was that he had to have her, but that he could not take her in the usual way. Suddenly decided, he put his hand underneath her, lifting her buttocks and driving first one finger, then two, deep inside her. He felt the anal muscle contract, then give way to the pressure, and he sighed with ecstasy. He would hardly know the difference, and she would still be virgin afterwards. She tensed at the invasion of her body, and closed her eyes. When she opened them a moment later he was staring at her breasts, eyes rapt, his breathing harsh and shallow.

"Richard," she pleaded. "Please, I beg of you, don't do this. You will regret it when you are sober."

He laughed, a warm pleasant sound that chilled her to the bone.

"You're wrong, Beth. I'm not drunk, and I will most certainly not regret it in the morning. Although I think you now regret defying me for so long. You have left it a little late to beg," he said. "But it's still good to hear."

He felt her trembling helplessly beneath him. The tears filled her eyes, such beautiful eyes, sparkling on her lashes and spilling down her temples. She would not fight him now. He had done it. After this, she would do anything he wanted, anything, without question. He moved his knees off her splayed legs, kneeling between them, and released her wrists while he pulled his shirt over his head, confident that even if she did try to escape him, which was unlikely, he could catch her before she reached the door.

The miracle had happened.

In one convulsive movement, Beth drove her heels into the mattress and threw her body up the bed, plunging her hand beneath the pillow in search of the object that she had kept there since her father had died and she had realised that she was alone, and therefore more vulnerable to burglary. In less than a second she had located it, and before he had done more than raise his arms above his head, a fistful of shirt in each hand, she had lunged forward and grabbed hold of his testicles with one hand, pressing the blade against the skin of the scrotum with the other.

"Now you be still, you bastard, or I swear to God I'll geld you." Her voice shook with the residue of terror and rage. He felt the steel cold and sharp against the delicate skin, and froze, his hands still above his head. He couldn't see anything because of the shirt. The lust vanished in a second, overridden by his survival instinct, and his mind cleared. Shame surged through him at what he had been about to do, mingled with anger at the position he was now in.

His erection vanished instantly, surprising her with the abruptness with which his penis shrivelled away to almost nothing. She had never seen a naked man before, although she had assumed that they had balls, like every male animal she had ever seen, and that they would not be happy at the thought of losing them.

"Beth…" he said, his voice muffled by the folds of linen.

"Don't move an inch," she said coldly. "Keep your arms where they are. Now you might be thinking that if you move quickly, you can disarm me." That was exactly what he was thinking. "But I warn you, I keep my knife razor sharp. You could shave with it. Are you willing to take the chance that you can take it from me before I can cut your balls off?"

He didn't answer her, but neither did he move. After a moment, she spoke again.

"Now, you are going to keep your arms above your head, and keep hold of your shirt, and you are going to, very slowly, move off the bed, towards the door."

She heard him swallow.

"I cannot see," he said. "If I miss my footing…"

"Then you will never have children. So you had better be careful." The icy rage in her voice left him in no doubt that she would carry out her threat if necessary.

It took nearly a minute for him to get off the bed, and to the door.

"Now keep your right hand and the shirt above your head, and reach down slowly with your left to open the door," she said. She did not want to even give him that opportunity, but had no choice. Both her hands were occupied. She squeezed her left hand slightly, and felt him tense at the uncomfortable pressure on his testes. He did as she had said.

"Open the door, and step out backwards into the hall," she instructed.

"Beth," he tried again. "I'm sorry." He was. He was appalled that he had almost ravished his own sister. He was sorry that he had drunk enough brandy to deprive him of his decency. But most of all he was sorry that he had allowed her to get him in the ridiculous position he was now in, standing naked on the landing with his shirt above his head.

"To paraphrase what you said to me earlier," she replied. "You have left it a little late to apologise. But it's still good to hear." She hesitated a moment, looked back at her room. Three steps away, and the door was wide open. She braced herself, then pulled down sharply with her left hand, squeezing as hard as she could at the same time. He screeched like a banshee, and doubled up instantly.

She leapt backwards into the room, slammed the door and locked it in one movement. Then she ran across to the heavy carved oak chest in which she kept spare bedding and with a strength born of desperation, pushed it across the room to barricade herself in. Once that was done, she felt reasonably safe against any attack he might make on the door during the night.

She dropped the knife on the bed, and leaned against the chest, panting for breath. She stood that way for almost a minute while her breathing slowed. Then the reaction set in. Her knees turned to water and her legs buckled beneath her. She just had time to crawl to the chamberpot that was kept under her bed before she was violently and copiously sick. After that she lay on the polished wooden floor for what seemed to be hours, grey and faint, the icy sweat of terror and despair soaking her shift. Finally, shivering with cold and reaction, she managed to pull the clammy cotton of her shift over her head, and drag herself into bed, where she lay staring at the chest that blocked the door, and, long after the candle had guttered and failed, continued to stare unseeingly into the dark.

* * *

Dear Cousin Richard,

I cannot tell you how delighted I was to receive your letter, which arrived by yesterday's mail. We are all so pleased that you and Elizabeth wish to re-establish contact with your family after so many years.

Beth gritted her teeth in anger. So he had had the cheek to write on her behalf as well as his own, without even bothering to inform her that he had done so.

Not surprisingly, she had not slept at all during the night, but had lain awake pondering the various options open to her. She had been both surprised and relieved that Richard had not attempted to force his way back into her room.

As soon as dawn broke she opened the shutters, and was now sitting at her writing table reading Isabella's letter in the thin grey early morning light. She leaned her elbows on the table and continued reading.

I am sorry to hear that your house is in such a bad state of repair, and will need extensive renovation before it is fit for you to live in or receive visitors. Of course I know that Uncle Henry was ill for some time before his tragic demise, and it is understandable that Elizabeth would have concentrated all her attention on caring for him rather than maintaining the house.

We would not hear of you staying in a hotel, when we have so much room here. My sisters and I would of course be overjoyed if you and Elizabeth would come to stay with us for a time. We live quietly here in Ardwick and have few visitors, so your company will be most welcome. Of course we will be removing to our London house for the season in the New Year, when life will be much more hectic. I have consulted with my brother, who says he feels it would be better if you could visit next week, in order that we may become re-acquainted, and we can then discuss the practicalities of your making an extended stay. We are at home each day from 10am until 2pm, and will expect you daily.

With very warmest wishes, both to you and dear Elizabeth,

Your cousin, Isabella.

Beth sat back in the chair. Her brother was not stupid. By saying that the house was in a dilapidated condition, he had both avoided the chance that the cousins would visit unexpectedly before he could reconcile her to them, and had managed to secure an invitation for them both to stay with their wealthy family, albeit a provisional one.

Beth scanned the letter again. Reading between the lines it seemed that her female cousins were bored with their life in the country, and would welcome the diversion of visitors. Cousin Edward was clearly more cautious and wanted to vet her and Richard before he consented to allow them to insinuate themselves into his household. Which Beth had to allow was understandable, although she still resented it, especially as she strongly suspected his reservations were about her rather than Richard.

Her father would not have hesitated to open his house to any relative in need, without feeling it necessary to meet them first. Her mother would, and indeed had, allowed any traveller who found himself stranded without a bed for the night to stay at the house. She had explained to Beth that in the highlands of Scotland where she was born, no traveller who requested hospitality was turned away, not even an enemy, although the guests were expected to reciprocate the treatment given by the host and behave in an honourable manner. Henry's illogical complaint that they would one day wake to find they had been murdered in their beds had cut no ice with his wife, and the worst they had suffered was the loss of some fine silver candlesticks.

A sudden flash of colour outside diverted Beth from her reminiscences, and she looked out of the window to see what it was, shrinking back when she saw her brother coming out of the stables accompanied by Graeme, who was leading Richard's horse. Once in the yard they stopped, and Richard took the reins, put his foot in the stirrup and swung up into the saddle. Beth, watching from behind the curtain, noticed that he sank into the saddle slowly and carefully, and felt a surge of satisfaction that in ejecting him from her room she had caused him some lasting, if temporary, damage.

Sitting astride the grey stallion, resplendent in his scarlet and buff uniform, Richard looked the picture of the refined gentleman soldier, his sole purpose in life to protect the country and its people from enemies, and Beth marvelled at how it was possible for someone to be so different in nature from what their physical appearance suggested.

I have lived a sheltered life, she thought. *I must become accustomed to meeting people who present a façade of themselves in public, when the reality is something else entirely. Indeed, I must try to learn to do that myself.* Richard spurred his horse forward and walked sedately out of the yard. He was not even out of sight before Graeme spat contemptuously onto the cobbles where the horse had stood just seconds before. Then he turned and walked back into the stables.

Beth had no idea where Richard was going, or how long he would be out. She did not think he would ride very far; clearly he was in some discomfort. As was she. Her wrists were swollen and black with bruising, her arms and shoulders ached, and the muscles of her thighs were stiff and sore. She had washed herself thoroughly several times with a cloth and water from the ewer and bowl in her room, but still felt soiled. A bath would be wonderful, but she did not have the time for that now.

She dressed quickly, cursing the current fashion that meant dress sleeves ended at the elbow, from which a series of ruffles covered part of the forearm but stopped well short of the wrist. She needed to speak to the servants, to tell them of the decision she had made, but she did not want them to see her injuries. She delved into the drawer where she kept her small collection of fripperies, withdrawing a pair of old-fashioned silk gloves. They would look a little strange but hopefully the news she had to impart would divert their attention from her appearance.

To her annoyance, when she tried to move the oak chest so that she could get out of her room it would not budge, and she had to resort to emptying it of its contents. Even then it took all her strength to push the heavy piece of furniture back to its normal place several feet along the wall, and she marvelled at the desperation that had enabled her to move it the night before. No wonder her arms ached, she thought.

When she reached the kitchen, Jane was the only occupant, although the pile of freshly baked bread rolls on the table, a large pat of butter and a slab of creamy white cheese told Beth that the others were expected at any moment. Jane turned from the fire and smiled when she saw who the visitor was.

"Richard has gone out," Beth said. "May I join you for breakfast?"

Jane laughed. "Since when did you have to ask such a question? Sit down. I'm a little late this morning, though. Sarah is ill, it seems, and is staying in bed. I'll go up to her later, but I haven't had time yet."

"What's wrong with her?" Beth asked.

Mary answered from the scullery where she was up to her elbows in hot water, washing dishes. Small for her age, she had to stand on a box in order to be able to reach into the sink, and Beth smiled as she saw her standing on tiptoe.

"She said she had a terrible headache and a bad stomach, Miss. She wouldn't even let me open the shutters, said the light would kill her, she did."

"It's come on very sudden," Jane said sceptically. "She was fine last night. If she's shirking I'll give her a bad head later, for certain. More likely she's been entertaining your brother, the little slut, begging your pardon, Beth, and wants to sleep late."

To Jane's surprise Beth whirled from the room without a word, and taking the stairs two at a time did not stop until she was outside Sarah's room. She stopped to catch her breath, and then without knocking, opened the door and walked in. The room was very dark, only a tiny amount of light showing at the edges of the ill-fitting shutters.

"Sarah?" Beth said softly, then listened. There was no reply, but she could tell by the irregular breathing coming from the bed that the maid was not asleep. She walked across to the window and fumbled to locate the latch of the shutters.

"Please don't open them, Miss," came the voice from the bed. "My head's aching something awful."

Beth ignored her and flung the shutters wide, letting light flood into the room. When she turned round, Sarah had pulled the sheet up over her head. Beth moved across to the bed and sat down gently on the edge of it. When she touched the sheet in an attempt to pull it down, Sarah gripped it so tightly her knuckles whitened, and she made an inarticulate sound of distress. Beth withdrew her hand. She was certain now that her suspicions were well-founded, and she hesitated before she spoke.

"Sarah," she said. "You know that I did not approve of your appointment. I'm sure you also know that the rest of the staff do not approve of you either. I know that when my brother employed you he expected you to provide other services for him in addition to the duties expected of a kitchenmaid. I have no doubt he also asked you to spy on me and the servants, and to report back anything of interest. I do not like you, I will be honest. But I do not blame you for seeking to improve your life, either." She hesitated for a minute, choosing her words carefully. She didn't want to reveal too much to the maid, who had become very still now.

"Last night," she continued, "Richard and I had an argument. When he left me he was extremely angry. I suspect that he has taken that anger out on you. I need to know, and I will not leave this room until I do. I'm not annoyed with you. If you have a headache I will send Mary up with some willow-bark tea. If you are injured I must know."

She moved to the foot of the bed and leaned against the bedpost, waiting. A few minutes passed, and Beth was just about to try again, when Sarah moved and slowly lowered the sheet, revealing her head and shoulders. Beth gasped.

One eye was swollen completely shut, black and maroon with bruising. Her lip was split and also swollen and had bled quite badly, judging by the dried blood on her chin. There were dark finger-shaped bruises at each side of her throat as well, and Beth's mouth twisted with rage.

"Tell me what happened, Sarah," she said softly

"I didn't do anything, Miss Elizabeth, I swear it!" Sarah said painfully, alarmed by the look on Beth's face. "I…he…came to my room. You were right, he does come sometimes, but not as often as everyone thinks. I could see he was angry and I tried to…er…console him. He just went mad." A tear trickled slowly down her cheek. "I don't know what I did wrong," she continued in a small voice. "I thought he was going to kill me."

Beth could imagine what Sarah had done to try to console him and how painful he must have found her attempts to caress him. Now she knew why he had not tried to re-enter her room. He had found another victim on whom to vent his rage, a more vulnerable one, one who would never go to the authorities, no matter how badly he beat her.

"Do you have any more injuries, Sarah?" Beth asked.

"He hit me in the belly, Miss, but not very hard. It's just a bit sore, is all. I'll be fine in a day or two."

Beth moved up the bed and took the maid's hand, startling her.

"I will ask Grace to come and tend you. She has a very gentle hand. You cannot stay here. You must leave as soon as you are well again," she said. When she saw the look on Sarah's face, she spoke again, quickly. "No, I'm not dismissing you. You did nothing wrong last night. He was angry with me, not you. But you must know him for what he is, Sarah. He's a bully, and he enjoys hurting people. You cannot still want to stay here, after this."

Sarah nodded her head, to Beth's amazement.

"He's no worse than many others I've known, Miss, and better than some. At least I've got a place to sleep at night and plenty of food. I'll be fine. Please don't make him dismiss me." Her tone was pleading, hopeful. He had clearly made her promises of some sort.

Beth tried to envisage the sort of life this girl must have endured for her to find her present situation an improvement. She released the maid's hand, and stood up.

"Richard will not be here for much longer, Sarah. Many things are going to change soon. I have no idea what promises he has made to you, but whatever they are, he is lying. He seeks to move up in the world and will discard you without a thought as soon as it suits him. Be realistic. You have no friends among the servants. Richard is protecting you from them. Once he is gone they'll force you to leave, one way or another. I know them, they're my friends, and do not suffer spies gladly."

Sarah's face crumpled and Beth felt a rush of sympathy and guilt that was almost physical. She had despised this girl, had made no attempt to try to befriend or understand her.

"I will promise you something, but you must give me something in return, Sarah. While I am here, I will do my utmost to make sure that Richard doesn't hurt you again. I will also ensure that he gives you a reasonable sum of money when you leave, enough for you to leave the area and maybe make a new start. I'll be honest with you. We are not rich, but I will do the best I can for you. In return I ask you not to report back to him anything the servants may say about him or anything else, for that matter."

"That won't be hard, Miss," Sarah said, trying to smile, and wincing as her lip cracked open again. "They hardly speak a word when I'm around. I hate being with them, but he told me I have to spend as much time in the kitchen as I can. He'll be angry if I don't."

"No, he won't," Beth said. "I will be giving him some very good news when he gets back. You can spend as much time as you want in your room. He has vented his anger on you now, and I don't think he will be fit enough to require your other services for some days yet. Now, I will go downstairs. I'll send Grace up to you later. Try to rest until then."

When she arrived back in the kitchen the others were halfway through breakfast. It was clear that Jane had told them that she was expected. A place had been set for her in her customary spot next to Graeme, and all eyes turned to her as she entered. She walked round the table and sat down.

"I've been upstairs to see Sarah," she said, looking at Jane. "Richard beat her quite badly last night. I told her I'd send Grace up to tend her. She'll be leaving once she is well enough."

Everyone looked relieved.

"Well, I can't say that I'm sorry she's seen sense," Jane said. "I'll be glad to see the back of her."

"She wanted to stay," Beth replied. "She said that this life is better than the one she knew before. I feel sorry for her."

"Yes, well, you always were soft-hearted," said Graeme, cutting himself a slice of cheese. "I've got no sympathy for her myself."

"You will have when you see what my brother's done to her," Beth replied. "She's a mess."

"Not as much of a mess as John was after being flogged, I'll be bound," he said callously, taking a huge bite of bread and cheese. "And with less cause for it, too," he finished in a muffled voice.

Beth couldn't argue with that, but even so she determined to do what she could for Sarah. John she could do nothing for. In spite of extensive enquiries nothing had been discovered as to the whereabouts of either him or Martha.

Grace had quickly finished her bread and cheese and now stood up, intending to go to Sarah.

"No, don't go yet, Grace." Beth held up a hand to stop her. "I have something to say, and it concerns all of you." Grace sat down again, and everyone looked at their mistress expectantly.

"Richard has written to my cousins asking to renew the acquaintance between us. Yesterday he received a favourable reply from Isabella. We are invited to visit next week, and if things go well, to stay with them for a time. I have decided to accept Isabella's invitation." Her voice broke slightly on the last word and she stopped, looking down at the empty wooden platter in front of her. The silence was profound, and when she looked up again a moment later everyone was still staring at her, their faces masks of shock. She swallowed, and opened her mouth to explain further.

"What has he done to you?" Graeme said harshly. Beth felt the sudden tears threatening and swallowed them back hastily.

"Nothing," she lied. "I've decided to renew my acquaintance with my family and that's all there is..."

"Take off your gloves," Thomas commanded suddenly. Beth looked at him in surprise. She had often heard him issue orders; that was what he was paid to do. But he had never used that tone of voice with her before. It was Graeme who was the master of plain, even abrupt speaking, not Thomas. She folded her arms defensively as though she expected him to force her to comply with his demand, and he sighed, his handsome face creasing with concern.

"You only wear gloves when you go riding," he explained. "I've never seen you wear them in the house, and certainly not when you're having breakfast. You're hiding something from us. If you've decided to make friends with your family, that's up to you, but you owe us honesty, Beth. We deserve that."

Beth flushed with shame. He was right. She unfolded her arms, but did not remove her gloves.

"You're right, Thomas," she said. "I will be honest with you. Richard told me about the letter last night, and we had an argument. He gripped my wrists and they're bruised. They look worse than they are, though. But I was afraid you would react like you did when he hit me in the barn, and so I wore these, hoping you wouldn't notice." Thomas raised one eyebrow. "Yes, I know it was stupid. You notice everything. And anything you miss, Graeme sees." She looked up at her neighbour, but he had not responded to her light-hearted tone; his tanned face was grim and forbidding, his bushy eyebrows drawn low in a frown. She cleared her throat uncomfortably. At times like this she wished she had maintained a distant relationship with her staff. They knew her too well.

"Let's see your wrists, then," Thomas said.

Beth took her gloves off and laid her hands on the table. Thomas's whole body stiffened, but he showed no signs of charging off to confront Richard, although Beth was still glad her brother was not at home. She reached over for a bread roll, trying to make light of the situation.

"As I said, they look worse than they are."

"What else did he do to you, Beth?" Thomas asked, his voice too quiet. Beth's heart somersaulted. She could not tell him. She was absolutely certain that if he and Graeme knew what Richard had tried to do to her they would kill him, or die in the attempt.

"Nothing," she said carefully. "He got the worst of the encounter."

"Kicked him in the bollocks, did you?" Graeme said unexpectedly.

Ben exploded with laughter, instantly extinguished when he caught sight of Jane's shocked countenance.

"Graeme!" she cried. "How dare you use such a word in front of ladies?"

He ignored her completely. "You did, didn't you?" he said, looking down at Beth. His face was still set in its grim expression, but his eyes were sparkling, sure that he was right.

He was close enough.

"Yes," she replied. "But how did you know?"

"I knew there was something wrong with him as soon as he walked into the stables. He walked very carefully, with his legs apart, as though he'd just shat himself. Sorry." He held up a hand to forestall a further outburst from Jane. "It's happened to me, and no, I'm not going to tell you why," he said, looking at Ben's and Mary's alert and curious faces. "Some stories are not fit for young ears. I'll tell you this, though, Beth. I'd have killed the person who did it to me if I'd caught them. It's a dangerous thing to do to a man. I'm surprised you've got no more than bruised arms."

"Yes, well, by the time he recovered, I was in my room with

the door locked and the chest pushed up against it. He took his rage out on Sarah instead."

"In that case, maybe I do feel some pity for the girl. Just a little," Graeme qualified, in case anyone should think he was going soft.

Beth was profoundly grateful to Graeme. He had unwittingly deflected Thomas's attention from Richard's attack on her. She spread butter thickly on her roll, and took a small bite. The bread was still warm, light and delicious.

"Why have you changed your mind about your family, Beth?" Jane asked. "I never thought you would. None of us expect you to."

"I know, but I must face facts. None of us can carry on like this. You are all miserable and…"

"We're fine," Jane said. "Don't give in to him on our account. We don't want you to do that."

"I know you don't," Beth said. "And I'm not. But the way things are going it's only a matter of time before one of us murders the other. I'm miserable too."

"But if you give in to Richard now and go begging to your cousins, surely that will encourage him in his violence?" Jane pointed out.

Graeme and Thomas both nodded agreement.

"Don't worry," said Beth determinedly. "I have no intention of begging. Nor am I giving in to him. I am going to compromise, that's all. And so is he."

* * *

To her surprise Richard did not return to the house until late in the evening. From her chair in the library she heard him come in. She put the book she had been attempting unsuccessfully to concentrate on down on the table, and waited for him. She was very tired, had been fighting drowsiness for hours, but when she heard the doorknob turn her mind cleared instantly and she was awake.

He had removed his coat and his boots, although he still wore his wig, which was slightly crooked. He took several steps into the room before he saw her. He stopped, clearly taken aback. His face reddened and he looked away, unwilling to meet her cool, level stare. That was good. He was ashamed of what he had done. That would help her to achieve what she wanted.

"Good evening Richard," she said serenely. "Come and sit down. I need to talk to you." He hesitated, obviously torn between a wish to leave and curiosity about what she was going to say. Curiosity got the upper hand and he took the chair opposite her by the fire, seating himself carefully. His face was sullen and guarded. Beth smiled.

"I have read Isabella's letter," she said. "And have decided to accept her invitation to visit, and to stay, if we are asked."

The transformation was instantaneous. His face lit up with a huge smile, his brown eyes sparkled, and he moved forward as though to embrace her. She jerked back in her seat, revulsion causing the bile to rise in her throat. She spoke quickly, before he could move any closer.

"I said I wish to talk to you. I have not finished. If you touch me I will leave the room immediately, and will not go to Lord Edward's, now or at any other time."

He sat back in his seat, the smile fading.

"I am sorry about last night, Beth," he began tentatively. "I had no intention…"

"I don't care what your intentions were, Richard, but as you've brought the matter up, I will tell you this. If you lay violent hands on me again, you will have to kill me. Because if you do not, I promise I will kill you at the first opportunity that presents itself." He smiled again, a little superciliously, she thought. "You may think this is an idle threat. You are stronger than me and enjoy violence, whereas I do not. But everyone is vulnerable at times. Everybody has to sleep, and your door has no lock." Her voice held no emotion. She was not threatening him. She was making a promise. The smile disappeared completely, but otherwise he did not react to her words. Beth was a little surprised. She had half-expected him to retaliate, and her hand, hidden innocently enough in her skirts, fingered the hilt of the knife secreted in her pocket.

"Now," she continued, when she was certain he was ready to listen. "I will come with you to our cousins' house next week. I will not beg, but I will be friendly. I will behave in a manner they will approve of. I will allow Edward to be condescending if he wishes, but if he insults my mother I will defend her. Don't interrupt me." Richard had opened his mouth to make an objection, but now subsided. He relaxed back a little further into the chair, and she continued. "I am willing to do a lot but I will not allow my mother to be slandered without retaliating. I will accept their charity if it is offered. I will go to London if we are invited. I will try to do whatever is expected of a lady. If a suitable man asks for my hand in marriage, I will accept. As part of the condition of acceptance I will insist that he purchase your commission for you and provide you with an additional lump sum to set you up in your officer's rank. If I am as irresistible as you seem to think, that will not be difficult." Richard cringed noticeably at her comment, but she ignored him. "I trust that you will by then have made enough connections to take your place in society without any further assistance from me." She stopped and rose, going across to the cupboard. She took out a bottle of wine and poured two glasses, handing one to him before resuming her seat.

He eyed her speculatively. "I assume you want something from me in return," he said cautiously.

"Of course, but it is not much, considering what you stand to gain in return. I'm not asking you to be false, to lower your pride, or to act against your principles, as you expect me to do."

"What do you want, then?" he said.

She took a sip of her drink before answering.

"I have written excellent character references for all of the servants. You will sign them. Anyone who wishes to leave will be allowed to do so immediately, and will be given three months' pay. If Martha and John can be found, they will be reinstated if they wish, and if they do not, will be given six months' pay. If any of the servants wish to stay they will be treated with the respect they deserve." So far, so good. Richard was listening attentively.

"When Sarah is well enough to leave the house, you will let her go. I have written a reference for her as well. You will give her twenty pounds to allow her to start a new life if she pleases." Now he reacted, as she had expected he would.

"What?! Twenty pounds? That's ridiculous! That's three years' wages for a kitchenmaid. Do you know what she is? She's nothing but a…"

"She's nothing but a woman who you came close to murdering last night because you were angry with me and ashamed of yourself. Yes, I know she's a whore and I know you have used her as such. But she didn't deserve what you did to her last night, Richard, and you will compensate her, even if you have to ask for a loan from your cousin to do it."

He inhaled deeply through his nostrils and the muscle jumped in his cheek, but he held his temper in check and did not object any further. Beth was surprised by how easy she was finding this. She had felt so sick with terror and disgust the previous night that she had not known how she would be able to face him again without vomiting or running cravenly from him. But now that she was actually in his presence she felt only an icy hatred and utter contempt for him. She emptied her glass then spoke again.

"When we are with my family, or in any public place, we will behave to one another as a brother and sister would who have been distanced by circumstances. I will not pretend any great affection for you. I'm not that good an actress. Once I am married and you have received your commission, you will remove yourself from my life. I do not wish to see you or hear from you ever again, as long as I live. You will communicate neither with me nor my husband under any circumstances whatsoever and you will to all intents and purposes be dead to me. Is that clear?"

He had the grace to look ashamed, and deeply uncomfortable.

"Beth, if I could turn back the clock, I swear I…"

"But you can't," she cut in brutally. "My conditions are not up for negotiation. You accept them all, or I will refuse Isabella's invitation and any subsequent invitations she may extend, and you can do your worst."

Richard looked at her, incredulous. This was not bravado. He had seen bravado; it was usually used to disguise fear. He had seen courage, too, many times; that was an acceptance and conquering of fear. But he had rarely seen what he was witnessing now; someone who had no fear at all, either of dying or living. She was truly indifferent. He had broken something in her, but it was not what he had wished to break. He had not cowed her spirit; instead he had irrevocably broken his hold over her.

She placed her empty glass on the table and stood.

"I would like to say one thing," he said, and she stopped, waiting for him to continue, her face composed and cold. "I think it would be better if you are known as Elizabeth from now on rather than Beth, which is somewhat informal and common, I feel. I am sure you have already noticed that the servants are addressing you as Miss Elizabeth. I will also call you Elizabeth, from this moment."

This was a pathetic attempt to reassert some authority over her. She looked down at him with contempt.

"I have no wish to be on informal terms with you or any of the Cunningham family," she said. "As long as once I am married you do not call me sister, between now and then you may call me the Queen of Sheba, if you wish. I care not." She moved away towards the door. "I will leave you to think over what I have said," she said carelessly. "Let me know when you have made your decision."

He had no choice. He accepted her conditions, and that evening wrote a letter to his cousin Isabella stating that he and his sister would be delighted to call on Thursday next, at twelve o' clock.

Chapter Four

Late November 1742

Brother and sister clattered down the road in a phaeton hired especially for the day from the landlord of the Ring o' Bells Hotel on Didsbury village green. Beth had complained that the expense was unnecessary; they could cut just as dashing a figure if they were to ride to Raven Hall on their own horses, especially as their cousins lived only five miles away, and the money saved could be used to repaint the windows and front door of their house.

Richard had argued that first impressions were all-important, and as he held the purse strings he got his way. As they entered the privately owned Ardwick Green, with its leech-shaped lake, known as 'the canal', and turned into the driveway of Raven Hall, Beth had to grudgingly admit that Richard had a point. She had forgotten how large the hall was. It was approached along a gravel driveway wide enough to take a carriage with ease, its formal lawns dotted with painstakingly trained and clipped topiary animals and birds, which alone denoted that the owner of the house had sufficient funds to employ an army of gardeners.

The hall itself was a Palladian villa, built of honey-coloured stone. Its portico was supported by columns of white marble, and its cornice ran around the house at first-floor level. Its many-paned windows glittered in the weak autumnal sunshine, and as they drew to a halt outside, the front door opened and the plump figure of Isabella, the eldest of the three Cunningham sisters, appeared in the doorway.

Richard, immaculate in his freshly-laundered uniform, leapt lightly down from the phaeton and reached up to help his sister, who ignored his hand and climbed down unassisted. His mouth tightened slightly but he showed no other sign of his displeasure, and the siblings walked up the steps side by side, Beth smoothing her voluminous yellow skirts as she went and composing her face into a mask of politeness as she drew closer to her cousin.

Isabella was wringing her hands and hopping about on the spot, as though uncertain as to whether she should come forward to greet them or not. Beth knew enough of polite etiquette to know that her cousin should really have waited in the drawing room until her guests were announced by a footman, rather than stoop to meeting them at the door herself. The fact that she had, showed how pleased she was to see them. Beth would also have laid a wager that Lord Edward was not at home.

"Oh, dear cousins, it is so good to see you!" Isabella gushed as Richard and Beth attained the top step, kissing each of them in turn on the cheek. Beth inhaled the faint aroma of lavender, then Isabella was turning away. "Do come in!" She led the way through a gloomy if spacious oblong entrance hall panelled in dark wood, into the drawing room, where her sisters Charlotte and Clarissa were sitting on velvet upholstered chairs, their faces masks of nervousness. Isabella motioned her visitors to sit down, and fluttered anxiously in the background, summoning a maid to bring refreshments.

"I trust you had a safe journey?" she said politely after a moment.

"Yes, thank you," Beth replied, when Richard showed no sign of doing so.

They perched stiffly side by side on the sofa where they had been directed to sit, Beth making sure she had no physical contact with her brother.

"Edward makes his apologies," Isabella said, confirming Beth's suspicions. "He has been called away on urgent business, but assures us he will return shortly."

"I trust it is not bad news?" Beth replied.

"No, no, I am sure it is not," cried her cousin, clearly clueless as to why her brother was absent.

There was a short silence. The clock that Beth remembered so well from her previous visit ticked ponderously in the corner. Isabella glanced towards the door, obviously praying for the appearance of the maid with the tea things.

Beth looked at the three women and realised with a start that they were more disturbed by this meeting than she herself was, although she doubted that they felt the resentment she did at having to lower her principles. Unexpectedly, she felt sympathy for her relations, who seemed uncertain how to begin a conversation. Richard, no conversationalist at the best of times, was clearly flummoxed at being in the presence of so many women. Beth had a mischievous urge to allow the silence to continue indefinitely, but remembering her bargain with Richard, took a deep breath, pasted a bright smile on her face, and plunged in.

"What a delightful room!" she said, looking around. It must have cost a fortune, she thought. Every wall was covered with expensive drab green wallpaper, printed with a pattern of Grecian urns. The floor was covered with an enormous carpet of dark red, and the uncomfortable mahogany furniture was upholstered in maroon velvet. The general effect was dark and oppressive, in complete contrast to her own cosy parlour, decorated in warm shades of yellow and cream.

"Oh, do you like it?" Charlotte spoke for the first time. "We chose the paper ourselves. Edward says it is too dark, but we like the colour. Green is so restful, you know. My dear Frederick always used to say that colours affect our moods."

"Indeed," Beth replied, too annoyed that she should share an opinion with a cousin she remembered as being boorish and pompous to ask who 'dear Frederick' was. "My bedroom is decorated in shades of green," she continued, omitting to mention that her wallpaper, a pale green originally, was now very faded, its original flower pattern almost invisible. The conversation pattered on for a few minutes, and just as it was in danger of drying up again the maid appeared with the tea things, and whilst the ladies were occupied in pouring tea and handing out tiny cakes, Beth took the opportunity to discreetly observe them.

They all had the Cunningham dark hair, deep brown eyes and sallow colouring. But whereas Isabella was plump, her pleasant face round and kind, her two younger sisters were painfully thin and looked as though they were just recovering from some terrible illness. Their faces were haggard, their skin already wrinkled, although they could hardly be out of their thirties, Beth estimated.

She was just about to enquire after their recent health, when Isabella, as though having read her thoughts, anticipated her. She seemed to have relaxed a little now that she had something to do with her hands.

"Charlotte and Clarissa always tell me that I eat too much," she smiled, deftly dropping a large lump of sugar into her teacup with the tongs, and picking up a cake. "I know it is the height of fashion to be slender as they are, but it is so tiresome to always have to refuse the tastiest food. And I have been told that men prefer ladies with a little…ah…roundness to them. What do you think, Elizabeth? I trust I may call you by your first name immediately, as we are related?"

"Of course," replied Beth, warming to her cousin in spite of her earlier determination to hate the family eternally. "But I really cannot venture an opinion on the matter. I think we must ask the gentleman present. What do you think, Richard? Do gentlemen prefer slender ladies, or those of more ample build?" She smiled sweetly at her brother, and waited.

Richard coloured furiously. Any man would be in a quandary over this query. He could not express an opinion without insulting someone, and he didn't have the social skills to deflect the question. The three sisters looked at him eagerly, as though he were the fount of all knowledge, and Beth rejoiced inwardly.

"I…ah…I am sure it would depend on the gentleman," he said lamely, after a pause. "Each man's tastes are different, you know."

He was not getting away with it that easily.

"Yes, I'm sure that's true," Beth responded. "But surely you must discuss the ladies with your dragoon friends. What would you say the majority prefer?"

Richard flashed her a look of pure hatred. He sipped his tea to gain time. The last thing he could talk about in polite company were his men's views of the female gender, which dwelt only on sexual matters and varied from the contemptuous to the obscene.

The door opened and Lord Edward strode in, an older, more portly version of Richard. The Cunningham blood was certainly strong, Beth thought, feeling out of place among all these dark relations. Richard had never been so relieved to see anyone in his life, and leapt to his feet to greet the peer. Beth rose more slowly.

"Sorry to be late," Lord Edward barked, sounding anything but. "Several hounds down with something, you know. The Master of Hounds is afraid they won't be fit for the meet next week. Had to go and reassure the fellow."

That's put us in our place, thought Beth. *A reunion with long-lost relatives takes second place to a sick dog.* Nevertheless she curtsied politely, and felt Edward's appreciative eyes surveying her from head to toe. He threw himself down in a chair and popped a cake into his mouth. Richard and Beth resumed their seats.

Isabella politely endeavoured to include her brother in the conversation.

"We were just discussing whether gentlemen prefer slender ladies like Clarissa and Charlotte, Edward, or more ample figures such as mine," she said.

"Neither," Edward replied without hesitation. He waved a hand at his pigeon-breasted sisters. "You two are too thin, and you, Isabella, are too fat,"

"My dear Frederick always used to say..." ventured Charlotte.

"Gentlemen prefer something in between," Edward continued as though she hadn't spoken. "A little roundness in the breast and the rump, that's all, not rolls of blubber, or sharp bones sticking out everywhere."

Beth bristled at his rudeness and even Richard looked uncomfortable. But the three sisters seemed completely unconcerned, and Beth realised that they were probably used to being addressed in such a manner. She envisaged months of having to endure her cousin's thoughtlessness without retaliating, and wondered how she would survive.

"So, I believe that Uncle Henry left your house in need of extensive renovation when he died," Edward said, addressing Richard.

"Er...there are repairs that need to be done, yes," Richard said.

"And you are hoping to come and stay here for a while?"

Richard looked to Beth for assistance, but she was gazing demurely into her lap. She had no intention of helping him here. She would be polite; she would endure her boorish cousin, but she would not beg, she had told him that.

"That would be very helpful," Richard replied. Sweat stood on his brow in spite of the fact that the room was distinctly chilly, the fire in the hearth doing nothing to counteract the draughts which pervaded the large room. "You see, father left us somewhat... impoverished, and we cannot afford the expense of a hotel."

"Ah, I see." *So you wish to come and sponge off us,* his tone clearly said.

"Father was very ill for some years before his death," Beth leapt in defensively. "He always managed his investments himself, and was unable to do so once he fell ill. As I had to nurse him alone, I did not have the time or the expertise to manage his financial affairs." Her emphasis on the word *alone* clearly reproved Edward for showing no concern over his uncle's illness, and he reddened slightly.

"The house is not mortgaged, but we find ourselves in somewhat straitened circumstances," Richard finished.

Lord Edward threw another tiny cake into his mouth and stood up.

"Well, I'm sure the ladies have no interest whatsoever in financial matters, and would prefer to talk about fashion or sewing, or suchlike," he said dismissively. "What say we repair to my study for a drop of port and discuss the situation?"

Richard stood, and remembering just in time to bow politely to the ladies, followed his cousin out of the room. Beth was torn between relief that he'd gone and anger at being so peremptorily dismissed.

"So, do you sew then, Elizabeth?" ventured Charlotte, following her brother's suggestion as to a topic of conversation.

"Yes, my mother was a seamstress, as I'm sure you remember. She taught me when I was a child," Beth replied, possessed by a mischievous demon.

Her three companions blushed, clearly embarrassed that the reason for her being ostracised for so many years had been brought up.

"Er...did you make your own costume, cousin? It is most becoming," Isabella asked.

She was being tactful, Beth realised; trying to put her visitor at ease. The bright yellow dress was old-fashioned in style and the colour hideous on Beth, making her hair look colourless and deadening her complexion. Even the unobservant Richard had commented on how unflattering it was when she had appeared that morning, but she had pointed out that she possessed only two dresses suitable for visiting, and the blue silk was dirty.

Beth gave in. She could not vent her anger on these ladies, who were only trying to be welcoming and kind and were showing not the slightest sign of condescension.

"You are too kind, Isabella," she said. "But I know the dress is out of fashion. I am afraid that I have not had the time to follow the latest styles. I have been too preoccupied with other things."

"Of course, I understand. It must have been so difficult for you, caring for your father, with no help at all. I did want to call but…" Isabella stopped abruptly, and Beth realised with a shock that her cousin had been about to say that she had wanted to call, but presumably her brother had forbidden it. This woman was not her enemy, and Beth tried to absorb the fact that if it had not been for the hostility of the male Cunninghams, the family rift would probably never have occurred.

"I have wonderful servants," Beth said, as though she had not noticed that Isabella had stopped half way through a sentence. "They were amazing. I did not feel alone at all."

"You are very lucky. Good servants are so hard to find these days." Isabella carried on, discussing the various merits and failings of the servants, and Beth listened with half her attention, wondering what Richard and Edward were talking about.

* * *

Richard had just finished outlining the provisions of his father's will, and had given a somewhat edited version of his ambitions to find a good husband for Beth.

"I realise that I may have to live in somewhat reduced circumstances, but I see no reason why Elizabeth should not make a good match, with her looks and dowry. She at least should be able to escape a life of penury," he said insincerely.

"You are too good-natured, cousin," Lord Edward put in. "Of course she needs a good husband. All women need a man to keep them on the right path. But I see no reason why you shouldn't profit by it as well. After all, *your* birth is impeccable. Both your parents were noble. I am sure a man can be found who will appreciate the high birth of his brother-in-law, and be suitably generous."

Richard tried to look as though the idea of profiting from his sister's marriage had not occurred to him until this very moment.

"Well, of course it would be very nice to be able to purchase a cornet's commission…" Richard began.

"At the very least, dear boy. Your sister is quite remarkable, you know, looks exactly like her mother. And even without a penny to her name *she* snared herself a lord's son, after all, didn't she?"

Richard was extremely grateful that his sister was not present. Edward's contemptuous tone left it in no doubt that as far as he was concerned Uncle Henry might have been in love, but his pauper wife had been out for everything she could get.

"I suppose you're hoping that I will help to launch Elizabeth into society, then?" Edward said.

Richard hesitated. He had not expected such bluntness, and was unsure whether he would gain more respect by responding in a like manner, or by prevaricating. He finally opted for the former, mixed with a little humility. After all, hadn't Lord Edward just pointed out that his birth was noble, and by inference that it was only his sister who was tainted?

"I would be most grateful if you were willing to do that, yes," he said.

"Do you think Elizabeth capable of behaving appropriately in more elevated circles?" Edward asked, eyeing Richard's empty glass with approval. He liked a man who could take his drink and didn't sip at it like an old woman. He replenished their glasses.

"Yes, I'm sure she can. She is very intelligent and well educated, and can speak on a variety of subjects, and I'm certain she is as anxious as I am to be accepted into the right company." That was true, at least.

"Hmm." Edward was not in favour of education for women; it made them dissatisfied with the domestic lives they were designed for. "Well, I think she may do. And you and I can always keep a tight rein on her, until she's married of course, after which we can leave it to her husband to control her. I think you should come and stay for a short while, see how things go. My sisters will enjoy having another woman around and will delight in making her presentable. If we all rub along well together I see no reason why you can't accompany us to London for the season."

Richard was ecstatic. He'd expected to have to use all his powers of manipulation and persuasion to get Edward to agree to take them under his wing. This had been so easy. He never stopped to wonder why, and when his cousin changed the subject to the proposed hunt on Saturday, Richard threw himself into the new topic without any further thought. Clearly Lord Edward was an altruistic man who had taken to his cousin Richard.

Lord Edward was nothing of the sort. He had been amazed by his lowborn cousin's beauty. Even in that hideous dress she was stunning. He was certain that his sisters would be delighted to groom her for London, which would get them off his back for a while, and once he let it be known that she was looking for a husband and had a considerable dowry to go with her looks, she would be besieged. All he had to do then was to make sure that the man chosen for her had some parliamentary influence. As a peer, Edward Cunningham automatically had a seat in the House of Lords but was right at the bottom of the pecking order of the nobility. The only way to secure more influence in government was to either buy the loyalty of MPs, which could be unreliable, and was hideously expensive, or to curry favour with a more prominent peer. An influential in-law could make all the difference, but his sisters were all past marrying age, and pig-ugly too. If she behaved herself Elizabeth could probably net a viscount at the very least. If necessary he would buy Richard's commission himself rather than let her marry a military man with no political pull. Of course he was not about to tell Richard that. If a suitor could be found who would both pay for a commission *and* get him political preferment, so much the better. Edward had not kept his fortune by spending money unnecessarily.

The pig-ugly sisters were delighted when they heard their brother's decision, and it was arranged that Beth and Richard would move in in two weeks, which would give them all a few weeks to get to know each other before travelling down to London.

For her part, spending an hour with her female cousins had reassured Beth on one point, at least; they were all genuinely pleased that she was coming to stay, and whilst they seemed somewhat empty-headed, they held her in no contempt at all. They were all kind and eager to make her feel welcome. Of Edward she was less sure, but she would cope with him when and if it became necessary.

* * *

All this did not make it any easier to leave home. She found herself spending more and more time with the servants and none at all with Richard, who reminded her every time their paths crossed that she would have to make a good impression on the Cunninghams if she expected them to take her to London. She reminded him of her promise, several times, and finally took to cutting him dead, walking away whenever he tried to speak to her. He did not attempt to touch her, for which she was grateful.

She went to visit Mary a couple of days before she was due to leave Didsbury. Saying goodbye to her friend, not knowing how long it would be before they saw each other again was difficult, but bidding farewell to the servants was even more heart wrenching. None of them had taken up the offer to leave with three months' pay, for which Beth was secretly grateful. It was comforting to know that she still had a body of friends that she could turn to at any time, even if technically speaking they were now Richard's servants rather than hers. She had promised them more than once that she would visit them before leaving for London, no matter what. They had briefly discussed King George's recent proclamation calling for extra men to volunteer for the militia. With much of the army engaged abroad, the militia would be needed to put down any local disturbances that might occur in their absence. As expected, Thomas said he would serve if necessary, but that he would not volunteer, to Jane's relief, who, Hanoverian as she was, had no wish to see her beloved husband die putting down a riot amongst his own neighbours. They all promised to step up their hunt for John and advise him to lie low if he wanted to avoid being enlisted. Vagrants were sometimes forcibly conscripted as a way of giving them employment. She had no idea whether John was a vagrant or not, but as he had never called to ask for a reference it was a distinct possibility. He would die rather than serve in the Hanoverian militia, she was sure.

On the morning of her departure Beth breakfasted in the kitchen. Everyone was too honest to put on an air of false gaiety and consequently the mood was sombre.

"It's not that bad," she said. "I'll only be a few miles away. I'll probably be able to sneak away more than once before we go to London. And if I do get married, I'll insist that you all come to work for me, if you want to."

"If your husband allows it," Thomas pointed out. "He'll already have his own servants."

"Well then, he can have some more!" Beth cried.

She was close to tears, but managed to swallow them down as first Thomas then Jane enfolded her in a warm embrace. Jane was a homely woman, plump and plain-featured, with mousy-coloured hair. Many people had wondered what Thomas had seen in her. With his handsome face, flashing green eyes, and muscular build, he could have had his pick of the village girls. But Beth had never questioned what Thomas saw in Jane. She was kind, loyal and level-headed, and absolutely devoted to him, as he was to her. It was a tragedy that in ten years of marriage Jane's womb had never quickened. They would have made marvellous parents, Beth thought, although if they were disappointed they never spoke of it in public.

"I feel better that Grace is going with you," Jane said, sniffing loudly. "At least you'll have a friend by your side."

Beth had been overjoyed when Grace had tentatively suggested that she accompany her as lady's maid, and had accepted the offer immediately. She could not think of anyone better suited for the post. Demure and polite, she could never cause offence, yet she would be unerringly loyal to her mistress.

Finally Beth turned to Graeme. To her surprise he made no move to embrace her, keeping his hands by his sides.

"You make sure you write, now," he said gruffly. "And don't you go marrying the first man that asks just to be rid of your brother. We'll always be here for you. Better be penniless with people who love you, than married to a lump of shite."

It was a measure of how upset Jane was that she made no comment on Graeme's language.

"Well, then," he said roughly, and stepping forward he crushed her to him suddenly, so tightly that her ribs creaked and her face was squashed against his chest. Then he released her, and turning, walked out of the kitchen without a backward glance.

Beth stood for a moment looking at the place where he'd been seconds ago. In all the years she'd known him, she had never seen him cry, not even when her mother and father died, both of whom he'd been devoted to. But in the moment between releasing her and turning away, she'd seen the tears standing in his eyes. It was too much. She broke down and sobbed.

* * *

Beth missed her home enormously, an abiding pain that lodged somewhere under her heart; sometimes dull, sometimes sharp, but never completely absent. The house at Didsbury was small, warm and cosy, if a little shabby. Raven Hall, in spite of its size and magnificence, was cavernous and draughty, its huge fires failing to penetrate the chill of the enormous, high-ceilinged rooms.

She blessed the contempt her lowborn mother had earned from Lord Edward; it was no doubt due to that that she had been delegated to a small, sparsely furnished bedroom. It was still twice the size of her room at home, but by Cunningham standards was poky. The bed was a huge canopied monster and the wardrobe and dressing table were so solid they would probably outlast the house, but the walls were decorated a warm shade of dusky pink, the size of the room meant that the fire had some effect on the temperature, and the window faced in the direction of her old home. At nights she would sometimes sit by the window, imagining an impossible world in which women had the same rights as men and did not have to be financially dependent on them, a world where she could live where she pleased, with whom she pleased, and do as she liked.

The servants seemed cool and distant, almost like ghosts. When she greeted them with a smile and enquired after their health they would merely mumble an incomprehensible reply, before bowing or curtseying and blending back into the surroundings. After a few days Beth discussed this with Grace, for whose welfare she was deeply concerned.

"They are really very friendly," Grace replied in answer to Beth's anxious queries as to their coolness. "They've made me very welcome. Of course there are a lot of them, and I haven't learned all their names yet, but the ones I've met are nice. They have to be distant with the family, though. That's what Lord Edward has commanded. They must remember their place. They would be dismissed if they were too familiar."

Beth was shocked. She now understood the mumbled replies to her friendly overtures. Presumably they were afraid that their tyrannical master would overhear and dismiss them on the spot.

"Does Edward beat them, Grace?" Beth asked, thinking of Richard and John, and wondering if her cousin was as brutal as her brother.

"No, I don't think so. But he is very demanding, or that's the impression I get. I don't think he is like Sergeant Cunningham." Her voice held a trace of bitterness.

That was the nearest Beth had ever heard Grace come to stating an opinion.

"You miss John, don't you, Grace?" Beth said.

Grace blushed and bent over the dressing table, searching for an imaginary hairpin.

"Yes," she admitted after a moment. "But I miss all of them, even Graeme and his terrible language."

"That's not what I meant," Beth persisted. Grace was so sensible and sober-natured, she sometimes forgot how young the girl was. Only sixteen, certainly young enough to fall in love with the charismatic stable boy. Beth turned in her seat at the dressing table and captured Grace's hands in hers.

"We will find him, Grace," she said gently. "Does he know how you feel for him?"

Grace shook her head, her face on fire. A single tear trickled down her face, and she squeezed Beth's hands.

"There was no point," she replied sensibly. "My parents would never allow me to marry a non-juror. That's the next worst thing to a Catholic in their view. And I think I would be too sober for him."

Beth thought of the commanding impulsive Thomas and his level-headed wife, and begged to differ. But there was no point in raising Grace's hopes. She was right. No self-respecting Protestant parents would want their daughter married to a member of a church that had refused to take the oath of allegiance to the Hanoverians. And John was more than that. He made no secret of his devotion to the Stuart restoration.

"Do you think you can be happy here, Grace? If not, you must tell me. You can go home any time you want," Beth said, changing the subject.

Grace considered for a moment.

"Yes, I think I will be content," she said. "And I want to stay with you for as long as you need me."

"That may be a very long time," Beth warned.

Gratifying as it was that Grace thought she could find contentment, Beth doubted she would ever feel the same emotion whilst living under her cousins' roof. There were benefits. She no longer had to fear Richard's violence or make excuses to avoid spending time alone with him. She had hardly seen him since they had moved in and Edward had spirited him away. The men spent the days riding and shooting pheasant, if the weather was fine.

The Cunningham women followed their own routine, a rigid timetable which had Beth paralysed with boredom after only a week. They would rise at seven, taking a dish of chocolate in their rooms. Then they would dress casually and go down for breakfast, after which Edward would appear briefly and read some carefully chosen illuminating verses from the Bible. He would then disappear, and the sisters would discuss the meaning of the holy writing. After this they would all go back upstairs and dress to receive visitors, which took at least an hour. From ten o' clock until two they would sit in the icy green drawing room, occupying their hands with a piece of embroidery or sewing of some kind, one or other of them leaping up at every noise in case it was a visitor, which it never was. No one had been near the house since Beth and Richard had arrived seven days previously.

At two they would repair to the parlour, which, if decorated in shades of dark blue every bit as gloomy as the drawing room's green, was at least a little warmer, being of much smaller dimensions. They would then read or write letters. If the weather was very pleasant they would take a short stroll in the gardens. Occasionally Clarissa would play the harpsichord, at which she was very proficient, technically at least. Then they would go and dress for dinner, which was served precisely at five p.m. After dinner, Richard and Edward would retire to discuss 'important business' and the ladies would be left to pass the interminable hours until bedtime, after which the whole routine would begin again.

Dinner was the most dangerous time for Beth, due to Edward's presence at the table. Having survived six of these events, Beth realised that her notion of dinner conversation bore no resemblance whatsoever to that of her cousins. It would seem that in society conversation consisted of the male head of the household pontificating on a subject for half an hour while the ladies dutifully agreed with everything he said. Towards the end of the meal Edward would ask the ladies in a disinterested tone how they had occupied themselves during the day, and would then cut their replies short, departing as quickly as possible to his bottle of port or brandy, Richard trailing in his wake.

Beth, faithfully keeping her promise to Richard, avoided being dragged into the minefield of commenting on Edward's views by keeping her eyes modestly cast down and concentrating fiercely on the food that was placed in front of her. Isabella had recently employed a French chef, who provided the ladies with the latest cuisine, while their regular cook continued to dish up the traditional fare Richard and Edward relished. This was a cause of some dissension, but for once the three sisters had stood their ground, hating the stodgy and fattening food that England considered patriotic, and Edward had given in to them, reluctantly.

On the sixth day, Edward, finding Richard's company excellent, as they clearly had many interests in common, and being reassured by Beth's demure demeanour at the dinner table, announced that he thought it would be perfectly acceptable for them to accompany the family when they went to London after Christmas. Richard had expressed his profuse thanks in an unctuous manner that made Beth's stomach turn. There had then been a pause, while Edward looked expectantly at her.

"You are most generous, cousin," she muttered, hoping that would be enough to satisfy him.

"Oh this is marvellous news!" cried Isabella. "We have no time to lose. We must call in the dressmaker immediately."

Edward looked somewhat alarmed.

"But surely you have enough clothes for the season? I have already spent a fortune on several new gowns that have not yet been seen."

"Yes of course, we have adequate fashionable clothing," his sister agreed. "But Elizabeth has only two formal outfits, which I am sure are sufficient for a retired life in the country but will never do in London. One is judged by one's dress, my dear," she said, looking warmly at Beth and then back at her brother, who was frowning ominously. Isabella wrung her hands, as she always did when nervous. "It would never do for a member of the Cunningham family to be seen in anything less than the height of fashion, Edward," she reminded her brother gently. "I am quite happy to spend some of my own allowance on ensuring that Elizabeth is suitably attired. In fact I would be delighted to."

Within a few days Beth realised that her cousin had only been speaking the truth. She took far more pleasure than Beth in selecting fabrics and suggesting trimmings, and went into transports of ecstasy over such details as buttons, lace and fans. They spent hours poring over drawings and tiny wooden puppets dressed in the latest fashions from France, trying to decide what would suit Beth's slender beauty. In spite of their dreadful taste in wallpaper, Beth was surprised to discover that the sisters had excellent taste in fashion, and in what would suit her fair hair and complexion, and left all the decisions to them. Only on one point did she put her foot down; she would not wear a wig.

"I absolutely hate them," she said when Charlotte advised her that her dear Frederick always used to say one was quite undressed without a wig. "They are hot and itchy and a breeding ground for lice."

Beth had, however, submitted meekly to the dressmaker, enduring standing for hours, being inadvertently pricked with pins and listening to the delighted exclamations of her cousins as the new outfits took shape. At least it was a change from sitting in the drawing room waiting for visitors who never appeared while the clock ticked away the empty hours.

Once the dressmakers and milliners had departed, life settled back into its normal routine. The outfits would be ready in three weeks, with another fitting probably being necessary in the meantime to make adjustments. Other than that, there were five more weeks to go until the date which had been set for their removal to London, weather permitting, in January.

Beth was in despair. Her proposal that they spend a day in

Manchester buying Christmas presents was greeted with horror. The weather was far too uncertain at this time of year to venture any further from home than the garden.

"But we can surely take the carriage?" Beth suggested, although she had intended that they walk; it was only a mile, after all.

"Oh, but then one still has to walk around the streets, in and out of shops, and if it should rain…" Clarissa said.

If it should rain, what? What would happen? Did the nobility melt in the rain? She had visions of her three companions dissolving into piles of slush at her feet, like slugs sprinkled with salt, and smiled, which her cousins took as a sign that she had realised the foolishness of her suggestion, and the matter was closed.

Chapter Five

"'But I would have you know, that the head of every man is Christ; and the head of the woman is the man; and the head of Christ is God,'" Edward intoned in a sombre voice, quoting his favourite apostle, Paul. "'For a man indeed ought not to cover his head, forasmuch as he is the image and glory of God; but the woman is the glory of the man. For the man is not of the woman; but the woman of the man. Neither was the man created for the woman; but the woman for the man. Let your women keep silence in the churches; for it is not permitted unto them to speak; but they are commanded to be under obedience, as also saith the law.'"

Edward closed the Bible reverently and beamed around the room. His sisters all looked suitably attentive, as he expected. His texts in the previous days had been chosen mainly with his cousin Elizabeth in mind. She seemed to be docile enough but it would do no harm to reinforce her submissiveness with a little of God's authority. He looked at her now, gazing as always at the floor. It disturbed him a little that she never met his eye, so he addressed a question directly to her.

"So, what do you think of these wise words of St. Paul, Elizabeth?" he said. Richard looked at her anxiously. It was the first time Edward had asked her opinion on anything. She looked mildly at him, folding her hands in her lap.

"If the words of St. Paul are correct, my lord, then surely it is not permitted for me to have an opinion, but to be regulated by a man?" Richard closed his eyes. Although her words were innocent enough, her tone was one of pure contempt. He waited for Edward's angry response, but to his surprise the peer merely smiled.

"Just so," he said. "Well, I will leave you ladies to discuss the reading further. Richard and I are to attend a cockfight in town but we will return in time for dinner."

Richard could not believe it. He knew his cousin was somewhat dense, but his sister's tone was so obvious that even the relatively stupid Isabella had started at it. The man really saw only what he expected to see. He was very easily duped, Richard thought gratefully.

An awkward silence descended on the room when the men had left. No one wanted to discuss the great wisdom of St. Paul, as it was obvious Beth held a dim view of it.

Beth looked longingly out of the window. She could not discuss her views with her cousins; if she could at least release a little of her pent-up anger in a brisk walk, that would be something.

"Why don't we take a stroll in the gardens?" she suggested.

Isabella looked doubtful.

"That would be a little irregular," she said. "We normally take a walk in the afternoon."

"But it will certainly rain this afternoon," Beth said desperately. "And a little fresh air would be just the thing." The mood she was in, she would be prepared to walk through a blizzard in her shift.

"And we are not yet dressed properly. What if someone were to call and see us in our informal wear?" Clarissa said.

"We have not had a visitor since I arrived," Beth pointed out. "You said yourself, Isabella, that most of your acquaintance is already in the Capital."

"That's true," conceded Isabella. "But Edward does insist on following Father's tradition that we all spend Christmas in the country."

"Yes, well, why don't we get our cloaks then?" Beth persisted.

No one moved.

"In that case," Beth said, teeth gritted. "Let us discuss St. Paul. In my opinion…"

The four ladies strolled along the paths of the formal garden, pausing to admire the topiary animals as though they had never seen such a phenomenon before. Beth's hood was down and the cold breeze blew about her face, reddening her cheeks and bringing a sparkle to her eyes. She quickened the pace a little, but slowed down when she heard the others' laboured breathing as they tried politely to keep up with her.

"Really, Adam does such amazing things with the shears," Clarissa said. "That eagle looks as if it could fly away at any moment."

Nobody commented. She said this every time they went for a walk.

They are bored, too, Beth thought. *But they have lived this way for so long they are accustomed to it. Will I be like them one day, uttering the same platitudes day after day?* Gloom descended on her suddenly and she shuddered, prompting Isabella, mistaking it for cold, to suggest they go back, and dress ready to receive visitors.

The cousins sat in silence, preoccupied with their embroidery. At least three of them were. Beth's expert fingers flashed in and out of the linen automatically, while her mind was in Didsbury, wondering how the servants were getting on and how on earth she was going to manage to get away to see them before January. Had they heard anything of John or Martha? She determined to write to them this evening and ask if there had been any news.

"Do you play, Elizabeth?" The sound of her name brought her back to the drawing room, and she looked up to find them all awaiting her answer.

Did she play? Play what? She looked from one to the other. Clarissa looked particularly eager. No doubt they were asking her if she played a musical instrument.

"No, I'm afraid not," she said.

The three sisters looked disappointed.

"Oh, such a shame," Clarissa said. "You see, we sometimes enjoy a game of quadrille and had so hoped you could make up a four. We used to ask one of the footmen to join us, but Edward was concerned that we were being too familiar and that Samuel would get ideas above his station, so we had to stop."

"Perhaps you would be kind enough to allow us to teach you?" Charlotte suggested. "After all, it will be a most useful skill to have once we are in London. Simply everybody plays cards."

Before Beth could respond to this kind offer there was a knock on the door and a footman entered.

"Sir Anthony Peters is here, milady. He apologises for calling unannounced, but asks if he may pay a short visit."

Isabella, to whom the footman had addressed his remark, being the eldest of the sisters, clapped her hands with joy.

"Of course, of course!" she cried. "Sir Anthony is always welcome to our home. Show him in at once." Isabella turned to Beth, who had brightened considerably at the thought of a visitor, who would maybe introduce some new conversation.

"Sir Anthony is always such delightful company," she said. "And he is so knowledgeable on the world of…"

Sir Anthony's expert field of knowledge remained unrevealed to Beth, as Clarissa was cut off mid-sentence by the door opening once more and the man himself entering the room. He looked across at them and executed a deep bow.

"I do declare, my dear ladies, your beauty is as always, utterly dazzling. I am quite overcome," he gushed. The three sisters rose as one to curtsey to him, covered in blushes at the compliment. Beth followed suit slightly belatedly, unused as yet to the custom of bobbing up and down to every person of rank who entered a room.

Courtesies completed, the party resumed their seats. Sir Anthony's eyes rested briefly on Beth. He was clearly about to ask her who she was, but was forestalled by the deluge of comments heaped upon him by her excited cousins.

"Oh, it is *so* wonderful to see you…"

"And it has been *such* a long time…"

"You cannot imagine how much we have missed you…"

"Where have you been hiding yourself all this time?"

He seized on the first question presented to him, and turning his gaze away from Beth, gave his attention to Isabella.

"I have been travelling a little, business you know, such a tiresome thing, but necessary. Once it was over I felt quite unable to return immediately to London, and have been recuperating in the country, my dears, away from the melee of the Court, enjoying the quiet life, hunting, shooting…" He waved his lace-covered hand airily about to indicate numerous hardy rural pursuits, before embarking on an anecdote about an unfortunate lady whose horse had unexpectedly dumped her into a bramble hedge during a recent hunt.

Whilst Sir Anthony spoke and the sisters simpered, Beth observed him with interest. She had heard about the effete dandies who frequented the aristocratic homes of England, but this was the first time she had seen one in the flesh. He was quite remarkable. Dressed from head to toe in embroidered lilac satin, his shirt frilled with layers of heavy lace which also protruded from his cuffs, covering his white-gloved hands almost entirely, he was the picture of pampered indulgence. His wig was elaborately curled and powdered, and his lilac shoes sported diamante buckles. A cloying odour of violets emanated from him as he waved his arms about to illustrate a point.

But the most fascinating thing about him was his face. Beth had never seen anyone so heavily painted in her life. His face was covered by a thick layer of white paint which made his mouth look unnaturally red. Two perfectly round spots of rouge decorated his cheekbones, and a crescent-shaped patch hovered at the corner of his mouth. Although he was above the average height, and appeared quite well proportioned, Beth could not imagine anyone less suited to the country life than this grotesque man.

She was drawn back to the conversation by the mention of her name.

"Oh, Elizabeth, is that not just quite the most amusing story you've ever heard?"

Beth hadn't heard a word of it, but she smiled politely and abandoned her close scrutiny of the visitor as his eyes rested on her once more.

"So Elizabeth is your name," he said, prompting a flurry from the others.

"Oh, I cannot believe…how remiss of me…I must apologise for not introducing you earlier, but I was quite overcome by your unexpected appearance…"

Beth listened to Isabella's sudden girlish breathiness with some amusement, and surmising that the older woman would probably continue in this vein for some time, effected the introduction herself.

"Elizabeth," she said brusquely. "Elizabeth Cunningham." She stood, and thrust out a hand to him. He took it in his, but instead of shaking it as she had intended, raised it to his lips. His blue eyes sparkled at her through the mask of paint.

"Enchanted," he murmured, before releasing her hand. She resisted the urge to wipe it on her skirt, and sat down again.

"Elizabeth is our cousin," Charlotte put in helpfully, while the other two women stared at Beth in shock for having had the temerity to introduce herself and give her hand to a stranger in such a familiar way. "She is recently orphaned and has come to stay with us for a time, with her brother. They will be accompanying us to London in January and are hoping to be introduced to the king."

Was it possible for a woman of twenty-two to be called an orphan? Beth wondered. This was the first she had heard of being introduced to the king and wondered how much plotting was going on behind her back.

The refreshments arrived, and Isabella busied herself with handing out cups of tea and slices of cake.

"Of course, our dear cousin has lived in the country all her life and is unused to the ways of polite society. We are hoping to coach her a little in the etiquette of the Court before she is presented," said Isabella, unaware of how insulting her remark sounded. Beth bristled visibly, and opened her mouth to reply to her cousin's comment. Sir Anthony intervened.

"You will certainly be the talk of the Court when you arrive," he said enigmatically. Whether he meant that the whole Court would be entranced by her beauty, or stunned by the manners of the heathen savage from the north, Beth wasn't sure. "But I am afraid you will find the Court of the old king very tedious, my dear," he said. "The Court of the prince of Wales is a far more amusing place for young people."

"Sir Anthony!" protested Clarissa. "How can you say such a thing!"

"Oh, I did not say that *I* find the king tedious," he said calmly. "I find his conversation most instructive. But it is no place for young, lively people."

He made himself sound as though he was as old as the king. Beth scrutinised his face as closely as she could without seeming rude. He could have been anything from twenty-five to fifty. With all that paint it was impossible to tell.

"Is it not true then, that King George has stated that anyone frequenting Prince Frederick's home is no longer welcome at St. James's?" Beth asked.

"Yes, that is true. But there are a very few of us who have the good fortune to be accepted in both circles," he replied, smiling at her with merry blue eyes.

"How on earth do you know that, Elizabeth?" asked Isabella. "I thought you had never been to Court."

Beth looked at her cousin impatiently. "No, but one does not need to go to Court to read the newspapers, which are always full of gossip about the king and his animosity towards his son."

Sir Anthony settled back a little in his chair, stretching his long legs out in front of him. "Are you interested in the affairs of the Court then, Miss Cunningham?" he asked.

"Not particularly, no, but I have an interest in politics, yes, and in the situation in Europe," Beth replied.

Isabella, Clarissa and Charlotte looked distinctly uncomfortable.

"What do you think then of the recent treaty concluded between Prussia and England?" he said.

"I know nothing of it, I am afraid, sir," she replied. "I used to read '*The Manchester Magazine*' and also a newspaper from London, but my cousins do not take a journal. I have read no news since I arrived here some weeks ago."

"Oh, but Edward does take the papers," cried Isabella, shocked that anyone should think the family so ill bred as to not keep up with events. Beth looked at her in surprise. She had not seen any trace of a newspaper, nor had Edward mentioned anything about an Anglo-Prussian treaty. "He takes 'The London Gazette' and is kind enough to tell us of any news which he thinks may be of interest to us."

A furious expression crossed Beth's face like a cloud.

"I beg your pardon," she said, her voice tight. "It seems that treaties between foreign powers are of no interest to ladies, Sir Anthony."

Charlotte stood up so quickly that she almost tipped the tea table over with her voluminous skirts. She looked out of the window.

"I cannot believe we did not hear your carriage approach, Sir Anthony," she said desperately.

Sir Anthony cast a sympathetic look in Beth's direction, before turning to Charlotte. "I asked John to put me down at the gate. I thought to stretch my legs a little by walking up the drive, but when I was half way along the path it started to spot with rain. I thought my coat would be quite ruined," he said, glancing down at imaginary spots on his lilac frock coat. "But it seems to have dried without leaving a mark."

"I was saying to my cousin as you entered the room, Sir Anthony," said Isabella, "that you are just the person to advise us on the latest fashions. Elizabeth has a whole new wardrobe for London. Perhaps you could advise us as to whether any alterations need to be made. You are so knowledgeable on these matters."

"Oh, how delightful!" the baronet trilled. "Perhaps you would care to model one of your new dresses for us, my dear?"

Beth rolled her eyes to heaven. She had hoped that his field of expertise would be politics or literature, anything that would ensure a lively conversation. Not fashion. She had already had enough of that to last a lifetime. She wanted to question him about the treaty, but the conversation had been moved on by Charlotte and Isabella.

"I am afraid my gowns are not yet ready," she replied. Even if they had been, she had no intention of parading up and down in her finery in front of this ridiculous scented man.

"But we have drawings of all her outfits, if you would be so kind as to give us the benefit of your expert opinion," Isabella said.

The next half hour was spent in poring over drawings laid out on the now cleared tea table, while Sir Anthony suggested the placing of a ribbon just so, and that this season's fashion was for a double ruff of lace at the sleeve rather than a single, and that feathers were so *a la mode* in France at the moment. Beth muttered agreement to every suggestion, wondering where Edward kept the newspapers and how she could get her hands on them.

For once she was actually relieved to see her brother enter the room closely followed by Lord Edward, cheeks flushed and wigs askew, having galloped home from Manchester to try to outrun the rain, which was now setting in in earnest. The scent of fresh country air breezed in on their clothes, dissipating the cloying smell of violets a little.

"Oh, Edward, look who has deigned to pay us a visit! Sir Anthony!" Isabella added, as though her brother was incapable of identifying the visitor for himself. "You must stay for dinner, Sir Anthony. Oh please say you will."

"How can I resist the entreaties of such a lovely lady?" he replied. "Unless it is too much trouble?"

"Oh, it is no trouble at all!" put in Clarissa. "We have so few visitors at the moment, everyone being in London, that it will be wonderful to have some new conversation, will it not, Edward?"

"Capital," said Lord Edward without enthusiasm, eyeing the satin-clad interloper with barely concealed disgust.

Beth had never heard the uncommunicative Clarissa utter more than a few words at a time, and realised with amusement that her cousins were vying with each other for the attention of the visitor, clearly finding him attractive.

Sir Anthony stood, and was introduced to Richard, who had taken his cue from Lord Edward, and displayed a similar hostile expression. With his sallow complexion, brown eyes and slightly less than average height, he, unlike his lovely sister, bore a marked resemblance to his homely Cunningham cousins, Sir Anthony thought, although Richard's thin mouth looked cruel rather than petulant as Edward's was, and the deep creases in his forehead coupled with the lack of lines at the corner of his eyes indicated that here was a man who did not smile often, and who took himself very seriously indeed. As the cousins shared a surname, Sir Anthony assumed they were related on their fathers' side. He surmised that Beth must take after her mother.

"Delighted to make your acquaintance, sir," he enthused, placing a limp hand in Richard's grubby brown one as briefly as propriety allowed before removing it. "I believe that your sister intends to be presented at Court. She will be an unqualified success, I assure you of that."

"Sir Anthony is on excellent terms with the king, Richard, and knows everyone of any importance at all. I am sure he will be of invaluable help in launching Elizabeth," Isabella said.

The difference in reaction between the siblings at this comment was as marked as their looks. While Beth struggled not to laugh as her imagination conjured an image of her gliding majestically ship-like down a ramp into an astonished Court, Richard's hostile demeanour evaporated immediately, and he eyed the overdressed fop with a new interest.

This interest continued for the duration of the meal. Richard questioned Sir Anthony closely regarding his friends at Court, asking whether the baronet had any acquaintance amongst the higher ranks of the military.

"Of course he has!" Edward butted in, disgruntled that his hopes of a cosy evening sharing a bottle of brandy with Richard whilst discussing the day's cockfight, at which he had won a hundred guineas, had been ruined by the appearance of this fop. "The man knows everybody. You'll be able to effect an introduction to anyone, from the lowest whore to God almighty, if you are well in with *him*." The last word was uttered with such revulsion that the table was rendered momentarily silent.

Sir Anthony alone of the company was completely unperturbed, seemingly taking Edward's remark at face value.

"Lord Edward is too generous." He addressed Richard amiably. "I only frequent the higher class of er…ladies, and I certainly cannot be certain of making the acquaintance of the Lord, either in this world or the next. Delightful cuisine, my dear Miss Cunningham," he continued, turning to Isabella with a smile.

Edward, embarrassed at having made his feelings toward Sir Anthony quite so obvious, now compounded his error. He moved the tiny spiced pancake around on his plate with the point of his fork, as though expecting a caterpillar to crawl out from underneath it.

"Delightful?" he said. "Ever since Isabella saw fit to engage that ridiculous French chef, we have been inundated with the most impalatable rubbish dressed up as works of art, in an attempt to disguise the fact that they are mostly composed of air. When will the man learn to cook a simple English dinner of roast beef and horseradish, with a fine suet pudding? Before I starve to death, hopefully, or before his salary bankrupts me."

"Edward," his sister remonstrated. "You know that Susan normally cooks a separate dish of roast meat for you, but I thought as we had company we could all eat the same fare tonight. Monsieur Blanchet is highly sought after. Why our table is the envy of society, I assure you."

"All I am assured of, sister," her brother retorted hotly, "is that I am put to the unnecessary expense of employing two cooks in order to have someone who understands that a man needs meat after a hard day. By God," he finished, "why we have to follow the ridiculous foppish customs of a country we're at war with when we have a perfectly good culture of our own, is beyond me!"

"Are we at war with France?" Isabella asked in a quavering voice.

Beth, who had remained silent until this point in the proceedings, now spoke.

"Well, it is true that the British forces are in Europe to assist Maria-Theresa of Austria against invasion. But as yet, as far as I know, there has been no formal declaration of war against France by Britain, although as Lord Edward thinks women incapable of understanding the newspapers, I am of course not au fait with the latest developments. Are we at war with France, Sir Anthony?" she asked, smiling innocently across at him.

"No, not as yet, my dear," he replied, highly amused.

"There you are then, Isabella," Beth said soothingly to the distraught woman. "I do not think that your excellent chef can be considered an enemy as yet."

Lord Edward looked at Beth as though she had just grown another head.

"If a nation wishes to undermine its enemy," he blustered, "what better way than to start by weakening its health?"

"So am I right then in thinking that you consider Monsieur Blanchet to be a hostile agent of France, trying to bring the country to its knees by means of sweet pancakes and spicy sauces? Should you not have him arrested, if that is the case?" Beth sounded sincere, and it was impossible to ascertain whether she was being sarcastic or was genuinely alarmed. Only the narrowing of Richard's eyes as he looked at his sister told Sir Anthony that the former was probably true.

"Well, no, of course not," Lord Edward said, aware that he was being made to sound a fool, but not quite sure how it had happened. "But I would like to see all of us eat the same meal – a good traditional roast dish. No wonder the two of you look half-starved," he said, glaring at Clarissa and Charlotte, who immediately looked as distressed as their older sister. "You haven't eaten a nourishing meal in months."

Beth glared at Lord Edward with absolute hatred. How dare he humiliate his sisters in company? She felt a wave of empathy with her silly cousins. They were all being dominated by the Cunningham men, and even though Edward seemed not to be brutal, his pomposity and tactlessness were still cruel. The evening hovered precariously on the edge of disaster. Beth could sense Isabella desperately hunting for an innocent topic of conversation to relieve the tension, but she was too upset to think clearly.

"So, Sir Anthony," Beth said smoothly, as though unaware of the strained atmosphere. "You said earlier that you have been travelling recently. I would so like to travel myself." This last was said with genuine longing. "Where have you been?"

"Oh my dear lady, I have been absolutely everywhere in Europe in my time. Such sights!" He clapped his hands together. "I cannot begin to describe them! But I am sure that with your beauty you will soon find a wealthy husband who will delight in showing you the wonders of Italy and Fr…the other countries," he hastily amended, with a quick glance at Edward's reddened complexion.

Beth looked as though a wealthy husband was the very last thing she wished to find.

"Recently however, being somewhat constrained by business issues, I have only travelled within this fair island of ours and do not have many exotic tales to regale you with, I am afraid. I have been exploring a little of the north in the last months, travelling up through Northumberland to Scotland, having had business to conduct in Edinburgh," Sir Anthony continued.

The three Cunningham sisters gave a uniform gasp of horror. Beth looked at them, perplexed.

"Oh but surely that was most perilous, Sir Anthony!" Clarissa gasped. "After all, Scotland is a hotbed of Jacobitism, surely?"

"There are Tories and Jacobites everywhere," put in the committed Whig Edward sourly. "The country is rife with the devils from top to bottom. You must have seen that if you travelled through Northumberland, Sir Anthony."

"Oh come come, sir, you frighten the ladies," Sir Anthony remonstrated, glancing at Beth, who looked interested, a little annoyed perhaps, anything but frightened. "It is true that some people talk of rebellion, but they are far too comfortable under King George to actually do any more than talk. The Hanoverians are in no danger from Northumberland, I do assure you."

"The same cannot be said for Scotland, though. After all, the Stuart kings were of Scottish descent. Many of the Scots are against the Act of Union and look to the damned Pretender to give Scotland its Parliament back."

"I don't think James will set foot on British soil again, after the debacle of the rebellion in 1715," the baronet replied. "The House of Hanover is too well established now to be uprooted by an old man and a few discontented Highlanders. Edinburgh certainly seems to be doing well out of the union. I stayed in the most comfortable lodgings and visited some excellent clubs whilst I was there. And the ladies! Ah, a positive delight to the eye! And Presbyterians, every one, loyal to King George."

"Oh, Sir Anthony," chimed in Charlotte, grasping at the first thing she had understood in the last few minutes. "Are the ladies of Scotland more handsome than those of England? My dear Frederick always used to say that nothing could compare with English ladies, but he never travelled in the north of Britain."

Edward looked askance at the enraptured Sir Anthony, and listened with impatience as he launched into a flood of overblown compliments about the ladies of the two countries. Really, the man was so easily diverted from interesting topics onto feminine trivialities. Yet in his political naivety he often let slip the most amazing and relevant information. The man had a knack with people that Lord Edward could not understand. All he could see was a classically educated dainty fop. Probably the man was a homosexual, in spite of all his talk about women. Most likely he was one of those perverts who enjoyed the favours of both sexes. It was disgusting. And yet he had a knack of gaining the trust of everyone he met. They would confide the most secret things to him. And he, all unwitting, would regale the company with tales of his conversations, letting slip tasty titbits all the time. As he was doing now. Lord Edward tried to turn the conversation back to the more interesting subject of the potential of the north to rebel.

"So, does your opinion that the Northumbrians are demoralised have any basis in fact, Sir Anthony, or is it just conjecture?" he asked.

"Oh no, my Lord, I spoke extensively with the most interesting people on my way to Scotland. Many of the people of Northumberland were most dissatisfied with the way the '15 turned out, and the fact that the Earl of Derwentwater was executed…well, many of the men I spoke to said that they would not put their lives at risk as he had for a lost cause. Why, even the

Earl's brother Charles has told me personally that he would not risk his life again for a young fop like Charles Stuart."

"What!" said Lord Edward. "Are you sure? After all, the man was sentenced to death after the '15 along with his brother, and if he hadn't had the luck of the devil as to escape to France, would have been beheaded. Is he back in Northumberland, then?"

"No, no, you mistake me," Sir Anthony said. "The man is in exile, you know, in France. I spoke to him there on my last trip. He is not impressed with the young Charles Edward, I can tell you. He said the pup couldn't lead an expedition to find a whore in a brothel, let alone a rebellion… begging your pardon, ladies, I merely quote the Earl, I do assure you…. But I am being diverted. The ladies of Edinburgh have a beauty of their own, but which cannot of course compare to that of the fair English rose, which is quite superlative." He scampered on, and Lord Edward let him alone, taking a few moments to digest the information he had just been unwittingly given.

This was heartening news indeed, and one which the king would be interested to hear. If even the fanatically Jacobite Earl of Derwentwater found the Young Pretender ineffectual, the chances were that many of the other potential leaders of a rebellion felt the same way. Lord Edward eyed the dandy with condescension. Perhaps it was the fact that the man so clearly did not have two political ideas to rub together that made both sides entrust him with their views. He would listen to everything with a sympathetic and interested ear, and understand the importance of nothing.

Beth sat in appalled silence, her face resolutely passive. She knew who the Earl of Derwentwater was. He was one of the most important English Jacobite nobles, unfailingly loyal. Beth could not believe that the romantic figure of her childhood stories could turn his coat, or if he had, that this utter idiot could let such a piece of news slip in this Hanoverian household, completely unaware of the damage it might do. Of course, if he had the ear of the king he was no doubt a committed supporter of the House of Hanover himself. She would have had more respect for him had he been aware of the import of his comment. As it was she felt nothing but contempt. And despair. Was the whole of English society composed of trivial women and imbecilic or blustering men?

When the evening finally ended and Sir Anthony announced his departure, assuring her that he would do everything he could to smooth her way into the Court circles, Beth smiled icily, and this time when he raised her hand to his red lips, she did wipe her hand on her skirt in a deliberately insulting gesture, although Sir Anthony seemed not to notice it.

Richard did, and Beth had only just got into bed when the door opened. She knew who it was immediately; he was the only person in the household who would be so rude as to enter her chamber without knocking. She cursed the fact that she had not locked the door.

"How could you do it?" Richard said without preamble. She did not pretend that she had no idea what he was talking about.

"The man disgusts me," she said. "He is an empty-headed, tactless fool."

"That empty-headed fool is a close acquaintance not only of the king and the prince of Wales, but also of his second son the Duke of Cumberland, and of Sir John Cope, all of them men who at a word could promote me to the stars if they wished. And you dared to insult the man? Have you forgotten your promise?"

"I remember exactly what I promised, Richard. I did *not* promise you that I would creep and toady to every overdressed nincompoop who was presented to me. He didn't even notice what I did, by the way. For your part, you promised that you would leave me alone and not enter my bedchamber ever again. Close the door on your way out."

She lay down and turned over on to her side, pulling the bedclothes up around her in a gesture of dismissal. She was aware of his every breath as he stood there, undecided. If he so much as touched her she would scream the house down, she decided. She had no knife under her pillow this time, but Charlotte's and Isabella's rooms were both within earshot.

After what seemed an interminable length of time, she heard his footsteps cross the room and the door close quietly. She made sure it was firmly bolted before she went to sleep.

* * *

20th December 1742

Dearest friends,

I received your letter today. It is so good to hear news from home, and I am determined to come to see you all before we leave for London at the beginning of January. I had hoped to come before Christmas, although that looks increasingly unlikely.

I am sorry there has been no news of either John or Martha. I am starting to think they must have left the area altogether, although I do worry about them, especially Martha, with her special circumstances.

Thank you for sending the newspaper article about the Anglo-Prussian treaty. I am glad that Richard forgot to cancel the papers when he left, and of course will not be reminding him of it. I do not think any good will come of concluding a treaty with Frederick of Prussia. After all, Britain is supposed to be supporting Austria, and Prussia is her main enemy! But the treaty will help to ensure the safety of Hanover, which is of course King George's main priority. It will be wonderful to discuss this with you when I call.

I have really tried to behave myself, and apart from a small lapse at the dinner table recently, as I told you in my last letter, I have been a model of propriety. It is driving me mad, and I must get out of the house soon. It seems that noble ladies are in danger of expiring at the slightest breeze, drop of rain, or snowflake. I can only assume that it is due to my mother's hardy Highland blood that I did not die the day I decided to find out if I could breathe underwater like a fish and fell in the pond. I think I was five at the time. Graeme will no doubt remember, as he dragged me out. It would have been the death of my cousins. Not that they would ever think to try such an experiment; if Edward told them they could breathe underwater, well then of course they would be able to. I have been thinking a lot about the past recently, and about how happy I was. I am not exactly unhappy now, but so bored and restrained. In some ways I am looking forward to going to London; at least I will meet some new people there.

I try to listen more attentively to my cousins now, as I have just spent the most excruciating time 'learning' how to play quadrille. I did not have the heart to admit that I had not been listening when Clarissa asked me if I played, and so have been perfecting the art of deceit instead, which I am sure I will need in London. I do not think the kind ladies suspected that I can in fact play cards very well. Sir Anthony Peters, who has now graced us several times with his flowery presence, insisted on sitting behind me, so that he could give me advice as to the proper cards to play. I do not think he was so easily fooled as the good ladies, as he commented dryly that I seemed to be learning the game remarkably quickly, although in fact I was too overcome by his presence to concentrate on my cards; his cologne is so strong it's quite nauseating, and when he was sitting in such close proximity during my first game, it was the most I could do not to be sick, or flee the room in order to get a breath of unperfumed air.

I wish you could see him. He has worn a different outfit for every visit, each one more outlandish than the last. Today's was of cerise velvet, richly embroidered with gold. He must be immensely rich. His conversation is amusing at times, although he is a true supporter of Hanover, is devoted to gossip, and has no sense of discretion at all. He is certainly well connected, though, and it is fun to watch Richard trying to hide his disgust of the man in order to cultivate his friendship. However, we will not see him now for at least a week, as he assures us he has business of a most tedious but pressing nature, which calls him away. I think it will take that amount of time to rid the house of his perfume, although I must admit the time passes more quickly when he is present.

I do miss you all so dreadfully, but be assured; Richard cannot hurt me here, and whilst Edward is pompous and domineering, he is harmless enough.

With all my love, until I see you soon,

Beth.

Chapter Six

Beth lay prone in bed, the covers drawn up around her. Her forehead was covered with a cool damp cloth. The shutters had been opened but the heavy cream velvet curtains were still drawn, filtering only a dim light into the room. On the table at the side of the bed stood a pot of pain-relieving willow-bark tea and a plate of bread, cheese and fruit, in case the patient should become hungry later.

Grace hovered uncertainly by the side of the bed. She was so unused to seeing her mistress unwell that she felt quite distressed. She had never known her to have such a bad headache before, and was worried that it might presage a fever.

"Can I get you anything else?" she asked.

"No thank you," came the weak voice from the bed. "I'm sure I will feel better if I'm left alone for a while."

"Very well. I will come to see how you are in an hour or so."

"No, you don't need to do that, Grace. I think I will probably sleep until this afternoon, and would rather not be disturbed."

"Oh, I will be very quiet. But I would not dream of leaving you alone all day. What if you were to get worse?" Grace said, her voice full of concern.

Beth discarded the wet cloth impatiently and sat up.

"Grace," she said. "I assure you, I will not need your attentions until…say, three o' clock this afternoon. I do not wish to be disturbed until then." Grace's mouth fell open at this sudden rallying of her patient. "However," Beth continued briskly, "if you would care to leave the outside door that leads to the back stairs ajar, I would be most grateful."

Comprehension dawned, and Grace's expression of concern changed to apprehension.

"Oh, Beth, what are you going to do?" she said.

"Nothing," said Beth, lying down again and retrieving the cloth, which had left a dark damp patch on the pink satin cover. She slapped it back onto her head. "If any of my cousins ask you later, you can tell them honestly that I said I had a terrible headache and asked to be left to sleep until three."

Grace was unerringly loyal. But she was also honest, and Beth did not want to put the girl in the position of having to tell Lord Edward an outright lie, if her plan was discovered.

"I'm sure I'll be quite recovered by then, and you can come and help me to dress for dinner," Beth said, in what was meant to be a reassuring manner.

Grace left the room, her face a mask of worry. Isabella, encountering her on the stairs, was most concerned and decided to inspect the patient herself. Beth, already out of bed and reaching for her stays, heard the gentle knock and leapt back under the covers just before Isabella popped her head around the door.

"I do not want to disturb you, Elizabeth, but your maid looked so worried…" she began.

"Really, I will be fine. I have had megrims like these before. If I am left in peace to rest until the afternoon, I am sure I will be recovered. As long as I am undisturbed."

Hopefully she would be left alone now, she thought. Just to make sure, she locked the door, and then hurriedly dressed in a simple brown woollen dress that she used to wear when she was working in the gardens or stables at home. Donning a pair of stout leather shoes and a cloak, she carefully counted the money her brother had reluctantly given her to buy any small items she might need. Nearly two pounds. She smiled and tucked it carefully into her pocket along with the bedroom key, and her knife in its brown leather sheath. If Grace forgot to leave the back stairs entrance ajar, or someone else closed it, she could probably force the lock with the blade. It was never bolted until the night time, and she intended to be back long before then.

The hoped-for family trip into Manchester had not materialised due to the inclement weather, and Beth was at the end of her tether. She was desperately in need of some freedom. She had hoped that if they all drove into the town together, she would be able to slip off unnoticed for a while. But this would be even better. A whole day of absolute freedom to do whatever she wanted. Bliss!

She parted the curtain and pushed the sash window up, blessing the person who had allocated this bedroom to her. Her window had a small wrought iron balcony outside. It was only decorative; there was no platform outside the window on which to stand and the space between the window and the railings was no more than a foot, but the ironwork butted up against the sturdy drainpipe down which Beth intended to make her escape. She had no fear of heights or falling, only of discovery. The coast was clear, and without considering any further she seized her chance and within a minute or so was sneaking furtively out of the side gate onto the dirt track which led to the main road into Manchester, little more than a mile away. She could already see the distinctive square tower of the collegiate church in the distance. She would be there in about twenty minutes.

As she walked along she blessed her parents for allowing her as a child to indulge her naturally tomboyish instincts, saying nothing when she came home with her clothes grubby and torn after having spent the day climbing trees or rolling down the slope behind the church in a madcap game with the village children. They had been grateful that she was healthy and robust; Beth would have had three younger siblings, but two of them were stillborn, and the third had lived only a few days. Indulged she might have been; spoiled she was not. If her mother and father had taught her the more eccentric skills of knife-throwing, tickling for trout and bareback riding, among others, she had also learnt to sew, to read and write, and various other accomplishments more traditional to a lady of birth. By the age of seven she was proficient enough in needlework to mend her own torn clothes, and was expected to do so.

Her father didn't hesitate to discipline her either, when necessary. Stealing apples from the farmer's orchard, dropping spiky chestnuts from a tree on to the heads of unsuspecting passers-by… She smiled as she remembered that her behaviour had been modified more by the knowledge that she had truly disappointed her parents, than by the half-hearted beatings her father had given her.

As she had grown older, she had started to understand that her upbringing was not the norm for a girl of her rank. Her father had tried to tell her of the way a young lady of the nobility was expected to behave, in case she was ever accepted back into the family, but it had seemed like a fantasy to her, unreal.

It was real enough now, she thought gloomily as she approached the town centre, panting slightly as she walked up the steep Market Street towards the Market Place, where she knew there would be plenty of stalls and shops from which she could select presents for her cousins and friends.

Once she reached the market, all her gloom was washed away in the joy of wandering through the stalls, exchanging pleasantries with the stallholders, and haggling over the price of items she was interested in. She saw no one she knew, and it was wonderful to be anonymous, her behaviour unscrutinised for impropriety. She bought a meat pie from a woman on the corner, making her choice from a large basket covered with a cloth to keep the heat in, and ate it in the street like any common person would, wiping her greasy hands on her skirt. With her plain homely clothes and her distinctive hair carefully covered by a scarf, she was mistaken for a maid who had been sent to purchase some trinkets for her mistress, and revelled in the joy of being able to unwind and relax, laugh and joke with good-humoured strangers in festive mood.

The buying of gifts took longer than she expected; by the time she had finished making her purchases, it was already afternoon. She would not have time to walk to Didsbury and back before three o' clock, and she dared not arrive home any later than that if she wanted her escapade to remain undiscovered. It was Christmas day tomorrow; her presents to the servants would be late arriving, but she was sure she could arrange a trip home at some time in the next few days.

Instead, reluctant to relinquish her freedom and return home earlier than necessary, she decided to stroll down Deansgate, perhaps pay a visit to Mr. Cox if he was in his office. She spent a penny on a handful of hot chestnuts, taking the opportunity to warm her hands at the seller's brazier while she waited for him to wrap them for her. Then she set off along the wooden-paved road.

She had walked for no more than a couple of minutes when it

started to rain. At first she ignored it, but then as it became heavier she took temporary shelter in a doorway, hoping that the downpour would soon blow over. It didn't, and the streets quickly emptied of people, except for a few who, dashing past her, disappeared down a narrow passage on the other side of the road, which led towards the River Irwell.

Comprehension dawned, and after hesitating for a moment and looking up at the cloud-filled skies in an attempt to estimate the time, she came to a decision, and plunged off down the passage herself, following the others down the slippery flight of stone steps which led to a dye-house on the banks of the river.

She had been here before, several times, although not as frequently as she would have liked. It was a risky place to be seen, and even more risky for her now, accepted as she was into the bosom of the devoutly Anglican Cunningham family, but she could not resist. What better way to end a rebellious day, than to attend mass? She had no idea how long it would be before she dare attend a Catholic mass again, to celebrate the mysteries of the faith with like-minded people.

A temporary altar had been set up on a trestle table in the corner of the dye-house. It was covered by a lace cloth, and a wooden crucifix stood atop it, along with two expensive beeswax candles and the pyx containing the host. Behind it stood the small slender figure of Father Henry Kendal, his round moon of a face beaming from above his vestments as he waited for the final stragglers to take their places before commencing. The congregation was not large. There were few Catholics in Manchester, and not all of them were able to attend every mass. Beth acknowledged the greetings of her neighbours, and noticed with disappointment that Mary was not present. It would have put the icing on the cake of this thoroughly enjoyable day if she could have seen her friend and been introduced to the wonderful Joseph.

She soon became lost in the comforting routine of the mass, the familiar responses, the dim glow of the candles reflecting off the polished surface of the pyx. The people assembled were dressed in their everyday clothes; they dared not wear their best for fear of arousing suspicion. Many of them had come straight from work and smelt of sweat, leather or horses, mingled with the odours of their occupation. The man next to her was a blacksmith; the sharp metallic scent of iron emanated unmistakably from his clothes. The Latin words wrapped themselves warmly around her like a blanket as she joined in with the creed, reaffirming her faith.

> *Credo in unum Deum, Patrem omnipotentem, factorem caeli et terrae…*

The service was simple; there was no choir, no organ, no magnificent building and rich music soaring to the rafters; but it was genuine and heartfelt, and all the more so because many of the people present probably risked dismissal from their jobs if they were discovered to be Papists.

And what do I risk? Beth thought as she left the makeshift church, resisting the temptation to stay and chat after the mass was over. *Complete, irrevocable alienation from my family, and the subsequent murderous wrath of my brother.*

She shrugged the thought off. She need not worry about her faith being discovered. What she *did* need to worry about, she realised with alarm as she emerged from the dye-house and looked up at the sky, was that either the mass had lasted longer than she thought, or she had estimated the time wrongly. It was still drizzling, but the darkening sky was due more to the fact that it was getting close to nightfall than to the miserable weather. Cursing inwardly, she set off at a brisk pace back along Deansgate. It must be close to four o' clock by now, and she estimated it would take her another thirty to forty-five minutes to get home. She tried to speed up even more, but, out of shape through her sedentary lifestyle of the last weeks, she was soon out of breath and had to slow down.

It was as she entered the maze of buildings and narrow passageways known as Smithy Door that she realised she was being followed. She walked on, hoping to reach the safety of the Market Place before the man overtook her, but as she heard his footsteps quicken behind her, she realised that he had no intention of allowing his quarry to reach sanctuary. Trying to look as though she intended to walk straight on, she suddenly veered off to the right, and the moment she was out of sight she took to her heels and ran, taking turnings at random, hoping to lose her pursuer in the maze of little alleys. It was growing ever darker and more than once she stepped into some unidentified slimy substance, wrinkling her nose in disgust, but not pausing to inspect her shoes. Finally, seeing no sign of her pursuer, she stopped at the entrance to a narrow alleyway to regain her breath. She peered into the gloom, trying to see if this way led back to civilisation. In her flight she had lost all sense of direction and was not sure where she was, but this way looked promising.

She started to make her way down the long narrow cobbled path, which was lined on either side by tall gloomy buildings in various states of dereliction, some dating from the Middle Ages. Most of them were shuttered and seemed deserted. No lights gleamed in the windows, and there was no sign of any habitation. The general atmosphere was not pleasant and Beth shivered, drawing her cloak closer around her, although in spite of her damp dress she was not cold. In fact she was sweating slightly, both from her recent exertion and from fear.

The overhanging buildings blocked out the little natural light that remained, and Beth did not realise that the alley was a dead end until she was almost at the end of it. She had two options; she could stay where she was and hope her pursuer would not explore the alley, or she could retrace her steps and then take another route, in the hope that she would emerge onto a street that she recognised.

Beth was always one who opted for action rather than procrastination; she turned round and started to make her way carefully back down the narrow thoroughfare. She was no more than a hundred yards from the end when a figure appeared at the head of the alley, his bulky shape dimly silhouetted by the last remains of the daylight. Beth shrank back against the wall, watching as he hesitated for a moment then slowly started to make his way in her direction.

He hadn't seen her yet, she was sure of that. She groped her way crab-like along the wall until she came to a recess, sliding silently into it. If she kept absolutely still as he passed by, she thought, there was a chance he would not see her. He was still some distance away, however, and she took the opportunity to reach through the slit in her gown into the pocket tied around her waist, and pull out the knife she carried in its leather case. She slid the blade out of its sheath, and felt the six-inch-long razor-sharp edge with satisfaction. At least if her pursuer caught her, she determined, she would not be an easy conquest. She stepped further back into the shadow of the doorway, and as she did so felt the wood behind her give slightly. Keeping her eyes on the alley, but reaching back, she gave it an experimental push. It opened inward. Quick as a flash she slid inside the building, closing the door silently behind her. The surge of relief made her legs wobble and she took a couple of deep breaths to steady herself. As her eyes became accustomed to the darkness she could make out the vague shapes of boxes stacked in the corner to her right. It seemed to be a storeroom of some sort, but if so it was very small. To her left was another door. There was a gap between the bottom of the door and the stone floor, which revealed a faint line of yellow light.

Light meant occupancy, but whether that was a good thing or not, she had no idea. She moved a little closer and was suddenly halted by a burst of male laughter. There were at least two men in the room, then. Something furry ran suddenly across her foot before pattering off in the direction of the boxes and she stifled a scream of fright. Her heart banged painfully against her ribs, and she waited a moment for it to slow before inching her way up to the door. If she could hear a little of what was going on behind it, she would be able to ascertain whether the occupants would be likely to assist her or not if she called on them for help.

The door was thin and somewhat rotten and when she was close to it she had no difficulty hearing the conversation that was taking place in the room. A few moments of listening told her that these were definitely not the kind of people who would be likely to help her, but although she knew she should retreat, still she stayed, mesmerised by the soft cadences of the foreign voices.

When the man opened the door, his fingers already undoing the buttons of his breeches preparatory to relieving himself, and saw the young woman standing there, it was difficult to ascertain which of the two was the more shocked. Both of them froze momentarily, then Beth's hand drove up forcefully, aiming for the soft area just underneath the sternum, at the same moment as he leapt sideways. The knife sliced through his shirt and tore into his skin, raking along his side.

He was fast. Before she could recover her balance he had grabbed her wrist and pushed her up against the doorframe, twisting her arm so hard up her back that her shoulder creaked alarmingly. She cried out in pain and he plucked the knife deftly from her fingers before spinning her round and pushing her into the room he had just been about to leave. He closed the door, and stood with his back to it. Her hip collided painfully with the edge of the wooden table which dominated the room and she almost fell across it, taking her weight on her hands and wincing as her abused shoulder protested at the sudden weight it had to bear.

Seated along both sides of the table were several men, who regarded her silently with surprise. The room was pleasantly warm and they were all in shirtsleeves, having removed their coats, which hung on the backs of their chairs, and several of them had rolled up their sleeves, exposing muscular forearms. Clearly they had been here for some time. A brazier glowed redly in one corner and two candles burned on the rough wooden surface of the table, which also held a number of pewter tankards and a large flagon of mulled wine. Beth shrank back a little, instinctively trying to disappear into the shadows, although her common sense told her how futile an action that was.

The solitary man seated at the head of the table nodded his head briefly at two of his companions, who stood immediately and left the room.

"Are ye alright?" he addressed the wounded man by the door, who had now taken off his shirt and rolled it into a ball, pressing it against the wound in his side.

"Aye, It's nobbut a scratch, but if I hadna moved, she'd ha' stuck me in the heart," he replied, a distinct tone of awe in his voice that such a fragile-looking woman had nearly killed him.

All of the men were bareheaded except for the one she presumed to be the leader, judging by his air of authority. He had thrown a cloak around himself and had pulled the hood low over his brow, casting his face into shadow so that she could not make out any of his features. The other men all had dark hair, except for one, whose hair was a mass of fiery red waves hanging loose to his shoulders. Their features differed dramatically, but they had one thing in common. They all looked extremely ruthless.

The shadowed man now turned his head towards her. She was

aware of his close scrutiny, although she couldn't see his eyes, and she ran her tongue around her lips nervously.

"Welcome to our gathering, lassie," he said mockingly. "Would you care for some refreshment?"

She shook her head quickly, once, and remained silent. Her breathing was fast and shallow and her hands were trembling violently. She pressed them into her sides in an attempt to stop him observing how frightened she was, and forced herself to stand erect. However terrified she felt, she was determined not to give these men the satisfaction of seeing it.

"Now then, it seems to me that ye owe us an explanation for coming upon us in so unexpected a manner,". the man said conversationally. As he spoke, he casually produced an object from the folds of his cloak and placed it on the table. Beth regarded the twelve-inch-long, razor-sharp tapering blade with something close to mindless terror. His hand rested lightly on the wooden hilt, which was intricately carved with an interlacing knotwork pattern.

"First of all, are ye alone? I'll have the truth, mind." His voice was deep, with a soft Scottish accent. In more favourable circumstances she would have found it seductive rather than menacing.

Normally when faced with extreme danger, there is a choice between fight and flight. Inability to decide between the two leads to paralysis of the mind and body. Beth had no such problem. Flight was impossible; she had no choice but to fight. Relieved of the necessity of making a decision, her mind cleared. She decided to opt for honesty, instinctively feeling it to be the safest option.

"Yes, I am alone," she admitted.

"Good," he replied, and she wondered if he meant that it was good that she had told the truth and he was now going to release her unharmed, or good because he could now kill her without having to deal with her companions as well. She glanced around the room again. All attention was fixed on her. None of the other men had spoken yet, and she found their silence unnerving.

"Now it seems to me a wee bit strange that a young lady should be strolling about this part of the town at night armed with a blade," the man with the knife continued amiably. "Are ye a whore?"

"No, I am not a whore!" she retorted in outrage. She stopped, brought her voice back under control, and started again.

"No, I am a respectable lady. I was exploring the town, doing a little shopping, and lost my way, that's all."

She looked at the man, trying to ascertain whether he believed her or not, but it was impossible to see his expression under the hood. He lifted his hand, pulling the hood further down over his forehead, and she realised that he did not want her to see his features. That was a good sign; if he intended to kill her, he would surely not care whether she could identify him or not. Of course the other men were not wearing headgear, and they didn't seem concerned that their faces were clearly visible in the candlelight, which was *not* a good sign. Why was he so bothered? Did he think she might know him? He spoke again, still in the same soft, casual way.

"Did you no' think it would make more sense to stay on the main road and ask directions, than to go skulking off down dark alleyways?"

"I was being followed," she replied. "By a footpad. At least I think that's what he was. There was no one around who looked as though they would help, so I decided to try to lose him in the alleyways. I didn't know it was a dead end, and before I could get back to the road, I saw him enter at the top. So I hid in here."

While she was talking she searched for any clues to his identity. She didn't know any Scotsmen. The only parts of him that were clearly visible were his brawny forearm with its dusting of dark hair, and the hand that still rested on the hilt of the dirk. It was a large hand with long, strong fingers, its perfection marred by the scar which snaked from his wrist to his fingers, bisecting the knuckles of his index and middle finger. It had been inexpertly stitched; she could see the thick raised ridge of scar tissue. A battle wound, perhaps.

"Do you always carry a knife?" She was concentrating so hard on the shadowed man that she jumped at this question, which came from the man sitting further down the table. He was a Mancunian; she recognised the dialect immediately. She turned her attention to him. He was examining her knife, testing its edge with his thumb. He nodded approvingly, and slid it down the table to the hooded man. Next to the dirk he was caressing, her blade looked like a toy. She looked back at her questioner.

"Yes, when I go out," she said. "I use it for all sorts of things, opening letters, sharpening quills, cutting flowers or rope, even prising stones out of my horse's hoof…" she realised she was in danger of babbling, and of losing control, and stopped.

"And where did you learn that particular use of a knife?" He nodded towards the injured man, who had now sat down and was gingerly examining his wound. "It's not a skill normally found in 'respectable' ladies."

"My mother taught me," she answered truthfully. "She told me that if I was determined to get into mischief at every turn, I might as well have the means of getting out of it as well."

The room erupted in laughter, and by the time it had died down the tension had abated considerably.

The shadowy man lifted his dirk from the table and replaced it in its sheath by his waist. He pointed to one of the seats vacated by the two men who had left the room earlier, and not yet returned.

"Sit down, lassie," he said.

She hesitated.

"Sit down," he insisted. "The others will be back in a minute. If you've told the truth, then you've nothing to fear."

She obeyed, and gratefully accepted the tankard of hot wine that one of the men poured for her. Her mouth was bone dry with fright, and she took a deep draught of the warming liquid. As she finished, the door opened and the two men returned.

"Well?" the Scot asked.

"There was a young gomerel sneakin' around in the alley wi' a knife, that's all," the taller of the two answered. He was slim but wiry, and his hair was long and fair, tied back with a leather thong.

"Will he live?" the hooded man asked matter-of-factly, in a tone that clearly said he didn't much care whether the answer was positive or not.

"Aye, I daresay. But he'll no' be doing much for a good while yet."

"Will that be your footpad, do ye think?" the shadowy man asked Beth.

"Yes, I think so. He was quite fat, with a blue coat, that's all I saw of him."

"It was too dark to see the colour of his coat, but he certainly enjoys his food," the fair-haired man replied with a smile.

"Well, then, lassie, delightful as it is to have the company of a beautiful lady, I'm sure your family will be getting a wee bit anxious about you by now. Where do ye think they'll be waiting for ye?"

"Er…if you could just show me the way back to the Market Place I'll be able to find my way home from there," she said.

"That's no' what I asked ye," the man replied. "Do I take it that your family dinna know you're in Manchester?"

She swallowed. Honesty had seen her this far, she might as well stick with it. After all, if they were going to kill her surely they'd have done it by now?

"No," she said, taking another gulp of wine, more to give her courage than to relieve her thirst. "My cousins live a…" she tried to think of an inoffensive adjective, "…sheltered life," she said finally. "They did not want to venture out in the rain. I wanted to buy some Christmas presents, so I… er…"

"So ye sneaked off without telling them," he finished for her.

"Yes," she admitted.

"Where do your family live?" he asked.

"Ardwick Green," she said. "But as I said, if you'll just see me to the road…"

"I'll do no such thing," he replied. He waved his scarred hand in the direction of the fair-haired man, who had resumed his seat but now stood again. "My friend here will see you home."

"But…" Beth was worried. She was almost certain that her disappearance would have been discovered by now. What would her cousins think if she arrived home in the company of a disreputable-looking Scot?

"Maybe we dinna look it," the blond man put in, "but I assure ye, we are all gentlemen. And no gentleman would think of allowing a lady to make her way home alone by night. Come on."

Beth stood, hardly able to believe that she was to be allowed to leave unmolested, and all the men rose politely. The fair-haired Scot offered her his arm as though they were about to dance, and she took it, the insane urge to laugh vanishing as he tucked it in his, trapping her elbow firmly against his side. She would not be able to relinquish his company until he chose to release her. With his other hand he took the pistol one of his companions offered him and thrust it through his belt. As they reached the door Beth turned back suddenly. Her knife was still lying on the table in front of the Scot, its mother-of-pearl handle giving it a decorative rather than a functional appearance.

"Could I have my knife back, please?" she asked politely.

The shadowed man looked at her from the depths of his hood. He picked up the knife from the table and seemed to be considering. In his large hands it seemed tiny, and Beth wondered why she had ever been crazy enough to think she could defend herself against any man with that. Although it had worked well enough against Richard. "It has sentimental value," she added dryly.

"Well," he answered finally. "I dinna see why not. Unless you want it for a souvenir?" He turned to the wounded man, who shook his head hurriedly.

"I'd just as soon forget that I was nearly killt by a wee lassie, thank ye all the same," he replied wryly

The other man threw the knife suddenly, and Beth's fair-haired captor caught it deftly.

"Gie it back to her when she gets home," the hooded man said. The other man nodded, and opening the door led the way out of the room. The door closed quietly behind them.

The men maintained silence until they were sure Beth was out of earshot.

"Christ, Alex, was that wise?" the red-haired man spoke now, for the first time.

Alex threw his hood back, before glaring at the man across the table.

"What would ye have had me do, man? Cut her throat?"

"No! Yes. Hell, I don't know. But was it wise to let her go? She knows what we all look like, and we have no idea how long she was listening at the door before Duncan was unfortunate enough to need a piss." Everyone laughed as the unfortunate Duncan vacated the room hurriedly, suddenly reminded by his bladder that he had not actually accomplished the deed.

"She canna have understood a thing," Alex said. "How many Sasannachs do ye ken who speak the Gaelic?" Everyone looked at the Mancunian. "Aye, well, you're the exception, Jack. Even if she does tell about what she's seen, we'll all be long gone from here by the time the militia arrives. But I'll wager she'll no' say a word."

"How in hell's name can you possibly know that?" Jack responded sharply. "She could have a husband in the militia for all we know. You know what women are like. If she arrives home in a fit of hysterics and announces that she's been ravished by a band of rogues, they'll turn the town upside down to find us. The rest of you might all be heading north tomorrow, but I live here. And so do you at the moment, Alex."

"Aye, I daresay we all ken what women are like," Alex replied, reaching back to untie the thong that held his dark hair back. It had come partially undone when he had removed the hood, and glossy tendrils were hanging in his face, the candlelight picking up its red highlights. He combed it back quickly with his fingers, then retied the leather lace. "I've had dealings wi' a great many in my time. But few of them, when confronted by a group of desperate men with no way of escape, would act as calmly as she did. She was shaking like a leaf, but she took considerable trouble no' to show it."

There was a general murmur of agreement amongst his companions.

"She's awfu' bonny," one of them commented wistfully.

"Aye, she is that," Alex replied. "And she's no got a husband in the militia, either."

All the men stared at him.

"Holy Mother of God, Alex, do ye ken the lassie?" Duncan said, having returned to the room in time to hear Alex's last words. The wound had stopped bleeding now, and he put his shirt back on. There was a large dark stain down one side.

"Aye, I do. She's a feisty wee thing. I didna ken she had such a skill wi' a knife though. That's rare among women. And it's one thing knowing the techniques of killing, it's quite another to be willing to put them into practice when it counts." That was true. Every man at the table had killed, several times, and they all knew how difficult it was to look another human being in the eye and take his life. "She's no' married, and her parents are dead. She's living wi' her cousins at the minute," Alex continued. "She's got an idiot of a brother in the dragoons who's looking to parcel her off to some man who can advance his career. He's no' going tae become an officer on merit, that's for sure. And she's no' going to tell him what happened here tonight. They canna stand one another."

"But if you know so much about her, she must know you, as well." Jack pointed out logically.

Alex smiled enigmatically, his blue eyes creasing at the corners. "Aye, we've met," he said. "But she doesna ken me at all."

"Could she recognise you again, do you think?" Jack asked.

"Christ, man, my own mother wouldna recognise me when I'm working. And why do ye think I wore this stupit thing?" he shrugged the cloak off his shoulders. "No, I'm safe. And wi' a bit of luck, yon lassie'll think twice before she goes wandering round the town alone again."

As they left Manchester behind and rode along the dark road towards Ardwick, bordered by fields and woods with no sign of life, yon lassie was already thinking twice about how safe she was in the company of the blond man. Was this apparently gallant gesture of taking her home just a ruse to get her alone on the road, where he could kill her? It made sense. If they had killed her in the room they would have had to dispose of the body, a risky business in the middle of a town. On the other hand, if the man sitting behind her on the grey horse, one powerful arm firmly wrapped around her waist, chose to strangle her now, he could just throw her body in the ditch by the side of the road. When it was eventually found everyone would assume a highwayman had done away with her, and serve her right for wandering about alone at night.

His silence did nothing to reassure her. He rode easily, but there was tension in his body that transmitted itself to her. It was unbearable. Perhaps if she attempted a little conversation she would gain his sympathy, make it harder for him to kill her in cold blood.

"I didn't introduce myself earlier," she said lightly, in her best drawing-room tone. "My name's Elizabeth."

"Pleased tae make your acquaintance, Elizabeth," he replied softly, amused.

There was a pause, while Beth waited for him to return the courtesy.

"May I ask your name?" she said finally, her nervousness making her sound prim.

"Aye, ye may," came the reply.

Silence. And no abating of the alertness quivering through the young man's body.

"Do you…?" Beth began.

"If it's all the same to you, lassie, I'd prefer it if ye'd hold your tongue," he interrupted. He felt her sudden stiffening, and realised how abrupt he'd sounded. "Pleasant as it'd be to chat wi' ye, I need to listen for noise. A lone horseman is a prime target for highwaymen, ye ken, and this isna the safest road in England." He found it amusing that he should be concerned about hurting her feelings, and realised that in other circumstances he would probably find this young woman very likeable. She was certainly desirable. That she had taken his words seriously he knew by her silence, and the wary alertness that now replaced the fear that had trembled through her before.

They were both somewhat relieved when they reached Ardwick Green, Beth because she was now certain that whatever recriminations awaited her at Raven Hall murder was not one of them, providing she could keep away from Richard, and the Scot because instead of walking his horse as he had done up to now, he could gallop hell-for-leather back to Manchester, pistol drawn, with little chance of being attacked.

When they reached the entrance to the driveway, Beth's heart sank. Across the gardens she could see that lights were burning in every room, and the front door was open, revealing the shapes of a number of men congregating on the steps. It was worse than she could have imagined. It seemed they were on the point of sending out a search party.

The young man rode past the gateway and stopped in the shadow of the wall. Before he could dismount to assist her down, she threw her leg over the neck of the horse in a most unladylike way and dropped noiselessly to the ground.

"I think it better if you don't accompany me to the door," she said unnecessarily. Her companion nodded.

"I'll bid ye goodnight, then, lassie," he said.

"I doubt I'll have one, but thank you all the same," she replied.

He laughed softly, and watched as she took a few steps along the path then turned and came back to the road. It was rutted from the passing carriages, and a large puddle of muddy water, several inches deep, had collected in the middle of the roadway. To the man's astonishment she walked straight into it up to her calves and splashed around, ensuring that the bottom of her skirt and cloak were thoroughly soaked.

"What the hell are ye doing?" he asked.

She emerged from the puddle and walked back to the gate.

"If I had just walked home alone and without a lantern from Manchester, then my legs and feet wouldn't be dry," she pointed out. "My cousins are unobservant, but my brother is not. He would notice that sort of thing. I'd as soon he didn't know about you and your friends, and I'm sure you would too." She glanced up into the shadows, and was rewarded with a brilliant smile.

"Aye," he said admiringly. "You'll do."

Then he turned his horse and cantered away down the green.

Beth watched him go, saw him spur his horse into a gallop as he reached the road, and illogically wished she was still mounted in front of him, riding back to the warmth of the room she had been so desperate to escape such a short time ago. Then she turned back to the Hall and braced herself to face the storm.

* * *

There were twenty men congregated around the front door, and they had just been issued with swords and lanterns. Richard had taken command of the search party and was issuing orders to them, which carried to Beth on the still night air as she walked unseen up the path, the sound of her feet crunching on the gravel drowned out by the noise of the men.

"It is likely that she either went into Manchester, or more likely to my house at Didsbury," he was saying. "So you will split into two parties, each party to take one road. You will search all the ditches, and if you should come upon my sister in the company of her assailants you are not to commit any action that would endanger her life."

His voice was clear, authoritative, demanding of obedience, and she would have been comforted by his words had she not known that his primary concern was not for her person, but for her dowry.

She emerged out of the shadows of the drive like a ghost.

"I am all right," she said, loudly and clearly. Several of the men jumped violently, and all of them turned in her direction. A momentary expression of the utmost relief crossed her brother's features, followed by another of absolute fury. She shivered, and not only from the cold which was seeping through her still damp clothes and settling in her bones.

"Where the hell have you been?" he said, his voice tight. There was not a trace of affection in his voice, only an icy, barely restrained rage.

I have spent the day in Manchester. I intended to return much earlier than this, but I lost my way," she replied, her voice containing a calmness she was far from feeling.

"Do you realise how much trouble you've caused?" he roared. She felt her temper rise to match his but knew that it was partly fuelled by guilt, and swallowed it back down.

"Have you been hurt in any way, Miss?" one of the men asked the question her brother should have asked. She smiled gratefully up at him, recognising him as one of the men who waited at table.

"No, Samuel, thank you. I am perfectly well. Just a little cold and tired."

Richard glared at Samuel, who was oblivious to the hostility he had just aroused in expressing his concern. He was astounded that Beth knew his name after such a short stay at the house. He had worked for Lord Edward for four years and was still addressed by him as 'man' or 'you'.

"You may all go," Richard announced curtly to the men. "Give your weapons back to the steward before you resume your normal duties."

The men filed away dutifully, and Beth tried to take the opportunity to sneak past Richard into the house, but he anticipated her and his hand shot out, gripping her arm painfully as she walked past him.

"Do you realise what you've done?" he snarled, his voice shaking with rage, his face pale.

She winced as his fingers bit into her arm, but could hardly remind him of his promise not to touch her, when she had just broken her side of their bargain so comprehensively. Even so, she could not bring herself to apologise to him.

"I intended to be back before my absence was discovered..." she started to explain.

"Lord Edward is beside himself with worry and his sisters are all swooning in the parlour. I would not be surprised if we were thrown out of the house this very evening!"

"Where is Edward?" she said.

"He is in his study interviewing your maid. But if I were you..."

She moved so quickly that she succeeded in tearing her arm from his grasp, and was up the steps and entering the study before he could catch up with her.

Grace was standing in front of Edward, her back to the door. She was shaking so violently that she seemed in imminent danger of collapse.

"I will ask you once more," Edward shouted. "And this time I expect a truthful answer..."

Both of them looked round as Beth opened the door. Edward's face drained momentarily of all colour, and then flushed an unbecoming red. The maid's face was blotchy, her eyes red and swollen with weeping.

"Oh, Beth," Grace whispered and, her knees buckling beneath her, she sank down onto the floor.

Beth was kneeling beside her in a second.

"Has he hurt you?" she said, taking Grace by the shoulders, but the girl was too occupied trying not to faint to answer. Beth looked up at her cousin standing in front of them, his feet planted solidly apart on the mustard-coloured carpet.

"Have you hurt her?" she said furiously. "Because if you have, I..."

"What do you take me for, madam?" Lord Edward roared, his face puce. "I have never struck a woman in my life! Although some women would clearly benefit from a good thrashing." He glared at her. "I was merely questioning her in an attempt to ascertain your whereabouts."

"I have never seen Grace faint in my life," Beth retorted. "You must have..."

"My God, woman, do you know how frightened we have been? We thought you had been abducted at the very least. And then you come strolling in, at," he glanced at the clock, "seven o' clock, as though nothing is wrong, and accuse me of assaulting your maid! How dare you!"

Beth helped Grace up from the floor and gently led her to a nearby sofa, where she sank down again, her face grey. Having made certain that the maid would not hurt herself if she were to lose consciousness, she turned back to her cousin.

"Please allow me to apologise on behalf of my sister, Lord Edward," Richard's ingratiating voice broke into the silence. "She does not usually behave so, I assure you. She is somewhat distraught by her recent bereavement…" His voice trailed off as he realised neither his sister nor his cousin were taking even the slightest notice of him. He hovered uncertainly in the doorway, unable to leave and yet equally reluctant to stay.

Beth was aware of Richard's presence, but was too preoccupied with Lord Edward's reaction to pay her brother any attention. His fleshy face was almost purple with outrage, but she could see the remnants of his fear in his eyes, and realised in that moment that she had misjudged him. He was angry, yes, pompous and domineering, certainly. But his blustering retort was partly an attempt to hide the genuine concern he had had for her safety.

"I am sorry," she said, and meant it. "I had no right to accuse you of mistreating my maid." She could feel Richard's hostile gaze boring into her back as he stood at the study door.

"No, you did not," Edward replied, glaring at her. His voice softened slightly. "Are you all right? Have you been molested in any way?"

To her horror, her eyes filled with tears and she felt the weakness of delayed reaction to the traumatic events of the day threatening to overwhelm her. She looked down at the carpet, saw the spreading brown stain of the muddy water dripping from her skirt, and fought off the weakness. She heard Edward ask Richard to go and inform the ladies that Elizabeth was safe, and the door close quietly. She felt better now that the waves of hatred lapping against her back had gone.

"No," she said, softly at first, and then more clearly. "No, I have not been molested. I am not hurt." She ignored the pain in her shoulder, which was still throbbing from when the Scotsman had relieved her of her knife. "I got lost, that was all. I only intended to spend a couple of hours shopping, and thought I would be home before anyone realised I had gone."

Unexpectedly, he moved across to her and took her by the elbow. He felt her flinch slightly away from him, but did not release her, instead steering her gently into a chair. He had no wish to see another woman collapse at his feet. He reflected that her father had probably had to beat her regularly to keep her in line. No doubt that was why she thought he had hit her maid.

"What possessed you to sneak out alone?" he asked. "Why did you not ask for the use of the coach? I am sure one of my sisters would have been willing to accompany you, if you wanted to go shopping."

It didn't seem politic to point out that his sisters were so nervous and pathetic that they were terrified of venturing further than the garden in case a raindrop should assault them. Now was the time to be humble. It was made easier by the fact that she knew she was in the wrong.

"I didn't think. I am truly sorry. I won't do it again, I promise."

That was an easy promise to make. They were leaving for London in two weeks.

"Well, I don't know," Edward said, as though he had read her thoughts. "I think I may have to revise my decision that you accompany us to the Capital. I cannot tolerate such improper behaviour."

Beth realised that she had to do something, quickly. Slumping back in the chair, she stopped trying to fight off the nervous reaction, and allowed the tears that had formed a lump in her throat to erupt.

"I am sorry," she sobbed, "I realise how inconsiderate I have been. I won't do it again, I promise. Oh!" This last came out as an exclamation of utter distress, but was in fact caused by the wave of sudden nausea which assailed her. She swallowed furiously, reasoning that while Edward might be moved by floods of feminine tears, he would only be revolted if she were to throw up at his feet.

"I have been so looking forward to wearing my new dresses and meeting all your friends!" she wailed.

Isabella, having heard the sounds of her cousin's distress, came rushing into the room. She knelt down beside Beth and enfolded her in her arms.

"What are you talking about?" Isabella said, her voice shaking with emotion. "Of course you are going to meet our friends. Oh, I cannot tell you how relieved we are that you are unharmed!"

Beth leaned into her cousin's embrace.

"I am so sorry for worrying you, Isabella. I didn't mean to. I so wanted to give you all presents tomorrow. I won't go off alone again, really. Please take me to London with you."

"Of course we will, won't we, Edward?"

Edward shuffled from foot to foot, feeling extremely uncomfortable in the presence of feminine tears.

"Er…well…I am not sure, Isabella," he said, trying against the odds to maintain authority. "I have made allowances for her parentage and upbringing, but really, her behaviour today was unforgivable."

"But all her dresses are ready!" wailed Charlotte from the door. "And Sir Anthony Peters has already promised to introduce her to the king!"

Had he? Beth's head shot up, then she lowered it again before Edward could notice that her eyes were now in fact, almost dry.

In the face of so much salt water, Edward crumbled.

"Very well," he said sternly. "But there are to be no more repeats of this ridiculous behaviour, or I will pack you straight back to Didsbury, do you understand?" He turned and walked from the room before she could reply.

Beth was then ushered up to bed, where a huge fire had been lit in the grate, and having been divested of her wet clothes by the much-recovered Grace, was forced to drink a large glass of mulled wine by Isabella, and then was fussed and cried over by the sisters for a full hour, before being finally, blissfully left alone to contemplate the events of the day.

In spite of the warmth of the room, she shivered uncontrollably for a long time. Part of it was due to reaction, she recognised that. But the sour taste in the back of her throat was not due to the bile she had swallowed down so frantically in the study. It was the nasty, bitter taste of duplicity, which she had never before had to resort to, but which she had used to such good effect tonight.

Get used to it, Beth, she told herself. *You will no doubt have to resort to it again, before long.* But only if absolutely necessary, she vowed. She was not proud of her actions this evening.

The shivering slowly subsided, and she lay watching the fire burn down to embers, contemplating the events of the day. She had been very foolish, she knew that, not, as the rest of the family thought, for going into Manchester alone, but for giving in to the temptation to attend mass instead of returning home at a reasonable time. All her misfortunes had occurred after dark, and she had no excuse; she knew that even her own village of Didsbury, which though innocent and beautiful enough by day, was a far more dangerous prospect once the sun went down. She should have known better, and if she had feigned distress to her cousins, she had nevertheless meant her promise – she would not go out alone after dark again.

Chapter Seven

"Thank you," Beth said. "I really appreciate this."

The man sitting opposite her in the coach brushed aside her gratitude with a languid wave of his hand.

"Think nothing of it, my dear. It is the duty of every gentleman to come to the assistance of a delightful young lady. Why, I feel positively Arthurian!" His chalk-white face creased into a smile, and his blue eyes twinkled. She expected flakes of paint to fall from his face like plaster, but his carefully applied make-up stayed in place.

The carriage rattled merrily along the road to Didsbury. Next to Beth on the black leather bench seat sat Grace, her hands folded demurely in her lap, her eyes sparkling in anticipation of seeing Jane and the other servants again. Beth herself was swathed in blankets and in spite of the chill January day was feeling decidedly warm. The carriage was very comfortable. The seats were well padded, there were numerous brightly-coloured velvet cushions for travellers to place behind their backs to soften the jolting, and leather blinds covered the windows, helping to prevent draughts from chilling the occupants. A small lamp hung above the door inside the carriage, which would give a cosy glow when lit at night. Beth had thought Sir Anthony's coach would be painted bright red or some such eye-catching colour, and had been surprised when she had first seen the sombre navy blue vehicle. No ornate family crest decorated its sides either. Another surprise.

She had almost despaired of seeing her friends again before the move to London. On Christmas day she had woken up with a terrible headache, but in spite of feeling distinctly feverish, she had managed to struggle downstairs for long enough to distribute the Christmas presents that had been so dearly bought, before being packed back off to bed by her cousins. She had lain there for a week, snuffling, sneezing and coughing, bombarded with honey and lemon drinks, bowls of nourishing gruel, and smothering affection. She found herself actually feeling worse than she would have done if she'd just been allowed to fight her way through it and carry on as normal. But it was a good excuse to escape from the hostile glares of her brother and the admonishing lectures that Lord Edward was clearly eager to deliver as to how young women of quality should behave.

She had finally emerged from the sanctuary of her bedroom, slightly red-nosed and snuffly, but otherwise fully recovered, only to have her pleas to be allowed to visit her servants received with horror. Isabella had pointed out that Beth was in very delicate health, and that if she wished to be able to travel to London next week, she needed to rest. When Beth had pointed out that she had had a cold, not pneumonia, and that she normally found fresh air and a brisk walk to be a great aid to recuperation, Lord Edward had delivered a resounding monologue on the delicate constitution of the female of the species, and the dangers of being exposed to the chill air and the lower orders whilst in a weakened state, from whom she would no doubt catch another, more fatal infection. In spite of the fact that this lecture was delivered in the decidedly frigid and draughty drawing-room, in the presence of three footmen and a maidservant who was tending to the fire, Beth did not point out the illogical nature of his arguments, knowing how precarious her position in the household was at the moment.

And then Sir Anthony had called, having now returned from his small business venture in York, and Isabella had mentioned Beth's dangerous and foolish wish. He had taken one look at the bitterly disappointed expression on the young woman's face and had swept into action. He had brushed aside the sisters' protestations with such a show of gallantry and flattery that before she knew it Isabella was waving them off quite light-heartedly from the door.

"Are you warm enough, Miss Cunningham?" Sir Anthony now asked, regarding her flushed face.

"Yes, thank you. In fact I am a little too warm, to be honest. If I may just remove this blanket…"

"Oh no, my dear lady, that would never do!" he exclaimed. "Whatever will your cousins think of me if I allow you to become chilled? I would never forgive myself if you were to fall ill again."

"I assure you sir, I am not the fragile flower that everyone seems to believe I am. Why, only last year I…" she had been about to tell him that she had accompanied John one overcast autumn day to the market in the village to sell some of their surplus eggs and butter, and the two of them, both full of a head cold, had laid bets as to who could go the longest without sneezing. She had come to no harm from her day spent standing in the cool fresh air, apart from being sixpence poorer due to losing the wager.

"You were saying?" Sir Anthony asked, after a few moments of silence.

"Nothing," she replied. She doubted that her family would appreciate her telling this gossipy man that she fraternised with the servants and held sneezing competitions. "I am…not used to such delicate treatment, that is all."

"Well, no, clearly not," he said. "Charlotte told me about your escapade in Manchester on Christmas Eve. Quite remarkable."

Beth was surprised. She had thought the family would want to keep her hoydenish exploit quiet.

"What did she tell you exactly?" she asked suspiciously.

"Oh, merely that you had risked walking the great distance into town for the altruistic purpose of buying Christmas presents for your family at the Market Place, and then somehow managed to get lost, arriving home in the middle of the night in an extremely fatigued and distressed state, whilst in the meantime half the men in the county were out frantically searching for your mangled remains."

Beth's lips compressed into a tight line. Trust Charlotte to make such a dramatic story out of it. What she would have made of the truth, Beth shuddered to think.

"And what did poor dear Frederick have to say on the matter, may I ask?" she enquired innocently.

Sir Anthony let out a whoop of mirth.

"Innumerable things about the dangers of night air, walking, highwaymen and ravishers…I must say, I think it most commendable that you would put your precious life at risk in order to purchase gifts for your friends. Far from being a fragile flower, you seem to be quite the Amazon, my dear."

"Oh for God's sake," she said, exasperated. "I assure you, I only did what hundreds of maidservants do every day. I had intended to leave Manchester during the daylight hours, but I lost my way. Admittedly I was a little late, but I hardly consider seven o' clock the middle of the night! I'm sorry," she added, realising that she had almost shouted the last words.

"No need to apologise, my dear," he replied, unperturbed. "But surely you must have felt a little apprehensive, being in the town and then walking home alone in the dark? Why, I confess, in your position even I, a man, would have been absolutely prostrate with trepidation!"

"Yes, I was frightened," she said, remembering the paralysing terror she had felt when the Scot with the scarred hand had produced the dirk from his cloak, "but I also felt more alive than I have since I can remember." She stopped, not having intended to say the last sentence out loud. But it was true, she realised suddenly.

"Another thing that I find intriguing," he continued conversationally, seemingly having paid no attention to her last comment, "is how you could possibly have lost your way. After all, the road from Ardwick Green leads directly to the Market Place. It commences to get dark at four-thirty at this time of year. I would have thought it extremely difficult for anyone to lose their way on a straight road for upwards of two hours, let alone a young lady who has lived her whole life in the area, and must surely be familiar with the route."

She looked at him as though he had just turned from a grass snake into a cobra.

"Have you said this to my cousins?" she asked warily.

He held his hands up in a pacific gesture.

"Of course not," he protested. "I am well acquainted with Lord Edward. I am in no doubt that you will have suffered enough from his moralising lectures, without me voicing my speculations and adding to your tribulation. No, no, I am the soul of discretion, I do assure you."

"And just what are your speculations, Sir Anthony?" she asked.

"Well…you are a most attractive young lady. I thought perhaps you had arranged to meet a young gentleman there, for…ah… romantic purposes, and had forgotten how swiftly time flies when one is in thrall to Venus."

She stared at him. His eyes were still innocent, full of sympathy and understanding for a warm-blooded young lady, but she could sense the acuity behind the guileless expression. He was on full alert.

"Stop the coach," she said, throwing off the blanket.

"My dear, my dear, please, do not distress yourself!" he cried.

"I am not distressed, Sir Anthony, I am angry," she replied hotly. "I went for a walk in Manchester and became lost in the back streets. It was, as I said, a disturbing experience." That was certainly true. "How dare you suggest that I would engage in secret liaisons with members of the opposite sex? What do you take me for? Now stop the coach at once."

The carriage rattled on.

"Please, please, accept my most effusive apology," Sir Anthony wailed, sounding genuinely distraught. "I see I have been terribly mistaken. But I did not mean to suggest you had engaged in any improper behaviour. Why, in London the ladies indulge in flirtations all the time. It is a most innocent pastime."

"If that is the way the ladies in London behave, then I begin to feel I should remain at home after all. I have been accused of many things in my time, sir, but lewd behaviour has never been one of them. If the London ladies choose to behave indecently, that is up to them, but I will certainly not be joining them." Even to her own ears she sounded absurdly puritanical, but she had, at all costs, to stop him from repeating his suspicions to the Cunninghams. She had no intention of telling anyone, least of all him, what she had been up to for the missing three hours.

She was grateful that he did not ask her what she *had* been accused of. Instead an awkward silence descended on the coach. If he expected her to break it he would have a long wait, she thought. But he seemed not to notice the strained atmosphere, and relaxed back in his seat as though he intended to take a nap. After a few moments though, he sat up and looked out of the window. They were approaching the outskirts of Didsbury. He curved his red lips into an ingratiating smile

"My dear Miss Cunningham, we are almost there, and I would not for the world spoil your much anticipated visit with your friends by having you meet them in a bad mood. Do accept my apologies, I beg you. I swear on my life," he placed his hand on his heart in a dramatic gesture, "that I will never utter one word against you to any member of your family."

In spite of his theatricality, his tone sounded absolutely genuine, and she gave in.

"Very well, I accept your apology," she said.

He uttered a great sigh of contentment, just as the coach halted in the driveway.

"Thank you. You do me the greatest honour. I will not forget it."

She could not wait to be away from him and his ridiculously overblown declarations. He leapt down lightly from the coach and reached up to assist first Beth then Grace down the steps. From the corner of her eye Beth saw Graeme in the distance. He was digging the vegetable patch over, but as they emerged from the coach he planted his spade in the soil and leaned on the handle, eyeing the purple velvet clad phenomenon with disbelief.

Sir Anthony waved merrily in the direction of the gardener.

"There, that will be one of your friends," he trilled, oblivious to Graeme's lack of response.

"I will show you to the parlour, Sir Anthony," Beth said politely, her voice still a little cool. "I am sure Jane can rustle up some refreshments for you."

"No, no," he said, carefully arranging the delicate white lace at his wrists, putting his hands together to make sure that exactly four inches of frothy material was protruding from each sleeve. "I would not dream of inconveniencing your friends. I shall go for a short drive, and return in two hours. Is that enough time?"

Gratified by his considerate gesture and that he persisted in calling them her friends, rather than 'the lower orders' or 'the domestics' as Edward would have done, she softened towards him a little.

"Two hours will be fine, thank you," she said, aware of how quickly that time would pass.

"Let us say three hours, then," he replied, climbing back up into the coach. "Enjoy yourself, my dear."

* * *

"Is that purple popinjay the sort of thing your brother'll be expecting you to marry, then?" Graeme said as the two women arrived within hearing distance of where he was standing, his brows drawn low into a frown.

Beth had known better than to expect a warm and friendly greeting from the gardener.

"If he does, then he'll be sadly disappointed," Beth replied as they made their way to the kitchen.

There she did receive a warm and friendly greeting, and was soon ensconced at the table while Jane bustled about preparing coffee and food, and Ben ran off to find Thomas. Once everyone had assembled Beth handed out all the presents, apologising for not having brought them earlier.

"When I'm in London," she said, "I'll write to you regularly. I'll try to post my letters myself. But if I can't, I'll write 'Dear staff,' instead of 'Dear friends', so that you'll know whether I'm being completely honest or not. I don't trust Richard not to read my letters before they're posted."

"I'll be able to post your letters for you, if you're worried," Grace said.

"I've been thinking about that," Beth said. "I don't think you should come to London, Grace." The slight flicker of relief in the maid's face before she opened her mouth to protest told Beth that she had made the right decision. "I'm very happy with you, you know that. And I'll miss you terribly. But you belong here. I have no right to take you away from your family or your friends."

"But what will you do?" Grace cried. "You can't do without a lady's maid."

"I don't know. I will have to look for someone else."

"But I can't leave you all alone!"

"I won't be alone. My cousins are not so bad," she assured them all. "I'll feel a lot better if you're living happily here, Grace, than knowing you're miserable in London with me." She forced a smile onto her face. At all costs she could not let Grace suspect how lonely she felt at the thought of facing her new life without a single true friend by her side.

"I can't deny we could do with the extra help," Jane said. "Since Sarah left it's not been easy."

"No, but Thomas is becoming a dab hand with a feather duster," Graeme observed.

Thomas glared at him.

"We've had to share Sarah's duties out between us," Jane pointed out. "Graeme's already doing John's work, and Mary and I are doing Martha's job…"

"So that leaves me to clean and polish," Thomas said, embarrassed.

"Do you wear one of Grace's lace aprons to keep your clothes clean?" Beth asked innocently.

"No, I do not!" Thomas snorted.

"I wish I'd known before. I'd have bought you 'The Housewife's Companion' for Christmas instead of a book about fishing," Beth said.

"Shall I go and make your bed up, Grace?" Thomas asked.

Grace looked shocked. "Oh no," she said. "I'll stay with Beth until she leaves for London."

"She'll not be leaving this kitchen if she carries on making comments like that," Thomas said, picking up the bread knife and eyeing it speculatively. For a moment, in place of Thomas's slender unblemished hand Beth saw a scarred one, and shuddered slightly.

"So, do you know where Sarah went?" she said brightly, hoping no one had noticed her reaction to Thomas's joke.

"Yes, she took a room next door to Mrs. Pelman's house in Manchester," Jane said.

"Mrs. Pelman's?" Beth said, puzzled.

"The whorehouse she came from before she started work here," Graeme supplemented. Jane closed her eyes in exasperation.

"But I made sure Richard gave her enough money to set up in a new life," Beth said.

"She has," Thomas replied. "That's why she's next door, and not *in* Mrs Pelman's. She's decided to set up as a lady's hairdresser. And good luck to her. Plenty of the 'ladies' next door are already using her services to make themselves look beautiful."

"She must be very talented, if she can make that lot of pox-ridden whores look good," Graeme commented acidly.

"The last time you spoke about her, you all hated her," Beth said. "What's made you change your minds?"

Graeme had the grace to look abashed.

"Hmm, well, maybe we were a bit hasty judging her. You were right, she just needed a chance."

"She was completely changed after you gave her that money, Beth." Jane said. "She came and apologised to us all, told us exactly what she'd said to Richard, and about some of the things she'd overheard that she hadn't told him. She had to tell him something so that he wouldn't beat her, but only told him the relatively harmless things. She worked like a Trojan for two weeks here before she left. And she thinks you're an angel from heaven, Beth."

"She'll not find it easy to make a living. There aren't enough gracious ladies around, and too many people know what her former profession was. But she's trying, I'll give her that," Thomas said.

Beth was greatly cheered. It was good to know she had rescued Sarah from the clutches of men like her brother. If only she could rescue herself.

"Any other news?" she said, painfully aware that the three hours were rushing by and Sir Anthony could return at any moment.

"I was going to write to you tonight," Jane said. "We have news of John."

Grace, who was halfway to the sink with a pile of dirty plates, froze. Beth looked up expectantly in time to see an enigmatic look pass between Jane and Thomas.

"What is it?" she asked.

"He's joined the militia," said Graeme bluntly.

The plates crashed to the floor. Miraculously, only two broke. Grace bent to gather them up, her face scarlet.

"I'm sorry," she mumbled.

Beth spoke quickly to give Grace some time to collect herself.

"Was he conscripted?" she asked. He must have been picked up as a vagrant, she thought.

"No," replied Thomas. "He volunteered."

Beth stared at him, open-mouthed.

"I don't believe it," she said finally. "John would never volunteer for the militia, not even if he was starving. Has he told you that?"

"Jimmy Taylor told me. They went to enlist together. He's been doing casual labour at the Vintner's Arms when they were busy."

"But what will he do if the Jacobites rise?" she said. It was a real possibility. Jacobite riots, although isolated and sporadic, did occur all over England, and Manchester was notoriously sympathetic to the Stuarts.

"Follow orders and throw them into jail, I expect," Thomas replied, his voice laced with disgust. "I know I never agreed with John's views, but I respected him, and liked him too."

"But none of us can respect a traitor to his cause, whatever cause that may be," Graeme said. Thomas nodded. Grace had by now swept the shards into the bin and sat down, white-faced. Beth still could not believe it. Not of John.

They all sat in companionable if gloomy silence for a while, until the distant sound of a carriage announced the return of Sir Anthony.

"Just before you leave," Jane said. "We all got you one Christmas present between us."

Beth was wrapping her shawl around her shoulders, and smiled.

"There was no need…"

"Yes, there was, and you've got to accept it," Jane said, thrusting an envelope into Beth's hand. Inside were six gold sovereigns. Beth looked at them all.

"I can't take this," she said. "I've persuaded Richard to give me a small allowance when we reach London, and you need this money a lot more than I do."

"It's not money," said Thomas. "It's the cost of a coach back to Manchester from London, including five days food and lodging. We'll have no peace of mind unless we know you've got the means to come back any time you want."

"It's as much a present for us as for you," Graeme added simply. "You're to keep it in case of need. And don't hesitate to use it, if that need arises."

Trust her friends to think of the one thing that would comfort her, that would help her to endure whatever London had to throw at her, she thought as they rode back in the direction of Ardwick. The knowledge that she could leave at any time would help to give her the strength to stay.

Grace hadn't said a word since she'd heard the news of John, and Beth reached now for her hand. It was trembling, and Beth knew Grace was finding it very difficult to control her emotion. So was she, for that matter. In spite of the comforting weight of the sovereigns in her pocket, she had no idea when she would see her friends again and what would happen between now and that day.

"Sir Anthony," she said suddenly, and he jumped, having been absorbed in gazing out of the window, respecting their need for silence. She had not thought he could be quiet for so long, unless he was listening raptly while someone revealed the latest gossip for him to spread. "I wonder if I might ask another favour of you, or do you have any appointments this afternoon?"

"None at all," he replied, smiling. "I am entirely at your disposal."

"I wonder if it would be possible to pay a brief visit to Manchester?"

"What a superb idea!" he enthused. "Perhaps we could partake of a little refreshment, if you ladies would be so kind as to grace me with your company?"

"We would be delighted," she lied. "But I need to make a brief call on a friend of mine first."

"Certainly." He leaned out of the window to instruct the coachman." What address shall I give?"

"The Vintner's Arms," Beth replied firmly.

* * *

"He's not here," the barmaid said, eyeing Beth suspiciously. "Why, who wants to know?"

"I'm a friend of his," Beth explained. "I wanted to speak to him, that's all. Do you know where he is?"

"No idea," the woman replied, turning away.

Beth sighed. She had had to argue all the way to Manchester to dissuade Sir Anthony from coming in with her, insisting it was a confidential matter. He had reluctantly agreed, on the condition that he wait outside within shouting distance. Although what he could do against the kind of clientele that frequented this establishment, she had no idea. Maybe they would be too weak from laughing at his appearance to attack him. Although there were not many customers at this time of day, she could feel the eyes of those there were boring into her from the shadows. A stench of stale beer, rancid mutton fat and tobacco smoke pervaded the room. This was just the sort of place the footpad of the other night would frequent, she thought. Or the men who had rescued her from him, for that matter.

"Look," she said, raising her voice. "I'm not a jilted sweetheart, and he doesn't owe me any money. He used to work for me. I need to know if I can send his character on here, and I would really appreciate a few words with him. If he doesn't want to see me, I'll go away."

The woman turned back, wiping her nose on the back of her hand.

"What's your name?" she said brusquely.

"Beth," Beth replied. "Beth Cunningham. Why?"

The woman's face lit up.

"Ah, well, why didn't you say so? He talks about you all the time," she beamed, holding out her hand. Seeing no alternative, Beth shook it reluctantly. "He's not here. But he'll be back, so you can send his character on if you want. Volunteered for the militia he did, the fool. He's off in Lincoln doing his training."

"It's true, Grace, I'm afraid," Beth said when she emerged from the pub, wiping her hand on her skirt.

"Is he there?" Grace asked.

"No, he's training in Lincoln. But he'll be back in a few weeks."

If Sir Anthony was curious, he showed no sign of it.

"Well, now we are here, ladies, why don't we repair to a more salubrious establishment and partake of some punch?"

John Shaw's Punch House, although very close by, could not have been more different. Both the room and the staff were clean and the air was rich with the fruity smell of punch. They sat at a table in one corner and Sir Anthony ordered a P from an enormous woman with forearms like trees.

"What's a P?" Beth asked.

"It's the larger size bowl of punch, my dear. The smaller size is called a Q, but if I may be so bold, I would say you both look in need of restoration, and John's punch is just the thing."

He was right. It was delicious, orange in colour, very fruity but with a distinctly alcoholic kick to it. Beth downed the first glass rather quicker than she had intended and made a conscious effort to slow down after that.

"So how did you spend your three hours, Sir Anthony?" she asked.

"Oh, I took the opportunity to explore your little village, my dear. Quite exquisite. And the food at the Ring o' Bells – well, what can I say? I have not tasted better outside London. In fact, I can honestly confess I have not tasted better inside London, either. I will be going down next week. I believe your family are travelling down on the nineteenth?"

"Yes," Beth said gloomily.

"You are not looking forward to it, Miss Cunningham?" he asked.

"I don't know," she said truthfully. "It is so far from all my friends."

"Oh, but you will be in the bosom of your family! And for my part, I would be ecstatic if you would allow me to facilitate your entrance into society. If I may presume so far, I would like to think we are becoming friends."

Would you? Beth thought.

"It will certainly give me the greatest pleasure to introduce you to those of my acquaintance with whom you may have…ah… how shall I put it…more in common than you do with your cousins. They are very dear ladies, but you are in need of a little more stimulation, are you not, my dear?"

Was it that obvious? She did not answer, taking refuge instead in her glass, which to her surprise was almost empty again. Sir Anthony, noticing, refilled it.

"London is a most stimulating place. There is not a dull moment to be had. You will be quite amazed at the difference in your cousins, I assure you. And of course, you will have your dear friend Miss Miller here for company as well."

How does he know her surname? Beth thought, at the same time as Grace explained that she would not be accompanying Beth to the Capital.

Beth would later blame it on three glasses of rather potent punch, but really the alcohol only gave her the courage needed to carry through an idea that had been in her mind all afternoon.

"Would you be acquainted with Mrs. Pelman's establishment, Sir Anthony?" she asked.

His blue eyes became round with astonishment.

"Certainly not!" he exclaimed. "It is a place of the lowest repute. I am deeply shocked that you have heard of it, Miss Cunningham." He fanned himself distractedly with his hand, and she supposed that he had blushed or gone pale under his inch of make-up. It was impossible to tell.

"Nevertheless, you have heard of it." It was a statement. "Is it nearby?"

"Well...yes," he admitted.

"There is a lady by the name of Sarah Browne, who lives next door. I would like to speak to her, if you would be so kind as to give me directions?"

He called his driver over, who was sitting in a corner with another coachman, enjoying a plate of jellied eels, and issued some instructions in a low voice.

"John will go and see if the young lady is at home. It reassures me only slightly that the lady you wish to speak to lives next door, rather than in the establishment you spoke of before. It is not a reputable area."

Both his words and expression denoted the utmost disapproval, but his eyes were merry.

They are beautiful, she thought, *a deep grey-blue, like a twilit sky.* She noticed for the first time how long his eyelashes were. Any woman would kill for lashes like that.

Sarah walked in and brought Beth to her senses. My God, she had actually found something about this dandy attractive for a moment! How potent was this punch?

Sarah's eyes lit up when she saw Beth, and she bobbed a curtsey before turning to Sir Anthony, a slightly perplexed expression on her face.

"You wished to see me, my lord?" she said.

"Oh, my dear, you do me too much honour. I am not yet elevated to the peerage, whatever my accoutrements may suggest!"

Sarah's face was a picture of perplexity.

"What the gentleman is trying to say," Beth explained, "is that he is not a lord, only a baronet. Allow me to present Sir Anthony Peters."

"Enchanted, my dear girl," he said, taking her hand in his lilac suede one and pressing his lips to it.

As soon as she saw Sarah struggle not to wipe her hand on her skirt when he released it, she knew she was about to do the right thing. But she needed to speak privately to her. She searched for an excuse to get away from Sir Anthony and Grace for a few minutes. The gentleman turned to Grace and smiled.

"Miss Miller, would you do me the honour of giving me your assistance in choosing a present for my goddaughter? It is her birthday soon, and I have no idea what would be suitable for a four-year-old."

Grace looked uncertain.

"I am right in believing that you have several young sisters?" he said.

"Yes, but…"

"And I have no sisters at all, being quite alone in the world. I really would be most grateful. There is a shop very close to here that sells numerous trinkets, but I have not the faintest conception as to what would be appropriate. We will be no more than five minutes."

Beth could have kissed him.

"You go, Grace. I will be quite safe," she said. She beckoned Sarah to sit down and remained silent until Sir Anthony and Grace had left, he taking her arm solicitously as though she were a lady of the highest quality instead of a maid. He really did have some very endearing qualities.

"We don't have much time, so I will be brief," Beth said. "You have used the money Richard gave you to set up as a hairdresser, am I right?"

"Yes, Miss, although I have only used a very little of it as yet."

"How good are you at dressing hair?"

"Very good, Miss, and I can apply make-up as well, and…"

"You will have problems, though, in obtaining a respectable clientele, won't you? Being known in the area as a prostitute? Graeme and Thomas tell me your main customers at the moment are Mrs. Pelman's whores."

Sarah blushed furiously.

"I am not trying to insult you. But I don't have time to dress my words up. I am going to London on the nineteenth with my cousins. I need a ladies' maid. Would you like the job?"

Sarah was thunderstruck.

"You're not serious," she said after a moment. "You don't even like me."

"Graeme has decided he was wrong about you, and that's good enough for me. If you accept I will expect you to behave impeccably, be absolutely loyal to me and no one else, and to be utterly discreet. If you are not, you will be dismissed. No second chances, although I will pay your coach fare back to Manchester. If you are as good as you claim, it could be the making of you. Not only will your past be completely unknown in London, but I will recommend you to every lady of distinction I meet. And it seems I am going to meet a great many. When I marry, or return to Manchester, you will be able to remain in London if you wish and set up a business there, which will have a far higher chance of success, especially as your abilities will already be known to the aristocracy, and your past will not. Do you need time to think about it?"

Sarah was used to thinking on her feet.

"Why me rather than Grace?" she said.

"Grace belongs here. Her family and friends are here and she is not a city person. You are. Your former life means that you must be adaptable, and capable of keeping confidences if necessary. I do not want my cousin or my brother to employ someone for me who will report back on everything I do. I think you now know Richard for what he is, and if Graeme is right, your loyalty is to me rather than him. Am I right?"

"Yes," Sarah said emphatically. "But if your brother is going to London too, won't he tell your family what I am?"

"What you *were*. No, he won't, because the moment I get home I am going to announce to the whole family that I have engaged someone who he employed as a kitchen maid, but who is eminently more suited for a better position, and that I am merely trusting in his superior judgement of character in engaging somebody he thought so highly of. And if you're worried about his violence, don't be. He's desperate to impress my noble family and is doing his utmost to behave like a gentleman. Just don't let him get you alone, where no one could hear if you screamed."

Sarah laughed out loud.

"My God, he got you wrong, didn't he?" she said. "He told me you were pathetic and weak, and would do whatever he said."

"I am, and I will," Beth smiled. "That is why I am employing you, because my dear brother thought so well of you. When can you give me your answer?"

"Now," came the reply as Sir Anthony and Grace walked back through the door. She spat on her hand and offered it to Beth. "You've got a deal."

Beth shook it, and this time she didn't wipe her hand on her skirt.

Chapter Eight

February, 1743

Dear Friends,

Thank you for your letter, which arrived last week. I have now barricaded myself into my room and refuse to emerge until I have replied to you. It is the only way I can get a moment alone. Sir Anthony (the purple popinjay!) warned me that London life was far different to that of the country. I wish I had believed him, although nothing could have prepared me for this.

Clarissa is still quiet and retiring, which is due more to shyness than snobbery, I think, but Isabella and Charlotte are transformed into true social creatures. Etiquette dictates that we make calls between noon and three, which would perhaps be pleasant if one could take the time to cultivate an acquaintance with the people, over an hour or two. But of course this would be too pleasant. Instead each call must last fifteen minutes precisely, during which you have no more time than to utter the most superficial platitudes about health and the weather, and perhaps a comment about Lord X, who is pursuing a secret affair with Viscount Y's wife before you dash off to the next house, to repeat the whole tiresome procedure again. In the course of three hours you visit eight or nine people, which is both tedious beyond belief and exhausting. And of course by the end of those three hours the whole of London knows about Lord X and Countess Y.

I miss you all more than you would believe. I can't help comparing our honest chats around the table with the insane artificiality of the so-called elite. Sir Anthony has assured me that once the initial rounds of visits are made things become a little calmer, but there seems no end to it at the moment. He is a regular visitor to the house, and I really have not made my mind up as to whether I like him or not. He is always considerate to me, and has an easy way of conversing that encourages confidences, although I do not confide in him, as I do not trust him. He can be very indiscreet at times. Having said that, he has said nothing about Sarah, although I am sure he suspects her past to be less than virtuous.

After dinner one can make yet more calls, or more often go to the theatre, the opera, or a concert, where the chief purpose of the audience seems to be to drown out the performance by talking as loudly as possible throughout. The whole aim is to be noticed. It does not matter if your head is empty; only that your mouth is full of nonsense, and your clothes are fashionable. Sir Anthony is always noticed, wherever he goes.

I have just re-read what I have written so far. I may be exaggerating a little, but at Raven Hall I was bored due to inactivity; here I never stop running around, yet I am just as bored.

Tomorrow I will be attending my first ball. Charlotte has told me that this is the sort of event where I will be most likely to meet my future husband, and that I will no doubt be inundated with admirers who are captivated by my beauty. To say nothing of my dowry, although of course no one would be so vulgar as to mention that. Lord Edward and Richard have been making separate visits to my cousin's male acquaintance, so I have no doubt that every bachelor and widower in London now knows that I come with a fortune. I expect to fend off a great many love-struck men tomorrow.

How are you all? Please tell me all your news, however trivial. It is like a breath of fresh spring air to me. Which is another thing – London smells so dreadful! I had not been prepared for that, although of course any town of half a million people is bound to smell, I suppose. Imagine that! Half a million people! I am glad Grace stayed at home. She would have hated it here. Even the servants have great airs and graces. Sarah is in her element, and is a great source of information about what is going on beneath the surface. The servants know everything. We are getting on well together, and she is keeping me sane with her humorous observations. Graeme was right, we had misjudged her.

I will write again, as soon as I get a moment's free time,
All my love to you all,
Beth.

When Beth descended on the evening of her first ball Sir Anthony was waiting for her at the bottom of the stairs, resplendent in sapphire-blue satin, his coat and waistcoat heavily embroidered with silver. She was already in a bad humour; her stays were too tight, her skirt was so wide as to be a danger to anyone who came within four feet of her, and her shoes were hurting her. She had not yet put on her social face, and scowled blackly at him as she reached the hall.

"My dear Miss Cunningham, how absolutely exquisite you look!" he twittered, holding his arm out to her and smiling sweetly. "I thought you might like to enter the room on the arm of someone with whom you are already acquainted, but if you think I am being too bold, please, do tell me."

She put her hand on his arm and leaned on it while she struggled to bend down and take off her shoe, which had something sharp in it.

"Oh, this is ridiculous!" she said after a few moments of futile battling against the restrictions of her clothing. "How can it be sensible to wear clothing which render it impossible to take off one's own shoe!"

"Allow me, my dear," he said, kneeling in front of her and managing to take off the offending item of footwear without touching her at all. He shook it, and a small stone fell out. "There!" he said, replacing the shoe onto her outstretched foot. He stood up and offered her his arm again. "Now I would suggest, dear lady, that you also take the sharpness out of your face and replace it with a smile, however painful that may be. Although you will no doubt be besieged by young men eager to make your acquaintance, regardless of your facial expression. Money always wears a smile."

She looked up at him.

"Does everybody know about my dowry then?" she asked.

"Of course, my dear. What do you think your cousin and your brother have been doing for the last days? Now, let us go in. I am so delighted that you chose to wear blue, and a shade which complements my own outfit so well! We will be the talk of the room."

"Why?"

"Well, as we are already acquainted, people will assume we have dressed in the same colour deliberately, as a way of stating that we are…sympathetic to one another, shall we say?" he beamed down at her, displaying a set of perfect white teeth.

She looked at him with horror, and his smile faded slightly.

"If you wish, you can announce that it is mere coincidence, but you may prefer to use the assumption to your advantage."

"What possible advantage could there be to me if people think we are sympathetic, as you put it, to one another?" she asked tactlessly.

"Well, when you find the constant attention and compliments a little overpowering, just signal to me, and I shall rescue you immediately. I promise not to say anything complimentary to you at all, and to pay you very little attention," he suggested, undismayed by her obvious abhorrence of him.

She smiled, in spite of her apprehension.

"Ah, that is better. You look so beautiful when you smile…but I have promised. No more compliments. You will have a surfeit soon enough."

"You are exaggerating, Sir Anthony," Beth said, determined that once she was in the room she would not go anywhere near him for the rest of the evening.

"We will see," came the reply.

Her resolve lasted just over two hours. Noticing her pleading look as she tried to fend off yet another young man who was begging her for the next dance and claiming that he could not live with the shame if she refused him, Sir Anthony left his companions and made his way across the room, bowing deeply to her and nodding perfunctorily to the pimply young man by her side.

"Ah, my dear Miss Cunningham, please do forgive me! I confess I was engrossed in conversation and almost forgot that you had kindly allowed me the next dance. Shall we?" She took his offered arm with alacrity, and almost dragged him away from the importunate young man.

"Thank you," she said, both relieved at his rescue and annoyed that she had had to ask for his help.

"Not at all. Now, am I right in assuming that you have not the slightest desire to dance?"

"You are." She had been whirled and swirled around, had her toes trampled on and her hand squeezed far too tightly since the moment she had entered the room.

"In that case, allow me to introduce you to some friends of mine," he said, as they neared a couple who were watching their approach with amused countenances. "Edwin is a committed Whig, and an MP, my dear," Sir Anthony continued as they came within earshot of the pair, "but that is not his fault. One day he will succumb to my entreaties that he take a cure."

Edwin laughed, and bowed to Beth. He was slim and pleasant-looking without being handsome. His moss-green eyes sparkled as he raised his head.

"I am delighted to make your acquaintance, Miss Cunningham. But I am told that I must on no account say anything complimentary about your appearance for fear of sending you screaming from the room."

"Thank you," said Beth. "I would appreciate it. I had no idea that eyes could resemble so many things, from stars to summer skies, to every kind of blue flower God ever made."

"Ah, and your hair!" Sir Anthony trilled, hand on hip. "Soft as spun silk, golden as a field of wheat on a summer's day, liquid moonlight…"

"You are breaking your promise," Beth growled warningly.

"Merely parodying your suitors, my dear," he said, resuming a more normal pose. "Allow me to introduce Edwin Harlow and his wife Caroline."

"I take it that you have not yet become accustomed to London life, Miss Cunningham?" said Caroline, looking down at Beth. She was tall, almost as tall as her husband, and willow-slim. Beth thought she had never seen such a classically beautiful woman, her upswept hair emphasising her long slender neck and perfect Grecian profile.

"I doubt I will ever become accustomed to this," she said sadly. "I thought the mad round of daily calls bad enough, but this…" she stopped, aware that she had committed a terrible *faux pas.*

"You were right, Anthony," said Caroline. She turned to Beth. "He said that you were a refreshing change from the normal empty-headed and frivolous girls who are launched on society as soon as they come of age. You have my sympathy, Miss Cunningham. I suffered the same ordeal before I was fortunate enough to be rescued by Edwin. At least I was prepared for it by my upbringing. But I am told that you have until recently lived quietly in the country."

"Yes," Beth replied. For the first time since she had arrived in London she felt relaxed, and sensed that here were two people she could possibly come to like.

"My commiseration on the death of your father, Miss Cunningham," Edwin said, bowing slightly. "Your brother is a sergeant in the dragoons, I believe. Is he here tonight?"

Beth looked around. "No," she said with obvious relief. "I cannot see him at the moment, but I'm sure he will make an appearance at some point. I will introduce you, if you wish."

"Not particularly," said Caroline bluntly. Beth looked at her, shocked, and then at Sir Anthony, who was wearing an expression of the utmost innocence.

"Just exactly what have you told Mr and Mrs Harlow about me, Sir Anthony?" Beth asked

He held his hands up in a defensive gesture.

"I have told them only what your cousin Edward has told the whole of London already."

"Which is what, exactly?"

"That following the death of your father, you and your brother have been happily reunited with the rest of your family, and that you are in London for the first time. And…ah…" He hesitated. Beth glared at him.

"What Anthony is afraid to tell you," Caroline said, "but of course you need to know, if you don't already, is that it is also common knowledge that you have a dowry of twenty thousand pounds, and that your brother and cousin will be willing to consider any suitor who can buy your brother a commission and your cousin a little more political influence in the House of Lords."

"Do I surmise by the expression on your face, Miss Cunningham, that some of this was unknown to you?" Edwin asked, perturbed by the angry flush that suffused Beth's face.

Out of the corner of his eye Sir Anthony saw the determined youth he had earlier rescued Beth from making a beeline across the room towards them. He placed his arm around her shoulders in a friendly way.

"So, my dear friends, what do you say we retire to the library for a spell, and we can continue this conversation over a glass of fine claret?" Without waiting for a reply, he began to steer her firmly from the room, Edwin and Caroline following.

"Will your brother and cousin not object to you leaving the party?" Caroline asked as they achieved the sanctuary of the library.

Forgetting propriety in her anger, Beth threw herself onto a chair and kicked off her shoes.

"To hell with Richard and Edward too," she said rudely. "Is that really what they've been telling everyone?"

Sir Anthony moved over to a cupboard by the wall and there was presently heard the pleasant sound of wine being poured into crystal. Edwin and Caroline sat down on a red and white striped silk sofa.

"Yes. Well, not quite as bluntly as Caroline has just put it, but the essence is true. Surely you knew?" Edwin said.

"I knew about Richard, of course, but I had no idea that Edward was looking to profit from my marriage. It seemed strange that he had accepted me back into the bosom of his family so quickly, but I was stupid enough to believe that he genuinely wanted to make a new start. I should have known there was an underlying motive. I am too naïve." Beth accepted the glass of wine Sir Anthony held out to her, and sipped at it thoughtfully. "It seems nobody does anything in society without a selfish motive," she said.

"Oh, I wouldn't say that," Caroline said. "Even though Isabella, Clarissa and Charlotte are not really my sort of people, they are kind and generous. I don't think they have any selfish designs. And there are other genuine people around. You just have to look for the signs."

That was probably true, but gave Beth little comfort, not knowing what signs to look for. She felt very downcast, and wondered if she would ever know whether anyone liked her for herself, or merely for the advantage she could bring them.

"What are the signs?" she said, depressed.

"This claret is a sign," Sir Anthony remarked suddenly, sitting down opposite Beth and holding the glass up to the candlelight. "By drinking this, we are showing the utmost consideration for our host, Lord Redburn. He suffers most dreadfully from the gout, and by drinking his secret store of fine claret we will be saving him from a severe attack of inflammation later."

"To say nothing of saving him from the embarrassing spectacle he'll make of himself at two a.m." Caroline said laughingly, drinking deeply.

Beth looked questioningly at the company.

"Lord Redburn is a drunken old sot and a glutton," Sir Anthony explained. "Every two months he throws a ball, to which he invites all the most beautiful young ladies. While they are all dancing and becoming intoxicated on the free-flowing champagne, he incarcerates himself in his room with a few male friends and a bottle of brandy. I have no doubt that is where Lord Edward and your brother are now."

"At around one a.m. he comes down to this room, and secretly partakes of several glasses of claret, to give him Dutch courage," Edwin continued. "Then he enters the ballroom and proposes marriage to the first unsuspecting girl he sees, in the hope that she will be drunk enough to accept him. If he is unsuccessful, he moves on to the next, and the next, becoming more belligerent as he goes. It happens every time. There will be a mass exodus of young women just after midnight, you'll see." He winked at her.

"Except that there will be no spectacle tonight, of course, due to the fact that we will have charitably deprived him of the necessary Dutch courage," Sir Anthony said, relaxing back. They all drank in silence for a few minutes. Beth's depression was lifting. She was thoroughly enjoying the company of these people, and felt that she could be herself for the first time in weeks.

"Ah, I feel a proposal coming on now," Sir Anthony said, draining his glass and reaching for a refill. Caroline swept the bottle from his questing fingers.

"Leave Miss Cunningham alone," she warned. "She's suffered enough tonight."

"That's true," he said sadly. "And I did promise to say nothing pleasant to you this evening. Although I think I may be right in assuming that you would not find a proposal of marriage from me to be a pleasant experience, my dear?"

"Your assumption is correct, sir," Beth replied. She was not alarmed. He was teasing her. "Is everything everyone does common knowledge?" she asked.

"Everything," Caroline said. "Believe me, it is impossible to keep anything hidden. If you don't inadvertently let your secrets slip to a friend, your servants will, and before you know it, all your private vices, infatuations, affairs and clandestine business dealings will be common knowledge."

"It is possible to prevent secrets from becoming common knowledge, although few people are capable of following the simple rule to ensure absolute confidentiality," Sir Anthony said. Although the comment was addressed to the room, his eyes were on Beth.

"And what is this simple rule, pray?" asked Caroline.

"Keep your secrets to yourself. Tell no one. Not your spouse, not your best friend, nobody. Simple, but impossible to do," he sighed.

As light-hearted as the words were, this was a warning, and Beth took it as such.

"Do you wish to return to the party, my dear, or would you like some more wine?"

Beth thrust out her glass immediately, and they all laughed. Sir Anthony filled it.

"Do I take it then that you are a Tory, Sir Anthony?" Beth asked.

Edwin roared with laughter, while Sir Anthony stared at her, his eyes wide with shock.

"I, a Tory, my dear, good God, no. What on earth gave you that impression?"

Beth faltered. "Well, when you introduced me to Mr Harlow you expressed a less than favourable opinion of Whigs, so I assumed..."

"Never assume, my dear. The Tories are nothing more than a nest of Jacobites, a lost cause if ever there was one."

Beth coloured hotly and just stopped herself from declaring that she was a supporter of this 'lost cause'.

"Of course, I apologise, sir," she said, her voice cold in spite of her efforts. "You have made it quite clear in the past that you are a committed Hanoverian."

"Have I?" Sir Anthony said, sounding no less shocked than when she had thought him a Tory. She looked at him, exasperated. Was he deliberately trying to confuse her?

"Yes," she said irritably. "I would think that anyone who declares themselves a close acquaintance of King George and his sons and who casts doubts on the loyalty of the Earl of Derwentwater, could be reasonably assumed to be a supporter of the House of Hanover."

His blue gaze met hers with remarkably perspicacity.

"A reasonable assumption, perhaps, but nevertheless incorrect," he said.

"You have found Anthony's Achilles' heel, Miss Cunningham," Caroline said, coming to Beth's rescue. "He prides himself on his utter impartiality. He is neither Tory, nor Whig, Jacobite nor Hanoverian. He is all things to all men, interested in everything, committed to nothing. He hates it to be thought that he has any partisan tendencies whatsoever."

To Beth, who had been reared on a diet of hotly debated opinions, this was incomprehensible.

"But how is it possible to have no opinions about anything?" she asked.

"Oh, I assure you my dear, in high society you will meet people every day who prove that to be eminently possible," Sir Anthony replied lightly.

She was not going to let him change the subject with a joke.

"But not intelligent people," she insisted.

"I will take that as a compliment. But as I recall, Caroline did not say that I was devoid of opinion, only that I do not espouse causes. Normally I prefer to play devil's advocate. It makes a conversation run on very merrily."

Of course, hadn't he just uttered an opinion, Beth thought; that the Jacobite cause was lost? Or was he just playing devil's advocate, trying to find out where her sympathies lay? If so she had almost fallen into his trap, lulled by the unfeigned honesty of Mr and Mrs Harlow. She was almost certain they were genuine. But she must never let her guard down with Sir Anthony, who in spite of the fact that he was a good friend of theirs, was a different kettle of fish entirely. He was infuriating. One moment she found herself warming to him, the next she hated him. She could not make him out at all.

The door opened and Lord Edward came in, Richard behind him.

"Elizabeth, we have been looking for you everywhere. Why aren't you dancing?" he said angrily.

Why aren't you searching for a suitable man, more like, she thought bitterly.

Sir Anthony leapt to his feet.

"Ah, I am afraid I am entirely to blame, Lord Edward," he said, bowing gracefully. "Your cousin was feeling somewhat fatigued, and I suggested we repair to the library for a moment's respite. Mr and Mrs Harlow accompanied us. We would not wish to be accused of any improper behaviour, you know."

"Ah, no, of course not," Edward said. "But I really think you should return to the ball now, Elizabeth. Several people have commented on your absence."

"Ah, Sergeant Cunningham, there you are!" Sir Anthony cried, as if seeing Richard for the first time. "Let me introduce you to my dear friends, Mr and Mrs Harlow."

Edwin and Caroline stood as Richard came forward to greet them. Their faces were closed and expressionless. They were the epitome of polite gentility.

Beth put her glass down and prepared to re-enter the fray.

"Oh, by the way, my lord," said Sir Anthony as they left the library together. "I took the liberty of recommending that, as this is Miss Cunningham's first ball, she might wish to leave a little early, whilst she still appears at her freshest. It would never do for her prospective suitors to see a wilted bloom, would it?" He ignored Lord Edward's frown and rattled merrily on. "Mr and Mrs Harlow have kindly volunteered to take her home in their carriage at midnight."

"Oh, we could not put you to that inconvenience," Edward muttered. He wanted Lord Redburn to meet Elizabeth. He was perfect: rich, a fool, influential and old enough to die while Elizabeth was still young enough to marry again. She would have to stay to the end, wilted or not.

"Oh I assure you, it is no inconvenience," said Caroline, laying her hand coquettishly on Edward's arm. "In fact, it is all arranged." This was the first they had heard of it, as Beth well knew. "Surely you do not think she will be in any danger from us, Edward?" Caroline continued, looking up at the peer's florid face in consternation.

"No, of course not," Edward said. "But…"

"Excellent, then it is settled," Caroline said crisply. "We will meet you by the front door at midnight, Miss Cunningham."

* * *

The endless round of meaningless calls continued, although in time Beth found herself able to distinguish Lady A from Lady B, as repeated exposure fixed their faces in her mind. The gossip she found difficult to remember, as she was really not interested in it and tended to drift off into a world of her own as soon as the words, "Oh my dears, you will not believe what I heard…" were uttered. This would infuriate Charlotte, whose sole purpose in life once the Cunninghams returned home was to regurgitate the day's rumour and speculate on its verity.

She should listen, she knew that. It would give her something to talk about when visiting, and it would teach her more about how society ticked. Everyone gossiped. It was the bedrock of conversation. But she couldn't help it. She hated gossip; it was usually malicious, often unfounded, and could cause untold misery.

Life had become more tolerable because of her rapidly developing friendship with Caroline and, to a lesser extent, Edwin, mainly because he was in Parliament all day, and she saw little of him. Because Caroline also rarely indulged in gossip and her husband did not possess a title, Beth's cousins expressed little interest in visiting her and consequently Beth was able to go alone, often spending the whole afternoon there. Caroline had accepted her from the first as though she were an old and trusted friend, and after a few visits Beth had plucked up the courage to ask her why.

"Anthony had already given you a glowing recommendation, and you've done nothing since I met you to prove him wrong," Caroline replied simply.

Beth thought back to the cold reception her brother had been subjected to at the ball, and wondered what Sir Anthony had told

Caroline and her husband about him. The baronet had never been anything less than friendly towards Richard.

"And you trust his opinion that much?" Beth asked.

"Yes. He's the best judge of character I've ever met. If he gives you his serious opinion of somebody, and is not merely being witty or playing to his audience, he's well worth taking notice of, believe me."

"I don't know how you can tell the difference," Beth said deprecatingly. "I don't think I've heard him utter a serious remark yet."

"You don't like him very much, do you?" Caroline commented.

Beth blushed. It seemed uncharitable to dislike someone who clearly had a high opinion of her, but she couldn't help the way she felt. She pondered the question for a moment.

"I don't know what to make of him," she said candidly after a minute. "He is amusing, and he's been very kind to me, but…" she faltered into silence, unwilling to tell someone who was a friend of his that she didn't trust him. "You have known him for years, of course, so you are better qualified to give an opinion of him."

"Not at all," said Caroline. "I've known him since he first arrived in London last year, that's all. Before that he was living in France. His family emigrated there from England when he was a child, after a family tragedy of some kind. But he has two faces, you must have noticed that, if you have spent any time alone with him. He's quite different when you get him on his own, if he likes you, than he is when in company."

Beth thought. He had been a *little* different from his normal superficial self when he had taken her to visit Didsbury, but then she had not really been alone, as Grace had accompanied her. She could certainly agree that he was two-faced, although that was not quite what Caroline had meant.

"I don't know," she said awkwardly. "Maybe when I get to know him better…"

"I heard a piece of gossip about you yesterday," Caroline commented, changing the subject in an attempt to alleviate Beth's discomfort. She poured the tea. "I must say I am deeply concerned about it, as I was hoping, now that we are becoming friends, to introduce you to some of my more intelligent acquaintance."

"What is this piece of gossip?" Beth asked.

"There are fears that you may be a little simple-minded."

"What?" Beth spluttered.

"It seems that when you make calls with your cousins, you have a tendency to behave in a somewhat vacant manner, staring into space, smiling to yourself, that sort of thing."

Beth burst out laughing.

"Oh dear," she said after a moment. "I think I have been making my boredom a little too obvious."

Caroline offered the plate of almond biscuits to Beth, who shook her head.

"Yes. You're adjusting quite well to society life, I must say. I have noticed that you are making great efforts to control your tongue, and your impatience, and even your temper."

Beth stared at her.

"I've been watching you. At the theatre last night you showed no sign of your impatience when Isabella kept chatting to you whilst you were trying to watch '*Othello*'. And you managed to sit quietly throughout the whole of Edward's ridiculous tirade about the inferiority of the female intellect at dinner last week. But it's not good enough to merely replace inappropriate emotions with a vacant expression, dear Elizabeth. You must do better than that. Why, some of your potential suitors are having second thoughts about asking for your hand!"

"In that case," Beth said dryly, "perhaps I should start drooling and muttering to myself as well as looking vacuous."

"Oh dear, is it that bad?"

Beth nodded. "Three proposals this week. All of them idiots. Two of the men I've never even met. How can you declare undying love for someone you've never even seen before? Luckily, they were all untitled civilians, otherwise Edward or Richard would be no doubt trying to fob me off on one of them."

"The attractions of twenty thousand don't need to be seen to be irresistible, Elizabeth. But if you think things are bad now, wait until you've been presented to the king. Still, at least being acquainted with royalty should deter some of the untitled suitors. You will put yourself beyond them if you make a good impression on George."

"I think it highly unlikely that I'll get to see the king," Beth said, sounding remarkably happy not to be meeting the sovereign. "None of my family has ever been invited to Court. Edward moans on about it constantly, trying to work out how to cultivate an opportunity to get into St. James's. I'm sure he thinks King George would take one look at him and say, 'Make the man a duke, at once!'"

Caroline laughed.

"But I've heard he's somewhat unsociable since the queen died," Beth continued.

"He's never been that sociable, but since Queen Caroline died St. James's has become unbearably dull. Everybody who is anybody usually dashes off to pay their respects as soon as they arrive for the season. It's only good manners, to visit the king first of all. Then after they've listened to him droning on about military tactics for a while, they make their escape, breathe a sigh of relief, and get on with enjoying themselves. Of course being accepted at Court still carries prestige, even though it is a chore."

Beth was shocked. "I thought you were in favour of the Hanoverian succession. Your husband's an MP in the government that put George on the throne!"

"I am," Caroline replied. "I would fight to my last breath to stop the Pretender regaining the crown and plunging the country into another civil war. But that doesn't mean that I have to personally like the man on the throne. He's ignorant and dull, and what's worse, he's proud of the fact."

"Do you really think there would be another civil war if James retook the throne?" Beth asked.

"Of course I do. It's nothing to do with personalities. King George is dull, the prince of Wales is more lively but incompetent, and Prince William Augustus has all the makings of a tyrant. Whereas from what I've heard, James is colourless, and so is his youngest son. The real danger is from the eldest son Charles. He's the only one amongst the whole shower who might be worthy to be called a king, if rumour is to be believed."

Beth gasped.

"Does Edwin know that you think Charles Stuart would be a better king than George?"

"Yes. We have no secrets from each other. But I didn't say Charles would be a better king than George. He has the personality fit for a king. He's rumoured to be a charismatic man, handsome and daring, although I have heard he's becoming a little dissipated now."

"Sir Anthony told you that, didn't he?" Beth said.

"Yes. He has connections everywhere, and hears a lot. But as I said before, it's not about personalities. It's about religion, and freedom. Not many people like King George or his family. But they like the thought of a Roman Catholic, French-influenced Britain far less. So George will stay. It's as simple as that."

Beth didn't think it was as simple as that, by a long stretch, but much as she was coming to like Caroline, she was not about to trust anyone with her deepest feelings on the matter of the Stuart succession.

"So what gives you the idea that I might be presented to the king?" Beth said.

"Sir Anthony told me that he intends to ask you to accompany him when he visits St. James's. He will be going as soon as he returns from his latest trip."

His trips lasted anything from a few days to a week or more. He had been away for over two weeks this time. There was a lot of speculation as to what his business entailed, the general assumption being that it was probably something to do with the clothing trade. Almost everyone assumed that he visited France on a regular basis, mainly because he always managed to drop a hint to that effect into the conversation; 'My dears, the very latest thing in France is…'

"Will he be welcome?" Beth asked. "After all, he's been in London for weeks. Surely he's breached the protocol, if he hasn't visited St James's yet?"

"Oh, it won't be his first visit. I thought you knew he was a regular visitor to St. James's."

Beth *had* heard that, but then he claimed to know virtually everyone. She had thought it an idle boast.

"Well, if he asks me I suppose I will have to accept, my cousins will never forgive me otherwise," Beth said. "But if you are right, I should do anyway, no matter how dull the king is. I'd visit the devil himself if it would reduce the number of fools that vow they can't live without me."

"Oh, I don't know if it will reduce them, but at least you'll attract a better class of fool," Caroline replied dryly.

In spite of, or possibly because of her conviction that George of Hanover had no right to be on the throne of Great Britain, she felt inordinately nervous at the thought of meeting him, and wondered when Sir Anthony would return and if, indeed, he would ask her to accompany him to St. James's.

In the meantime she tried to concentrate on looking less vacuous and appearing more interested in the conversation during the daily round of calls. However, by the end of the week, she had other things than Sir Anthony and the king to think about.

For at a small soiree given by Lady Ann Morley, she had met Lord Daniel Barrington, eldest son of the Earl of Highbury, for the first time. He was titled, handsome, intelligent, witty and irreverent. And she was smitten.

Chapter Nine

Joshua White paced half the packed dirt floor of his dimly-lit cellar in a mixture of apprehension and anticipation. The other half of the floor was stacked with boxes of tea and several bales of high quality silk, along with two hundred broadswords and a hundred muskets. He had helped to unload this cargo from a cutter landed at Hastings a few days earlier. All the goods were contraband. If he was discovered to be storing these items, he would be heavily fined. If it was discovered that he was a newly-accepted member of the notorious Stanbridge gang of smugglers, he would be transported, at the least.

These thoughts were certainly enough to keep any man worriedly pacing a room, but the prospect of being apprehended by the authorities did not even cross Josh's mind. He was safe here, he knew that. The cellar's entrance was hidden behind a false wall in the kitchen and was accessed by a steep flight of wooden steps wide enough to permit the descent of only one man at a time. Cumbersome when carrying the boxes of contraband up and down, but easily defended from below. Behind another wall in the cellar a tunnel led to the nearby woods, facilitating escape if necessary. These precautions were not, however, the reason why Joshua felt so safe. The village of Stockwell, though only three miles from London, was beyond the rule of law. Almost every occupant was involved in the smuggling business in one way or another, either voluntarily or by coercion, and in addition he was protected by his membership of the gang. No one would threaten him now.

The frown which creased his thin, sharp-nosed, foxy face was caused not by anything he had done, nor by his conscience pricking him over the men he had killed and betrayed in the past, but by what he was about to do. He had gone over the plan several times, how he was going to approach the subject and how he would cope with the possible reactions of the young man he would be meeting soon.

No, he thought. *He won't give me any trouble.* Josh was a good judge of character. His life had depended on it more than once. He had dealt with the handsome young Scot known as Jim several times. It was not his real name, Josh knew that. Nobody used their real names in this business. Jim was brave and reckless, but also good-humoured and naïve. Still, better to approach the subject in a public place, surrounded by people who would assist him if the boy tried anything rash, than in his own house.

He mounted the cellar steps and, putting on his blue woollen coat, which was made of good material but had seen better days, he left the house. The weather was fine though cold, and the single street that comprised the small hamlet was dry. The sun was setting. In an hour or so the villagers would be coming home from the fields, but for now the few scattered cottages were deserted. As he walked down the street his spirits lifted and he started to softly whistle a bawdy tune. The plan would work. It was already working with two of his other clients. Soon he would have a steady regular income, and without being soaked to the skin while unloading cargo, or running the risk of being caught by excisemen every few weeks.

When he arrived at the pub his client's horse was already tethered outside the squat, whitewashed building. Josh entered the stuffy interior and acknowledged the pretty barmaid's desultory greeting with a perfunctory nod of his head. He was not a popular man, although that did not disturb him at all. He preferred to be feared rather than liked, and at any rate the villagers' opinion of him was irrelevant; in a few short days, if all went according to plan, he would be able to move to the Capital and set himself up in style.

He looked around the room. The young man he sought was sitting in the dim recesses of the inn, a pewter tankard of beer in front of him. To Josh's surprise there was another tankard on the table opposite the blond man. He looked up and smiled as Josh approached and sat down, his back to the room.

"Very kind of you to stand me a beer," Josh said, taking a deep swallow of the foaming brew. "Were you expecting me imminently, then, or are you very thirsty?"

Jim seemed about to say something, and then desisted, a small smile playing about the corners of his mouth. He relaxed back into his seat.

"I called in for a beer, as I always do, and the landlord told me ye'd sent a message to say you wanted to meet me here rather than the house. Why? Are we discovered?"

"No, nothing like that. Everything is in the cellar, as usual. I just thought it would be more convivial to meet here over a drink, that's all." Josh looked sharply at his companion, but he showed no suspicion. On the contrary, he seemed quite amused by something. Maybe he had just propositioned the barmaid and been accepted. His athletic figure, glossy blond hair and merry blue eyes were just what Jane would go for. Even as he thought this, Jim cast a glance over Josh's shoulder in the direction of the bar and winked, slowly and seductively. Josh didn't need to look round to know who he'd winked at; Jane's clear tinkling laughter rang out across the room seconds later.

"Well, pleasant as it is to share a drink with ye, I'd just as soon conclude our transaction immediately and be on my way, if it's all the same to you," Jim said.

"Do you have the money?"

"Aye, of course, man. I always pay for the goods up front, you ken that well. What's the matter with ye? You said there's no' a problem."

"No, but the price of the particular goods in question has…changed a little. Due to their dangerous nature, you realise."

Jim's blue eyes narrowed slightly.

"We agreed the price beforehand, and the goods havena become more dangerous in the shipping. What's changed, then?"

Josh took a deep breath and his hands moved beneath the table to loosen the dagger concealed inside his coat from its leather sheath. He leaned forward slightly so as not to be overheard.

"Have you ever heard of a man by the name of Sir Anthony Peters?" he said.

The Scot's eyes widened and his hand clenched convulsively around the tankard of beer, the knuckles showing white. But he did not leap to his feet and draw his sword, and that was a good sign. Josh leaned back again, relieved. His plan was going to work.

No sooner had his spine touched the back of the chair, than a hand settled lightly on his shoulder and he shot to his feet, knife in hand, whirling to meet his attacker. The man leapt back, hand upraised in a conciliatory gesture, a look of fear on his face.

"I'm sorry, man, I had no wish to frighten you," he said.

Josh maintained his aggressive stance, trying to keep both Jim and the newcomer in sight. His mouth opened to call for help.

"This is an acquaintance of mine, Mr Smith," Jim said, making a conscious effort to relax his death grip on the tankard. "He goes by the name of…Abernathy." He looked at the half-empty tankard in front of Josh. "You were drinking his ale, but I doubt he'll mind."

"I am truly sorry, Mr Smith," said Abernathy. "Jim asked me to lend a hand with moving the merchandise. I just popped away out to relieve myself, and didna want to disturb ye at your conversation, but Jim had told me to come straight back and no' mess around outside…"

The man was babbling in his eagerness to appease him, and Josh relaxed a little. Whoever this man was, he was no threat. If anything he appeared a little simple-minded. No doubt Jim had chosen him for his brawn rather than his intellectual capacity.

Abernathy turned now and took a chair from the next table, drawing it up beside Jim's and plopping down into it.

"Your friend and I were just having a private conversation, Mr Abernathy," Josh said, trying to sound authoritative. He looked at the two men sitting opposite him. They were closely related, that was clear, probably brothers. They had the same dark blue eyes, straight noses and strong mouths, the edges turned up slightly at the corners as though permanently about to smile. They were both tall as well, but Jim's frame was still boyish, whereas Abernathy already had the muscle that Jim would one day possess. He didn't seem dangerous, but it was impossible to tell. Josh looked for a way out. He would never have broached the subject of Sir Anthony if he'd known Jim was not alone.

"It's all right, Mr Smith," said Jim amiably, as if reading his mind. "Ye can say anything in front of Abernathy here. He's a wee bit daft in the heid, but he's trustworthy. Mr Smith had just asked me if I kent of a man by the name of Sir Anthony Peters, Abernathy."

Abernathy's face instantly became a mask of fear.

"S…Sir Anthony Peters?" he stammered. "What would we have to do wi' him?"

Josh's heart exulted. He was certain now. Although Abernathy was older than Jim, he was obviously feeble. Dismissing him completely, Josh turned his attention back to the young man.

"He is your sponsor, isn't he?" Josh said.

"I have never heard of…"

"How do you know?" Abernathy spoke at the same time as Jim. Jim raised his eyes to heaven, but did not rebuke his friend for revealing that Josh was right. The foppish, seemingly Hanoverian Sir Anthony Peters, close confidant of the king, was a secret Jacobite, paying for arms to be smuggled into the country! Josh could retire on this, if he played his cards right.

"Let me just say that you were seen entering a certain establishment in London with a package, and Sir Anthony left very soon after, clutching a package of the very same size. You've been seen meeting in this way on more than one occasion." His voice was strong and confident now. In fact, he had seen the blond Scot and his dark-haired 'friend' Abernathy go into a pub in Covent Garden only twice, but on both occasions Sir Anthony had left soon after. He must have already been inside, waiting for his friends. On the second occasion Josh had gone into the pub enquiring after Sir Anthony, pretending he had an urgent message for him, and had been told that the baronet had been entertaining some acquaintances, and had just left. He had known that someone must be sponsoring the Scot to bring in arms, and had guessed that Sir Anthony was the man. He had hoped by Jim's reaction to the name to verify his suspicions, which the loose-tongued Abernathy had just done.

The loose-tongued man in question now looked anxiously around the room, and Jim finished the last of his beer and turned the empty tankard upside down on the table.

"I'm sure you'll appreciate, Mr Smith, that this is a verra sensitive matter and not one I'd be wanting people to eavesdrop on. Can we no' go somewhere a wee bit more private? I'm sure we can come to some sort of agreement." Jim's voice was raw with worry.

Josh took them to his house, ensconcing the simple-minded Abernathy, who expressed a fear of going down into the dark cellar, in the parlour with a glass of wine.

"You'll have to forgive him," Jim said as he followed Josh down into the cellar. "He's always been afraid of cellars ever since his father used to lock him in one as a bairn when he'd done wrong."

He looked around at the boxes stacked about the room, barely visible in the light from the lantern Josh carried. A strong smell of tea filled his nostrils. "Is everything here?"

"Yes, of course," said Josh. "I'm a man of my word."

"Aye," said Jim mildly. "A man of your word who follows other men about, prying into their secret business."

Josh eyed the young man warily, but he was examining a bolt of beautiful chiné silk absent-mindedly, and showed no signs of incipient violence.

"I'm certain we can come to some arrangement," Josh said. "Everything has its price. I'm sure that Sir Anthony wouldn't want his friends to know that he's a closet Jacobite and traitor."

"I'm sure he would not, indeed," replied Jim. "Just what sort of arrangement are ye proposing? I assume that this involves Sir Anthony paying a large sum of money for you to keep your mouth shut?"

"Oh, in view of what he has to lose, I would not consider it a large sum," said Josh, sitting down on a bolt of silk and laying his hands on his knees. He was enjoying himself now. "Shall we say…ah…ten thousand pounds?"

He had expected Jim to protest, but he only inhaled loudly through his nose. Josh cursed to himself. He should have asked for more.

"Ten thousand pounds," the Scot echoed. "And how much will it be costing to pay off all the people ye've let into the secret?"

"I haven't told a soul," Josh said. "I am the soul of discretion."

"For ten thousand pounds Sir Anthony would expect a lot of discretion."

"He would get it, sir, I assure you."

"It is a great sum of money, Mr Smith," said Jim, prevaricating. Where the hell was his brother?

"A man has to live, Jim," Josh said, spreading his hands on his lap.

"Indeed he does, although it would seem that you yourself have no wish to do so," came a voice from the cellar steps.

"Is everyone dealt with?" the young man asked his companion, relief etched in his voice.

"Aye," said Abernathy, coming into view as he reached the bottom of the steps, miraculously cured both of his fear of the dark and his simple-mindedness. "There was nobbut a couple of servants. They'll no' be giving us any bother for a while."

Josh leapt up from his seat, fumbling for his knife, but in two strides the dark-haired Scot had reached him and drove a fist hard into his stomach. The air rushed from his lungs and he collapsed back onto the silk, gasping for breath. The blond man kicked the knife Josh had dropped away into a corner.

"Abernathy?" Alex said to his brother, reaching into his coat and withdrawing his dirk. "Where the hell did ye get that from?"

Angus's merry laugh echoed incongruously around the cellar. "Christ, man, I dinna ken. It just seemed right at the time."

Both men looked at the wheezing figure of the seated man. His wig had fallen off, revealing a mop of greasy black hair. He looked up beseechingly at the two men looming over him and tried to speak, but nothing other than a strangled gasp came out. After their previous encounter, Angus had expressed a mistrust of 'Mr Smith' but had admitted it was based on no more than instinct. However, Alex, whose trust in instinct had saved his life more than once, had taken Angus seriously and offered to accompany him to this meeting. Angus was now extremely glad he had, in view of the way things had turned out.

"What do we do now?" he asked quietly, all trace of merriment gone from his voice.

"I dinna see we have a choice in the matter," Alex said. He reached out and grasped Josh by the hair, dragging him to his feet. Turning him round, Alex wrapped his arm round the man's throat, pulling him against his chest. Alex was a full head taller than Josh; the back of his head rested against the Scot's shoulder. He raised his hands instinctively to defend himself, but then felt the cold steel of the dirk at the base of his throat and subsided.

"Now," said Alex quietly, "you're going to tell me a few things that I need to know. How many other people ken about Sir Anthony?"

"He's already told me that he didna tell anyone else," Angus said, before Josh could answer.

"Do you believe him?" Alex asked.

Angus considered for a moment.

"Aye. He's greedy. He wouldna want to share ten thousand pounds with anyone else."

Josh felt Alex's head nod slightly behind him. He tried to move his head, but the iron-hard arm tightened warningly. He knew now that he had vastly underestimated both of these men. The man standing behind him was clearly no simpleton, but a soldier, battle-hardened and ruthless. And the blond youth standing casually nearby seemed to have no qualms about violence either. He fervently wished that he had told twenty others, or at least had said he had. Then there would be no point in killing him. He tried to collect his wits, no easy task when twelve inches of razor-sharp steel are being levelled at your throat and you are alone.

"Please," he whispered. "Let us talk. What do you say we just forget I ever saw anything, and you can have the weapons and the silk for nothing. By way of an apology." His voice was pleading, craven, but he did not care.

"It's no' the money that's the problem," Alex said. "It's trust. Ye ken well ye had no business to be snooping around, trying tae find out about us."

"I wasn't snooping!" Josh said desperately. "It was pure chance that I saw you, that's all."

"That'll be two pure chances, then, at least," Angus said dryly.

"Ye see, I'm right, ye canna be trusted. Even now, when there's no point in lying, ye're still doing it. How many other people are ye blackmailing?" Alex's voice was cold.

"None! None, I swear it." Josh lied. "It was the first time I've tried it, and I'll never do it again. I've learnt my lesson." He was trembling, his body shaking uncontrollably in the big man's grip.

"You can see his eyes better than I, Angus. Is he lying?"

Angus raised the lantern, moving closer to examine the man, and Josh lost control of his bladder. In that moment he knew he was going to die. Not because the young man was scrutinising him so coldly, and not because of the knife at his throat, but because the man holding him had called the other by his proper name. It no longer mattered to them if Josh knew their real names, and that could only mean one thing.

Angus stepped back.

"I canna tell for sure if he's lying or no'. Does it matter?"

"Aye, it could. I'll ask ye one more question, man. Do ye have a wife and bairns?"

The question was so unexpected that Josh forgot the shameful urine trickling warmly down his leg and puddling at his feet for a moment. Then he grabbed at the lifeline he thought was being offered him.

"Yes!" he cried. "Yes! I do. Five children, and the eldest only eight. If you kill me, they'll starve. Please, have mercy!"

"I'm sorry, man," Alex's voice was soft, regretful. "But I promise ye this. I'll no' let your bairns go hungry, nor your wife either. I'll make sure they're provided for." He removed the dagger from Josh's throat and flexed his bicep, cutting off Josh's air supply and almost lifting him off his feet.

"For what it's worth, ye were wrong," Alex said softly into Josh's ear. "Sir Anthony Peters isna my sponsor."

Josh's hands came up instinctively as he started to choke, his fingers scrabbling at the Scot's brawny forearm. His mind was concentrated solely on releasing the pressure on his windpipe so that he could breathe, and he didn't feel the dirk until it slid between his ribs into his heart. His eyes widened, and he coughed softly, once. One hand reached blindly for the dirk which was buried to the hilt in his chest, but he had no strength to draw it out. His body spasmed violently before going limp. Alex went with him, lowering the body gently to the floor, where it twitched feebly for a moment before the brown eyes slowly glazed over, and all movement stopped.

"Have ye a kerchief, Angus?" Alex said to his brother, who was standing stock still, eyes wide, face ashen. He fumbled in his coat for a moment and produced a square of linen, which he handed to the man crouched on the floor. Alex wadded it up and wrapping it round the base of the dirk, slowly withdrew the weapon, pressing the cloth against the wound. Angus watched in horrified fascination.

"We dinna want to leave the house covered in blood," Alex explained. "This will soak it up, and no' leave so much of a mess." He stood up, sheathing the dirk, and scrubbed his hand through his hair. He looked down at the body of the man at his feet. "Christ, why the hell did he have to do that? Could he no' be satisfied with the money from the smuggling?"

Receiving no answer, he looked at Angus for the first time, and his eyes widened in alarm.

"Sit down, man, for God's sake." He took his white-faced brother by the shoulders and sat him down on a bale of cloth, shoving his head roughly down between his knees. "Breathe slowly. It'll pass in a minute."

"'M a'right," came the muffled voice a few seconds later. Alex released him, and Angus sat up, still pale but no longer looking as though he was about to faint.

"I'm sorry, but I thought ye kent I'd have to kill him. You've seen me kill before. Ye've even killed men yourself, more than once," Alex said, sitting beside his brother and putting an arm round his shoulder.

"Aye, I did, and I have," Angus said shakily, ashamed now by his reaction, but still leaning into his brother's comforting warmth. "But it's one thing killing someone who's trying to kill you, when your blood's up, and another watching your brother kill a man in cold blood."

Alex examined his right hand, splayed on his lap, the heavy ridged scar pale against his tanned skin.

"You're right," he said softly. "It's no' the same thing at all. But if I'd let him live, he would have killed me, Angus, and you and Duncan too. Not to mention all the others whose names would likely have been tortured out of us before we were executed. And if they connected me with Sir Anthony…" Alex shuddered. "I couldna let him live, ye must see that."

"Aye, I see that, right enough," Angus said, sliding his arm round Alex's waist and squeezing, realising with a slight surprise that his seemingly invulnerable older brother needed comfort too. "But there isna any danger now, surely?"

"No, I think you're right," Alex mused. "I dinna think he told anyone else. But I want you to ride straight to The Three Crowns anyway and tell Rose what's happened. And warn Duncan too. I think it'd be better if we find another place to meet. Probably better we dinna meet at all for a few weeks." He stood up, galvanised into action. "I'll move the body into a corner. It's too risky to chance getting rid of it now. Can you and Duncan move the stuff?"

"Aye, I've the horse and cart ready, and we're expected at the storehouse in a couple of hours."

"Are ye feeling well enough to go straight away?" Alex asked.

"Aye, nae problem. I just went queasy for a moment, but I'm fine now."

Alex looked at his youngest brother. The colour had returned to his cheeks and he was already moving purposefully toward the boxes of arms, putting the killing of the man out of his mind with all the carelessness of youth. Alex felt a pang of envy. He wouldn't sleep well for a few nights to come. No matter that he had had no choice; he had just taken a life, and widowed an innocent woman.

"Good. I'll be off then." He moved towards the stairs, feeling suddenly weary.

"Where are ye going?" Angus asked, surprised.

"To keep my promise."

* * *

Alex reined in his mount and looked up at the whitewashed inn with some trepidation. Yellow light spilled from the windows and the yeasty smell of beer assailed his nostrils as he approached the door. Someone was playing a pipe inexpertly, and there was a burst of laughter as he opened the door and entered the warm, welcoming atmosphere of the Swan Inn. He would rather have been anywhere on earth than here.

When he had told his brother what he was going to do Angus had tried to dissuade him by every means possible. But once set on a course of action that he was certain was right, there was no dissuading Alex, and Angus had finally desisted, wishing his brother luck as he rode off into the afternoon and wondering if he'd ever see him again.

It was the only honourable thing to do, Alex thought as he shouldered his way to the bar and asked if he could have a word with Mr Foley regarding a friend of his known as Mr Smith. The barmaid looked at him suspiciously but disappeared, and ten minutes later Alex was standing in a well-lit, comfortably furnished upstairs room, the merriment from the pub below muffled but unmistakably jolly and raucous, quite at odds with the tense atmosphere in the room as the two men cautiously assessed each other.

Gabriel Foley had risen to his feet as Alex entered the room, and he knew at once that this man was quite a different prospect to the small, sly, fox-faced 'Smith'. Foley was of no more than average height, several inches shorter than Alex, but massive of shoulder and thick-waisted. He reminded Alex of a bull pawing the ground warningly, debating whether to charge. His face was ruddy, a jolly face, but the grey eyes that weighed Alex up now were shrewd and intelligent, and the expression was wary rather than good-humoured. Instinctively Alex recognised that this man was worthy of respect, and fervently hoped he would not have to kill him.

"You have chosen a very late hour to pay your respects, Mr Abernathy," Foley said. His voice was deep and rich, the tone neutral.

"I didna choose the time, Mr Foley, it was forced upon me by circumstance."

"Are you armed?"

"I gave my sword to the man at the door."

"I know that, but nevertheless I rarely travel at night with only a sword for company. And I've not yet met a Highlander that wasn't armed to the teeth even when doing nothing more risky than visiting his maiden aunt. You *are* a Highlander, are you not?"

Alex smiled, and opened his coat. He took the pistol and dirk from his waist and laid them on the table.

"Aye, I am," he said carefully.

Foley waved a hand at a chair.

"Take a seat, Mr Abernathy," he said. "Can I get you a drink? You look like a man who has ridden hard and fast."

Alex gratefully accepted a glass of claret, and watched Foley's eye drift towards Alex's armpit as he sat down opposite him, almost as though he could see through the layers of cloth to the small *sgian dhu* strapped under his arm. The man was shrewd, and very knowledgeable. No doubt that was why he'd survived over ten years as the leader of a gang of smugglers, a profession not known for its long-term prospects.

Alex was not about to surrender his only remaining weapon without a fight, and to his relief the smuggler did not ask him to.

"So, Mr Abernathy, what can I do for you?"

"I didna come to ask for your assistance, sir, but to give you a piece of information."

He could see the respect in Foley's eyes turn to contempt. He thought Alex had come to sell information, perhaps to betray a supposed friend. He came straight to the point.

"I have killed a man tonight, Mr Foley, who claims to be a member of your association. I thought you should know of it."

Gabriel sat back, but Alex was not deceived. Every muscle in the man's body was tense, ready to spring into action at a moment's notice. Alex felt his own muscles tighten in response.

"You are either very brave or very stupid, sir, to come here alone and tell me you have killed one of my colleagues. Which is it?" Their eyes clashed, and both men recognised the force of the other's personality.

"Neither," Alex replied bluntly. "I made the man a promise just before I killed him, and I am here to honour that promise."

"Ah, honour," Gabriel said. "I have heard that Highlanders place a high value on honour." Alex tensed, but there was no mockery in the man's tone. "Well, English though I am, so do I, Mr Abernathy. Relax, sir, I'll hear you out. Tell me who you have killed, and why."

"I've been dealing with Mr Smith for some while, bringing in various items of merchandise. I kent that he had links with your people, and I also ken that you are no' entirely unsympathetic to my cause."

"I take it you mean the Jacobite cause. You are well informed, Mr Abernathy. Go on."

"Tonight he attempted to blackmail me to the tune of ten thousand pounds. He has been following me, and had learnt various things about me that would put my life and the lives of others I hold dear in jeopardy. Because of this, I felt it necessary to kill him. I did it as quickly and painlessly as possible."

"I take it then, that he was stupid enough to tell you this in a private place, where no assistance was to hand?"

"He seemed to feel I didna represent a threat, Mr Foley," Alex replied.

Gabriel raised his eyebrows as he viewed the tightly-coiled body of the tiger sitting sipping claret opposite him. The man radiated violence from every pore, and what was more, a dangerous, controlled, icy violence.

"Well, I would say such a fool probably deserves to die. Smith, you say? Describe him to me."

Alex did, while Gabriel leaned over to replenish his glass before offering the bottle to his visitor.

"Yes, he is, or rather was, a new member of my group. I confess that I was not sure of the man, but he was an excellent sailor, and knew the part of the coast around Hastings like no other. However I know well the value of anonymity, as I'm sure do you. My men are trustworthy. They ask no more questions about a man's business than they need to know to ensure they are paid for their services. If you speak true you have done me a favour."

"I canna prove what I have told you is true, sir, as I am sure you realise," Alex replied.

"I do realise that. And you seem an intelligent man. You must have known that before you came here, and the risk you took if I did not believe you. What is this promise you spoke of?"

"Before the man died, I asked if he had a wife and bairns. He said he did. I promised I wouldna let them go hungry. With me I have only the money to pay for the goods Mr Smith procured for me, which I will give to you now. However, if you'll give me the details of his family I'll ensure that a regular sum is paid to them. I'd also ask ye sir, to convey my deepest apologies to them. I didna wish to kill the man, but he gave me no choice."

Gabriel looked at Alex, open-mouthed.

"My God, you really mean it, don't you? You risked your life to come here and confess to killing one of my men, offer to pay for goods you could have taken for free, and to support a whole family for years? What manner of man are you?"

"An honourable one, I hope, sir," said Alex. "I do only what any of my clansmen would do, and for that matter, many other clansmen too. Ye must know that, an ye deal with Highlanders often?"

"I don't deal with them often, although I wish I did if they're all like you. I just recognise the accent and know where they keep their weapons." He passed the dirk back to Alex, blade first. Alex took it, and sheathed it. For the first time since entering the pub, he relaxed. It was a good feeling.

"They're no' all like me," Alex admitted. "There are rogues and saints in every nation. I'm closer to a rogue than a saint myself. But I'd no' see bairns starve because they had a fool for a father."

"You won't see any children starve. The man was a bachelor. If he has any children they were born on the wrong side of the blanket and I've no knowledge of them, but I doubt it, ugly runt that he was. He no doubt hoped you'd spare him if you thought he had a family."

He watched with amusement as Alex slumped back in the chair with relief.

"Christ, I'm glad to hear ye say that, man. It wasna easy, thinking that I'd widowed a woman and left five bairns fatherless."

"I don't know if you'll be glad to hear me offer you a bed for the night as well, Mr Abernathy, but I'd suggest you take it. The weather is not conducive to a long ride through the night, I'd say."

A shower of hail battered against the window as if to confirm Gabriel's words. And Alex found himself saying that he'd be delighted to stay the night, in a place that an hour ago he'd gladly have ridden through hell to avoid, had honour not compelled him to do otherwise.

Chapter Ten

Early April, 1743

"I don't know why you have such a mania for taking the air, Beth," Lord Daniel said a little grumpily, shivering in spite of his layers of clothing. "It's freezing. I shouldn't be at all surprised if it were to snow later."

They were walking arm in arm down the long thoroughfare of Birdcage Walk, which though full of fashionable pedestrians in the summer months, was now almost empty. Beth stopped, inhaling gratefully the fresh crisp air blowing across from the wide green spaces of St James's park to her left. In spite of having now lived in London for over two months, she still had not become completely inured to the smells of the city, and took every opportunity she could to visit green places.

"You are being dramatic, Daniel," she said. "It is far too cold for snow." She glanced up in time to catch the look of horror that crossed his features, and couldn't hide a smile.

"You are joking with me," he said peevishly. "You are too cruel, when you know how sensitive I am to the cold." He snuggled deeper into his heavy fur-lined coat.

"You spend too much time huddled round the enormous fires in your mansion, or drinking in stuffy coffee houses," she admonished. "You need fresh air. It brings roses to your cheeks, and the exercise is good for you, if you walk at more than a snail's pace, that is."

"You're being unfair," Lord Daniel said as he handed her up into the waiting carriage, before jumping in himself, grateful to be out of the biting wind that Beth seemed to barely notice. "I do nothing but exercise all summer. But the winter is a time to take stock, and allow oneself a little relaxation. There is some compensation for the last hour's suffering, though," he said, looking at her fondly as she took off her gloves and rubbed her hands together briskly to warm them.

"What's that?" she said, glancing across at him.

"You have never looked lovelier than you do right now," he said warmly.

It was true. Her cheeks were rosy, her blue eyes sparkling with happiness. She smiled at him, and his heart did a somersault. God, she was lovely. He leaned across and kissed her lightly on the tip of her nose, and she felt a warm glow spread through her body, banishing the cold.

She had felt the chemistry the first time she had seen him, nearly six weeks before. They had been at an unspeakably dull card party. She had wandered desultorily from table to table, restless and praying for the evening to be over. Then their eyes had met across the room, and her life had changed forever. He had felt it too and they had drifted towards each other, magnetic north and south pulled irresistibly together. He had abandoned his game, they had spent the evening chatting, and by the end of it she had been certain of a new friend, at least. The next day he had called to the house and begged leave to court her. Since then they had spent as much time as they could together.

She had the Cunninghams' blessing; the Earl of Highbury was indecently rich and very influential, just the sort of person both Edward and Richard wanted to cultivate. With her family's encouragement everything was made easy. They attended the opera and the theatre together, sitting in the Earl's permanently reserved box. To Beth's delight Lord Daniel did not chatter throughout the performances, but listened carefully. During the interval he would talk about the piece, commenting on the actors' or musicians' proficiency. He had seen many plays and been to innumerable concerts and once he realised how much she loved the theatre, he took her at every opportunity.

She could have loved him for that alone; but he was also amusing, intelligent, and seemed to share almost every interest with her, with the exception of taking long outdoor walks in cold weather. He preferred to sit in coffee houses during the day or spend time at his club, which was banned to women.

In looks they were opposites; his hair was dark, his eyes a warm light brown. He was taller than her by some six inches, broad of shoulder, but slender of hip, and his legs were long and well shaped. He was perfect, and latterly Beth had found herself leaning towards him when he was talking to her, longing to kiss his smiling mouth but afraid to do so in case he should think her too forward. He was a model of propriety, and whilst she knew he was behaving that way out of respect for her rather than a lack of interest, it had become increasingly frustrating as the weeks passed and her feelings for him strengthened. He was considerate and attentive, showering her with compliments and presents, flowers, books, and lately jewellery; a pair of pearl earrings, a gold bracelet. But he had made no move toward her until last night, in the comparative privacy of an alcove during a ball.

More than half of the becoming flush of her cheeks today was due to the memory of that kiss, gentle and warm, but with the promise of much more to come. At the first touch of his lips desire had raged through her blood and when he had pulled back reluctantly, she had been shaking and breathless, totally defenceless against the unfamiliar sensations which had possessed her.

"If I did not know better," he had said, smilingly. "I would say that was your first kiss." His hands were resting lightly on her shoulders; she could feel them burning through the thin silk of her dress.

"It was," she had admitted, blushing. She had read about kisses, she had seen her mother and father kiss each other, but nothing had prepared her for this. A footman had walked past at that moment, and they both shrank instinctively further behind the large palm plant that sheltered them from public view.

"Ah," he said, a note of satisfaction in his voice. "Then may I assure you that it is much less painful the second time." He chuckled to himself, but before she could ask what was amusing, he had taken her in his arms and kissed her again, this time far more thoroughly, his mouth demanding on hers, his arms crushing her to him in an embrace that was almost painful. This time when he broke away from her he was also breathless, whilst every bone in Beth's body seemed to have turned to water and she leaned helplessly against him for the support that her legs were unable to give her.

He had felt her slight weight and the erection straining against his breeches, and had been tempted to push her up against the wall, lift her skirts and take her now. The risk of discovery would only add to the pleasure. But if they were discovered his prudish father would kill him. This was no servant girl to be tumbled in a cupboard and forgotten about. She was virgin, the girl he hoped to marry. He moved away from her reluctantly and peeped round the side of the plant, surreptitiously adjusting his breeches, which had grown somewhat uncomfortable around the groin.

"I think we had better leave separately," he suggested, slightly huskily. "I wouldn't want anyone to think I had compromised your virtue." He had slipped out of the alcove silently, Beth reappearing a few minutes later when the blush had faded from her cheeks.

Remembering that now, her cold cheeks flamed, and Daniel, noticing, smiled fondly at her.

"It really *was* your first kiss, wasn't it?" he said softly. She nodded.

"Yes. Do you mind?"

"Mind? God, no. I feel privileged. I just find it hard to believe that no one has tried to kiss you before."

"Oh, plenty have tried," Beth replied, pulling her gloves back on. "You are the first that has succeeded, that's all."

"Then I feel doubly privileged." He leaned forward and took her hand in his. "I intend to write to my father today and ask him if I may bring you to meet him."

Her eyes widened. "Are you sure?" she asked.

"Yes," he said. "But I don't want to do anything without your agreement."

"Do you think your father will approve of me?" she asked.

"How could he not?" Daniel smiled. "He will love you at first sight."

"And will you tell him what I have told you today?" she asked, looking him straight in the eye. This morning, sensing that their relationship had taken a more serious turn, she had told him about her mother's origins. Her origins, but not her religion or political sympathies. She had half-expected Daniel to back off, but to her surprise and relief he had not turned a hair, telling her it was her he cared for, not her family background.

"No, not immediately," Lord Daniel said. "I think it is something that would be better told in person. But once he sees you he will have no doubts that you will make a perfect wife for me, of that I'm certain. You need not be ashamed of your mother, my love."

Beth pulled her hands from his grasp.

"I am not ashamed of my mother!" she said hotly. "I will not have you deceive your father."

He softened his tone, aware that he had upset her.

"Nor should you be ashamed. I would love you no matter what your birth. But my father is of a different generation. Once he has met you he will see at once that you are a lady indeed. I have no intention of deceiving him, but let us wait for the right time to tell him." He took her hand again and squeezed it gently, relieved when she did not withdraw it, although she did not return the pressure.

"Come, my love, let us not argue," he said. "You know that I love you. But one day I will be the Earl of Highbury. I will have you for my wife, but I must tread carefully with my father. We have only known each other a short time. I know that you are the only woman I want but if I tell my father that, he will think I am being indecently hasty. We must take things slowly, convince him that we have taken the time to get to know each other, before we tell him we wish to marry. I will tell him only that I have met a lovely girl and that I would like him to meet her and give his blessing before we pursue our relationship. That will please him."

He looked tired, she noticed. Maybe the kiss had disturbed him as much as it had her. She had not slept well last night.

"And what if he says no?" she asked.

"He will not, believe me," Daniel replied.

Later at home she realised that he had not answered her question. What would he do if his father disapproved? What would she do, for that matter? On a practical level, Lord Daniel was a perfect match. From a noble, influential and wealthy family, he could easily afford to purchase Richard's commission in the dragoons and provide him with enough money to buy his way further up the ranks as positions became vacant. And his father was one of the most influential peers in the House of Lords. Edward's standing would be vastly elevated. Yes, if she sought a husband merely to escape from Richard, she could not do better. But she had not anticipated falling in love with her rescuer. It weakened her judgement, she was aware of that. But try as she might, she could see no faults in him. His father *would* like her, she determined; she would make him like her.

She could understand why he was reluctant to tell his father about her mother's low birth before he had met her. She too had not confided totally in Daniel yet, but only because she did not want to deluge him with information. She would tell him about her Catholic and Jacobite leanings before she agreed to marry him. It would not bother him unduly, she was sure. Once she was married, she could be herself. He loved her for what she was, not for her money, that was certain. To the son of the Earl of Highbury her dowry of twenty thousand pounds would be a drop in the ocean, of no importance at all.

Lord Daniel was also in his room, pacing the floor like a caged lion. He was tired and irritable, angry with both himself and Beth, although he realised that was irrational. It was not her fault that he had been both inflamed and frustrated by the kiss in the alcove. So inflamed that after leaving the party he had made his way straight to the stews of Covent Garden, where he had quenched his lust in a young whore, closing his eyes as he climaxed in a vain attempt to conjure up Beth's perfect delicate features instead of the coarse painted face and rotten teeth of the girl he panted and sweated over.

Nor was it Beth's fault that he had met an old acquaintance as he left the whorehouse, a man he had vowed to his father that he would never speak to again, and that the man had invited him to a card game that was about to start at his club. It was not her fault that he had then gone on to lose a great deal of money, his whole year's allowance, in fact. But he was still annoyed with her for tempting him with her fresh, innocent beauty. If he did not blame her, he would have to take the responsibility for his own actions, which would never do.

He stopped pacing and sat down at his writing desk. If he

wrote to his father now he could catch the early post. He dipped his quill in the inkpot and bent wearily to his task.

* * *

Sir Anthony sprawled languidly on the green velvet chaise longue, long crimson satin-clad legs crossed delicately at the ankle. At his elbow was a small spindly-legged gilt table, on which were a glass of wine and a plate of juicy purple grapes. He popped one into his mouth, and looked at Caroline with amusement.

"Do close your mouth, my dear. It is most unbecoming," he said. "Have you not seen chiné silk before?"

"Yes," Caroline replied, running her fingers reverently over the luxurious cream silk, woven with a pattern of red flowers and green foliage. The outlines of the flowers were blurred, giving a watercolour effect. She tore her eyes away from the roll of material reluctantly. "I have never seen such a fine one as this, though, and such a length. There is enough here for a whole dress!"

"Well of course there is. I could not see you walking around in public dressed in only half a gown. What would people say?"

She threw a cushion across the room at him, which he caught deftly and placed in the small of his back.

"Ah, that is better," he sighed blissfully. "Coach travel is *so* uncomfortable these days, the state of the roads being what they are. I swear that every bone in my body has been put out of joint by the infernal jolting."

"You know full well what I mean," she said, expressing no concern for the alarming state of his skeleton. "I have never seen a dress made from one length of this silk before. There is always a seam, somewhere. But there is enough here to make…" she stopped. "What have you been up to?" she said, eyeing her companion suspiciously.

Edwin walked in just in time to hear his wife's last words and to catch Sir Anthony's look of injured innocence.

"What *have* you been up to, then?" he echoed.

Sir Anthony clapped his hand to his breast, an expression of the utmost distress on his face.

"Oh, you have wounded me mortally! What a terrible state of affairs when those who profess themselves to be one's friends are suspicious of the most altruistic acts. I declare, I am quite overcome with grief." He slumped dramatically backward into the cushions.

Edwin raised one eyebrow.

"Now I *know* you've been up to something," he said, bending over to pick up a grape from the plate next to his guest. "What do you suspect him of, Caroline?"

"It's more than a suspicion," she said, folding the length of silk carefully. "The reason I've never seen a dress made of chiné silk without a seam is because it's only imported into England in short lengths. Too short to make a full gown. You have been smuggling, have you not, Anthony? Or at least dealing with those who have."

"Oh my dear, I will not deny that I have…ah…associates in all echelons of society. Merely by chance I happened to run into an acquaintance who expressed a desire to rid himself of a large quantity of silk at a most economical price. I thought to make you a present of it. But if you do not want it, then…" He reached out a hand towards the shimmering fabric, and she slapped it away.

"I did not say that," she said, and all three of them laughed. "Would this acquaintance of yours happen to be an English smuggler, or were you still in France at the time?"

Sir Anthony popped a grape into his mouth.

"I do not ask the nationality and profession of every gentleman I meet, Caroline. That would be vulgar. But no, his accent proclaimed him not to be of this fair land. As for the country I was in when the transaction took place…well, one piece of land is much the same as another, don't you think?"

As half the countries of Europe were now engaged in full-scale war because they considered their piece of land to be very different from the others, or because they felt another piece to be extremely desirable to them, this was not a viewpoint shared by his companions. Indeed, Edwin had just spent a long and weary day in the Commons defending a motion he did not personally agree with, that foreign troops defending the piece of land known as Hanover, so dear to King George, should be paid for by the British parliament. He loosened his stock and sat down.

"I don't think I want to know any more about how this piece of cloth arrived in our drawing-room, my love, and whether our friend here is a smuggler himself or merely buys from them," he said to his wife. "Just say thank you, or return it and let's leave the matter there."

"Thank you, Anthony," she said, moving to stand behind Edwin. Placing one hand on each shoulder, she began to massage the tense muscles. He sighed blissfully.

"I have another length of a different pattern, which I had intended for Elizabeth. But in view of what you told me before, I am not sure it would be wise to give it to her," Sir Anthony commented sadly.

"Why?" said Edwin. "Is she possessed of greater moral fibre than my wife? Ouch!" Caroline dug her thumb hard into the side of his neck.

"No, you fool," she said. "To be honest, whilst I'm sure Elizabeth would love such a present, I doubt she would appreciate its value. I have never met a woman so disinterested in fashion. She would have no idea that it cannot be obtained in such quantity by legal means, either. But her suitor would definitely understand and would probably jump to the wrong conclusion."

"What? You think that Lord Daniel would see *Anthony* as a threat? Ha!" Caroline paused in her massaging to raise her eyes to heaven, and Edwin realised his mistake. "Oh, I'm sorry, old fellow," he said. "I didn't mean it the way it sounded. It's been a long day and…"

"Quite all right, no offence taken. I agree. Lord Daniel is most attractive, and titled as well. And I have heard nothing bad about him as regards his conduct towards the ladies," Sir Anthony said. "I would be a very poor prospect next to him."

He sounded almost wistful, and Edwin glanced up at Caroline. Clearly they were thinking the same thing.

"You like her, don't you, Anthony?" Edwin ventured.

The baronet, who had been obviously thinking of other things, jumped slightly.

"Yes," he said frankly. "Not romantically, of course," he amended quickly. "I am not interested in marriage. To anyone. God, no. Hideous thought." He glanced up at his friends. Twin looks of scepticism greeted him. They had never heard him utter such a series of staccato phrases before. "I admit, then, I am becoming fond of the girl. Who would not? She is lovely, innocent, unaffected."

"Everything you are not," put in Caroline bluntly.

"Exactly. Quite unsuitable. But I would see her make a good match, and not tie herself to the first man who seems viable, just to get away from her ridiculous family."

"She's in love, Anthony," said Caroline, planting a kiss on the top of her husband's head and coming round to sit next to him. "She's positively glowing with it. If you thought her beautiful before, she is irresistible now."

"Glowing is certainly something you seem to know a good deal about yourself at the moment, Caroline," Sir Anthony commented. "Have you then also taken a handsome lover, or is your bloom more maternal in origin?"

The fact that Edwin was still in the room when Sir Anthony made his enquiry told the couple that he did not suspect the former to be the case at all. Caroline blushed prettily, confirming the baronet's suspicions.

"How on earth do you know that?" Edwin asked, astonished. "Caroline only told me last night." Edwin looked at his wife suspiciously.

"No I didn't!" she exclaimed, guessing his thoughts. "You ought to know better than to think I would tell anyone else such a thing before I told my own husband."

"Please, please, don't argue because of my intrusive comment," their friend pleaded. "I assure you, Edwin, Caroline has not even hinted that she is *enceinte.* But it is my business to be observant and I have seen enough women who are expecting a child to recognise the signs. I am sorry if you did not want anyone else to know. But it can only be a matter of time before they do, anyway, you know," he finished.

This could not be disputed, but Edwin and Caroline still felt a little disgruntled. They had wanted to keep the news to themselves for a few days before it became public knowledge.

"Is it that obvious?" Caroline asked.

"No, not at all," Sir Anthony reassured her. "No one else will have the slightest notion until you tell them. Most of our acquaintance are so self-obsessed, that I doubt they will notice until you are at the point of delivery. The signs are subtle. I assure you most sincerely that I won't tell a soul, and will affect the deepest surprise at the news when you do announce it. If I may just offer my sincere congratulations, then I will speak no more of it." He beamed at his friends, who looked only partly mollified. "So," he continued brightly, "our Elizabeth is in love. Does she prattle on incessantly about Lord Daniel in that tiresome way women in love for the first time do?"

"No, although I'm sure she would like to," Caroline replied. "She keeps a lot to herself. She is not one to prattle about anything, you know that. But as soon as he enters the room she lights up like a torch. Charlotte is making up for Elizabeth's reserve. She chatters endlessly to anyone who will listen about how romantic it is, and that it was exactly the same for her and her dear Frederick."

"Poor woman," Sir Anthony said, not elaborating as to whether he meant Charlotte or her lovestruck cousin. "This has all happened very suddenly. Does Elizabeth know about Lord Daniel, then?"

"Does she know what about Lord Daniel?" Edwin asked.

"Why, that his father banished him into the countryside to cool his heels for a while after he ran up enough gambling debts to feed the population of London for a week. He was only allowed back three months ago after he promised faithfully to reform his ways. In all fairness, he seems to have kept his word up to now."

"How do you know all these things?" Edwin asked incredulously, his irritation with Sir Anthony's acuity banished by curiosity. "We were all under the impression that he had been visiting Italy to improve his knowledge of fine art."

"As I said, dear friends, I have associates in..."

"All echelons of society," Caroline and Edwin said together, and laughed. The atmosphere lightened.

"Well if that's the case, we will just have to hope that he has learned his lesson and mended his ways. Because we dare not warn her. I am certain she is too infatuated to accept anyone speaking ill of her beloved Daniel," Caroline said.

"Elizabeth is more level-headed than you give her credit for," Sir Anthony replied.

"No one is level-headed when they are in love, Anthony, as you will no doubt find out one day."

Sir Anthony shuddered theatrically.

"Me, my dear, never! If I am ever in danger of marrying for love, please, I beg of you, just shoot me in the head and save me years of untold misery."

"Caroline and I married for love," Edwin pointed out.

"Exceptions only prove the rule, dear boy, and are rare. I do not expect to marry at all, but if I do it will certainly be for practical reasons, not for love. Horrible, restrictive thing. Deprives one of all reason. Quite unfathomable."

The silk remained in Sir Anthony's possession, and Beth remained in love with Lord Daniel. They both waited for the Earl's reply, and in the meantime their romance was the talk of London society.

Now he had returned, Sir Anthony resumed his visits to the Cunningham household, and as far as the family was concerned nothing had changed. He was still as friendly and chatty, his violet cologne still smelled as strong, and the white lead paint covering his face was still as thick. The general assumption was that it was concealing the horrible scars of smallpox, although no one would be so indiscreet as to ask him directly. It was well known that his return from the continent to England just over a year ago had been precipitated by the death of his whole family due to smallpox. Quite understandably he did not talk about this tragedy, and no one was ill-mannered enough to ask. Beth watched him closely in the drawing room as he chatted to Isabella about the horrors of sea voyages, and how his addiction to the vagaries of fashion that necessitated his trips to France would be the death of him one day. It was possible, she thought. Many people did survive smallpox, although the resultant scarring could be hideously disfiguring. The paint was certainly thick enough to fill in the holes caused by the disease. Although no matter how badly scarred, he couldn't possibly look worse than he did with this grotesque mask.

He felt her gaze on him and looked up at her, smiling briefly before continuing with his tale. He had changed towards her since his return from France. It was subtle, but obvious to her. He rarely addressed her directly, did not offer to accompany her into the dining room, and was no longer on hand to rescue her from unwelcome suitors. Presumably he now realised that was Lord Daniel's job. She was grateful. She had not thought Sir Anthony particularly tactful and had worried that he would anger Lord Daniel with his flippant informality and meaningless endearments. But he had kept his distance. If anything, he had become more distant than was strictly necessary.

She let the conversation drift on around her. How long did it take a letter to get to Berkshire? How long would the Earl take to reply? She supposed he would have to think about it before answering. A week, maybe two. The waiting was intolerable. Surely he would not refuse to see his son's choice of wife? Lord Daniel had not actually proposed to her yet, but that was only a formality. Did the Earl already have a bride lined up for his heir? A titled woman, with lands? She frowned.

"Will you then be free next Friday, my dear Elizabeth?"

The mention of her name jolted her out of her speculations.

"Of course she will. She will make herself free," Lord Edward said.

"Free for what?" Beth asked, her mind still half on the unpleasant prospect of the Earl of Highbury's censure. She looked up to find the whole Cunningham family eyeing her disapprovingly and Sir Anthony watching her with amusement.

"Really, Elizabeth, I give up. Do you never listen to anybody?" Richard said irritably.

"Do not be hard on your sister, Richard. I'm sure she has far more pleasant things to occupy her mind than listening to my tedious conversation," Sir Anthony said.

Edward did not protest that Sir Anthony's conversation was far from tedious.

"Sir Anthony is taking you to be presented to the king next Friday, Elizabeth. You are most honoured," he said imperiously.

Am I? she thought, bristling with anger that Edward thought himself competent to know how she felt. She glared at Sir Anthony, who held up his hands in defence.

"I did not command your attendance, my dear, as your cousin suggests. I merely asked if you will be free. I intend to visit the king and would be delighted if you could accompany me. But if you have another appointment, I am sure his Majesty will understand."

Even if his Majesty would, it was very clear her family would not. She sighed and gave in. She might as well get it over with. Maybe the earl would look more favourably on her if she made a good impression on the monarch. She brightened at that thought.

"I would be delighted, Sir Anthony," she said, and almost meant it.

Chapter Eleven

"Oh come on, man, let your hair down for once. There's nae harm in it."

Alex rubbed his hand roughly through the hair aforementioned as he always did when irritated, and inhaled sharply through his nose in frustration as the thong binding it broke and chestnut locks cascaded around his face.

"I'd beg leave to differ with ye on that, Angus, but that's no' the point," he said, catching the ribbon thrown to him by Duncan in mid-air and tying his hair untidily back. "I didna take the risk of coming here to meet you just so that I could empty my balls in some pox-ridden whore."

"Aye, but since we're here…" Angus said hopefully.

"Just what did you take the risk of coming here for?" Duncan interrupted, aware that his older brother was irritable and that Angus's flippant attitude was not likely to restore his temper.

Alex had sent a message to his brothers' lodgings, stating that he needed to meet with them urgently at nightfall. The maze of alleyways that lay between the Strand and Drury Lane were ideal. Ill-lit as they were and populated by numerous denizens of the criminal world, the three men sitting quietly in the corner of a disreputable back street inn would attract no attention. The only prostitute who had earlier made her way jauntily towards them, hoping for business, had recoiled at the ferocious look in Alex's eyes as he noted her progress across the room. He had jerked his head sharply at her and she had scurried quickly away.

"There are problems at home," he said, his voice soft so as not to be overheard. "The arms near Stronmelochan have been discovered."

"What?!" Angus exclaimed, and then seeing his brothers' disapproving looks, lowered his voice. "How?"

"I had a letter from Donald. It was waiting for me at the coffee-house when I went there this morning. It had been there for three days. It seems that ten days ago a pack of redcoats found the cave. Wee Davy Drummond happened to be there, and heard them coming frae miles away. Ye ken what a racket the redcoats make. Anyway, he hid himself in the gorse and watched them come to the top o' the hill, then rootle around a little until they found the cave. Then he slid off backwards down the hill and ran to tell the others, although there was nothing they could do."

"They could have gone and fought, surely? How many redcoats were there?" Angus said.

"It doesna matter how many there were," Alex said through gritted teeth. "Think, man. If the men had all rushed up the hill, maybe they'd have killed the redcoats and saved the weapons, aye. And within less than a week every British soldier in Scotland would have descended on the glen and wiped us out. As it is, the cave is actually on Campbell land, so the MacGregors are unlikely to be suspected – no' immediately, at least," he said thoughtfully. "The British'll no be eager to accuse a powerful clan like the Campbells, being halfway up George's arse as they are. While they're investigating, we can be on the other side of the glen and out of harm's way. They did the right thing in not attacking the soldiers, Angus. Swords and pistols can be replaced. Men cannot."

"Ye're thinking that it was no accidental discovery then, Alex, that the redcoats knew where the cave was already?" Duncan said, his grey eyes troubled.

"Aye, although Donald doesna' ken for certain. It seems awfu' strange that a pack of English soldiers should be strolling aimlessly around a barren rocky hill in the pouring rain, though. And Davy did say as they made straight for the area where the cave was, moving wi' a purpose."

Duncan whistled through his teeth.

"Christ," he said. "I canna believe it. What's the world coming to, when first smugglers'll break their honour, and then your own clansmen?"

"We dinna know for certain what's happened yet," Alex pointed out. "I need someone to go and find out. It should be me, as chieftain, but I canna leave London again so soon without attracting suspicion."

"I'll go," volunteered Angus. His brothers looked at him, their faces twin masks of disbelief. Duncan opened his mouth, and Alex, hearing the tactless words before they were uttered, leapt in.

"No, man, I need ye here, doing what you do best, talking in taverns, finding out where our supporters might be found and how ready they are to rise if it comes to it. No, Duncan, it'll have tae be you. I'm sorry, you've only just now got back."

Duncan nodded. "It doesna signify," he said. "I'll leave tomorrow. If I find out who it is, do I have your permission to deal wi' the man?"

"Aye, ye do," Alex interrupted, his eyes cold, chips of blue ice reflected in the light of the tallow candle which was pushed into a blob of wax on the rough wooden table. "In any way ye see fit."

There was a silence while the three men gloomily contemplated the almost unbelievable idea that a member of their own clan could have betrayed them to the enemy. Then Angus finished his tankard of ale and stood up.

"Well, now the business is concluded, it seems a shame to waste the evening, especially when Mother Meredith's house is only a few steps away. I'll just take a piss while ye finish your beer."

He walked off across the room, pausing for a moment to say something to the comely barmaid that brought a smile and a blush to her cheek, and then disappeared out of the door. Alex watched him go and then shook his head.

"*Bas mallaichte!* Was I that careless when I was his age?" he said, half to himself.

"I dare say you would have been, but you had to grow up fast after Father died afore his time, Alex," Duncan said. "He's young and reckless, that's all. But there's nae harm in him."

"I'm no so sure about that," Alex replied.

Duncan's eyes widened with shock.

"Christ, Alex, ye canna mean to say that you think Angus would hurt the cause?"

Alex picked up his tankard of ale and stared into its amber depths.

"No," he said. "No' intentionally. I'd trust him wi' my life. I *am* trusting him, and you, wi' my life. He'd die before he'd betray us. He's brave, and a good fighter. There's no one excepting yourself that I'd rather have by my side in battle. But he's wild, and reckless, like ye said, Duncan. He doesna always think before he acts, and that's what worries me."

"Och, dinna fash yourself, Alex, he's young, that's all. He'll grow up fast enough, when the time comes."

Alex forbore from saying that the time was already here, and his youngest brother showed no signs of maturing at the moment. Instead he took a deep swallow of beer. Duncan eyed him knowingly across the table, his grey eyes warm with affection.

"Ye've a lot in common, ye ken," he said softly. Alex looked up from his beer. "Ye've both got a way wi' people. Ye can make friends of nearly anyone, and get them tae tell you the most amazing things. You both thrive on danger. And ye both attract the ladies like wasps round a sugar bowl."

Alex laughed.

"Christ, I ken that well enough," he said. "I'm besieged by the silly creatures. I think they sense I've no notion of marrying, and see me as a challenge. It's awfu' wearing, though. But you're right about Angus. That's why I want him here. And there's one thing he's got that I havena. I never kent any man who was so unaffected by the drink."

That was true. Angus seemed to be immune to the effects of alcohol, which was a distinct asset in his current profession. He could match his companions drink for drink and remain clear-headed while they were drunkenly babbling all their most treasured secrets in his ear. No one to Alex's knowledge had ever seen Angus the worse for drink.

The subject of their conversation now returned to join them.

"Come on!" he said impatiently. "If we're quick, we'll get there before all the decent lassies are taken."

They didn't, and rather than have what was left, Angus and Duncan chose to wait until the choicer girls had finished with their current clients. All three men had been to Mother Meredith's before. It was a somewhat better class of whorehouse than many in the Drury Lane area, and the brothers relaxed on burgundy velvet-covered chairs in the salon, drinking brandy while they waited.

"So, who do you have your eye on tonight, Alex?" Angus asked. "I'm after Rosalind, myself, if I dinna have to wait too long."

Rosalind was one of the newer girls, small and slender, with long blonde hair and thick-lashed blue eyes. She still retained the vestiges of country innocence about her, but Alex knew it wouldn't last long. No woman could survive in this profession for more than a few months without becoming hard, a hardness which soon showed in her face.

"No," he said. "I'm no' in the mood. I think I'll pass for tonight."

"Oh come on," coaxed Angus. "Ye canna do anything about the situation in Scotland by moping about it, man. There's no better way tae take your mind off your troubles than a good shag."

"He has a point there," Duncan conceded.

"Tell ye what," Angus said, "I'll let you have Rosalind. I'll take Clara instead."

"That's generous of you indeed," said Duncan. "Ye always have Rosalind."

"Aye, well, she reminds me o' yon bonny lass that came upon us that night in Manchester. God, but she was lovely," Angus said wistfully, staring unseeingly at the wood-panelled wall of the room, clearly reliving that night four months ago. "I can still feel the soft curves of her body in front of me on the horse, my arm wrapped round her waist to stop her leaping off. She was so slender, I could hae…" His voice trailed off as he saw the expression of fury on his brother's suddenly pale face. Alex's hands were curled into fists at his sides, and Angus instinctively shrank back in his seat.

"Dinna compare that lady wi' a whore to me, not ever," Alex said, very quietly.

Angus ran his tongue nervously across his lips.

"I'm sorry," he said. "I didna mean any harm. I had nae idea ye were soft on the lassie."

"I'm no 'soft on the lassie' as ye say," Alex replied, his words clearly at odds with his reaction to Angus's observations. "But she's a lady, respectable, and I'll no' have her maligned."

"Ye still see her then," Duncan said.

"Aye, from time to time."

"Are ye after marrying her yourself, then, Alex?" Angus said cheerfully, clearly not believing his brother's protestations of indifference to her.

"No, I am not. She's niece to a lord, destined to marry high. She'd no' look at the likes o' me. If I was interested," he added hastily. "Which I'm not." The firmness of his tone brooked no dissent. The subject was closed. Angus's face was alive with questions, but there was no point in asking them, he knew that. All he'd succeed in doing was angering his brother more, and he knew from past experience how unwise a move that was.

The sound of doors opening and closing upstairs announced the imminent appearance of the more select ladies. Angus drained his glass in one before standing. Duncan pulled roughly at his sleeve.

"For God's sake, man, sit down," he said. "If they ken how eager ye are, they'll double the price."

"Rosalind willna," said Angus confidently. "She looks forward to my visits as much as I do. She's tellt me so, more than once."

Duncan and Alex exchanged a knowing glance. She no doubt said that to all her customers. Or all the clean ones, at least. Duncan shrugged his shoulders. Let Angus keep his romantic illusions, while they did no harm.

"Are ye sure ye'll no' change your mind?" he asked his older brother.

"No," said Alex. "I'm no' in the mood. I'll wait here for ye." He sat back in the chair.

When the two brothers returned to the salon an hour later, Alex had gone. They waited for him for a short time before leaving, slightly puzzled, but not worried. Alex could look after himself, they knew that. Most likely he had got bored of waiting and had made his way home.

* * *

Beth had agreed under duress to make a brief call on Lady Winter with Isabella.

"You have made excuses not to come on the last three visits," Isabella pointed out. "If you do not come this time, she'll think you don't like her."

"I *don't* like her," Beth had replied.

"Oh, Elizabeth, how can you say that? She always speaks so highly of you!" Isabella had cried.

Only when my back's not turned, she wanted to say. The woman was a malicious gossip and delighted in destroying the reputation of anyone who was unfortunate enough to cross her. Beth conceded defeat though, pragmatic enough to realise that fifteen minutes of listening to vitriol was a small price to pay to keep in Lady Winter's good books.

When she got there, however, she found herself dragged into a ladies only party in full swing in the drawing room.

"All the men have gone to see the bear baiting," Lady Winter explained merrily. "So we ladies decided to have a little impromptu get together. I was about to send a man round to invite you, but you've saved me the trouble. Isn't it wonderful?"

"Yes," said Beth unenthusiastically. She gritted her teeth and plunged in.

She knew that everyone would want to ask her about Lord Daniel, and within moments of entering the room her fears were confirmed. Was he about to propose? Was she going to meet his parents? Was his father going to come to London soon? What a beautiful bracelet. Had he bought it for her?

She fended the questions off as well as she could, smiling vacuously, hiding her impatience behind a façade of blushing romantic innocence. She looked around the room for Caroline, seeking shelter from the storm of questions, but to no avail. She took refuge in a corner hoping that the others would take the hint and leave her alone, but she was soon joined by several other ladies, Isabella amongst them.

"Emma was just saying that the gardens at Ranelagh and Vauxhall will soon be open, now that spring is almost upon us," Isabella said. "I am sure Lord Daniel will want to show you the delights to be found there."

"Oh, have you never seen the pleasure gardens, Elizabeth?" asked Anne Maynard, a buck-toothed stick of a girl with lank brown hair which was currently covered by an enormous powdered wig.

Of course I haven't, you idiot. I only arrived in London for the first time three months ago, as you well know.

"No," Beth said, smiling with her mouth while her eyes

remained expressionless. "I have not had that pleasure as yet."

"You must of course go to Ranelagh, rather than Vauxhall," another lady put in. "Why, any rabble can get into Vauxhall now. Maidservants go there, acting the lady in their mistresses' hand-me-downs. It is becoming impossible to distinguish between the mob and people of quality. Why, when I was a young girl a lady would not dream of passing good clothes on to the servants. She would throw them away first. It does no good, giving them ideas above their station." Her beaked nose quivered with indignation.

Beth, who had already passed on the yellow satin dress that looked so hideous on her to Sarah, kept quiet. She was certain her maid would be at Vauxhall the moment it opened. She was having the time of her life in London. Beth swallowed the urge to make a challenging reply to the beaky woman's comment and looked around for an escape route.

"So, I believe that Lord Daniel has written to his father, asking permission to take you to Skelthorpe Hall to meet his family," Lady Winter said.

"Yes," Beth admitted, wondering how the nosy cow had found that out. Surely Daniel hadn't told her?

"Oh, I have heard such wonderful things about Skelthorpe Hall. You must tell me all about it when you've been," Isabella said, clearly assuming it was a foregone conclusion that the earl would approve of her cousin. "I have heard that one room is covered from floor to ceiling in gold leaf! Imagine that!"

"It sounds quite…unique. If you will excuse me for a moment," Beth said. "I really must use the privy."

Once outside the drawing room she leaned her forehead against a pillar in the vast hallway, the cool marble soothing to her skin. She had not seen Daniel for three days, nor had he sent a message to explain his absence. She could not understand it. For the last month they had seen each other almost every day. On the rare days that he had been unable to meet her he had sent flowers and notes to say how much he was missing her. Now, suddenly, nothing. Her mind was in turmoil. Had his father replied expressing his disapproval, and Daniel was afraid to tell her? Had he changed his mind, met someone else, decided he didn't love her any more? The thought tore through her like a knife and she closed her eyes against the pain. No, it wasn't possible. He loved her, she was sure of it, and she loved him. Whatever had happened, that much was certain. But the niggling doubt remained. Could his love for her withstand his father's displeasure? She wished he would just come and tell her, whatever it was. Anything was better than not knowing.

"Are you unwell, my dear?"

Beth's eyes snapped open. A vision in russet velvet stood about four feet away from her. One of his parents must have been a cat, she thought; she had not heard his approach across the echoing hall, in spite of her acute hearing.

"What are you doing here?" she said rudely. "I thought all the men were at the bear baiting." His violet cologne belatedly assailed her nose, and she wrinkled it in disgust.

"I have no interest in watching an animal torn to pieces for no good reason," Sir Anthony said, not at all ruffled by her rudeness. "I called to leave my card, and Lady Winter kindly invited me to join the party. Speaking of cards, I have left mine at your home for the last three days. I need to speak with you about a most urgent matter, but Isabella told me you were indisposed. Indeed, you are remarkably pale, my dear Elizabeth. Are you ill?"

"No. That is, yes. I…" She was on the edge of tears. She had not slept well last night, or for the last three nights, in fact. She had refused to see Sir Anthony when he had called, asking Isabella to say she was ill. Suffused with love and worry about Lord Daniel, she had felt unable to tolerate Sir Anthony's idle chatter, and felt in no mood to do so now, either.

"Perhaps if you would be so kind as to spare me a few moments now?" he ventured. "It really is most…"

"No. Not now. Go away," she said bluntly. "Please," she added belatedly, swallowing convulsively. She looked around wildly, trying to remember which of the ten or so identical doors that led off the hall was the one for the privy.

"Very well," he said, and turned towards the drawing room. "Ah…the third door on the left, if I assume rightly," he said over his shoulder, before opening the door to be greeted by feminine exclamations of welcome.

Following his directions, Beth attained sanctuary and closed the door with a sigh of relief. *How does he do it?* she thought. It was not the first time he had seemed to know what she was thinking, and she found it very disconcerting. As much as she and Daniel loved one another, he had never shown the slightest indication of being able to read her mind. How many men would think it pleasurable to be invited to an all-female party? Most men she knew were vastly uncomfortable in the presence of more than three ladies, unless they had another male to provide moral support.

Her composure restored a little, she splashed water on her face, smoothed her hair back, pasted a pleasant expression on her face and made her way back to the drawing room.

She had been away for longer than she thought; several ladies had left, and only ten or so now remained. Any hopes that Isabella might be looking to leave were dashed by Miss Maynard, who came across to tell her that Lady Winter had taken Isabella upstairs to show her the main bedroom, which though not completely covered with gold like the room at Skelthorpe Hall, had a simply divine ceiling, covered with gilded plaster cherubs.

Beth resigned herself to enduring at least another half hour or so before Isabella reappeared and she could persuade her to leave. Perhaps if she pleaded a headache…The ladies moved in her direction again, and Beth steeled herself.

"Oh, my dears, I must tell you the most amazing thing that I heard the other night!" Sir Anthony's voice trilled from somewhere behind Beth. She didn't turn towards him, although several of the other ladies did, eager for the latest gossip.

"Of course, it is a little *risqué,* and I'm not at all sure I should tell you. I would not wish to offend your delicate sensibilities." This statement ensured the attention of every lady in the vicinity, and Beth was sudden bereft of companions.

"Oh, come, Sir Anthony!" said Lydia Fortesque, a lady whose considerable beauty was diminished by her excessive awareness of it. She tapped him playfully on the arm with her fan. "I am sure we are all ladies of some experience. We are all married, or well of an age to be." She glanced across at Beth, who refused to be drawn and instead feigned interest in a particularly badly executed portrait of one of Lord Winter's sour-looking ancestors.

"If you are sure," Sir Anthony responded, although his voice was still a little doubtful. A chorus of female encouragement persuaded him.

"Well, then. I am a little ashamed to admit that last night I stayed overlong at my club. To be precise, it is not exactly my club, but since the darling Marquis of Tweedale was so kind as to introduce me, I have been a regular attender, although not actually a member at present. Of course I do have hopes…but I digress, ladies, please accept my apologies. Where was I? Oh yes. So having stayed overlong at my club, I found that upon leaving there was not a carriage to be seen. It being a most clement night, I decided to walk a little of the way in the hopes of picking up a hackney along the road."

"Why, were you not in your own chaise, Sir Anthony?" asked Anne.

"No, I had given my man the night off. I was confident I would be able to obtain a conveyance home, you see, as I had not intended to leave later than ten of the clock."

"Oh, you are really too kind to your fortunate servants!" Anne twittered. He beamed down at her, and the other ladies tutted in exasperation, not only at the fact that Miss Maynard was taking the opportunity which they had missed to flirt with the bachelor, but also that she was delaying him from getting to the interesting part of the story.

"You are very sweet, my dear Anne!" he cooed.

Beth moved on to the next painting, an overly sentimental rendering of an improbably large-eyed child standing by a summerhouse, acres of what was presumably his future inheritance stretching away in the distance behind him.

"As I was walking along the Strand, who should I meet but one of my footmen, in the greatest of hurries. I was most surprised, and asked him where he was off to in such unseemly haste. He told me that he was following a certain young noble of our acquaintance, who has until recently shown somewhat of a penchant for cards, but now claims to have renounced them. My footman told me that he had been in a house of ill repute earlier, and had espied Lord…ah…X, shall we say, in the company of a most disreputable man. He had decided to follow him, in case the man should lead Lord X to a dark alley and there rob him."

A little gasp of shock ran around the company. Beth froze in front of the painting. Every decent instinct told her to leave the room rather than listen to malicious gossip, but she could not bring herself to move.

"Surely you do not mean the Earl of Highbury's son?" Lydia gasped.

"It would be beneath me to disclose any names, my dear, in view of what I am about to tell you. Of course, seeing that my footman was engaged on a most noble errand, I told him to proceed immediately and even gave him a little cash and made him the loan of my sword in case he should have need of it. My man disappeared into the night and later told me what had transpired."

He paused for dramatic effect, and Beth, still ostensibly admiring the painting, closed her eyes. Surely he was not about to lightly declare that Lord Daniel had been stabbed to death in an alley? Her heart seemed to constrict in her chest, and she held her breath, waiting for him to continue.

"It seems that Lord X and his companion went straight to Beecham's club, where there was an all-night card game in progress. My footman had a most diverting time there, drinking an exceptionally fine port, at my expense, I might add, and conversing with Mr Ashworth. He is a delightful man, who has recently been in Italy, you know. When he was in Florence…" Beth let out the breath she'd been holding. He was safe then. Whatever nasty gossip Sir Anthony had, it could not hurt her if Daniel was uninjured.

"But what of Lord Dan…Lord X?" One lady asked impatiently.

"Who? Oh, of course. Well, he sat down to a game of Loo, which he played without cease into the morning hours, and won not more than three or four tricks in all that time. He finally left at around four o' clock, looking most distraught."

"Oh, the foolish boy!" cried Lydia. "If he continues to lose money gambling, his father will be bound to find out."

"Indeed, I do not think his father can fail to discover his son's lapse. After my lord left, my footman made some discreet enquiries," Beth's snort of disbelief that Sir Anthony could be discreet about anything went unnoticed by the entranced circle, "and I discovered that he lost over four thousand pounds."

Several of the ladies cried out in shock, for which Beth was very grateful, for in spite of herself, she had also gasped with horror.

"Four thousand pounds!" cried Anne. "Oh no, surely that cannot be true, Sir Anthony!" It could. The frenetic nature of Loo with the stake doubling at every trick could make it one of the most expensive games to play.

"I am afraid it is. The proprietor of the establishment himself told my man so. But had it been one hundred pounds, it would have been as dire. The poor boy is already impecunious. I know for a fact he has not paid his tailor's bills for some time, and the man has now refused to extend him any more credit."

"How do you know that, Sir Anthony?" asked Emma.

"He had the temerity, once he had been turned away from his own tailor, to approach mine. But of course people in the profession talk to each other, and my Mr. Johnson was far too perceptive to be taken in by Lord X's plausibility. After all, it is not the first time, nor indeed the second, that Lord X's father has had to bail out his son. His supposed trip to see the renaissance art of Italy last year was nothing more than a device of his father's to free him from the clutches of the very man in whose company he was two nights ago, and to try to break him of his ridiculous addiction to cards. In fact the young man did not go to Italy at all, but was rather despatched to one of his father's more remote country estates for a time. It seems, however, that he has learnt nothing and is determined to ruin himself. I am certain his father will not help him again. Indeed, he has said on more than one occasion that he will not. If the boy is to obtain the money to discharge his debts, he will have to seek elsewhere than his family for it." Sir Anthony glanced across at Beth, who was staring fixedly at the child's portrait, her face white.

Daniel had told her about the trip to Italy, had enthused about the works of Botticelli, Michelangelo. They had trusted one another. They did trust one another. Sir Anthony was lying. She did not know why, could think of no reason why he would wish to hurt her so, and in public too. At that moment she hated him even more than she hated her brother. Her hands curled into fists and she unclenched them with effort. She had to leave, now. A giddy panic washed over her, and she placed a hand against the wall to stop herself from reeling.

"But, ladies!" Sir Anthony called in his gratingly high voice. "I must beg your opinion on an important matter! If you will excuse a small lapse in etiquette!" The ladies, eager to ascertain Beth's reaction to this news of her lover, had turned as one in her direction, but now their attention focussed back onto the only gentleman in the room. He removed his coat with a flourish before executing a little pirouette. "What do you think of my waistcoat, ladies? I had it from my tailor this very morning. Is it not delightful?"

The ladies all eyed the waistcoat with approval. For Sir Anthony, the colour was dull, a beige-coloured velvet with a darker brown pattern of flowers and scrolls. It was exquisitely cut, as were all his garments.

"It is beautiful, Sir Anthony," ventured one of the ladies.

"The colour is most fetching," said another.

"Ah, I am gratified that you think so," the gentleman said. "For, in truth, the colour is the only thing I had reservations about."

"I am sure your complexion would suit any colour, Sir Anthony!" gushed Anne. This was taking flattery too far; under all the paint, Sir Anthony could be a negro for all they knew. No one had ever seen him without his make-up, and even the most patient of the ladies present were exasperated at this point with the ridiculous Anne.

"But that is not what I wish to draw your attention to. Do you not see, come, look closer." Every lady except Beth was now gathered closely around him, and he lowered his voice so that they had to give him all their attention.

"It is *à disposition,* ladies," he whispered confidentially. "The velvet has been woven to fit the shape of the panels! Is it not perfect?!"

The ladies bent closer to observe the perfect matching of the pattern across the panels of the waistcoat.

"It is French of course," he announced proudly. He looked around the room to ensure all eyes were on him, revelling in the attention of so many beautiful ladies. Beth was nowhere to be seen, having taken the opportunity to slip out of the room unnoticed. Sir Anthony bent over and retrieved his coat from the table he had placed it on.

"But I must apologise for my state of undress," he said, deftly donning his coat. Various ladies declared that they had not been at all offended. "Well, I will not take up any more of your time. I am sure I am becoming tedious, and the gentlemen will be angry when they return and realise that I have spent the entire afternoon in the company of their ladies." He made an elaborate bow. "If you will excuse me."

"What a delightful man," sighed Anne, after he had departed. There was a soft murmur of agreement as every woman in the room compared the interesting and sympathetic Sir Anthony with their hunting, shooting and politically obsessed husbands, to the latter's detriment. Many of the ladies wished they were single again. Not one of their husbands would have known or cared what *à disposition* was.

Neither did Beth. Having slipped silently out of the room, she had dashed across the hall, to the consternation of Isabella and Lady Winter, who, having concluded their inspection of the bedroom ceiling, were descending the stairs to rejoin the company.

Beth stopped in her tracks, white-faced and trembling with rage at Sir Anthony, and disgust at herself for half believing his evil gossip.

"Are you ill, Elizabeth?" asked Isabella, moving quickly to her cousin's side.

"Yes," cried Beth. "I have the most terrible headache. I think I must go home immediately." She was not lying. Her head had indeed started to pound, and she felt distinctly nauseous.

Within half an hour she was at home, in bed, alone with her thoughts. Thoughts which kept her awake again, well into the night.

* * *

"You have a visitor, Beth," Sarah said, popping her head round the door the next morning. Beth had dragged herself out of bed, determined not to be affected by Sir Anthony's gossip. She had spent the sleepless night going over every word he had said. His story seemed plausible enough and if he had witnessed the events himself, she might have been tempted to believe him. But he had the story second-hand, from a footman. No doubt the servant had been up to something unsavoury himself, and had made up this preposterous story to divert his master's attention from his own behaviour. Well, Sir Anthony might be gullible enough to believe the word of a servant, but she was not.

"If it's Sir Anthony, Sarah, tell him to go away," she said, examining the dark shadows under her eyes with a grimace.

"No, it's Lord Daniel," Sarah said, coming up behind Beth. "A little rice powder will hide those," she said practically.

Beth started up in joy, almost dropping the hand mirror.

"Tell him I'll see him in ten minutes and…what's wrong?" Sarah wore a worried expression.

"It's nothing, really. Only he seems very…distracted, somehow. Not himself at all," she said.

Beth didn't care how he seemed. He was here. He would be able to give the lie to Sir Anthony's tale.

"He must have had a reply from his father. Show him into the parlour, Sarah. I'll be down directly."

"Do you think he's going to propose to you? He seems very nervous."

"No. We've already decided to take things slowly, I told you that. It's very important that he gain the approval of his father. He won't do that if he proposes formally to me before his parents have even seen me. No, it must be something else." A cold finger of doubt touched her heart, but she dismissed it. His father must have made a negative reply. It was not insurmountable. She had not seen Daniel since Sir Anthony had invited her to meet the king, but she would tell him today. That would be sure to impress the earl.

When she opened the door he was pacing up and down the parlour like a caged lion, but stopped as she entered the room. She looked at him, surprised, understanding now why Sarah had been worried. His clothes looked crumpled, as though he had slept in them, and his forehead was creased in a frown. He moved forward to greet her and she smelt the unmistakable odour of stale tobacco. Daniel did not smoke, but he had obviously spent some considerable time in the last hours in the company of men who did. She suffered him to kiss her, although his breath smelt sour. It was so unlike him to be anything less than immaculate that she knew something was seriously wrong, and when he moved away from her, Beth's face wore a frown to match his.

"What is wrong?" she asked. "Have you received an unfavourable reply from your father?"

"What?" he asked distractedly, as if he had no idea to what she was referring. "Oh, oh, yes. No, he has not yet replied. No, I have come to ask you…" he faltered, "something else."

Now she was seriously alarmed.

"Now you are frightening me, Daniel," she said. "What has happened?"

"Nothing!" he exclaimed with exaggerated brightness. "Only…I did not sleep well last night, and I am a little tired. Er…do you think we might have some tea?"

She called for tea, and by the time it was served Lord Daniel had regained a façade of composure, at least, while Beth was becoming more unsettled by the minute. She waited impatiently while he drank one cup of tea, but when he reached again for the teapot she could stand it no longer.

"For God's sake, Daniel, what have you come to tell me?" she cried.

He put down his cup and stood up, moving across to take her hands in his.

"Forgive me, Beth," he said, attempting to smile reassuringly. "I am very nervous. I have come to ask you if you will do me the honour of marrying me."

He was so certain she would say yes that her reaction took him by surprise. She pulled her hands from his grasp and her face drained of all colour.

"I'm sorry," he said. "I know I should make a speech, go down on my knees. But you know I love you, and I am so nervous, that if I kneel I don't think I'll be able to get up again!" he smiled at her, and she looked away, swallowing hard.

"I thought you wanted to take things slowly, Daniel," she said emotionlessly. "What has changed?" She looked at him, praying that he would give a good reason, a plausible explanation for his sudden proposal.

"Nothing!" he exclaimed again. "Only I have not seen you for three days, and they have been excruciating. I realised then that I couldn't live without you and decided I must marry you now, before someone else tries to take you from me."

She closed her eyes, trying to tell herself she was imagining the insincerity of his tone. A lump came to her throat and she swallowed again.

"Where *have* you been for the last three days, Daniel? Why didn't you call on me if you missed me so? I have been here, waiting for you."

It was his last chance, although he did not know it. If he had told her the truth then, she would have forgiven him, would have married him against all common sense, so much did she believe herself in love with him.

"I have been busy getting my affairs in order, to be sure that I could afford to make my proposal to you. And I wanted to see how long I could endure not seeing you." She willed him to look her in the eye, but his gaze slid past her, fixing on an object somewhere over her left shoulder.

"I see," she replied. She desperately wanted to believe him, but his dishevelment coupled with his extreme nervousness and his inability to look her in the eye, told her he was lying. Sir Anthony's poisonous words of the previous day echoed in her head; "If the boy is to obtain the money to discharge his debts, he will have to seek elsewhere than his family for it." She felt sick and numb, but with a monumental effort composed her face into a mask of politeness.

"And have you succeeded in setting your affairs in order?" He opened his mouth to answer, but she hurried on before he could lie to her again. "Four thousand pounds is a great deal of money to find, when your father is unwilling to give it to you. How did you obtain it?" Her voice was cool, matter-of-fact, although the hot blood surged through her veins. She wanted to fly at him, tear him limb from limb, hurt him as he was unknowingly hurting her now.

At last he looked directly at her, his mouth falling open with shock.

"How did you find out?" he asked automatically before flushing, obviously regretting the words as they left his mouth.

"Sir Anthony told me," she said, half hoping that Daniel would later call him out and kill him. "But it's common knowledge by now. As is the fact that you did not go to Italy earlier this year, but were banished to the country by your father in an attempt to break you of your mania for gambling."

He sank down into a chair, his blush vanished, his face now as pale as Beth's. Then he looked up at her, clearly trying to find a plausible explanation.

"I would suggest that instead of trying to invent another story, you tell me the truth," she warned him, her voice still emotionless. Her heart thumped leadenly in her chest.

"I love you, Beth, that is the truth, and I do want to marry you, I swear it!" he declaimed passionately. "I am sorry. I didn't want to lie to you, but I thought you would despise me if you knew I gambled. I have mended my ways now, though. I will never go near a card table again, I assure you."

He sounded genuine. But then he had sounded genuine when he had told her of the beauties of Florence and Venice, beauties that he had not seen, of the interesting people he had never met last summer, of the glorious warm weather he had not enjoyed.

"I am not asking you to marry me for your dowry. I love you, surely you know that?"

"I'm very happy to hear that, Daniel," she said. "In that case, I think we would do better to stick to your original plan, and wait until your family have met me. I am in no danger of falling in love with anyone else, I promise you." At this moment she thought she would never love anyone, or trust anyone, ever again in her life. But if he passed this final test, accepted her suggestion, she could at least walk away from this meeting with some vestige of belief that his declaration of love had not been a total lie.

"But you must marry me!" he cried, panicked. "There is no other solution!" He sprang to his feet and would have embraced her, but she backed away so hurriedly that she collided with a small table, knocking a vase of flowers on to the floor. The delicate glass shattered, and water splashed up her skirts unheeded. She was certain now. He wanted her for her dowry. Whether he loved her or not was immaterial; she no longer believed he did. Her fragile control threatened to fragment as the pain welled up in her heart. "I cannot live without you!" he added passionately.

"I am afraid you will have to. The answer is no, Daniel. I will not marry you. Not now, not ever. I am sorry." She turned away blindly, desperate to be away from him, to be alone, where she could break down, scream, wail, tear her hair out. Her satin-shod feet crunched unheeding through the broken glass as she dashed for the door.

He ran in front of her, blocking her exit.

"You cannot do this to me, Beth. I thought you loved me!" he pleaded.

"Yes," she said, her voice trembling. "I thought so too. But I was wrong. You have betrayed my trust, Daniel, and you have lied to me for no good reason. I do not love you any more, and that is all there is to it." She swept past him and left the room, walking straight-backed up the stairs without looking back, leaving a trail of bloody footprints and a distraught Lord Daniel behind her.

By the time she got to her room she no longer wanted to weep and wail. She felt drained, and sank down on the bed, willing herself to sleep, seeking escape from the heartbreak that she knew would overwhelm her if she let it. Sarah, alerted by the blood, appeared a few minutes later and to Beth's intense relief did not express any curiosity as to what had transpired in the parlour. She merely examined Beth's feet and left the room silently, returning after a short time with a bowl of hot water, some tweezers and strips of clean linen. She extracted the splinters of glass, washed and bound her mistress's feet and then picked up the bowl of bloody water and ruined shoes.

"Do you want me to stay or would you rather be alone for a while?" she asked softly.

Beth looked at the maid for the first time. Sarah's face was a mask of concern.

"I would like to be alone for a time, Sarah. I won't do anything foolish, but I need to be on my own just now." Her voice broke, and she turned her face into the pillow. She heard the door close quietly a moment later, and then she could hold the pain of betrayal and loss back no longer. She curled up on the bed and let the hurt, the misery and finally the tears come, huge racking sobs that tore through her body until she thought she would die. She had not felt so bereft since her father died, and vowed in that moment that she would never again let anyone get close enough to hurt her like this.

Chapter Twelve

Beth stayed in her room for two days, giving her inability to walk due to lacerated feet as an excuse for not going down to face the barrage of questions from her family that she dreaded. In fact, although her feet did indeed hurt when she put weight on them, in the past she had shrugged off minor injuries, any discomfort subdued by her zest for life.

Now, however, she possessed no zest for life to act as a painkiller, and moped around her room, eating sparingly and drinking rather more wine than was wise. Sarah attended her, at first sympathetically and then increasingly disapprovingly as she started to suspect, quite rightly, that her mistress was now unhealthily and uncharacteristically wallowing in self-pity.

Isabella visited her once, and Beth explained that Daniel had proposed marriage to her and gave the reasons why she had refused him in an unemotional voice, after which she had lapsed into a moody silence, unbroken until Isabella took the hint and left.

"It won't do, you know," Sarah said suddenly on the evening of the second day, after she had made up the fire, lit candles and closed the curtains, while Beth sat on a chair chewing her fingernails and staring into space. Beth looked up.

"What won't do?" she said.

"This," Sarah said flatly. "Locking yourself away from the world. The longer you stay here, the harder it'll be to go out and face the world again."

"I'm not ready yet. Give me another day or two and I'll see how I feel," Beth replied listlessly.

Sarah snorted through her nose.

"In a day or two you'll feel worse. I know how you feel, Beth, but…"

"Do you?" Beth said, suddenly animated. "Do you really? Have you ever been in love, trusted someone absolutely and been utterly betrayed?"

"Of course I have!" Sarah exploded. "Why do you think I ended up on the streets before Richard found me? Because I fell in love with a man who promised me everything and then as soon as I was pregnant disappeared, that's why! I found out later that he was already married with three children. So yes, I do know how it feels!"

Beth looked at Sarah in astonishment.

"I'm sorry," she said. "I didn't know."

"No, well, you never asked, did you?" Sarah said, in a softer voice.

"What happened to the child?" Beth asked. She was ashamed of herself. Sarah had been with her for months now. They had become good friends. But she had never talked about her past, and Beth had never thought to ask her.

"She died," Sarah said, in a tone which stated clearly that she didn't want to talk about it. "If you sit around here moping, you'll never get better. I know you don't want to go down and face the gossip, but it'll be going on anyway whether you're there or not. You might as well get your version in."

"Is there a lot of gossip?" Beth asked.

"I don't know. I've not been out of the house for two days. The only thing I do know is that Lord Daniel has left London, so you don't need to worry about meeting him."

"You're right," Beth said. "I have been feeling sorry for myself. I'm pathetic. I'll get up tomorrow." She looked at Sarah's sceptical face. "I promise."

In the morning she felt far from ready to get up, but she had promised Sarah, and besides, she *was* being pathetic. She had always prided herself on being a fighter, and in many ways she was. But this was the first time she had trusted and loved someone and been betrayed by them. Richard's treatment of her had frightened and enraged her, but she had never loved or trusted him.

She got up and washed herself with a cloth and water from the bowl on the dressing table. She dressed informally; she would spend today quietly in the house with her cousins, and then tomorrow would throw herself back into the social whirl.

She was brushing her hair when there was a gentle knock on the door, and Sarah's head popped round it.

"Ah, Sarah, there you are!" Beth said in a bright tone she was far from feeling. "Can you help me to dress my hair, please?"

"Er, yes, but you have a visitor," Sarah replied, coming a little further into the room. "Sir Anthony Peters is here to escort you to see the king."

Beth flushed scarlet.

"Tell him to go to hell," she said. "I have no wish to see him, now or ever again."

Sarah went down to the drawing room, where Sir Anthony was waiting in the company of Isabella and Richard, and relayed her mistress's message, using a somewhat more tactful wording.

"Oh," said the baronet, rising from his seat. "Well, if Miss Cunningham is still indisposed, I am sure the king will understand. Perhaps another time." He prepared to leave. Isabella fluttered after him into the hall. Richard sat tight-lipped for a moment, his fists clenched at his sides, then slowly got to his feet. His intentions were written clearly on his face.

Sarah made a rapid assessment of the situation and sent up a silent prayer to heaven that she was about to do the right thing. She hurried out into the hallway.

"Miss Cunningham is much better," she said. "In fact, she is up and dressed, although not for Court. I think she is only a little shy of meeting the king." She reddened under Sir Anthony's unblinking gaze, and looked demurely at the floor.

"Oh Sir Anthony, if she is dressed, then you must go up and persuade her not to miss this wonderful opportunity!" Isabella cried.

"Er…I am not sure that is wise, my dear," Sir Anthony ventured.

"You could charm the birds from the trees with your eloquence, Sir Anthony. Please, I beg of you."

Richard appeared in the hall, his face set. He looked up the stairs.

"Well, if you are sure, Isabella," Sir Anthony said. He mounted the stairs reluctantly, followed by Sarah, who showed him to the correct door. She knocked gently, then stood back to allow him to enter.

"Come in!" Beth said without looking round, recognising the maid's knock. "Can you help me to get this mess into some sort of shape?"

Sir Anthony looked at the cascading silver-blonde waves with admiration.

"Yes, if you wish, but I am not sure it would be proper, my dear," he said.

Beth spun round on her stool, her face flushing red.

"What the hell are you doing here?" she said. "Get out!"

"Ah…Isabella thought I might be able to persuade you to…"

"Get out!" she shrieked again, cutting him off in mid-sentence, and reaching for the first object to hand.

He managed to regain the safety of the landing and close the door a fraction of a second before the heavy silver-backed hairbrush thudded into the wood where his head had just been.

"I think my persuasive powers are somewhat lacking this morning," he said jovially to Sarah, who was still standing on the landing. "Perhaps it would be better if I were to try another day, when your mistress is in a calmer frame of mind."

Richard, who had been halfway up the stairs, had witnessed Sir Anthony's hasty withdrawal. He now joined them on the landing.

"If you would be so kind as to wait in the drawing room a few moments longer, Sir Anthony, I am sure I can persuade my sister to change her mind," he said with a cold smile, and marching past the baronet and the maid, opened the door of his sister's room without knocking and walked in, closing it firmly behind him.

Sarah made an instinctive move to follow him, and then hesitated. She was clearly very alarmed. Sir Anthony looked at her, and then took up a position by the door, leaning nonchalantly on the wall. He beckoned Sarah closer. She moved next to him and listened. From inside the room she could hear the murmur of voices, although she could not make out the words.

"Be at ease, my dear," he whispered to Sarah. "If your mistress requires assistance, we will know by the tone of her voice and can rush to her aid immediately."

They stood outside the room, silent, listening. The murmur of voices continued for a time, the tone rising and falling, but never showing signs of alarm or violence. Hearing a sudden ominous silence, Sir Anthony shot from his post, seizing the startled Sarah by the arm and dragging her down the landing, and a few seconds later when Richard opened the door the two were standing by a flower display deep in conversation about the technical aspects of arranging blooms.

"Of course, Miss Charlotte is far more of an expert than I, Sir Anthony," Sarah said, improvising wildly. "I am sure she'd be delighted to instruct you in how to arrange flowers correctly, if you wish to learn."

"I do," replied Sir Anthony. "And I will remember in future to cut the stems on a slant, as you suggest,"

She nodded approvingly, although she had suggested no such thing, having only had time to utter the one sentence before Richard emerged from the room.

They looked up as he approached them, his face still flushed from his interview with his sister.

"Your mistress requires your assistance to dress for Court, Sarah," he said formally. "Sir Anthony, if you would be so kind as to wait a short while longer, Elizabeth will be delighted to accompany you to see his Majesty the King."

Beth appeared in the drawing room twenty minutes later, a vision in the pale green silk dress her cousins had ordered specifically in case she should be lucky enough to gain an audience with the king. Her hair was elaborately dressed and powdered, diamonds sparkled at her ears and throat, and the obligatory four-foot-wide skirts brushed the edges of the door as she walked into the room, limping slightly. Her eyes glittered with a cold fury as her gaze passed between Richard and Sir Anthony, and her mouth was compressed into a tight line. She looked anything but delighted to be accompanying Sir Anthony to see the king, but he rose and bowed elaborately to her in homage to her beauty.

"Oh, Elizabeth!" gasped Charlotte and Isabella together. "The king will be enchanted!"

"Of course he will," Sir Anthony said. "Who could not be by such incandescent beauty?" He offered her his arm, which she pointedly ignored.

"Shall we go?" she said coolly. "It would never do to be late." She swept from the room, twitching her skirts sideways to pass through the door, and he followed in her wake.

In spite of the difficulties she had getting into the carriage, encumbered as she was by her clothing, she refused the assistance of her companion and finally managed to settle herself, arranging her billowing skirts around her. Sir Anthony sat opposite, and they rode in silence for a while, she looking pointedly out of the window to avoid having to speak to him.

"You are angry with me because I told you of Lord Daniel's gambling debts," he said finally. "Would you rather not have known?"

She turned from the window and regarded him icily.

"You are wrong, sir," she replied. "I am not angry with you because you told me of Daniel's gambling debts. I am angry with you because you called yourself my friend and then took pleasure in humiliating me in public."

He sat forward so suddenly, bracing his hands on his knees as though he was about to lunge at her, that she flinched back instinctively. She had never seen him even so much as irritated before, and to her surprise a shiver of fear ran down her spine. He suddenly seemed large, threatening.

"I assure you, madam," he said in tones as cold as hers, "that I got no pleasure from what I did. But you gave me no other choice. I tried to…"

"Spare me your excuses, Sir Anthony," she interrupted. "If you are worried that I will behave inappropriately at St. James's because of my hatred of you, you can rest assured that I will give the performance of my life. But know this. I have no wish to meet this king of yours; I am doing it because my cousins and society in general seem to think it important, and because my brother will dismiss all my servants in Manchester if I do not." She paused, aware that in her anger and unaccountable fear she had said more than she had intended. She took a deep breath, and continued more slowly, thinking before she spoke this time.

"Once this visit is over, however, I would be obliged if you would terminate our acquaintance. I understand it is inevitable that we will meet from time to time, and I shall be polite when we do. But I have no need of friends such as you, who stab me in the back for the thrill of being the first to pass on a piece of juicy gossip."

He sat back again in his seat, and regarded her intently for a moment in silence. Then he looked away.

"As you wish," he said dismissively.

The return journey passed in uncomfortable silence. Beth had indeed given the performance of her life, but had switched off her vivacity like a tap the moment she re-entered the carriage. Sir Anthony's mood echoed hers, and he sat tapping his fingers lightly on his knee, whilst looking intently out of the window. He had behaved in quite a different manner to his normal flowery affected self when in the presence of the king, and she observed him now discreetly. She had never seen him dress so soberly, in cream breeches and hose, with a tasteful navy blue waistcoat and frock coat, unadorned with his usual lavish embroidery. There was not even a hint of violet cologne about his person, and in spite of the customary heavy make-up, he had seemed positively masculine when discussing military matters in flawless German with the bluff, war-obsessed King George. She wondered, not for the first time, just what kind of man the real Sir Anthony was. He had probably been playing so many roles for so long, he didn't even know who he was himself any more, she thought.

The carriage rattled to a halt, and Beth looked out of the window in surprise.

"Why are we stopping?" she asked.

"I promised Caroline that we would call round for tea after St James's," Sir Anthony replied. "I realise now that you will find my presence distinctly unpleasant, but I thought you would perhaps enjoy a little light conversation with Caroline before returning home. I will not be coming in," he added. "I have business elsewhere, but will send the carriage back for you in an hour."

He got down from the carriage and took her hand, releasing it the second she was safely on the pavement. His manner was stiff and formal.

"Thank you," she said, still hating him, disturbed by the fact that he had been considerate enough to realise she would not want to return home immediately after meeting the king, and that Caroline was the only person whose company she would not find onerous after such a stressful morning.

"May I express my sincere regret that you will be forced to accompany me one more time to the Palace? I assure you I will do my best to make it as painless as possible for you," he said.

Beth had been dismayed when the king, having left her to the lascivious attentions of his son the Duke of Cumberland, to whom she had taken an instant dislike, while he conversed enthusiastically with Sir Anthony in German, had suddenly turned back to her.

"Miss Cunningham, I was telling Sir Anthony that I am having a musical evening next week, and would be happy if you would grace us with your beauty."

The duke's eyes had lit up and Beth's spirits had sunk, but she had had no choice but to accept his Majesty's gracious invitation.

Sir Anthony accompanied her up the steps to Caroline's house, then retired to his carriage before the door opened.

Caroline was in the cosy cream and blue decorated parlour when Beth was announced. She looked slightly puzzled, but made no comment on the absence of Sir Anthony.

"Sit down, Beth, before you fall down," she said. "You look exhausted. Was it that dreadful, then?"

She could have been referring to anything, from Daniel's marriage proposal to her rift with Sir Anthony, to her visit to St. James's. Beth chose the latter to comment on.

"Yes," she said, sinking down into a chair, and gratefully accepting a cup of tea. "I hate having to act a part. I must be getting good at it though. The king has invited me to a musical evening next week."

Caroline whistled softly. "You must have impressed him," she said. "He issues few invitations these days, except to close friends."

"I didn't think I had," Beth said, relaxing into the chair as far as her enormous hooped skirt would allow her to. "After telling me he was delighted to make my acquaintance, he ignored me completely for over half an hour while he chattered away to Sir Anthony in German. I hadn't realised they were such good friends." She remembered the king throwing an arm companionably round Sir Anthony's shoulders as he led him off to a nearby table, on which were spread numerous maps.

"Oh, I wouldn't say they were good friends, exactly. But

Anthony does have the advantage of speaking fluent German, which most of George's British subjects do not. He can also listen for hours apparently enthralled to the king's incessant repetitions of the glorious military days of his youth, which he's hoping now to repeat in his old age."

"Is he?" Beth asked, surprised.

"Yes, of course. It's common knowledge that the king intends to lead his troops in person. He is preparing to leave for Holland in a couple of weeks. I believe Prince William Augustus is going with him. Of course, you have been occupied with other matters for some weeks, otherwise you would have known that."

Beth circumvented the subject Caroline was obliquely referring to.

"Prince William Augustus was there too," she said. "I certainly made an impression on him. I thought his eyeballs were going to drop out into my bosom, he stared at it so much."

Caroline laughed.

"Your breasts are certainly displayed to their best advantage in that dress," she said, looking at the considerable expanse of creamy white bosom revealed by the low décolletage.

"It's not the dress, it's the stays pushing them up," Beth said. "Sarah laced me so tightly, I'm surprised my breasts didn't pop out of the dress altogether. Perhaps that's what the duke was hoping for. I have never worn anything so cumbersome and uncomfortable in my life as this ridiculous gown. I can't wait to get out of it."

"I think you may have to get used to it, if you have taken the eye of the prince. You will no doubt be invited to all manner of royal functions in the future."

"Oh, God, I hope not," Beth groaned.

"Didn't you like the prince, then? Many of the ladies find him most attractive," Caroline commented.

Beth looked at her incredulously.

"I find that hard to believe," she said. "Although on second thoughts, maybe not. I never cease to be amazed at what women find attractive."

"Titles and money are powerful aphrodisiacs, my dear," Caroline said, in an uncannily accurate mimicry of Sir Anthony. A shadow crossed Beth's face briefly.

"It is as well that William Augustus has those, then, because he's distinctly lacking in looks and personality," she said. She had found his incipient obesity, his wet red lips and his protuberant blue eyes repellent. His remarks had been innocent enough; the state of the weather, polite requests as to how she was enjoying her first season in London; but every comment had been addressed to her bosom, and she had the strong conviction that apart from wanting a quick tumble with her, he felt that women were beneath contempt.

"Never mind. I am sure Anthony will protect you from any dishonourable intentions the prince might have. He's an expert at bumbling innocently into any uncomfortable situation, just when the lady is most in need of rescue." Caroline paused to refill her cup, then gave Beth a look of shrewd appraisal.

"Every time I mention Anthony's name you look as though you're eating a lemon. You might as well tell me what has happened. I assume you are still angry with him for telling you about Lord Daniel's gambling problem?"

"That's what he thought," Beth said crossly. "No, I wouldn't have been angry with him for telling me that. I would have been upset, but I needed to know, especially in view of what happened later…But he didn't tell *me*, Caroline, he told the whole room of stupid babbling gossips while I was there, and took the greatest pleasure in doing so. It was horrible." To her horror her eyes filled with tears, and she realised just how emotionally fragile she still was. She sniffed loudly, and looked down at her teacup.

"You are doing him an injustice, Beth," Caroline said. "He took no pleasure in what he did, I assure you."

"Is that what he told you?" Beth said hotly. "Well, I was there. Believe me, he relished every moment of it. He couldn't wait to humiliate me in front of as many ladies as possible."

"I can't argue with you on that, Beth. You're right, I wasn't there. But I do know this. He called to see you twice a day for three days once he found out about Lord Daniel, but Isabella told him you were ill and could see no one. He was terrified that Daniel would propose to you at any moment and you would accept without knowing the reason behind it. We were all frightened of that. We knew how infatuated you were with him. To be honest, I thought he would persuade you to marry him anyway, regardless of the fact that it was clear he only wanted you for your dowry. It was Anthony who said you were more level-headed than I thought, and he was right. He could hardly force his way in to see you. He took the only opportunity he could to tell you."

Beth looked suspiciously at Caroline's face, which was flushed with emotion.

"Is that why he brought me here and then drove away? So you could argue his case for him, and persuade me to forgive him?" she said.

"No it isn't," Caroline snapped. "I thought he would come in with you. For God's sake, Beth, I know how distraught you are about Daniel's betrayal, but don't assume everyone is like him. Anthony would be appalled if he knew I was defending him to you. He would no doubt prefer you to make up your own mind about the reasons for his behaviour. But I won't sit here and let you accuse him unjustly. He is my friend, and so are you. We're here for you, if you want us. But don't take your anger and hurt at Daniel's behaviour out on Anthony, or on me for that matter. It's unfair."

Beth looked at the carpet, unable to speak. Caroline's words had hurt her, and her first impulse was to lash out. But her friend was right. Beth had been infatuated with Daniel, had been able to see no wrong in him. And now she was trying to avoid more pain and humiliation by seeing the worst in everyone.

"I'm sorry you've been hurt, Beth, I truly am," Caroline continued in a gentler voice. "But I cannot say I'm sorry that you've seen Lord Daniel for what he is. Neither Edwin nor I thought he was suitable for you, in spite of his title. I wanted to tell you that. This may surprise you, but Anthony was of the view that you should decide for yourself, and we should not try to influence you. It was only when he discovered how much debt Daniel was in that he decided to warn you. He had to, and you would not see him privately. I know you don't like him much, but he cares about you, Beth."

Beth still sat unmoving, her head bent. A huge tear suddenly splashed onto the pale silk, then another. Her shoulders heaved as she tried to swallow back the deluge, and then Caroline was kneeling beside her, her arms around her, and Beth leaned into the comforting warmth of her friend and gave in to her grief.

By the time Edwin came home, Beth had almost recovered, although her eyes were still red and swollen from the torrent of weeping. He strode in on the emotional feminine scene and stopped uncertainly three paces into the room.

"Ah," he mumbled. "Er, is Anthony in the library, then?"

"No," his wife replied. "He didn't come in with Beth."

"Oh," Edwin replied, puzzled. "His coach is outside, so I thought..."

Beth started up.

"Oh!" she said. "He said he would send the coach back for me in an hour. I had completely forgotten. I must go."

"You will do no such thing, until you're ready. And I have something to tell you, once we have sorted out what to do about Anthony," said Caroline.

"Shall I leave you in peace?" Edwin said, clearly eager to be away from this torrent of disturbing female emotion.

"No, sit down, you may be able to give some advice," Caroline said.

He sat down on the edge of a chair.

"Beth has told Anthony in no uncertain terms that she wants to terminate their acquaintance," Caroline explained.

Beth reddened.

"Er...what I actually said was that I had no need of friends who would stab me in the back for the thrill of being the first to pass on a piece of gossip."

"Ah, I see," said Edwin uncomfortably. "Well, that should do it, right enough."

"He was very cold to me after that, apart from the spectacular act we put on for the king, of course," she said in a small voice.

"Well of course he was," said Caroline. "You have hurt him. If you'd been a man he probably would have called you out. That's how men usually deal with insults, isn't it?" She looked at her husband.

"Er...yes, it is one way, although of course it's not looked on favourably by the authorities. Would you like some more tea?" he said brightly.

"No. Stay where you are," Caroline ordered. "The question now, is, do you want to terminate your friendship with Anthony or not?"

"I don't know what I want," Beth said honestly. "I know I don't have the high opinion of him that you do, but it seems I've been unfair to him when he was trying to help me. I can't just leave things as they are."

"She will have to see Anthony again next week, Edwin. The king has invited them to a musical soiree at the Palace."

"Has he, by God!" said Edwin. "Your act must have impressed him, Beth."

"Yes, yes," said Caroline impatiently. "The question is, should she leave it until then to apologise, or should she write to Anthony beforehand?" Both women looked at Edwin.

"Em…well, by next week, he will certainly have calmed down, I would say. Perhaps it would be wise to wait until then. On the other hand, it could do no harm to send an appropriately worded letter in the meantime." He smiled at the ladies.

"Now you know why Edwin is a politician, Beth," Caroline said. "He's an expert at not answering questions. Let me put it more directly, my love. What would you do if you had insulted Anthony in the way Beth has?"

"Probably bleed profusely all over Hyde Park," Edwin mused. "It may surprise you, but Anthony is remarkably adept with a sword. I've seen him practising on occasion. I wouldn't want him to challenge me to a duel."

"I give up," said Caroline, exasperated. "Go on then, we will have more tea."

Edwin was out of the room in seconds.

"What was this matter you wanted to talk to me about earlier?" said Beth.

Now it was Caroline's turn to look uncomfortable.

"It can wait. I didn't realise just how upset you would be about Daniel. On the other hand, it's probably better you hear it from me than anyone else."

"You're starting to sound like Edwin," Beth said. She felt more cheerful now that she had had a good cry. It was nice to have people she could relax with and speak her mind to. "Tell me what it is. If it's something upsetting, I'd rather hear it from a friend, than a malicious old cow like Lady Winter."

"Lord Daniel has left London, and returned to his father's estate," Caroline said. Beth nodded. "Before he left, he let it be known that he had visited you, and that there had been an emotional scene."

"That's right," said Beth. "He proposed to me and I refused him. We were both upset.

"That's one version of the story," Caroline said. She took a deep breath. "His version is that he discovered your mother was in fact a whore from the Highlands of Scotland who your father was duped into marrying. He said that once he discovered that, he came to tell you he could not marry you, and you begged and pleaded with him to change his mind." She looked at Beth's shocked countenance. "I'm sorry," she said. "Perhaps I should have waited, after all."

"No," said Beth, her voice trembling with rage. "You were right. It was better I hear that from you." She gripped the sides of the chair so hard her knuckles whitened. "By Christ," she said in a low voice, "I wish I was a man. I would kill him for that. In fact, if I get the opportunity, I may do anyway." She looked at Caroline, and then at Edwin, who had chosen that moment to reappear with a tray of tea.

"Just so that you both know the truth," Beth said. "It is true that my mother was from the Highlands of Scotland. Her name was Ann MacDonald. She was poor. I was stupid and trusting enough to tell Daniel that. But she was not a whore. Nor was my father duped into marrying her. They loved each other, very much. I could not have had a better mother. And I could not have a worse brother. When this rumour reaches his ears, he will kill me."

Edwin and Caroline exchanged alarmed glances. It was clear that Beth was not joking, or exaggerating. Anthony had told them he thought Richard to be brutal. Was he really that bad?

"No he will not," Caroline said.

"You don't know him, Caroline," Beth replied. "I haven't told you half of what he's done."

"No, but I do know that while he thinks you have a chance of a superb marriage to a man with military influence, it is in his interests not to hurt you, isn't it?"

"Yes, but once this rumour gets round, no one will be interested in me," Beth said.

"Nonsense! You're still worth twenty thousand. And who will

believe the malicious words of the out-of-favour son of a mere earl, when they know that the woman who rejected him has now caught the eye of none other than Prince William, Duke of Cumberland, a man who, I might add, has more military influence than any man in the country, except perhaps the king himself?"

Beth and Edwin both looked at Caroline.

"Don't look at me like that," she said. "I'm not telling any lies. I think your brother, rather than wishing to kill you, will worship the ground you walk on when he hears this. And of course, the king and the duke will both be leaving the country soon, and will be too occupied with military matters in the meantime to condescend to refuting such rumours, should they get to hear of them. I think I'll throw a small dinner party tomorrow. Just a few select friends. I am so sorry you'll be unable to attend, Beth."

"Thank you, Caroline," Beth said.

"Think nothing of it. It will be my pleasure. I never liked the spoiled brat Daniel anyway. And I must confess to not liking your brother much, although he's never done anything to me."

"I am not thanking you for that, although I should. Thank you for telling me what Daniel said about my mother. You have quite cured me of my infatuation for him."

It was true, she thought as the coachman assisted her into Sir Anthony's waiting carriage a few minutes later. Her former love and hurt had been transformed into a slow-burning anger. She sank back onto the seat. What a long day! It seemed to have gone on forever! She could hardly believe it was not yet even four o' clock. She had aged ten years today, she felt. She had certainly grown up. It would be a long time before she would give her heart again. She had learnt a good deal about betrayal and vindictiveness over the last days. And she had been guilty of both too, she thought uncomfortably as the carriage bounced down the rutted road. She had not given Sir Anthony a chance to speak, had condemned him out of hand and insulted him. And he had still treated her with the utmost courtesy in the presence of the king, had conveyed her to Caroline's, knowing that she needed the comfort of a friend, and then had sent his coach back for her. She could not wait until next week to set things right between them. She would write tonight, tired as she was.

She sat for a few minutes, musing on how she could word a

letter. Then she knocked on the roof of the coach, bringing it lurching to a halt.

* * *

The man who opened the door to Beth's knock was dressed in green livery, and looked down at her in that slightly superior manner that all footmen worthy of their salt affected.

"Good afternoon," she said briskly. "I have come to see Sir Anthony, if he is at home." She almost hoped he wasn't. She had ordered the coach to turn round and drive to the Peters' household on impulse, and was already starting to regret it.

"Is he expecting you, Miss…?"

"Cunningham," Beth said, looking more closely at the man's face. Although he had only spoken a few words, his accent was unmistakably Scottish. She looked down at his hands, but he was wearing beige calfskin gloves. She could hardly ask him to take them off, or enquire as to whether he had a scar on his right hand.

"No," she continued, bringing herself back to the current matter. "But I am sure he will see me. It is a matter of the utmost urgency."

He surveyed her in a manner she found most insolent, taking in her elaborate Court costume, and then seemed to come to a decision.

"If ye'd care to wait in the hall, Miss Cunningham, I'll see if Sir Anthony is at home to visitors."

He disappeared up the polished wooden stairs, and Beth sat down on a velvet-upholstered chair, looking around with interest. She had never been to Sir Anthony's house before. He had told her he rented a house for the season in common with many other gentlefolk, but she had expected that he would have added some personal touches. Almost every house she had been in had family portraits hung in the hall and on the stairs, showing the impressive ancestry of the family in residence.

The only painting in Sir Anthony's hall was a rather indifferent landscape, depicting a few shaggy-haired cattle grazing on a piece of barren moorland. The stairs were bare of any pictures at all. With nothing to focus her mind on, she started to run through what she was going to say, trying and rejecting different opening lines. As time went on she started to feel unaccountably nervous, which was ridiculous. She didn't even like the man that much. If he rejected her apology, well, at least she could leave with a clear conscience. Caroline and Edwin would still remain her friends. Her life would be no poorer without Sir Anthony's affected mannerisms.

A sudden polite cough roused her from her reverie, and she jumped to her feet. Sir Anthony was standing at the bottom of the stairs, his expression neutral. She had no idea how long he had been there observing her, and in her confusion her carefully rehearsed opening lines flew from her mind.

"Oh! Er…I am sorry to disturb you, Sir Anthony," she faltered. "I hope I have not called at an inconvenient moment."

She expected him to either invite her into the drawing room for tea, or make some gushing comment about how improper it was for her to visit him unchaperoned. He did neither, instead regarding her silently for a moment.

"You said the matter was of the utmost urgency. What is it?" he said brusquely.

This was so unlike his usual attitude that she was completely unnerved.

"I, er, I have come to apologise, Sir Anthony," she said.

He raised one eyebrow but said nothing, waiting for her to continue.

"I accused you unjustly of taking pleasure in hurting me, and I realise now that I was wrong. Caroline explained that you had been driven to such a measure by the fact that I refused to see you in private, and…"

"She had no right to say that," he interrupted. "Did she also tell you to come here and apologise to me?"

"No!" Beth exclaimed. "I would never apologise to anyone because I was instructed to do so! Caroline merely helped me to see your side of the situation. I refused to let you explain to me, for which I am also sorry. When I expressed a desire to apologise, she suggested I write a letter, or wait until next week."

"I see. And why did you not take her advice? It is somewhat irregular for an unmarried lady to call upon a bachelor alone. A letter would have been the more respectable way."

She stared at him, cold, forbidding and unyielding. He was not going to accept her apology. For some unaccountable reason she felt distressed at the thought. *I am overwrought, that is all,* she told herself. *The slightest thing would upset me at the moment.*

"You are right," she said, trying to match his cold attitude. "I did not wish to wait to put matters right between us. But I see the damage cannot be undone. Goodbye." Her voice wavered on the last word and she cursed inwardly, walking past him toward the door. Her fingers were on the knob when he reached past her, putting his hand on the door to stop her opening it.

"Why?" he said softly. "Why did you not wish to wait?"

She turned round. He was standing very close to her; she had to tilt her head right back to look into his eyes. They were a lovely shade of slate blue, with tiny flecks of gold in the irises. He held her gaze, earnest, intent, and her mouth was suddenly dry. Without the overpowering cologne he smelt of fresh linen and an attractive clean male smell. She tore her eyes away from his with difficulty, looking instead straight ahead. She focussed her eyes on the silver button of his waistcoat.

"Because I never like to leave any difficult matter unresolved for any longer than I have to," she said.

"Is that the only reason?" he asked.

"Yes, of course. What other reason could there be?" she replied, her voice more confident now.

He stepped back, away from her, and seemed to diminish, to shrink into himself.

"Well then," he said, and before her eyes the Sir Anthony she was more familiar with repossessed him. "Let me reassure you my dear, there need be no more difficulty between us. I accept your apology. Let us put the whole unfortunate incident behind us, and speak no more of it. Now, I would dearly love to invite you to dine with me, but I do not think it would be wise to risk the speculation that would ensue if I did."

"No, indeed," she replied, wishing nothing more than to get out of the presence of this extremely disturbing man.

"My carriage is, of course, at your disposal. My man will take you home immediately. Your family will no doubt by now be wondering where you are." He smiled.

How does he do it? she thought as she rode home. How did he put on and take off personalities so easily? She had seen three, no four, different sides to Sir Anthony today, and was still no closer to knowing the real man than she had ever been.

Chapter Thirteen

June 1743

Dear Friends,

Thank you for your letter, and the very useful information regarding the accounts, and the sale of surplus butter, which of course Richard and probably Edward too read before passing it on to me. It has been wonderful for me to be able to write to you from the heart (thanks to Sarah), but very frustrating not to be able to receive replies of the same kind. Knowing you are well and that the hens are laying profusely is all well and good, but I am sure you have a great deal more to tell me than that! I am writing to tell you that I now have a secure address, where I can receive letters without my family being any the wiser.

I have mentioned Edwin and Caroline before, and have now confided my difficulties to them. They have suggested that you write to me care of their address, and they will pass on your letters unopened. I trust them implicitly, and you may write anything you wish to them in complete security.

It goes without saying that Thomas will have to continue writing his polite letters to this address, and I will reply to those as I have been doing.

Life has been going on here as normal. I have not seen Lord Daniel since I refused him, and hope I never have the misfortune to run into him again. Sir Anthony and I are once again good acquaintances, although I still cannot bring myself to trust or really like him, in spite of Caroline and Edwin's assurances.

The scurrilous lie Daniel put about regarding my mother seems to have been negated by the fact that it is now common knowledge that I am in the good graces of both the Elector and his hideous son the Duke of Cumberland. I was relieved beyond measure when the musical evening was postponed due to the indisposition of Mr Handel, and as both George and William are now abroad, and look to be so for some time, (I could wish it to be a permanent state) I can bask in the glory of my royal favour without any danger of encountering them.

Neither Richard nor Edward have mentioned the rumour about my mother. I think they must have heard it, even though Caroline did squash it almost immediately.

Well, I must give this letter to Sarah, and look forward to hearing from you very soon. I miss you all.

Your friend, Beth.

* * *

"Are you sure these are the latest thing in France?" Beth said, clutching the tiny embroidered bag to her chest. Isabella and Clarissa were carrying the same fashion accessory, a present from the gentleman Beth was now addressing, but in a far more careless manner than their cousin.

"I assure you, my dear Elizabeth, the reticule is the very height of fashion," Sir Anthony simpered.

"They are the very height of stupidity," she said, scowling at the other shoppers on the Strand, expecting an urchin to fly out of a back alley at any moment and relieve her of the useless article. "Either there is very little theft in France, or the ladies there are extremely careless of their possessions. I feel much safer keeping my valuables in a concealed pocket."

"You worry too much, my dear," came the reply. "No one would dare to molest either you or your charming cousins. Not with myself and the formidable Sergeant Cunningham to protect you."

The formidable Sergeant Cunningham leaned against the shop doorway, wishing that a group of thieves would carry off not just the ladies' reticules, but also the ladies themselves, and thus relieve him of this purgatory. He couldn't think what had possessed him to agree to Edward's suggestion that he accompany the ladies and Sir Anthony on a shopping trip. He had just spent four of the most boring hours of his life traipsing round shop after shop, whilst his companions exclaimed over a ridiculous assortment of useless and overpriced trinkets, and he had had no opportunity at all to take Sir Anthony to one side and try to re-establish his acquaintance with him, which had unaccountably cooled of late. He couldn't stand the man, but as Edward had pointed out, he *did* have considerable connections. Why, it was even rumoured that the king himself had taken the time to write to him from his temporary base in Hanover. He sighed, and followed reluctantly as Isabella plunged into yet another shop, which sold a selection of hat trimmings and hair decorations.

Beth was already inside, paying for some ribbons and decorated hair grips, which she intended to give to Sarah as a birthday present. She fumbled angrily with the clasp of the reticule.

"This is the most ridiculous…!" she began, then lunged forward as the clasp sprang open and the contents threatened to tumble from the purse. She succeeded in rescuing her possessions, except for a few coins, which cascaded to the floor and rolled merrily off under the shelves.

"That's it!" she said. "I am sorry, Sir Anthony, please don't think me ungrateful, but this is the most useless present I have ever received."

"Well of course it is," he replied, not offended in the slightest. "It is not intended to be *useful,* it is a fashion accessory. I would suggest that in future you carry no more than the money you require for the day's purchases in it, and keep everything else in the concealed pockets you're so fond of. Allow me." He leaned across and paid the shopkeeper with a coin he had produced from the far more practical pocket of his waistcoat. "Now, may I suggest we all repair for a little refreshment before we indulge in any more shopping?" He leaned over confidentially to Richard, who was frowning ominously at his sister, although she was too preoccupied to notice. "I have received the most interesting news from Hanover, and would like to discuss it with you over coffee, if you would be so kind, Sergeant Cunningham."

After dinner, to which Sir Anthony had been invited, the men retired to Lord Edward's study and the ladies to their rooms, exhausted by the excitement of the day's shopping. Beth was far from exhausted, but took the welcome opportunity to spend some time alone, and before going to her room went to the library to choose a book. She still had the ridiculous reticule with her. The ladies had arrived home late; dinner had already been delayed, and as Edward had been in no mood to wait any longer, they had eaten without changing first. Beth had placed her bag behind her on her chair. She had no wish for the thing to spring open and shower its contents all over the dining table. Sir Anthony had been right. She should not have put her most treasured possession in the bag. She would not do that again. She must find a secure hiding place in her room, where a maid could not accidentally come upon it. Either that or continue as she had been, carrying it with her at all times in a secure pocket tied around her waist under her skirt.

She searched the shelves for an interesting book, her eyes finally coming to rest on a likely title. Reaching up onto her toes, she attempted to reach the volume, but the tips of her fingers stopped several inches below the bottom edge of the shelf where the book was sitting, leaving it tantalisingly beyond her grasp. She tried an experimental jump, but the books were too closely packed on the shelf for her to retrieve the volume whilst in mid-air. Knowing herself to be alone, she cursed in a most unladylike manner under her breath, before looking round for a suitable piece of furniture which could be used in lieu of a ladder.

Dismissing the spindly-legged and distinctly fragile table, which looked barely capable of supporting the decanter of brandy and two crystal glasses that were currently residing on it, her eyes settled on one of the upholstered chairs which was placed close to the fire.

She was halfway across the room when the library door suddenly opened and Richard walked in, pushing the door closed behind him. For once Beth was glad to see him.

"Ah, Richard," she said, abandoning her progress towards the chair. "I've been trying to get a book off one of the shelves, but it's just a little too high for me to reach. Could you get it down for me, please?"

"Where is your reticule?" he asked brusquely, ignoring her request completely, his back to the door as though to prevent anyone else from entering.

"What?" she said, confused by the unexpected question.

"Don't prevaricate with me. Where is it?" His stance was aggressive, his tone abrupt. She had no idea what interest he could have in her reticule, but his attitude roused her temper immediately, and her response matched his tone.

"It's none of your business!" she retorted, but her eyes instinctively darted to the mantel where she had placed the small embroidered bag after entering the library.

Perceptive as ever, he intercepted her glance and marched straight over to the fireplace to pick the bag up, undoing the little clasp and turning it upside down to shake the contents out over the Aubusson rug in front of the hearth.

"How dare you!" she cried in outrage, running across the room and bending down to retrieve her small personal possessions, which she scooped back into the bag that he had also dropped on the rug. His sudden silence alerted her to danger, and she looked up from her crouched position to see him standing menacingly over her, holding a small green leather case in his hand. Spilling out of it over his fingers was a rosary, its amber beads joined by delicate silver links. The crucifix swung gently to and fro, gleaming in the firelight.

Beth straightened up very slowly, her reticule lying forgotten on the floor.

"A mo niggan loo-a…" Richard read haltingly the words embroidered on the silk-covered leather. "What the hell language is this?"

"*A mo nighean luaidh,*" Beth repeated fluently. "It's Gaelic."

"What does it mean?"

"It says, 'to my darling daughter,'" Beth answered, watching with satisfaction as his eyes widened with shock. He opened his mouth soundlessly then closed it again, and Beth took the chance to snatch the beads from his hand while he was off guard. In doing so the case was also dislodged from his fingers and she caught it neatly in mid air as it fell, pouring the rosary back into it and buttoning it closed.

"Are you trying to tell me you're a bloody papist?" Richard gasped.

"I'm not trying to tell you anything at all," she replied coolly.

"Then what the hell are you doing carrying a rosary around with you?" He didn't seem to notice that she had not answered his question. She weighed up her chances of escape, but he was between her and the door. Beth resigned herself to giving him an explanation of sorts.

"They were my grandmother's," she said. "She gave them to my mother on her confirmation, and when she knew she was dying, she gave them to me." They were the only physical reminder she had of her mother, and were her greatest treasure, but she was not about to tell him that.

"And has it not occurred to you that carrying papist prayer beads in a case covered with Gaelic around in public, may be just a little dangerous?" He spoke slowly as though to a child, but his voice trembled with rage. He had a point there, but she was not about to concede it to him.

"No one knows about them," she countered.

"How do you think *I* knew about them?" his voice rose in volume, and without waiting for an answer, he continued. "I saw them trailing out of your reticule when you were at the haberdashers!"

She remembered now, just a couple of beads had made their way out of the corner of the case as the bag had sprung open. But she had pushed them quickly back into the case, and no one else had noticed. Except him. None of her companions would have been able to identify them as a rosary anyway just from that glimpse, and judging by the look on his face a few moments ago, neither had he.

"I remember that," she said. "Nobody else saw them at all, and even you with your hawk's eyes didn't know it was a rosary until just now, did you? You thought a secret admirer had bought me some jewellery, someone who might interfere with your ridiculous plans to marry me off to a crusty old general who would further your career."

"My career and your hopes for any marriage at all will be in ruins if anyone sees those, to say nothing of our lives," he cried dramatically, gesticulating wildly at the hand still holding the offending item. "You might as well sew a white cockade on your hat and declare for the Pretender now, you stupid bitch!" His face was red, his fists clenched, and she swallowed back her retort that she had no intention of marrying anyone of his choosing and couldn't give a damn about his career. She had come to know him well in the last months; he was close to violence and it would be unwise to provoke him any further.

"I know you avoid being alone with me," he continued. "But as we are alone now I will tell you this. I am not at all satisfied with your conduct at present."

"What do you mean?" she said.

"Don't think I haven't heard the story Lord Daniel put around about your mother. You told him what she was, didn't you? How could you be so stupid! Or was it perhaps deliberate?"

"What are you talking about?" she replied angrily. "Of course it wasn't deliberate. I was stupid, that I will admit. I should not have trusted him. I assure you, I will never trust or confide in anyone again."

"Are you sure of that?" he asked. "I am not so sure this is not just a ploy to avoid having to marry anyone at all. Don't think I'm taken in by that preposterous suggestion that your crony Caroline has put around that the duke of Cumberland has his eye on you. Beautiful as you are, the prince is hardly going to ask *you* to marry him. And if you continue to publicise your Catholic connections, no one will! I'll tell you this. If you think I will wait for seven years while you hide behind Edward and avoid marrying anybody, you are sorely mistaken."

"I am not hiding behind anyone," Beth said, enraged, "least of all that pompous idiot Edward. If you are talking about Daniel, you know full well why I didn't marry him. If I had, my dowry would have been swallowed up by his debt. You would certainly not have got your precious cornet's commission from him!"

"I am not talking about Lord Daniel. But you have had sixteen marriage proposals in the last four months, Be…Elizabeth, and you've said no to all of them."

"You've actually been counting?" she said, incredulous.

"Of course I have! It's in my interests to see you well married. But you must admit I have not interfered, or tried to get you to accept anyone against your will."

"Huh!" said Beth. "Only because none of them suited your purposes. Or Edward's, for that matter. I promised you I will marry if I find someone suitable, and I will."

"Yes, but you are doing your level best to make sure nobody suitable asks you, aren't you, flaunting the fact that your mother was a bloody Highland savage!"

"Be careful what you say, Richard," she said, her voice suddenly low and threatening. "I will tolerate a lot from you for the sake of our bargain, but do not push me too far."

"That is the problem, I think," he declared haughtily. "I have not pushed you at all since we came to London. But it is high time you found a husband, Beth, and if you do not do so soon, Edward and I will find one for you."

Beth had started to bend down to retrieve her reticule from the carpet, but at these words she stood up again.

"You already have someone in mind, don't you?" she said. "Who is it?"

"Lord Redburn is very well connected, and is actively seeking a wife."

"Lord Redburn!" she shrieked. "That decrepit drunken old fool! I would rather shoot myself than marry him!"

"Then you had better find a suitable husband before Lord Redburn throws his next party in two months, or resign yourself to him. Otherwise you will find yourself out on the streets, you and your precious servants. I will not support you indefinitely, and neither will Edward." Richard's face was puce with anger, and the muscle jumped in his cheek.

"That's twice in a matter of weeks that you have used the servants to threaten me, Richard," she raged. "If you do it again, I swear to God that the next time I meet the king, I will declare for the Pope and King James and stab the stupid old fool through the heart myself! Then we'll see how your precious military career goes!"

He stared at her. She was serious. She had gone mad. No, she was calling his bluff, that was all. Wild and stupid as she could be, she was no Jacobite. Even if she was, she would never attempt such a suicidal act. Would she? To his horror, he realised that he was not absolutely certain *what* she would do if pushed too far. He had no doubt that she would have castrated him if he had tried to disarm her that night in Manchester.

He fought down the impulse to strangle her on the spot, and cleared his throat.

"I would suggest then," he said, controlling himself with difficulty, "that you make yourself more amenable to prospective suitors, and find a husband within the next two months."

"Very well, you are right," she said through gritted teeth, which diminished the conciliatory effect of her words somewhat.

"I will not carry the rosary beads around with me any more. I will secrete them in my room where they will be safe from discovery. Does that satisfy you?"

He didn't answer, and taking his silence for acquiescence she bent down to retrieve her reticule from the rug.

In a flash his fingers had entwined in her hair, pulling her back to her feet, and with his other hand he snatched the precious leather case from her grasp before she had time to react. She swung her fist at his face, but he ducked his head back so the intended blow barely grazed his cheek. Still holding her hair in his fist, he pulled her head back, forcing her to look up at him.

"No," he growled. "That does not satisfy me." And with one flick of his wrist he sent the leather case spinning into the back of the fire which burned merrily in the hearth.

"No!" she screamed in anguish, fighting for release, heedless of the pain of her scalp as she pulled against his grip in a desperate attempt to retrieve the case from the flames. He wrapped his free arm around her, pinioning her flailing arms to her side.

"Ahem!" came the theatrical cough from the doorway, seconds before the cloying scent of violets assailed the nostrils of the struggling siblings. Richard spun round, still holding Beth, who had not noticed the intruder, so intent was she on trying to escape.

Sir Anthony minced into the room, resplendent in peacock blue coat and breeches and cerise silk waistcoat.

"I do hope I'm not disturbing anything," he said. "I decided to go for a short walk to assist the digestion of the excellent meal. Only it is so excruciatingly cold out of doors and I simply had to get warm before I could take another step. I declare I would have fainted away otherwise."

"I am having a private discussion with my sister, sir," said Richard icily, releasing his grip on Beth's hair, although he kept a firm hold on her arm. She had ceased to struggle, recognising even through her anguish that the discovery that she owned a rosary by a man who was not only one of the king's friends, but was also indiscreet enough to regale the whole of society with his find, was extremely risky to both of them. In spite of her dramatic threat of a moment ago, in reality she had no wish for her religious views to be revealed to the world.

"Carry on, my dears," Sir Anthony said, waving a gloved hand airily about as he made his way to the fire. "Don't take any notice of me." He stood with his back to the flames, absorbing all their heat. He obviously had the sensitivity of a carthorse, and was not going to take the hint and leave Richard and Beth alone.

Richard sighed, and retaining his firm grasp on Beth's arm, dragged her from the library.

"Close the door behind you, dear boy, if you don't mind," Sir Anthony called cheerily from the fireplace.

Once outside the room, Beth glanced around once to make sure no one was observing them, then rounded on her brother, tears of rage and misery sparkling in her eyes.

"I will never forgive you for this," she hissed at him.

"*You* will never forgive *me*?" he retaliated. "You had better pray, sister, that your precious memento has melted beyond recognition in the fire, and that that empty-headed nincompoop doesn't find it. If he does, you will beg me for forgiveness before I've finished with you."

He stalked off, leaving her standing by the library door. She dared not go back in to retrieve her precious beads. All she could do was to wait and return later when Sir Anthony was gone. Maybe some of the amber would survive the fire, at least.

She went to her room and paced up and down impatiently for an hour, by which time she assumed Sir Anthony would surely have warmed himself and left the library. The man was a butterfly; he was sure to have gone off in search of company and gossip by now.

The library door was closed when she returned, and she opened it carefully. To her consternation Sir Anthony was still in the room, seated by the dying fire, a book on his knee. He was gazing vacantly into the embers, but looked up as she tried to retire unnoticed.

"Ah, it is the delightful Elizabeth! Come in, come in! You left your reticule here, you know. Clarissa was kind enough to offer to return it to you. Although perhaps you would rather I had thrown it away." He gestured to the chair opposite him, but Beth did not take up his offer of a seat, although she did move further into the room, thinking it would be highly suspicious were she to flee.

"No, I would not be so ungrateful as to throw it away. It was a gift, after all," she replied.

"You are too kind, my dear, but I assure you I will not be offended if you pass it on to someone who would derive more pleasure from it than you have." He paused for a moment. "I presume you have finished your discussion with your brother, then?" His dark blue eyes were innocent and friendly in his painted and rouged face.

"Er…yes, thank you. We were having a little disagreement, but it has been resolved now." She moved a little closer to the fire, trying to peer into its depths surreptitiously. She couldn't see any sign of the remains of her rosary, but there was a lot of ash on the hearthstone under the grate. Perhaps it was there.

"Are you cold? Come, come a little closer, warm yourself." He placed his book on the table and started to stand, obviously intending to usher her into a seat. She backed off hurriedly.

"No, I'm not cold," she said, trying to come up with an explanation as to why she'd returned. In a moment of inspiration she seized on her previous reason for entering the library, which had been completely forgotten following the altercation with her brother. "I came to get a book. I have been told that Pamela by Samuel Richardson is a most interesting story."

"Well, it is certainly a weighty one," he replied.

"Have you read it?" she asked, pretending to peruse the shelves in search of it, although she remembered exactly where it was.

"Oh, good Lord, no. It is far too lengthy for me. Why, I fall asleep sometimes just reading the periodicals!" he retorted.

She could believe it. Although clearly well educated, fluent in German, and French and Latin too from what she had heard, it appeared he had not opened a book since leaving university. She wandered around a little more, and then turned to him.

"I have found it," she said. "But it is a little too high for me to reach. If you would be so kind?"

"But of course, anything to assist a cherished friend," Sir Anthony gushed. He leapt to his feet and came across to her, reaching up to retrieve the volume.

"It doesn't seem particularly weighty to me," she said, looking at the book in his hand.

"Ah, but it comes in four parts," he replied, glancing along the shelf before reaching up again to retrieve another volume, "although the third and fourth parts are a later addition. If, after you have read the first two, you wish to continue," he sounded as though he doubted in the extreme that she would want to, "then I am sure I can procure the others for you." He smiled down at her, and weighed the book carefully in his hand before passing it to her. "I would keep this tome by me at all times, if I were you, my dear," he said. "Then if you have another…ah…discussion with your brother, you can always use this to emphasise your point if necessary." His eyes twinkled merrily as he looked down at her, and she smiled back politely.

"Thank you," she said, choosing not to respond to his comment. She was about to make her excuses and leave, but after a moment he yawned theatrically.

"Well, I must admit to feeling a little tired. This always happens to me after indulging in exercise and then a little perusal of a book."

To say nothing of a few glasses of brandy, she thought wryly, noting the depleted contents of the decanter.

"If you wish to read your book in peace, you may stay here. I will not be so rude as to impose my company upon you," he added. He paused, seeming to be waiting for her to contradict his statement and plead for the pleasure of his sparkling conversation.

Silence reigned.

"Make yourself at home, sweet child. I shall make my weary way to my house, I think." He bowed. "I bid you goodnight."

After the door had closed, Beth waited, forcing herself to count slowly to a hundred, certain he would suddenly reappear to regale her with a *bon mot* of some sort. Then she threw the books onto the chair and crouched down by the hearth, rooting frantically through the ashes with the poker.

There was not the slightest fragment of either amber or silver in the ashes. There was no hope for the leather case, and the silver had probably melted into a blackened lump, indistinguishable from the tiny fragments of charred coal. But she had hoped that something would be left of the beads. Did amber melt in fire? She had no idea, but one thing was certain. The last tactile memory of her mother was gone, and Beth sank down on to the hearthrug, finally allowing herself the luxury of tears, which did nothing to ease the knot of absolute misery that had lodged in her chest.

* * *

By the end of the week Richard was breathing a little easier. Sir Anthony could have heard nothing of the altercation between him and Beth, he thought. He must have appeared at the door at the very moment they saw him. Otherwise he would surely have told everyone. He had not discussed his concern with his sister. In fact they had not spoken to each other since the incident, maintaining a polite distance by mutual consent until their tempers had cooled enough for them to at least be civil to one another.

Beth had also given the situation some thought. Unlike Richard, she knew from Sir Anthony's dry comment about the books that he had been fully aware of the fact that there had been nothing affectionate about the embrace he had caught them in, although she had no idea how much he had overheard.

She observed the behaviour of the ladies at every opportunity, watching for signs that Sir Anthony had let slip that dear Elizabeth and her brother hated each other; the curious glances, the comments behind hands followed by a surreptitious glance in her direction. Nothing.

When Sir Anthony visited the house a few days later, he was his usual gregarious self, flitting around the company in his obscenely gaudy costume and painted mask of a face, alighting on one group for a time, rousing them all to laughter with his malicious humour before flitting off to the next to repeat the experience, trailing a cloud of violets and admiring women in his wake.

Instead of fruitlessly pondering Sir Anthony's motive for keeping quiet, Beth resolved instead to concentrate on how to persuade Richard and Edward that Lord Redburn would *not* make a suitable husband for her. She had not been proposed to for a few weeks. Presumably that meant that either Daniel's slur on her mother's character had been believed, or alternatively, that any interested gentlemen were leaving the way clear for his Royal Highness the Duke of Cumberland. She was certain that Lord Redburn would have no such inhibitions. If Edward or Richard were to hint to him that she would be amenable to a marriage proposal, he would be down on one knee like a shot. She shuddered. No. She would refuse. No one could force her to marry him against her will. But would Richard carry out his threat if she did? He was far more capable of it than she was of carrying out hers. That had been empty bluster, and he would have recognised it by now.

She thought of her ticket home, the six sovereigns wrapped in a cloth now hidden in a hollowed-out Latin grammar in her room. Could she do it? Could she resign herself and her servants to a life of poverty by deserting London and alienating the Cunninghams forever? No, she thought, not yet. After all, Lord Redburn had not yet proposed. Richard had given her two months. Anything could happen in that time. It was only in her quiet moments that she felt the desperate misery of her restricted life, when the breathless claustrophobic panic that she would never be free again threatened to overwhelm her. She would have to make sure there were no quiet moments. Not difficult to achieve in the heady rush of social engagements that comprised the London season. She could continue dissembling for now, she resolved; after all, it was fast becoming second nature.

The resolve lasted a week.

Chapter Fourteen

The dinner party was in full swing. In spite of the fact that Britain was now most definitely, in spite of the lack of a formal declaration, at war with France, and everyone was talking of the king's magnificent victory at Dettingen at which he had led his troops in person, no one, not even Lord Edward, commented on the fact that the meal had obviously been prepared by a French chef.

Isabella was in her element. Everything had gone without a hitch. The company had all been carefully invited with regard to their breeding and ability to keep a constant flow of interesting conversation going. She beamed down the table at her guests. Lord and Lady Winter were there of course, and Miss Anne Maynard, so enamoured of Sir Anthony, who was seated to her right with Richard on his left. Opposite Richard was his sister, and next to her was Mr Jeremiah Johnson, a po-faced man of almost puritanical leanings who Isabella hoped would be a good and sobering influence on her young cousin Elizabeth. The friendship with the somewhat forthright Caroline Harlow was something to be discouraged, however, and Isabella had refrained from including her among the party this evening.

The main topic of conversation was of course the breaking news of the Battle of Dettingen.

"The casualties among the French were considerable, I believe," commented Lord Winter smugly.

"Presumably so," said Richard. "Although in his despatch, Lord Carteret did not specify numbers, merely that twenty-five thousand of the enemy had passed the main, and considerably fewer repassed it later."

"I am surprised that you have not been recalled to barracks, Sergeant Cunningham," said Sir Anthony. "Would you not wish to have participated in such a glorious event?"

Richard frowned. "Indeed I would, sir," he said. "But it is always necessary to keep some regiments at home, in case of Jacobite insurgency whilst the king is away. In that event I could rejoin my regiment within a day."

"Quite. Although there must be little likelihood of that now, with the king showing his true colours. England could not wish for a finer monarch. The Jacobite traitors must be trembling in their shoes." Mr Johnson spoke for the first time.

"I am sure they are, my dear sir," Sir Anthony replied smilingly. "Although the British have also suffered casualties, I believe."

"Yes!" cried Miss Maynard. "Poor General Clayton is killed!" She spoke as though she was a close friend of the general, although she had never heard of him prior to reading the newspaper yesterday.

"The duke of Cumberland was also wounded, was he not, Elizabeth?" put in Lady Winter. "That must have caused you some concern."

"Of course," Beth replied smoothly. "But it was only a leg wound, and did not touch the bone. I believe there are no fears for his life."

"Oh, but many men have died of such wounds!" exclaimed Anne.

"I am sure we need not worry. The Duke will receive the best of attention. It is the common soldier who risks the most and is most likely to die of infection if he is wounded, is it not, Richard?" She looked at her brother, who surveyed her warily. She had changed subtly since the incident in the library, was quieter, more moody. The sooner he got her off his hands, the better.

"Yes. But common soldiers are easily replaced," he replied. "The duke is unique."

"He certainly is," Beth agreed.

"I must say that I am most relieved that the king saw fit to leave some of his troops in England," Miss Maynard said. "Goodness, one cannot even travel the roads in safety any more! There are no end of robbers lying in wait for innocent travellers. Why, only yesterday I read of a respectable businessman who was robbed of over three hundred pounds by a highwayman in broad daylight!" She shuddered.

"It is not the job of the dragoons to patrol the roads for highwaymen, Miss Maynard," Lord Edward replied. "But you are right. These villains are becoming bolder by the day. Something must be done about them."

"I read the account you speak of, Miss Maynard, and I cannot help but think the victim partially deserved his fate," Beth said thoughtfully. Lord Edward glanced sharply at her, and she looked innocently back at him. "Mr Harlow does not think ladies incapable of understanding the news, Edward. I read the newspapers with Caroline."

Before Lord Edward could reply to this remark, Sir Anthony cut in.

"What makes you say that, my dear? Surely you are being a little hard on the poor man?"

"The newspaper published a description of the highwayman as being over six feet in height, with a black wig, red breeches, and a patch on his eye. He must have looked most disreputable."

"Quite so. Horrible!" Anne Maynard trembled, inadvertently placing her hand on Sir Anthony's arm in her agitation. Uncharacteristically he started at her touch, looking down at the small hand, pale against the dark brocade of his coat, as though he had never seen such a thing before in his life. Then he remembered himself, and placing his gloved hand on hers he patted it absently but continued to give his complete attention to Beth, to the other lady's consternation.

"And yet not only was the gentleman, Mr Highmore I believe his name was, riding alone with a large sum of money and no armed escort," Beth continued, "but when this highly suspicious-looking man suggested that there was a better way to a destination Mr Highmore no doubt travels regularly to, the idiot accompanied him down a secluded lane without the slightest hesitation! How stupid can anyone be!"

"Do you not think it a sad state of affairs when no man can trust his neighbour?" Mr Johnson said.

"Of course I do! But in the real world it is folly to trust disreputable strangers. In fact, in my experience I have found it unwise to trust anyone at all." Her gaze rested on Richard for a moment, then turned to Lord Edward. She smiled pleasantly, her eyes cold.

There was a short silence, during which Lord Edward excused himself and went to use the privy and Richard tried to think of a pretext to remove his dangerously unpredictable sister from the room. Clarissa coughed nervously.

"So, my dear Elizabeth, how are you getting along in your reading of 'Pamela'?" Sir Anthony said brightly.

"I have finished it, sir," she said.

He raised a carefully pencilled eyebrow. "Really? It is a most weighty volume. You must read very quickly."

"I didn't find it challenging reading. The most difficult part was in staying awake to read it."

"So, you did not enjoy it enough to continue on to volumes three and four, then?"

"I enjoyed the first part of the book, although I fail to understand why Pamela didn't leave immediately after the hero's first attempt to seduce her, as she said she intended."

"But the girl sought to retain her position in the house. She was of a very poor family, and had reason to believe that her master had reformed," Mr Johnson put in.

"I don't see what reason she had to believe he'd reformed," Beth countered. "If she valued her virtue as much as she claimed, she would have left immediately. Her family were supportive, after all. Instead she stayed long enough for him to abduct her."

The whole table now became involved in the conversation. Everyone had read the novel. It had been a sensation when published, and had caused great controversy.

"Oh, but then it is so romantic!" Charlotte put in. "After all, she reforms him with her virtue, you know. It is every woman's duty to show a good example by her behaviour. Not of course that my dear Frederick needed a good example to follow." There were murmurs of agreement from the ladies.

"So what would you have done, had you been abducted by such a rake?" Sir Anthony asked.

"I assure you sir, that any man who tried to enter my bedchamber with evil intention would have a very unpleasant reception," Beth said vehemently. She glanced across at her brother, who, to Sir Anthony's curiosity, reddened and looked the other way.

"Oh, but what can one do against such a man!" cried Anne Maynard. "We are all so helpless in the hands of man's greater strength!"

"It strikes me that some ladies are more helpless than others," Sir Anthony commented, keeping his eyes on Beth. "But as dear Miss Maynard says, what can a woman do against such a determined man?"

"If we follow the advice of the author Mr Richardson, presumably wait until he miraculously reforms and proposes marriage, whereupon she can instantly become the most appalling creature, bemoaning her unworthiness to occupy such a privileged position from morning till night." Beth's voice was laced with disdain.

"I would that all women were so virtuous and sensible of their role," said Mr Johnson pompously. "I often find it to be the opposite case. Many women continually tempt men by their lewdness into imperilling their souls."

"Ah, but sir, if you will persist in your acquaintance with the ladies of Drury Lane, what can you expect?" Sir Anthony commented. A snigger ran along the table. None of the company, the Cunninghams excepted, liked the self-righteous Mr Johnson. Every one of them was regularly subjected to one of his lengthy improving lectures, with the exception of Sir Anthony, who had been heard to proclaim in a loud voice that if he wished to hear a sermon, he would go to a minister, not a hypocrite. Mr Johnson had given the baronet a wide berth after that, and looked at him now with a hatred most unbecoming in a man of professed faith.

Blithely disregarding his enemy, Sir Anthony proceeded to address Beth.

"I take it from your expression that you don't consider Pamela to be so virtuous after all? She does resist him, under the most trying circumstances."

"Yes, but she deliberately puts herself in those trying circumstances. But you told me you had not read the book, Sir Anthony. You seem to know a lot about it."

"Yes, well, I thought I would make the effort after all, in the hope of engaging you in a discussion. I was sure that your opinions would be diverting."

Everyone at the table except Beth pricked up their ears at that.

Sir Anthony had never expressed interest in any particular woman before. Was he smitten? Only Beth failed to notice, having not been brought up in a society so obsessed with matchmaking. She was still pondering the character of Pamela.

"I think she is hoping for marriage all along," she continued. "I find it most unconvincing that she spends the first half of the book denouncing the hero, only to suddenly discover she has been in love with him all along the moment he proposes marriage. I think all in all they deserve each other, for she is the most unctuous mercenary thing, and he shows all the makings of an absolute tyrant."

Lord Edward had entered while Beth was talking and now took his seat at the head of the table, muttering apologies as he came for his tardiness. The master having reappeared, the second course was now served.

"So who are you talking about? Who is unctuous, and who is a tyrant?" he asked.

"We were discussing Mr Richardson's novel, 'Pamela,' Edward," said Isabella. "Elizabeth was giving her opinion of the hero and heroine."

"Ah, you take the view of Henry Fielding then, cousin," he stated.

"I have not read Mr Fielding's comments on the novel," she said.

Edward smiled, pleased to have read a book his over-educated cousin had not. "He wrote a parody on the novel, entitled 'Shamela'. Most diverting. But of course this is what happens when a man marries beneath his station. The hero is most fortunate that his family and friends do not cast him out, as they should have done." He looked sharply at Beth, who coloured. "Still, at least *Pamela* remained humble, and was truly grateful for the honour bestowed upon her."

"But does that give Mr B. the right to be a tyrant?" Beth retorted.

"He has the right to be whatever he wishes. He is well born, whereas she is not. She would do well to remember it, as would any woman who finds herself with the opportunity to marry above her." He took a forkful of venison, chewing it with gusto.

It was clear that the conversation had suddenly moved from

the general discussion of a novel to something of a personal nature between the Cunningham family. Sir Anthony glanced at the various members. Richard looked smug, but wary. The three sisters appeared a little nervous and fluttery; everyone else seemed slightly bemused, clearly not fully comprehending the undertones. Sir Anthony sat back to observe, his face impassive.

"And yet did our Lord Jesus Christ not say that, 'He that is least among you all, the same shall be great?'" Beth said. "And, 'Whosoever of you will be the chiefest, shall be servant of all?'"

"Are you seriously telling me you believe that everyone is born absolutely equal?" Lord Edward glowered. He leaned back in his chair and beckoned imperiously to one of the footmen standing nearby. "Here, sir, what is your name?"

"Samuel, my lord," replied the man, astonished that after several years of being ignored in his service, his master should now address him personally.

"Well, Samuel, what do you think to replacing me as Lord Cunningham, eh? My cousin seems to think you worthy of the post. What do you say?"

The unfortunate Samuel opened his mouth and then closed it again, at a loss for words.

"Come, come, man, don't be shy," the lord barked. "Do you think you are up to the job?"

"I…I am sure I am happy where I am, my lord. I would never presume to rise further…" he stuttered, clearly wishing the ground would open up and swallow him.

Beth had been about to change the subject before Lord Edward unfairly attacked his servant. She had noticed the nervous reaction of her female cousins and the puzzled expressions on the faces of the rest of the company, and realised that she had overstepped the mark. Although Lord Edward was behaving boorishly, he was both the head of the family and the host of this dinner party, and convention dictated that she owed him respect and deference as such. But the sight of the humiliated red-faced footman stammering, while her cousin eyed him with a mixture of contempt and triumph was too much. Outwardly calm, inwardly she raged at the injustice, and flung propriety to the four winds without a care.

"You are being unfair, Edward, in attempting to humiliate a

man who cannot answer back," she remarked icily. "You do yourself no credit to behave thus."

Her comment had the desired effect. Samuel was forgotten and retired gratefully into the shadows.

"Tell me then, madam, who clearly consider yourself my equal to speak to me in such a manner, do you think this Samuel is capable of replacing me?" asked Edward angrily, his attention now fully back on Beth.

"No, of course not. Some are born to poverty and low position, and some are born to high position, as God wills."

"I am glad to hear you think that way, because..."

"But it is the duty of everyone born to high position to behave in a manner befitting the honour God has bestowed upon him," Beth interrupted. "If he thinks that noble blood gives him the right to be a pompous, ignorant tyrant, then he does not deserve the position. Add to that the fact that the highborn person has access to the most improving education and company, and he has even less excuse for being a despot. A man may be born to an exalted position, but that does not make him a gentleman, or deserving of respect. Respect can only be earned by gentlemanly conduct." Her tone made it very clear that she felt Lord Edward had not earned *her* respect, at any rate.

The noble had gone purple with rage, and Richard was subtly but fruitlessly trying to attract his sister's attention, no doubt in an attempt to stop her inflaming her cousin's anger further.

Isabella broke nervously into the momentary silence that followed. "I am sure, though, that those who are born to privilege would never seek to abuse it. I am certain that I always try to set a good example to others in everything I do and say."

"I know you do, my dear Isabella," Sir Anthony reassured her kindly. The poor woman seemed to spend her life humouring her arrogant brother, and he pitied her. "But unfortunately I must agree with Elizabeth, that not everybody shows such a good example."

"Even if they do not," blustered Edward, riding roughshod over his sister's feeble attempts at conciliation, "who are we to argue with what God has ordained? Are you saying that we should promote beggars to replace peers of the realm who behave in an unsatisfactory manner?"

"No, of course I am not saying that, cousin," said Beth, in a deceptively humble voice. There was a little sigh of relief from Isabella and a few other ladies at the table. "But I do think that more of the company in fact agree with my views than you think. Indeed, I believe that you yourself secretly subscribe to them."

"What?!" How can you possibly justify that?!" her cousin exclaimed. Several people leaned forward, disregarding the servants' attempts to take away their empty plates. All eyes were on Beth.

"How else can you justify the replacement of a king born to his position by divine right, with a distant relation who had no hereditary right at all?"

The silence was profound. Even the servants froze.

"My God, woman!" roared Edward, leaping to his feet and knocking over his wine glass in the process. A red stain spread slowly across the immaculate snowy tablecloth. "Are you telling me I have a bloody Jacobite traitor in the midst of my family?"

Only Beth and Sir Anthony remained apparently calm amongst the uproar at the table. Isabella and Clarissa looked about to faint. Mr Johnson spluttered his mouthful of wine across the table; Richard appeared about to assault his sister. Indeed he half-stood, his hand moving automatically towards the sword he had forgotten he was not wearing. Sir Anthony reached across and laid a restraining hand on the other man's arm. Richard shook it off angrily, but he subsided back into his chair.

"I said no such thing, Edward," Beth replied sweetly once the noise had subsided a little. "I did not state that I thought it wrong to replace an unworthy king. I do not hold the view that every man deserves to hold his place regardless of his conduct. You however, do hold such a view. I therefore asked you, a devout Hanoverian, in all seriousness how you can justify the removal of a divinely ordained monarch, according to your stated principles?"

"It is a completely different matter altogether," Edward spluttered, aware that he had been wrong-footed somehow. He sat down again, and motioned a servant forward to clean up the spilled wine. "James was incompetent. He had to go. The man was a papist, for God's sake! If he'd had his way we'd all be kneeling to Rome by now, and the pope would be head of the country."

"Hear, hear," said Mr Johnson.

"So, then, you agree that the country is fully within its rights to remove an incompetent king, but an incompetent mere lord cannot be challenged in any way by those beneath him?"

"I did not say that!" Edward said.

"Yes, you did. To quote your exact words, uttered not five minutes ago – 'who are we to argue with what God has ordained?' Yet you agree with a parliament who did indeed argue with what God had ordained. James was the hereditary heir to the throne, competent or not. If I, who am, as you insinuate, not your equal," her voice was thick with scorn, "have to endure the dictates of my *superiors* regardless of their moral or intellectual right to be called so, then should not you follow the same rule with regards to *your* superiors? You cannot claim right by birth for yourself, but deny it to others when it suits you, my lord."

Lord Edward was clearly stumped. He gulped at his refilled glass of wine, trying to gain time before having to answer.

"James abdicated his throne voluntarily," he said sullenly after a pause. "A king who will not fight when challenged is not worthy of the title."

Sir Anthony laughed out loud, drawing attention away from the duelling cousins.

"Come, my lord, that is not true. James may not have fought to retain his crown, but he did not abdicate, everybody knows that. But you prevaricate. The lady has a point. Will you not answer her?" He was in his element. He had never thought he would see the day when Lord Edward was bested by a woman. He usually surrounded himself with sycophants or people who depended upon him for their livelihood, or who could be easily bullied. Clearly he had got more than he had bargained for when he had taken his cousin under his noble wing.

"She is no lady, sir, surely that is obvious by her impertinence? Her father may have been my uncle, but her mother was nothing more than a…"

He got no further, as the carefully controlled rage suddenly exploded. Beth jumped up and threw the newly replenished contents of her wineglass straight into Edward's face. Isabella gave a little shriek of horror. Beth stood facing her cousin, who had also risen from his chair and looked about to strike her. She was white-faced, but with anger, not fear.

"You may call *me* anything you wish, cousin," she said. Her voice shook with emotion. "But you will not insult my mother while I am present to defend her. If you are coward enough to do so when I am not present, that is your prerogative." She turned to the sea of shocked faces looking up at her. Only Sir Anthony was smiling. "You will excuse me if I leave the table now. I beg your pardon if I have ruined your meal."

"On the contrary, dear lady. I for one feel you have considerably enlivened it," said Sir Anthony merrily.

She hardly heard him through the fire that roared in her blood. She turned, straight-backed and swept from the room, closing the door behind her.

There was a short silence, broken only by the servants ministering to their drenched lord.

"Well, are we to have the next course, or are we all to die of starvation first?" Sir Anthony asked.

"Oh…of course. I beg your pardon." Isabella clapped her hands and the servants who had frozen along with the diners while Beth and Lord Edward argued were galvanised into action. Plates were removed and the next course brought in. The rattle of crockery and cutlery masked the awkward silence, and by the time the plates were filled, sporadic conversation had started up again in which any topic that touched on noble birth and hereditary rights was carefully avoided. Lord Edward left the room temporarily to change his waistcoat. A semblance of normality returned to the evening.

Only Richard remained unpacified. His face was red with anger, and his fists clenched under the table. A muscle worked in his cheek. Sir Anthony had started a conversation with Miss Maynard on his left, and sensed rather than saw Richard start to rise.

"So, sir," he said, laying a gloved hand on Richard's arm. This time when the dragoon tried to shake it off, Sir Anthony maintained his hold. "I find your sister a most intoxicating woman, and must confess to being half in love with her. You must tell me more about her background. She never speaks of her childhood. Tell me everything, I will not be gainsaid."

This had the desired effect. Richard was not about to throw

away the chance of fostering relations between Beth and a wealthy and influential suitor, not even for the satisfaction of giving her a beating, which he had been about to go and do. He spent the next half hour painting a glowing portrait of his sister and her genteel upbringing, which bore no relation whatsoever to the woman Sir Anthony had observed so far, but to which he listened with apparent fascination and vapid exclamations of rapture, while Miss Maynard was sadly obliged to give all her attention to her lemon mousse.

By the end of the evening Richard was well satisfied. Sir Anthony was a better proposition than Lord Redburn. More generous with his money, for one thing. And, in spite of his inferior title, far more influential and respected. Beth would marry him, if he proposed to her. Richard would make sure of it.

* * *

The drawing room was quite tastefully appointed; its wood-panelled walls had been painted cream, the elaborate carvings gilded. A series of portraits of the owner's ancestors hung around the room, gazing down austerely on the assembled company. A riot of gilded plaster garlands festooned the ceiling, breathtaking in their detail for anyone who cared to crane their necks and examine them.

This beautiful workmanship was completely wasted on the men who were scattered in small groups around the room. Some were sitting round small walnut card tables; others stood in twos and threes conversing in hushed voices, as though in church. They were dressed in hardwearing woollen or leather breeches in shades of brown or dark green. Their shirts were of coarse material, their shoes of stout leather, unadorned with silver or diamante buckles. Only one man was dressed appropriately for the setting, in the green livery of a footman. The others looked incongruous in the elegant room. An air of unease and anticipation pervaded the room, and although they knew each other well, their conversation was halting, desultory.

After a few minutes of this, the door opened. The buzz of conversation stilled, those who had been seated stood, and all eyes turned to the man who now appeared in the doorway. He hesitated for a moment on the threshold, his eyes scanning the room, then he located the person he was looking for and moved purposefully across the room toward him.

The men who had been standing with Angus now moved away from him, as if by unspoken accord. The man halted for a moment in front of his ashen-faced brother and looked at him coldly. Angus raised one hand, palm forward, as if in supplication.

"Alex, I…" he began.

Alex's fist crashed into his brother's face, sending him reeling backwards against the wall. Angus splayed his hands against the painted wood to steady himself and shook his head to clear it. Then he moved away from the wall and stood straight, making no move to defend himself as Alex hit him again, this time in the abdomen. His breath shot from his lungs with a whoosh and he doubled over, managing by sheer effort of will not to fall to his knees. The next blow took him in the ribs.

The men watched in silence, their faces impassive as the beating was administered. It was systematic, designed to inflict maximum pain but no permanent damage. Finally, after what seemed an eternity, Alex moved back and flexed his fingers to ease the pain of his bruised knuckles. He stood tall, menacing, as pale now as Angus, who had finally fallen to his knees, one arm wrapped round his bruised ribs, the other braced against the floor. His head hung down, his long fair hair obscuring his face.

"You have disgraced yourself and shamed your clan," Alex said clearly and loudly in Gaelic, as though addressing an assembly of hundreds in an echoing hall, rather than twenty men in a genteel London drawing room. "If you do it again I will kill you, brother or no." He turned away, and looked at the other men for the first time. "Find yourselves seats, we've things to discuss. I'll be back directly."

He shot one more look at his brother, who had now sat back onto his haunches, his breathing laboured, and then walked from the room. Duncan hesitated for a minute, glancing from his injured sibling, now trying painfully to regain his feet, to the doorway through which the other had just gone. Motioning to two of the nearest men to help Angus to a chair, he made his decision, and followed Alex downstairs into the kitchen.

There were no servants in the house tonight and Alex had ostensibly gone to fetch refreshments for the men. But when

Duncan entered the room his brother was sitting at the table, his head in his hands. He looked up sharply, then seeing who it was, resumed his position.

"Are ye all right, man?" Duncan said, although it was clear Alex was not. He sat down beside him and waited.

"Mother of God, Duncan, what possessed him to do that? Rob an innocent man in broad daylight, risk his life and the lives of all of us, for the sake of what? Three hundred pounds?" Alex said after a minute.

"Three hundred and forty. I dinna think he saw it quite like that at the time," Duncan replied hesitantly. "He did say as he'd originally intended just to accompany the man along the way for a wee while, no more. But he angered him so much wi' his blethering on about how wonderful King Geordie was, and how he was going tae use some of the money he had with him to sponsor militiamen to put down any o' they damn Jacobite bastards that took it into their heads to riot while the king was out of the country. So he decided tae relieve him of his burden and ensure it was put to better use. I can understand him." Alex looked at him darkly. "I didna say I agreed wi' him," Duncan continued hastily. "I said I understand him. He said he couldna believe it when the man agreed to go down a dark lane wi' him, and that he felt then that he was doing the man a favour, in a manner o' speaking, because in future he'd think twice before trusting a stranger, which might save his life next time. He didna harm him, ye ken, just tied him up, that's all."

Although Duncan was uttering the words, this was so typically the light-hearted Angus speaking, that Alex smiled in spite of himself.

"Aye, that's as maybe, but what would he have done if the man had produced a pistol, Duncan? Would he have let himself be taken, or would he have killed him, a man who'd done no wrong apart from to be over trusting and express an opinion contrary to Angus's? An he'd done that, he'd have hung, and I'd no' have lifted a finger to prevent it." He looked at his brother, his face anguished. "And it would have fair broke my heart, Duncan. It hurt me greatly just to beat him like that," he finished softly. He would not have admitted this to any other living man, and Duncan nodded his head in acknowledgement of the honour.

"He kens that well," Duncan said. "I explained it to him. He'll be relieved that you only beat him. He was expecting a flogging, at the least. He'll no' do such foolishness again."

"I surely hope not. He'll be the death of me if he does. D'ye ken where I heard it? At a bloody dinner party given by Lord Edward Cunningham. I nearly died when I heard the description of the highwayman and recognised the stupit disguise Angus wears sometimes when he's travelling. God knows how I didna give myself away there and then. Luckily everyone was diverted somewhat by a stramash between the lord and his cousin." He ran his hands through his hair again and stood up, reluctantly. "Aye, well, we'd best be getting back. The others'll be wondering where we are."

By the time they arrived back in the drawing room, armed with several bottles of brandy and a tray of glasses, the men had moved the chairs into a rough circle and were sitting chatting while they waited. The tension had dissipated somewhat. Apart from the presence of the young man sitting hunched awkwardly in a chair, one eye swollen shut and a bloody handkerchief clutched to his mouth, no one would ever have known that a brutal, unpleasant scene had so recently taken place.

Alex passed the glasses and bottles around, and took a seat.

"I asked ye all here tonight for several reasons," he said. One had already been addressed. No one mentioned it. The punishment had been administered, Angus had accepted it as just, and had already apologised to the assembled MacGregor clansmen. "As ye're no doubt aware, we were relieved of a cache of arms by the redcoats a few weeks ago. As I couldna go myself to find out who betrayed us I sent Duncan up in my stead, with instructions to dispose of the traitor an he discovered him." He looked at Duncan, who nodded, and took over.

"I found out who it is," he said. "But there's a wee problem. It's no' a man, but a woman who betrayed us."

"Where's the problem in that?" one of the men asked. "Death's the punishment for betrayal, no matter who does it." There was a murmur of assent from the assembly. Different punishments were meted out to men and women who committed offences against the clan. But the punishment for betrayal was the same for both. No mitigating circumstances were taken into account for such a serious crime.

"Aye, but the woman in question is Jean MacGregor."

Four of the men in the room blanched instantly, and there was a deathly silence.

"I'm sorry, lads," said Alex softly. "I kent it'd be hard, her being your sister, an all."

"Are ye sure?" one of the pale men asked in a strangled whisper.

"Aye, I'm sure," Duncan replied. "She was caught...em...in close company wi' the soldier, you might say." There was no doubt from the expressions on the faces of the men that everyone understood exactly the nature of the position in which she'd been found. The four black-haired brothers of Jean wore identical shocked expressions, and Alex's heart went out to them. He'd be very glad when this day was over.

"What did Kenneth say about this?" one of them asked. Kenneth was the woman's husband.

"Kenneth has asked my permission to kill her himself. I've agreed provisionally," Alex said. "But I wanted you to have the chance to speak before the deed is done."

"You're our chief, man. We'd go along wi' whatever you said, ye ken that," The first man pointed out. His pallor was especially noticeable against the raven darkness of his hair.

"Aye I ken that, Dougal," Alex said. "But there's a difference between going along with me and agreeing with me, an' I'd no' have dissent among us, if I can avoid it."

"Would ye let her live, if we asked?" the youngest of her brothers asked.

Alex shook his head.

"No, I couldna do that," he said, not without regret. Jean MacGregor was a beautiful woman, black-haired and grey-eyed like her brothers, with an infectious laugh and a lovely singing voice. She was also vain and susceptible to flattery, which had no doubt been her undoing. "But you've the right, as her brothers, to demand that I carry out the sentence personally, rather than let her husband do it."

From the direction of the hall came the unmistakable sound of a knock at the front door. Everyone froze.

"Are ye expecting anyone?" Duncan asked quietly.

"No," replied Alex. "Iain, see who it is, if you please."

The man dressed in footman's livery stood, smoothed down his coat, adopted the necessary superior air and left the room, closing the door behind him. The others sat in various states of casual readiness, hands on dirks.

Minutes ticked slowly by. Then the footman reappeared clutching an ornately embellished pink card, which he handed to Alex.

"Lady Wilhelmina Winter, to see Sir Anthony Peters," he said formally.

"Who is unfortunately away from home at present," Alex said in a mock aristocratic English accent, breathing a sigh of relief.

"Just so," replied the footman, grinning. "She was most disappointed and will call again tomorrow. She's gone. I watched her drive away, to make sure."

The danger over, the men relaxed as far as was possible in the circumstances. The four brothers of Jean had taken the opportunity to have a whispered discussion.

"We've made a decision," Dougal now announced, standing up. "Under normal circumstances, we'd ask you to carry out the sentence. But these are no' normal circumstances. You're over three hundred miles from home, and besides, if Jeanie was caught as ye say, Duncan, then she's wronged the clan, aye, but she's wronged her husband too. We'll be satisfied for him to do it. We'll no' speak of her again." He sat down again and looked at the floor, his face set.

"Thank you." Alex was relieved. He had no wish to personally strangle a beautiful woman, or any woman for that matter, although he would not have hesitated to do so had her brothers asked it of him.

"In that case," he said, "we've got one more consignment of arms to come in from France, and then ye can all go home, except for Duncan, Angus and Iain." He glanced at the footman. There was a collective sigh of relief. "I'm expecting to be here for a few more weeks, if all goes according to plan, and then I'll be off to Europe for a wee while, a month, maybe two."

"Will ye be seeing the prince during your travels?" one man asked.

"Aye, I expect I will, although I confess I was hoping to see him without crossing the water myself."

"Aye, it's a wonderful opportunity he's missing, wi' Geordie and his son an all away fighting, and the throne lying empty," Dougal said wistfully. His colour was returning slightly now, but his grey eyes were still moist with the tears he would not shed for his sister.

"True. But he canna do anything if the French willna help him, and the English Jacobites willna rise unless they do," Alex pointed out practically.

"Ah, tae hell wi' the English!" Jamie MacGregor cried suddenly. "Scotland'll rise for him, if he'll lead us!"

"Some of Scotland'll rise for him," Alex corrected. "But no' enough, if he doesna have the French to back him. The Protestant clans, apart from the Episcopalians'll no' follow him. The Campbells will fight for George, and much of the lowlands too. That's one of the things I'm going to talk about with him, if he'll see me."

"All the more reason for us to fight for Charlie." Angus spoke for the first time, his voice emerging thickly through his split lip. "What more can we ask for than to kill both the Campbells and the English, and all in a noble cause?"

Several men laughed at that, and there was a cheer of agreement. The Campbells were the sworn enemies of the MacGregor clan, and had been for centuries.

The meeting broke up a few minutes later, the mood generally cheerful. Although the men were upset about Jean, they were relieved that the traitor had been found and vastly relieved to be going home so soon. They left in ones and twos through the rear door, disappearing silently into the back streets without attracting attention.

Duncan, Angus and Iain remained, and settled to finish off the last bottle of brandy. Alex drained his glass as though it were water, sitting back and closing his eyes wearily. He felt deeply sorry for having to raise the subject of Jean's betrayal in front of so many men, but there was no help for it. He had needed witnesses to ensure there would be no later dispute about the punishment, or the fact that her husband rather than himself was administering it. Angus drained his own glass almost as fast as Alex, wincing slightly as the alcohol stung his injured lip.

"Are ye all right, man?" Alex said gently. Angus looked at him through his one good eye.

"Aye, I'll do," he said. "Though I doubt I'll be helping to bring the next shipment in. I think ye cracked one of my ribs." There was no accusation in his tone. "I'll not give you cause to do that again, Alex. I was wrong, and I'm sorry."

The four men drank in silence for a time.

"You didna say anything to the men about the other matter in hand," Duncan said eventually.

Alex ran his hand through his hair, as he always did when worried or irritated. Several strands were pulled loose by the gesture and glinted copper in the candlelight.

"No point in bothering them unduly. They had enough to deal with tonight, without me worrying them wi' something that might not happen."

"Aye, but on the other hand, it might. Are you sure you're doing the right thing?"

"I'm sure. I've been watching for a long time. And hesitating. But if I dinna move soon, it'll be too late. There's a slight risk, but I'm willing to take it."

"I'm no' so sure I'd be willing," Duncan said. Angus nodded agreement. "But I'll stand by ye if you're determined to go ahead. But will ye no' think again, before you make your final decision?"

Alex looked at his two brothers.

"I've nae choice in the matter," he smiled helplessly, his eyes suddenly soft. "*Tha gràdh agam oirre.*"

His three companions exchanged sympathetic glances.

"Ah. Well," said Angus. "I guess there's no more to be said, then."

Chapter Fifteen

Beth lay on the bed, the letter Sarah had just given her clutched to her breast. She felt a shiver of excitement thrill through her, like a small child faced with a brightly-wrapped Christmas present. The last week had been hell, with Lord Edward, face set and grim, refusing her the loan of the carriage to visit Caroline. When Beth had expressed the intention to walk to her friend's house he had actually stood in front of the door, barring her way, Richard smiling nastily in the background. Her cousin had pompously told her that he felt it better if she only went out in the company of his sisters until she had learned to behave in a more genteel manner. Although furious, she had, with difficulty retained the presence of mind to weigh up the situation, looking from her cousin to her brother. Edward would not hurt her, she knew that. But in his expression she could also see that he would not prevent Richard from restraining her in whatever manner he thought fit, were she to lose her temper.

She opted for disappointing Richard by acquiescing meekly to Edward's demands, and had been a model of perfect behaviour ever since, to the whole family's intense relief, although she had not apologised to Edward as he had hoped. She had to keep some of her principles intact, although it had cost her dear. She was finding it increasingly difficult to fight off the depression that threatened to overwhelm her and sap her strength.

There was one small ray of light in her life, which came in the form of her maid. She blessed the day she had decided to employ Sarah, who had managed, while performing a small errand, to hare round to Caroline's, give a brief explanation of her mistress's current situation and pick up the waiting letter. Beth now carefully opened the sheet of paper and started to read.

Dearest Beth,

How wonderful it is to address you by your proper name! As I said in my other letter, which your brother will by now certainly have shown you, we are all well. Even Graeme's joints are much better, although we feel this is due to the dry weather rather than any improvement in his general health. We all miss you terribly, as I am sure you know.

We were very sorry to hear about Lord Daniel. We were hoping that you could marry a man who would bring you happiness as well as relieve you of the burden of your brother. But it is far better that you knew what he was beforehand, thus escaping a terrible fate.

As for Lord Redburn, Graeme became most agitated on hearing of him, and said he would abduct and marry you himself before he would let you fall into the hands of such a drunken fool! I am sure you will be able to outwit your brother in his designs. But I urge you to keep in mind the present we gave to you when last we saw you. Do not hesitate to return to us if you need to. We are all agreed on this.

The words suddenly misted and blurred, and Beth stopped reading for a moment to wipe her eyes. Then she continued.

Now we have some news for you, regarding John, although whether you will welcome it or not is another matter.

Some three weeks ago, it being a fine day, Thomas, Graeme and I walked into Manchester, on the excuse of buying provisions, but really to enjoy the lovely weather. We had been there for some short while, when who should come marching up the street but the militia, fresh from their training in Lincoln. They looked very fine with their muskets, bayonets and swords, some of them in blue coats and buff belts, which seemed to be an attempt at uniform. Needless to say, Graeme was not at all impressed by this show of strength, and made numerous derogatory comments in a rather loud voice, which attracted not a little attention from the marchers.

Of course we looked for John, although expecting he would try to avoid us. To our surprise, he did no such thing, but on seeing us, waved merrily and abandoning his position without a care, came over to us. Before I could do more than greet him Graeme had launched into a tirade of insults, saying that he was amazed John even had the cheek to breathe the same air as us. John tried to explain something, but could not get more than two words out before Graeme told him that he had no wish to listen to those who abandoned all their principles and deserted their true King for a coat and 6d a day. (John was one of those fortunate, or unfortunate enough, depending on your view, to have been issued with a new coat.)

John then lost his temper, and becoming very hot, declared that if Graeme believed him to have betrayed the Jacobite cause, then he was an even bigger fool than he thought him to be. Whereupon Graeme listened to no more, but struck John a mighty blow in the face, which, taking John by surprise, knocked him down. He would have followed this up with a further assault, but that Thomas and I, having noted that others were now showing a great interest in the proceedings and that some of the militiamen, having marched past, were now looking curiously back, seized Graeme and dragged him by main force into the back streets, where we managed to calm him enough to get him home without further trouble. Since then he has spoken no more of the incident. In truth, I do not understand John's motives, as he was always so fervent in the Jacobite cause. I would never have believed him capable of betraying it, but can see no other explanation for his actions.

At least from this account you know that John is well, apart from the possible loss of a tooth and a bloody nose, and that Graeme shows no signs of mellowing with age.

I will write again as soon as I receive your reply assuring me that the address is still safe.

Your friend,
Jane.

Beth lay back and closed her eyes. She could almost see the incident in her mind, the dust kicked up by the marching feet, the sun glinting on swords and bayonets, Graeme's weatherbeaten face red with anger, John's shocked expression as he landed in the dirt…she opened her eyes quickly. Like Jane she could not understand John's motives, but she understood far better now how easy people found it to betray each other. Sir Anthony had been right. Trust no one. That she was not suited to society life she made no bones about. But she had told no one of her desperate loneliness, of the strain of coping with the boredom and hypocrisy, the meaningless conversation and backstabbing, without a single true friend in whom she could confide.

True, she had Sarah. But although the maid listened sympathetically to Beth, she had no empathy with her. Sarah would eagerly have swapped places with Beth at a moment's notice, considering marriage to an alcoholic ancient lord a small price to pay for the title and luxury she would gain. Of course, thought Beth with a smile, Sarah would not hesitate to take a lover if she saw fit, or to deceive her husband at every opportunity. In fact she would relish it.

I want too much, thought Beth. *I want a loving man, who I can trust, and who will love me for myself. If I had that, I could cope with this artificial life, if I had to.*

She thought she had found that in Daniel. Now she knew she would not find it in anyone.

She opened the letter again, intending to re-read it to divert her mind from the depression that she was rapidly thinking herself into. She was half way through it when she heard Sarah's voice outside the door, speaking with unusual loudness and clarity.

"I am not sure if she is dressed to receive a visitor, Sergeant Cunningham," she was saying. "If you will just let me enquire…"

Knowing that Richard would allow Sarah to do no such thing, Beth jumped off the bed and lifted the mattress, pushing the letter well underneath it where it was in no danger of slipping out. When Richard walked in she was sitting on a chair by the fire deeply absorbed in a book. She looked up in surprise. Sarah had obvious intentions of following him into the room, but he shut the door in her face.

Beth put her book down and eyed him warily, although her tone when she spoke was neutral, if formal.

"Well, Richard, I assume this is not a social call. What is the matter?"

"I need to speak to you on a matter of the utmost importance," he said pompously. His eyes were eager and he was clearly very excited about something. Beth's heart sank. Whatever it was, she was sure she would not share his enthusiasm.

"What is it?" she asked tiredly.

"Sir Anthony Peters wishes to make a proposal of marriage to you."

Beth stared at him.

"You are joking with me, Richard. You must be," she said after a moment. "If you wished to find an excuse to talk to me and reconcile matters between us, you could surely have fabricated a better story than that."

"I'm not trying to reconcile matters between us," Richard retorted impatiently. "Well, I do want to, of course," he amended, rather insincerely.

"A simple apology for destroying my property would suffice," she suggested coldly, knowing he would offer no such thing.

"Yes, well, of course I am sorry for causing you any distress, but I acted as I did in the interests of both of us, you must have realised that."

Beth was astounded. With one notable exception, she had never heard her brother apologise for any action he had taken, no matter how violent or outrageous. Even though he had qualified his apology, still it put her immediately on high alert.

"You're not joking, are you? He really *has* proposed marriage."

"Not exactly, but he does intend to. He came to me this morning to ask my opinion as to how you might receive a proposal from him."

"And what did you say?"

Richard had the grace to look at least a little embarrassed before he answered.

"I told him that I was sure you would be honoured, and that you would give it serious consideration."

"I see," Beth replied. Richard could surely not believe for one minute that she would entertain this proposal, and would be expecting her to lose her temper. If she could remain composed she had a chance of wrong-footing him.

"Did he tell you why he wishes to marry me?" she asked. "After all, he has a permanent entourage of silly girls who would jump at the chance of marriage to him, and who are eminently more compatible with him than I am."

"He only told me that he finds you very beautiful, and that he is quite overcome by affection for you."

This was so obviously a quote from the horse's mouth that Beth laughed out loud.

"How many gesticulations did he use to embellish his words?" She placed the back of her hand on her forehead and threw her head back. "My dear boy, I positively think I shall *die* if she refuses me," she drawled in a creditable imitation of Sir Anthony's slightly high-pitched voice.

Richard watched her, his face stony. Beth sighed. He must have inherited his lack of humour from his mother, she thought. Papa would have roared with laughter at the whole idea of his daughter marrying such a feeble-minded popinjay. She was unexpectedly assaulted by a wave of grief at the realisation that she would never hear her father laugh again, and sank back down into her chair, rubbing her hand fiercely across her face to fight back the tears that threatened.

"What has he promised you?" she asked bluntly. When Richard opened his mouth to deny that he had been promised anything, she hurriedly continued before he could speak.

"Don't lie to me. Let us be honest with each other, for once. If I can make a good marriage and in doing so end my financial dependency on you, I will. But I will not marry that affected molly, Richard, not even to escape you." Her voice was soft, but steely.

She saw his face redden and his fist clench, and determined that she would not lose her temper, no matter what he did. She had the advantage this time; he wanted something from her. He seemed to realise this, and unclenched his fist with obvious effort.

"Elizabeth," he said. "The man is reported to be immensely wealthy. He certainly dresses as though he is, and he has influential friends in very high places."

"I seem to remember we thought the same of the earl of Highbury's son, and look what a mistake that turned out to be," his sister replied.

"Yes, but Sir Anthony is quite a different proposition to Lord Daniel."

He most certainly was. In spite of the fact that he amused her at times, the thought of any intimate physical contact with him made her shudder with horror.

"You're right. But then you must agree that you cannot assume Sir Anthony is rich just because he spends a fortune on clothes. Do you know if his tailor's bills are paid regularly?"

"They are," Richard replied immediately, thereby betraying

that he had been expecting this proposal for some time and had done at least some research into the man's credentials. "Everyone knows of his background, although I'll research into it further if you wish. And no one can deny that the man is influential. Why, even the king himself thinks very highly of him!"

"The king is taken in by him, Richard, as is everyone else. Who would not be amused by such a witty chameleon? But you can save yourself the trouble of looking any further into his family tree. I am not going to marry him. Why, I cannot spend more than an hour in the man's company without him irritating me, let alone the rest of my life!"

"Beth, please, don't dismiss him out of hand. See reason. We are not titled or wealthy. Father worked hard to provide you with a dowry. You owe it to him to make a good marriage."

All Beth's pacifistic intentions almost foundered in her anger that he would dare to use her father's love to persuade her. But her tactic was working. Her coolness was keeping her brother's temper under restraint. Either that, or Sir Anthony had promised him the moon. She was quite enjoying listening to her brother plead with her. This was really important to him.

"What did Sir Anthony promise you, Richard?" she asked again.

This time he answered the question.

"He has promised to buy me my cornet's commission, and provide the funds for a lieutenant's commission as soon as a place becomes vacant. He promised to mention me to the duke of Cumberland when next they meet. He will also use his influence to help Lord Edward as far as he can. And he's also agreed to finance some of the repairs and improvements to our house in Didsbury."

Beth whistled through her teeth, ignoring Richard's look of disgust at her unladylike gesture. She couldn't care less about his promotion, but it would be wonderful to see her house restored to its former glory. But what was she thinking of? In spite of Richard's words, the house was no longer theirs but his and his alone, as he delighted in reminding her on a regular basis.

"No, I'm sorry, but I won't do it. You will just have to tell him that I decline his proposal." She had carefully moved into position as she was speaking, and now had her hand on the door handle, ready to run if he should react. But he made no attempt to assault her, although he was looking at her with murder in his eyes.

"I can't do that," he replied. "I've already told him that you'll meet him in the drawing room at four. You'll have to refuse him yourself, if you're going to. But remember, if you say no to him, you *will* say yes to Lord Redburn. Both Edward and I are determined on that."

He brushed past her and stalked out of the room, leaving a pale-faced Beth even more determined not to marry Sir Anthony, and trying unsuccessfully to convince herself that she could withstand both him and Edward with regards to Lord Redburn.

* * *

"I can't believe I'm doing this," Beth gasped as she arrived at the door of the drawing room. Sarah had helped Beth to dress for her meeting with Sir Anthony, and had insisted on lacing her mistress's stays so tightly that she could hardly breathe. In Sarah's view, it seemed a hand-span waist was a crucial aid in rejecting an unwelcome marriage proposal.

She paused a moment in the hall to compose herself, and then, standing erect and raising her head, she opened the drawing room door and entered, closing it firmly behind her.

Her rose-pink skirts rustled as she moved into the room and Sir Anthony, who had been standing by the window looking out across the square with his hands clasped behind his back, turned round at once.

He can't have been waiting long, she thought. Any room he spent more than five minutes in reeked of violets, and she couldn't smell his obnoxious cologne at all.

"My darling Elizabeth!" he piped, coming towards her and taking her arm. "How beautiful you look! Do sit down." He ushered her into a chair and moved across to a table in the centre of the room, which had been set with a number of plates of small cakes and dainty biscuits along with a teapot and two delicate Sevres cups and saucers, chatting as he went.

"Isabella was kind enough to provide the most delightful fancies for us and even a pot of the finest Bohea tea, which is prohibitively expensive, as I'm sure you know. She has assured me that we will not be disturbed, so we can have a most pleasant chat." He lifted the teapot. "I have so been looking forward to this meeting. Shall I pour you a cup of tea, my dear, or would you care to partake of a cake first? Or perhaps a biscuit? They are the most exquisite little things, and…"

Beth had stood up and made her way across to the table. She placed her hand flat across the top of the cup he had been about to pour tea into, and only his quick reflexes stopped him from pouring the hot liquid over her hand.

"Why?" she asked. She stared him straight in the eye, and he met her look for a moment before turning away and replacing the pot carefully on its stand. She could still smell no trace of violets, and realised with surprise and relief that he was not wearing perfume today. *He must feel naked,* she thought, amused, although he had not stinted on his powder and rouge. Beth repressed a shudder of distaste as he reached delicately for a cake, placing it on his plate with precision before addressing her question.

"Why does anyone eat such dainties, my dear? For the pure indulgence of the senses…"

"That was not what I was asking. Why do you want to marry me?"

Sir Anthony put his hand on his breast, shock written all over his face.

"My dear Elizabeth, do you not think you are being a little previous? I have not actually proposed to you yet, you know."

"No, but we both know you intend to. After all, that is the only reason we are here. Why?"

"You confound me. I had planned the most beautiful speech, designed to win over the most recalcitrant of ladies, and you have destroyed the moment utterly." He did not look *that* distraught, Beth thought, although in truth it was difficult to ascertain any but the most extreme of expressions on his face. The delicate changes in colouring that told her whether someone was shocked, embarrassed, about to lose his temper, were completely concealed on Sir Anthony under the heavy layer of paint. The man could be positively beetroot with distress and she would not have the slightest inkling of it.

"I am sorry if I have ruined your flowery speech. But it seems you have anticipated that I would be recalcitrant, and I assure you I appreciate plain speaking far more than lengthy monologues devoid of any content or genuine feeling. So I ask you again, why do you want to marry me?"

Sir Anthony sighed. Picking up the teapot again he poured them both a cup, briskly, without any of his customary affected gestures. He handed one cup to her, retaining the other for himself. Motioning her to be seated, he took the chair opposite her, arranging his coat carefully to ensure that it didn't crease. Beth stirred her tea and waited while he considered his reasons.

"Very well," he said at last. "I have lands in the north, and the lease on a house in London, which you would be the mistress of. I can promise you adventure, travel to interesting places, and the acquaintance of stimulating people, which I know you crave. We would, of course, have to consummate the marriage, if I may be so indelicate as to mention it, although you did ask for plain speaking, did you not? But after that, I assure you that if you find my continuing attentions distasteful I will not press them upon you, although if we remain together I would of course demand that to outward appearances we retain the semblance of a devoted couple. And, what is probably of greatest importance to you, marriage to me will free you to a great extent from this life you hate so much and which you are finding increasingly difficult to endure. It will also free you entirely from the machinations of your self-seeking bully of a brother." Sir Anthony sat back in his chair and sipped his tea, regarding Beth over the rim of his cup with a pair of slate-blue eyes that suddenly seemed to hold a great deal more intelligence than they had a moment before.

"Caroline has told you all this," she said in a shocked voice.

"Not at all, my dear. She would never divulge a confidence. I have eyes in my head. I have observed you closely over the last weeks. You are most dreadfully unhappy, and are fast reaching the point of collapse."

"And you think marriage to you will prevent that?" she asked mockingly.

"Most assuredly so," he replied calmly, taking a tiny bite of his cake.

Beth was speechless. She had expected an overblown declaration of love, promises of undying devotion, not this list of practicalities coupled with a highly astute and intensely disconcerting knowledge of her personality and family relationships. Now she knew what it must be like to be an insect pinned to a board and inspected minutely. Feeling the blush rise steadily up her throat to her face, she looked away from him, trying to regain the upper hand. When she looked back she detected a distinct sparkle of humour in his eyes, which disappeared almost immediately.

"I see I have embarrassed you, my dear Elizabeth, which I assure you was not my intention at all," he said. "If you had only let me do as I wished, and propose to you in the proper manner…but you did insist on plain speaking and it is of course a prospective husband's duty to indulge his lady in everything. Please do not be angry with me, I could not bear it."

Ten minutes before she would have taken his words at face value, but now she wondered if he was being sarcastic, and looked at him suspiciously. But neither his voice nor his expression held the slightest trace of insincerity. She pulled her scattered wits together and tried again.

"You have still not answered my question," she said.

"Have I not?" he asked, his face all innocence. "What more reason could you need to consider my proposal?"

"You have told me why I might wish to marry you. But you have not told me why *you* wish to marry *me,* which is quite a different thing."

"Yes, of course. Well then, let me consider. You are, as I'm sure you know, a most beautiful and vivacious young woman, whose talents I both respect and would like to encourage. I would like to see you develop to your full potential, and it would delight me to help you to do so." He held up a hand to stop her as she was about to interrupt him. "I assure you that whatever you may believe to the contrary, I am speaking the truth. Please allow me to proceed. I do, most assuredly, hold you in deep regard. I am aware that you do not feel the same for me, but I have hopes that you may come to think differently towards me once we are married. Of course, there are also practical considerations, and I will not insult your intelligence by denying that. There is the matter of your dowry, which is a not inconsiderable sum. And there is also the fact that I am heartily sick of being pursued by women in whom I have not the slightest interest, and of having my pedigree and status investigated by hopeful parents. It would be most pleasant also to have children eventually, but that is a secondary motive, and will depend on how our relationship develops. As I stated before, I most certainly will not force my attentions upon you. I also promise you that whilst you are married to me, you will have my full protection against anyone who tries to hurt you. And of course as my bride, you will remove me from the marriage market, for which you will have my undying gratitude." He smiled at her, before offering further refreshments.

She accepted his offer of another cup of tea and a cake, and whilst he was occupied, considered his words. Her first instinct, in spite of her earlier resolve, was to accept him. His arguments were very plausible, if they were genuine, but she was also aware that he had unbalanced her by his unpredictable behaviour, and she did not want to make a decision that she would regret as soon as she had left the room.

She dithered, eating her cake and drinking her second cup of tea in silence. He did not press her for a decision as she had half expected him to do. Instead he resumed the position he had been in when she entered the room, looking out of the window.

After a few minutes, she could stand it no longer. She stood, and returned her cup and plate to the table.

"Sir Anthony," she ventured. He turned round at once, waiting politely for her to continue. "I am sorry, but I find I cannot give you an answer immediately. I need a little time to consider your proposal."

"I quite understand, my dear Elizabeth. After all, marriage is a life-changing decision. You would be foolish to commit yourself without due consideration. Take a few days to think about it, and give me your answer when you are ready."

She turned at once to leave the room, anxious to be away from this confusing man.

"Oh, I nearly forgot," he called when she was almost at the door. "I have a little present for you." She turned back to see him fumbling in the pocket of his coat. He produced a small package, wrapped in tissue and tied with silver ribbon.

"You are most kind, Sir Anthony, but I really couldn't accept a present, especially when I have not consented to your proposal." She held her hand up in a gesture of refusal as he tried to give the gift to her.

"You have not declined my proposal either," he pointed out

reasonably. "And I was going to give this to you in any case, whatever your answer. Please, it would make me very happy." His eyes were eager, and she gave in. He had shown her the utmost courtesy. It would be churlish of her to refuse his gift.

"Thank you." He stood back while she opened it, untying the pretty ribbon with care. Inside was a small case of supple blue leather, tooled with an intricate interweaving Celtic pattern. She opened the tiny button that closed it and looked inside. Nestling in the little case was a rosary, of amber and silver.

The shock was so enormous she forgot to breathe for a moment, and when she tried to inhale in a desperate attempt to recover her equilibrium, her over-tight stays prevented her from taking in the air she so desperately needed. The colour drained from her face and tiny white lights swam at the edge of her vision. She struggled again unsuccessfully to fill her lungs with air, forgetting to take shallow breaths, which were all the corset would allow, and felt her knees buckle under her as panic overtook her.

Sir Anthony caught her as she fell, lifting her easily and dumping her unceremoniously onto a nearby stool before tilting her forward slightly. She was dimly aware of something cold and smooth sliding down her back, then he gripped her shoulders and gently lifted her back into a sitting position. Crouching down on the floor at the side of the stool, he supported her back with one arm.

"Now breathe, slowly and deeply," he commanded.

To her great relief she found that the restriction around her chest had eased, and she sucked in a great lungful of air, holding it for a moment before exhaling slowly. After a few moments she had recovered enough to realise that the reason she was able to breathe so easily was because he had cut the laces of her stays.

He removed his arm from her back once he judged her capable of supporting herself, and knelt on the floor in front of her.

"I am sorry," he said. In his hand he held the little case with its treacherous contents. "I only wished to please you. I am afraid that the leather was quite blackened and ruined by the fire, too much so for me to ascertain its original colour. I hope the new one is acceptable to you. But the contents were quite undamaged. I thought you would be happy to have them returned. I know they are of great sentimental value to you."

He had heard every word of the argument between her and Richard in the library, she now realised, and with his 'gift' was warning her of what he would do with his knowledge if she refused him. She reached out slowly and took the case from him, raising her eyes to his, expecting to see triumph there. But the dark blue gaze held only warmth and concern.

Which shows how easily duplicity comes to him, she thought, knowing now that all his extravagant promises were nothing but lies. Not only was he a weathervane, but an extremely dangerous one, and she was now facing the consequences of having underestimated him completely. Flashing him a look of utter hatred, she rose to her feet and left the room quickly and silently, leaving him kneeling on the floor in front of the empty stool as though in supplication.

Once in her room she bolted the door to ensure that no one would enter unexpectedly. Then she took out the rosary, running the translucent golden beads through her fingers. They were her greatest treasure; never would she have believed that she would be sorry to have them returned to her. After a moment she bent her head and began to tell the beads, holding each tiny golden sphere between her thumb and forefinger as she recited the Hail Mary softly, moving on to the next as she finished, and repeating the prayer. The rhythmic chanting of the familiar words soothed her, as they always had, but as she recited them she was not calling to mind the Blessed Mysteries, as the Church bade her do, but was allowing the import of the last hour to sink into her mind, hoping a solution would present itself.

Having finished, she kissed the tiny tortured figure of Christ on the cross and replaced the beads back in their case. Then she sat on the bed with her hands in her lap, calm now, and contemplated her options.

She could refuse Sir Anthony's proposal, which she so desperately wanted to do. Would he denounce her if she did? Whatever he may claim to be, Sir Anthony was most definitely a supporter of the Hanoverian succession. Although he seemed to show no particular interest in their politics, he was regularly to be seen in the company of prominent Whigs, and King George certainly thought highly of him. Both the timing of his return of her rosary, together with his words, were a warning, of that she was sure. He knew that the rosary was particularly precious to her, which meant he had probably overheard her reading the Gaelic inscription. He therefore knew that her mother was of Scottish extraction and a Catholic, and probably suspected that Beth herself was one, too. On its own that was not enough to get her into trouble with the authorities, but it would arouse suspicion that she had Jacobite sympathies. As rumours of an imminent Jacobite rising continuously circulated in England, leading to a paranoid suspicion of all Catholics, and Scottish ones in particular, the revelation that Sergeant Richard Cunningham's sister was possibly both would not do him any favours in his military career, and would certainly result in them both being ostracised from society. The thought of returning ignominiously to Didsbury along with a vengeful brother who enjoyed inflicting pain and with no friends powerful enough to protect her from his wrath, made Beth shudder.

On the other hand, the thought of being blackmailed into marrying a devious, effeminate fop was equally abhorrent to her, although possibly less life-threatening. Once they were married, she would be safe. Sir Anthony could not then denounce her without incriminating himself. She knew what her decision must be. There was no point in wasting time hunting for a way out. There *was* no way out.

The next morning she sent Sarah to Sir Anthony's house with a note, stating that she had given his proposal some thought and had decided to accept it. She did not sign it, nor did she add any endearments. They both knew why she had accepted him. Let the victor claim his prize, but if he expected any joy from his conquest, he was to be sadly mistaken.

Chapter Sixteen

As soon as Beth's feminine cousins heard about her betrothal to Sir Anthony Peters, the preparations for the marriage got under way. Charlotte in particular was in her element, chatting away for hours about her own wedding day to dear Frederick, and the subsequent if brief bliss she had enjoyed before his untimely death a year later.

Sir Anthony had expressed a desire to be married as soon as possible, certainly within the next six weeks, as he said he would like to take his wife on a short journey before the winter rendered travel impossible.

"If you will indulge your husband, my dear Elizabeth," he had simpered. "It would give me the utmost pleasure to show you the sights of Europe. I thought we could spend maybe six weeks abroad, perhaps a little longer if the air agrees with you. What do you say, my dear?"

Beth had said that she couldn't care less. If she was going to marry him, it may as well be sooner than later. He had not shown any discomfort at her distinct lack of enthusiasm, and had merely pointed out that in that case they would need to depart the country before the end of August. He would arrange their passage, foreign itinerary and accommodation, and would leave all arrangements for the actual wedding ceremony in her capable hands.

The date was set for the first week of August, which gave a bare three weeks for the preparations to be made. As a result of this the house was filled from morning till night with dressmakers, caterers and florists. Lord Edward's only contribution to the proceedings was to suggest that they have a private ceremony by licence at the Cunningham house rather than a huge public church affair. Although this was common enough amongst genteel brides, Beth suspected that Edward's motives for suggesting it were financially motivated. She agreed with alacrity, and without consulting her bridegroom. He had, after all, left everything to her, and she had hardly seen him since the proposal.

To Beth's relief she was no longer restricted in her movements by Richard and Edward, who now spent as much time as possible at their club to avoid the female hysteria which had overtaken the house. She indulged her cousins. It was nice to see them so animated. She had not made things easy for them, she knew that, and felt a little guilty about it. Now she made reparation by allowing them a free rein with her wedding, in which she had no interest at all, although she did her best to feign enthusiasm, certainly managing enough to satisfy Isabella et al.

When it all got too much, she would repair to Edwin and Caroline's house, with whom she had an agreement not to mention the word 'wedding' or anything associated with it. If Caroline found this a little difficult to do at times, she showed no sign of it, making no mention either of marriage or Sir Anthony, for which Beth was extremely grateful.

Instead they chatted happily away about politics and crime, the latest scientific discoveries, and the uncomfortable early effects of being pregnant. The couple had finally announced the pregnancy just over a week ago, and it was a relief to Caroline to share the details with a genuinely interested audience who did not regale her with lurid tales of agonising childbirth experiences.

Back at the Cunninghams' Clarissa took charge of the music, Charlotte the flowers, Isabella the catering, and all of them had a hand in the making of Beth's dress, an elaborate confection of cornflower-blue silk, which shade exactly matched the bride's eyes. The bodice and skirt were heavily embroidered with silver thread and crystals, and the whole ensemble was so heavy that Beth wondered how she would manage to stagger down the stairs and across the drawing room to take her vows without collapsing along the way. She had no doubt that it would be considered most becoming for the ecstatic bride to faint at the altar, as it were, but she had no intention of doing so. She wanted to look Sir Anthony straight in the eye when she exchanged vows with him and let him know that although he may have coerced her into the wedding, she would not prove to be a submissive partner.

The happy groom turned up unexpectedly one day, and was shown into the drawing room by a footman. He eyed the seating plans spread out on the floor with interest, before accepting Charlotte's invitation to sit down. If he found it strange that the three sisters were poring avidly over wedding plans whilst his bride-to-be was ensconced in the corner with a book, he did not comment.

"I seem to have called at a most opportune moment," he addressed the company with a beaming smile. "It is the guest list that I wish to discuss."

"Oh, Sir Anthony," Isabella cried. "Have you overlooked some member of your family, or a friend? I am sure we can find space for a few more people, if we are careful." Her brow knitted as she looked at the plans, crowded with names.

"No, no, my dear Isabella," Sir Anthony hastened to reassure her. "No, as you are no doubt aware, I am the sole survivor of the Peters family, thanks to the smallpox epidemic in France. If only we had thought to vaccinate, but Mother thought it a risky operation…but there is no point in speculating on what might have been," he said sadly. "If I have any distant cousins, I am not aware of them. As for friends, well, I have noted that it seems more than half of the guests are my friends." He paused. The fact that the remaining guests were all friends of Lord Edward and his sisters hovered in the air unsaid. In fact the only people Beth had invited were Edwin and Caroline, and they could more properly be numbered amongst Sir Anthony's guests, as he had known them for longer. "It seems a little…ah…unfairly distributed. I thought perhaps Elizabeth would like to invite some family members."

Beth put her book to one side, although she did not move from her corner.

"I appreciate your consideration, Sir Anthony," she said. "But all the Cunninghams have been invited, as far as I know."

"Indeed they have," trilled Clarissa. "We are but few, Sir Anthony, but great-aunt Arabella is expected to attend with her son."

"Yes, but then of course there is another side to the family.

Are there no relations on your mother's side who you would like to invite, my dear?" He looked at his fiancée expectantly.

Every muscle in Beth's body tensed.

"My mother's family were Scots, as you know," she answered tightly.

"I am aware of that. But I see that as no bar to them being invited. I have attended more than one wedding in Scotland myself, and assure you the natives of the country certainly know how to celebrate."

Beth was sure they did. As sure as she was that even if she were in contact with any of her mother's family, they would not be welcome at this particular wedding.

"I do not correspond with any of my mother's kin. In any case, they live in the Highlands. It is a long way to come for the wedding of a cousin they have never met." Hopefully he would leave it there.

"What is your mother's clan?" Sir Anthony continued gaily, ignoring the fact that Isabella and Charlotte were uncharacteristically silent.

"Her surname was MacDonald," Beth supplied curtly. She took up her book again, a very impolite sign that she considered the conversation to be at an end.

"MacDonald. Ah, but there are several branches of the MacDonalds, are there not? Keppoch, Glencoe, Clanranald, to name but a few." He looked at her innocently. Why was he doing this?

"You seem to know a great deal about the Scots, Sir Anthony," Charlotte ventured nervously.

"Indeed, I have numerous connections in Scotland, and find it a most hospitable country," he replied.

"My mother's family were not from Edinburgh, sir," Beth said scathingly. She remembered him once telling her he had been there on business. No doubt he thought the whole of Scotland to be like its capital city. Beth, who had never been north of the border, felt she knew the country better through her mother's reminiscences than he, the quintessential fop, ever could. The English-speaking people of Edinburgh considered the Gaelic-speaking Highlanders to be no less lawless and barbaric than the English did.

"I am not talking about Edinburgh," Sir Anthony waved his hand airily about, "as beautiful as it is. No, the weddings I have attended were both far north of that fair city. And I have had other dealings with Highlanders."

"Oh, Sir Anthony, you are very brave!" cried Isabella, while Beth was trying to imagine what the warlike, hard-drinking clansmen would have thought of her betrothed as he mincingly danced a minuet at their weddings. "Were you not afraid to deal with such savage…" her voice trailed off and she looked nervously at Beth, no doubt expecting an explosion.

Beth had hardly heard her cousin's words. She focussed only on Sir Anthony. In spite of his air of casualness she was certain there was a hidden agenda. What was he trying to tell her? That he did not consider it a matter of shame that half her blood was barbaric? Or was he trying to find out her mother's clan so as to discover how involved they had been in the Jacobite rebellions, to gain a further hold over her? That was the most likely reason, she thought.

"I do not wish to invite any Scottish relatives I may have to my wedding. And although I have friends in Manchester whom I could invite, I do not think they would care to be present at such a…" she had been going to say farce, but managed to stop herself just in time, "an occasion," she finished, her tone making it very clear that she would discuss the subject no further. She picked up her book and resumed reading.

"It is such a shame," said Charlotte wistfully, "that the king is out of the country at the moment. I am sure he would wish to be present at the wedding of such a close friend as yourself, Sir Anthony."

The baronet perused the crowded seating plan with interest. Richard had been placed next to Beth at the top table. He glanced at his bride-to-be, who appeared completely absorbed in her book. It was doubtful that she was even aware of what was certainly a faux pas on the part of Isabella.

"Perhaps you would wish to delay the wedding until his Majesty returns?" Isabella asked doubtfully. Sir Anthony observed her anxious frown, and smiled reassuringly.

"Oh, my dear Isabella, I would not be so bold as to call myself a *close* friend of the king's! I would not dream of spoiling all your exquisite plans, unless of course, my darling fiancée would prefer to postpone our nuptials in the hope that the king would condescend to attend our modest affair."

His darling fiancée looked up, enraged. How dare he provoke her this way? The last thing she would want was for the usurper to the throne to attend her wedding, as he well knew. He also knew that she could hardly say so outright, in front of her innocent and well-intentioned cousins.

"Oh, I see no sense in delaying the wedding," she replied. He smiled, and she lowered her eyes modestly to lull him into a false sense of security. "After all, the king has been over the water for some considerable time, and shows no sign of being able to return at present. Although of course, with his son's assistance, we may hope for an earlier return than expected."

Beth smiled a challenge at her fiancé, ignoring Isabella and Clarissa's twin gasps of shock. They at least had realised that while this remark could apply to George and William Augustus, it was in actuality more appropriate to the exiled James Stuart and his son Charles. Indeed, the only man ever referred to as 'the king across the water' *was* James, and he was only referred to as this by Jacobites.

Sir Anthony nodded slightly in acknowledgement of this hit. He glanced up at the pale faces of the cousins, then back at Beth. His eyes sparkled, and even before he spoke she knew she had not succeeded in discomfiting him.

"Indeed, if you wish so much for the king and his son's blessing on our union, I see no reason why we may not make a slight detour to visit them whilst we are on our travels. Would you like that, my darling?"

Beth had no desire whatsoever to be his darling, or to further her acquaintance with the Elector of Hanover and his overweight second son, as her husband-to-be well knew.

"I hardly think the king will be disposed to entertain his subjects at such a crucial moment in his life, sir," she replied coldly. She flashed Sir Anthony a look of dislike, and to her surprise he looked puzzled, even hurt momentarily, before he lowered his gaze back to the paper spread out before him.

"Well, then," he said brightly after a moment, favouring Isabella with his most charming smile. "It seems that none of us need to alter our plans in any way. My dear fiancée is most considerate, is she not?"

Beth returned to her book. Isabella bit her lip uncertainly.

"Although I do think, my dear Isabella," he continued smoothly, "that as the senior lady of the Cunningham family, it would certainly be more appropriate for you rather than Sergeant Cunningham to sit next to the bride. I am sure he would not mind being moved."

Beth's eyes flickered, but she did not raise them from her book.

"Oh, what an excellent suggestion!" enthused Charlotte, who had realised that the atmosphere in the room had become uncomfortable after she had mentioned the king, but had no idea why. "When I was married to my poor dear Frederick, Isabella remained at my side all day. I could not have done without her. The excitement, you realise…"

Isabella blushed, Sir Anthony beamed, and if anyone noticed that the bride took no further part in the resultant lively discussion of the seating arrangements, no one commented on it.

* * *

Dear Friends,

I am writing to tell you that I have finally accepted a proposal, and am to marry Sir Anthony Peters on the fifth of August. I have accepted him, because, if I had not, I would certainly have been forced by my brother and cousin to marry Lord Redburn. I am truly unhappy, so much so that I feel increasingly desperate. The days drag endlessly by, and…

Beth crumpled up the expensive sheet of paper and threw it to the floor. She laid her pen to one side, and put her head in her hands despairingly. She had to tell Jane, Thomas and Graeme, she knew that. She had waited a week, and could delay writing the letter no more. But she had to tell them in a way that would not cause them to worry unduly. She sighed, and busied herself with trimming another quill while she tried to order her thoughts.

Dear Friends,

I am writing to tell you that I have accepted a proposal of marriage from Sir Anthony Peters, and am to be married on the fifth of August. I have considered my situation, and think it to be the best thing. I will not pretend to you that I am in love with the man. You have seen him, albeit briefly, and know how unlikely it would be that I could become infatuated with such a creature. However, I have come to know him in the last months…

She paused, her brow furrowing, then carefully inserted two words into her previous sentence.

I have come to know him a little in the last months, and he seems to be kind, and in no way a violent man. Everyone seems to feel that he cares for me, and he can be very amusing and witty. He has assured me sincerely that he will allow no one to hurt me, and that he will not force me to do anything against my will. Of course, it goes without saying that he will pay for Richard's commission. And once I am married, the hold Richard has over all of us will be gone. I would urge you to seek other positions. I have spoken to Sir Anthony about the possibility of him employing you all, so that you could remain together, but he has regretfully said it is not possible at present. He did rather enigmatically state that he has a possible solution to the situation, but refuses to discuss it until after the wedding, by which time he says he will be more certain as to whether the solution is a viable one. He will not be drawn further on the topic, but I assure you that as soon as we are married I will pursue the matter relentlessly.

I have not invited you, or any of my friends to the wedding, as I cannot pretend it will be a happy event for me. Instead, after my honeymoon (six weeks or so in Europe), I hope to travel up alone to visit you, when we can have our own party to celebrate my liberation from Richard. I will look forward to that, more than you can imagine.

She put her pen down, and re-read the letter. Yes, it would do. She picked up her pen again, and settled to the more simple task of describing the wedding preparations, her outfit, and caricaturing the various characters who would be appearing at the performance, as she thought of it. Certainly there would be more play-acting on the fifth of August than had ever been seen at a Drury Lane production.

* * *

Sir Anthony moved gracefully down the carpeted corridor that led to the duke of Newcastle's private apartments, looking around with interest at the Palladian décor. Statues of Roman Emperors long deceased stared severely at him from alcoves, and elegant marble columns made a pretence of supporting the ornate plastered ceiling. Certainly designed to impress and intimidate, Sir Anthony thought, as the footman stopped at a set of double doors and rapped imperiously three times. A voice from within barked a command, the doors were opened and Sir Anthony was ushered in to a private interview with Thomas Pelham, Duke of Newcastle, Secretary of State and brother to the current First Lord of the Treasury.

Sir Anthony looked to be neither intimidated nor particularly impressed. He now ceased his perusal of his surroundings and turned his attention to the imposing figure of the man who rose from his chair by the fire and came to greet his visitor. Every inch of him screamed ancient aristocracy; the aquiline nose, the mouth, narrow but finely shaped. His wig was old-fashioned, long and curling past his shoulders, and his clothes exquisitely tailored but a sober brown in colour, in startling contrast to his visitor's canary yellow breeches and waistcoat, and royal blue frock coat. If he was surprised to see such a garish display of finery, the duke was too well bred to comment on it. Instead he accepted the deep bow of his guest with a nod, and beckoned him to a chair.

Sir Anthony sat, arranging the skirts of his coat fussily, and waited for the duke to tell him why he had been summoned to see him.

"Well, Sir Anthony, I suppose you wish to know why I asked you to attend me this morning," the duke began, after having waited a short time for the baronet to ask the question.

"I must confess to a mild curiosity, yes," Sir Anthony admitted, deliberately understating his feelings considerably. He relaxed back a little in his chair and waited for the duke to continue.

"I would like to congratulate you on your impending marriage, sir," Newcastle said. "I have not yet had the pleasure of meeting the bride, but have been told that she is the most beautiful woman in London. You must be very happy."

"Thank you," Sir Anthony replied politely. "I would say that you are not misinformed as to my fiancée's appearance, although as the devoted groom, I would be bound to think her the finest woman in the capital."

"Yes, yes, quite so," said the duke, clearly having no more than the most superficial interest in the lovely Miss Cunningham. "I believe you intend to make a Grand Tour with your wife directly following the happy event."

Sir Anthony smiled. "Oh, I would hardly call it a Grand Tour, my lord. We only expect to be away for a short time, two or three months, perhaps. It depends entirely on Elizabeth. One must indulge one's partner, particularly in the early days, do you not think?"

"Certainly," said the duke enthusiastically, who only indulged anyone when it was in his own best interests to do so.

There was a pause. The duke of Newcastle had certainly not asked him here to merely make casual chit-chat about his forthcoming nuptials. Sir Anthony waited for him to come to the point, amusing himself by not giving his host any assistance.

"Ah… which countries are you intending to visit?" Newcastle asked casually.

"I have not yet fixed my itinerary. Would you perhaps care to make a recommendation, my lord?"

"I believe Rome is a most beautiful city, with many works of art that would delight even the most discerning lady."

Ah, here it was, then. Sir Anthony bent his head, as if considering the idea.

"I do not know, my lord. I had thought of Italy, it is true, but intended to confine our sojourn to the north – Venice, perhaps. I have been told that Rome is lovely, but it is of course so very…Catholic, would you not agree?" He looked up innocently at the duke, who turned away and began to pace the room.

"I understand that you may find Rome a somewhat distasteful place to visit, holding such staunch Anglican beliefs as you do. Indeed, it is greatly to your credit that your family succeeded in living for so many years in France without succumbing to the corruption of the Romish faith."

"We lived also in Switzerland for a goodly number of years," Sir Anthony informed the duke, although clearly he already knew that; he had no doubt that the man knew almost everything there was to know about the Peters family.

"Yes, yes," said the duke impatiently, waving a hand dismissively. "I will come to the point, sir. Both myself and the First Lord, to say nothing of the king himself, would be greatly indebted to you if you could see your way to including Rome in your itinerary."

"Oh, well, if you put it that way," replied the baronet, obviously deeply impressed by the fact that the king was thinking of him in the midst of his preoccupation with the foreign war. "I would be only too delighted to oblige. I will of course make detailed observations of all the beautiful buildings and monuments to be seen in that fair city. I take it that the king is thinking to visit the city himself then, at some point in the future?"

Newcastle looked sharply at his guest.

"Of course not, sir! The king would never dream of visiting the centre of popery! He has no interest in architecture and idolatrous art. I will make myself plain. We would like you to pay a call on James Stuart and his son, and report back anything that you think may be of interest to us."

Sir Anthony's face was immediately a picture of the utmost horror. He leapt to his feet.

"My God, how can you ask me to do such a thing! Visit the Pretender! I could not do it, nor could I ask my wife to endure the company of such a villain!" His hands fluttered wildly. "Besides, it is against the law! I would not dream of breaking the laws of this fair land. Why, my family would be disgraced forever!"

The duke looked at the quivering baronet with barely concealed distaste. He knew this was a mistake, and had told his brother so, in no uncertain terms. He was a master of the espionage game, operating a huge network of spies across Europe. This man was an empty-headed fool, in spite of his university education, and indiscreet too, which was worse. Left to his own devices, the duke would have abandoned the whole idea at this point, but the king had recommended Sir Anthony most forcefully.

"Nothing is against the law if the king himself sanctions it," Newcastle pointed out. "Your wife need never know you have made such a visit. Indeed, it would be better if she did *not* know. All the king asks is that you pay your respects to the Pretender, and express an interest in seeing his restoration to the throne." Before Sir Anthony could object, as he was obviously about to do, the duke hurried on.

"The king feels that you may be especially qualified to cultivate the friendship of the Pretender's son. You are of an age, are you not?"

"No," Sir Anthony said, still clearly shocked, but now starting to recover a little. He patted his face delicately with a scrap of lace from his pocket, taking care not to smudge his make-up. "He is some six or seven years younger than I, I think."

The duke made a dismissive gesture.

"Nevertheless, you have much in common, from what I am led to believe. Charles is also a f…" he stopped himself just in time from using the word 'fop' and continued smoothly, "fashionable man. All we ask is that you attempt to engage the boy in conversation, befriend him if possible. And then report back anything he says that may be of interest, or anything you note regarding what manner of man he is, and most particularly what his intentions are for the immediate future. We would be most grateful." Seeing that Sir Anthony still looked gravely doubtful, the duke continued. "I assure you, men who perform such services are considered to be the greatest of patriots. Your family will go down in history as being among those who helped to rescue England from the greatest danger she has ever faced."

"Well, I am not sure." The baronet was wavering, and Newcastle pressed home his advantage.

"You would of course be made a generous allowance for expenses, sir. I know that would not influence the decision of a man of honour such as yourself, but this should; I know of no man as fitted for the purpose as yourself. Your country is depending on you, sir, to find out more about this jumped-up puppy who dares to challenge the king, and to help us foil any plans he may have to restore the throne to his popish father."

"Oh, well, now that puts things in quite a different light," Sir Anthony said, preening noticeably. "I am sure I can include a short trip to Rome in my itinerary without any difficulty. I am greatly honoured that you think me fitted for such an important task, my lord." He smoothed down his coat and beamed obsequiously at his host.

"It goes without saying that we would expect you to behave with the utmost discretion. Not a word to anyone. You will, of course, submit a report of your findings to our representative in Florence, Sir Horace Mann, on your way back. I will write to him to inform him of your mission," the duke advised. He had not told anyone else. Only the First Lord and the king knew that Sir Anthony had been approached. If anyone else mentioned that Sir Anthony had been recruited as a spy, he would know where the rumour had come from, and would abandon the whole venture, being sure as he did to cast severe doubt on the loyalty of the baronet himself, and effectively ruin his reputation.

He was to be pleasantly surprised. In spite of ensuring that everything Sir Anthony said in the week between the interview and his wedding got back to him, the duke heard not a word about his private interview or its purpose. He did, however hear that Sir Anthony had expressed a desire to include Rome among the destinations to be visited, stating that he had heard it to be a most delightful city, in spite of its doctrinal errors. His wife-to-be had not been consulted on the matter, seeming in any case to be remarkably indifferent as to where her husband chose to take her on their honeymoon.

The duke felt this to be a good start. In spite of the spies that constantly hovered around the Stuart Court in Rome, none of them had succeeded in gaining the confidence of the Pretender's son. Perhaps a fool would succeed where the more polished and astute spies had failed. It was worth trying, at any rate. After allowing the man a reasonably generous expense account, he dismissed Sir Anthony Peters from his mind temporarily, and addressed himself to more pressing matters of state.

Chapter Seventeen

"There!" said Beth, inserting a final pin into her companion's elaborately dressed hair. "Now, stand up and let's see how you look."

Sarah stood and turned around slowly while her mistress looked her over critically.

"You look wonderful," Beth said honestly. She did. Dressed in a gown of rose-red *gros de tours* silk woven with trails of white roses over a hooped petticoat, her lustrous brown hair decorated with tiny white silk rosebuds and her slender neck circled by a rope of pearls borrowed from Beth, she was miraculously transformed from a ladies' maid into a lady of quality.

Sarah looked down at her dress, fingering the expensive silk with awe.

"You didn't need to do this, you know," she said.

"I know I didn't. I wanted to. It's the least I could do after everything you've done for me. I couldn't have wished for a better maid. I'm going to miss you terribly."

Sarah swallowed.

"I don't have to stay…" she began.

"Yes you do," Beth said briskly. "This is your opportunity to make something of yourself. If you come to Europe with us you'll lose the chance of the lease on the shop you've had your eye on." She didn't mention that Sir Anthony had been strangely reluctant for Sarah to stay on as Beth's maid once they were married, although he hadn't expressed it in so many words. "It's in a perfect spot, and you have enough recommendations now to ensure a select clientele. I will certainly be visiting you when I return to London."

"You better had," Sarah said shakily. "And I won't take a penny from you when you do."

"Just don't fall for the first handsome young man who comes calling. There'll be plenty of them hanging around once you start to make money."

Sarah curled her lip in disgust.

"I have no intention of ever getting married," she said. "I've seen enough of men and what they are under their fancy wigs and perfumed clothes to last me a lifetime." She paused, realising that this was not the most tactful thing to say to a young woman about to be married to a man she was not in love with. "Are you nervous about tomorrow?" she asked Beth as she slipped on her high-heeled cream leather shoes. She winced slightly. They were a little tight, but it didn't matter. They would only be walking a few yards from the coach to the theatre and back again.

Beth considered for a moment.

"Yes," she said, "I am. Not of the actual ceremony, but of putting myself in the power of another man, and a man I don't really know at all. Still, I think he's better than Richard, at least. And I don't have much choice really."

"It wouldn't be difficult to find a man better than your brother," Sarah said disdainfully, taking the ivory handled fan Beth offered her. "But Sir Anthony does have something else in his favour, apart from his wealth and his wit."

"What's that?" Beth asked.

"He's the only man I've ever met who doesn't look at a woman as though she's a brood mare."

Beth laughed. It was true, although she hadn't thought of it until now.

"Now that could mean one of two things," Sarah continued. "Either he has respect for women, or alternatively has no sexual interest in them at all and is more inclined towards men. Which means that in the bedchamber he'll either be considerate and attentive, or completely disinterested. What more could you ask for?"

A lot, thought Beth, although she knew she wasn't going to get it.

They settled themselves in Lord Edward's coach, and Beth tapped on the roof to signal to the driver that they were ready to leave.

"I'm really looking forward to this," Sarah said excitedly, settling her skirts around her. "I've never been to the opera before."

Beth was glad she had decided to spend her last night of freedom giving her maid a taste of luxury instead of enduring the ladies' card party Isabella had suggested. She had reserved their box at the King's Theatre in the Haymarket, and arranged for champagne and cinnamon cakes to be served in the interval. She felt Sarah's excitement start to infect her, giving a new novelty to what had over the last months become a chore. At least she would be able to concentrate on the performance tonight, instead of having to listen to the incessant chatter of her companions. Sarah would want to savour every moment, that was certain. And it would be a relief to get away from the mounting hysteria of her cousins' pre-wedding nerves, which were threatening her thin veneer of composure.

"Will I understand what's going on?" Sarah asked after a moment.

"No, because it's sung in Italian," replied Beth. "But you can buy programmes that tell you the story before the piece starts. I'll get one for us."

The coach lurched unexpectedly to a halt.

"We can't possibly be there already," Beth said, lifting the leather blind and looking out. The driver had jumped down.

"What's the matter, Tom?" Beth asked.

"One of the horses is limping a little, Miss," he said. "It's probably a stone, but I'd rather check, if you don't mind."

Beth pulled the blind back down.

"It's all right," she reassured Sarah. "We've got plenty of time. We'll still…"

The coach door opened suddenly and a man jumped in, sword in hand. He looked at Beth, and then at Sarah, who had uttered a little scream of shock.

"Get out," he said to her brusquely. When she didn't move, he leaned over and grabbing her arm, began to drag her across the seat.

Beth had at first thought their intruder was an opportunist thief who had seen the coach stop and was seizing his chance. But although the man had a black silk scarf tied round the lower part of his face, she recognised his voice at once.

"Daniel," she said. "What on earth are you doing? Let her go at once!"

His eyes widened at the mention of his name, but he offered no explanation. Instead he hauled the maid to her feet and pushed her roughly out of the carriage, slamming the door shut behind her, before turning back to Beth. She had started to rise from her seat, but subsided when he levelled his sword at her breast.

"Stay where you are," he said, and sitting down opposite her, he banged hard on the coach roof. It set off immediately at a brisk pace.

Sarah, who had landed on her hands and knees in the street, watched the coach disappear round the corner, noting the direction it took. Then she was on her feet, careless of the filth and slime that covered her beautiful gown, careless of the pain from her swelling knee. She picked up her skirts and ran in the opposite direction as fast as she could, pausing only momentarily to kick her shoes into the gutter, before speeding in the direction of Smith Square.

* * *

"I thought I'd lost you," Daniel said conversationally as the coach lurched along. "I couldn't believe my luck when I found out that you'd decided to go to the opera on the eve of your wedding, with only your maid for company."

"What are you talking about?" she asked. "Where are you taking me?"

"I thought we'd bring your wedding forward a bit. To tonight, to be precise. And there'll be one or two changes, the most important one being the bridegroom."

She stared at him. He had lowered his sword from her chest, but hadn't sheathed it, and was sitting opposite her, his handsome features relaxed and smiling.

"Are you telling me you intend to marry me?" she gasped.

"But of course. I am a gentleman. I wouldn't dream of ravishing you without the benefit of the law," he grinned.

This sort of thing didn't happen in real life, Beth thought frantically, only in the romantic novels Charlotte was so fond of reading.

"This can't be legal," she said. "No court in the land would uphold such a farce."

"Oh, I assure you they would. I have the ring," he patted his pocket, "and the minister is waiting. Everything is ready. All we have to do is make our vows, and then we can retire to the room I've rented to consummate our happy union."

She looked at him incredulously. In spite of his light-hearted tone, he was deadly serious.

"Don't you need to at least obtain a licence?"

"Oh, my love, in spite of your precocity, which I am looking forward to taming by the way, you are woefully ignorant of certain echelons of life. You don't need a licence to get married if you have the money and know where to go. Don't worry yourself, everything is prepared. And you do look enchanting," he said, eyeing her aqua silk gown with approval.

"You seem to be forgetting that I refused you six weeks ago. And nothing has happened to make me change my mind since then," she said coldly.

"Oh, come on," he said. "You can't possibly prefer that Frenchified perfumed fop to me. And he's only a baronet, for God's sake. If you marry me you'll be a Lady now, and a countess when my father dies and I inherit the earldom."

"Which will probably be many years from now," she replied. The coach was slowing slightly. Would she be able to get out of the door before he caught her? He would not be expecting her to try to escape before the coach stopped. She changed position slightly to give her better access to the door. "And in the meantime," she continued. "I believe he's refused to pay your gambling debts. I would rather be a rich baronet's wife than a lady pauper, thank you."

"But we won't be paupers," he pointed out. "Your dowry will pay off my debts and my father will reinstate my allowance once he knows I'm married. He has a soft spot for beautiful women. He would never let you starve."

He had really thought it all out. And he was absolutely convinced that she would be swayed by his looks and title into agreeing to his ridiculous proposal. She looked at his arrogant, petulant face and wondered what she had ever found attractive about him. Anger and indignation rose in her, but she swallowed them down with an effort. It would do her no good to lose her temper. The coach had slowed to a walking pace now. Beth made a sudden lunge for the door.

She almost made it. She was halfway through it before his fingers got enough purchase in her hair to wrench her backwards. She cried out as he tore her away from the door and threw her into her seat. Jewelled pins flew in all directions and her hair tumbled down around her shoulders.

His smile had vanished, and they locked gazes, his hot and brown, hers cold and blue.

"I will not marry you, Daniel," she said very clearly and slowly. Her scalp was on fire, and tears of pain stood in her eyes.

"Yes, you will," he replied, gripping her arm and pulling her to her feet as the coach came to a halt. The driver had jumped down, and caught Beth as Daniel pushed her roughly out of the door. Her suitor jumped down after her, and one on either side of her, the two men held her firmly by the arms so she could not attempt to run.

"Because if you do not," Daniel continued pleasantly, "then this will be my new home from tomorrow. And I have no intention of spending any time here, not when there is such a pleasant alternative available." They started to walk towards the entrance of a large gloomy building, half dragging, half carrying Beth between them. She looked up in horror at the unmistakable shape of the Fleet debtors' prison.

* * *

The card game was well under way when the filthy dishevelled woman dashed through the open front door and burst into the drawing room before anyone could stop her. Several ladies screamed in terror, and some of the gentlemen leapt to their feet.

Lord Edward was horrified at this intrusion into the sacred portals of his home by what was clearly a madwoman of some sort. She skidded to a halt a few feet into the room and stared wildly around, until her eyes rested on Sir Anthony, who, having declared himself too nervous to be able to concentrate on cards tonight, was standing behind Isabella, observing her game.

"Beth…" she tried to say, but no sound came out. Her chest was heaving with the effort of running at full pelt in inappropriate clothing. The whalebone of her stays cut into her waist, and she had an agonising stitch. She pressed her hand to her side and willed him to understand what her eyes were trying to say.

"How dare you barge into my house like this?" Sir Edward roared. "John, remove her from the room and call a constable at once!"

To the horror of the company, before the footman John had taken more than two paces in the intruder's direction, Sir Anthony shot across the room, drawing his sword as he ran. It seemed as though he was going to run the woman through, but before anyone could stop him he had reached Sarah, and turning her round he took hold of the neck of her dress and pulled hard, tearing it down the back from neck to waist. Raising his sword, he slashed through the laces of her stays expertly, without drawing a drop of blood.

"This is getting to be a habit," he muttered to himself.

Isabella fainted, landing on the floor with a crump, but no one took any notice. The spectacle before them was far too interesting for anyone to take their eyes away from it long enough to attend to their swooning hostess. Had Sir Anthony gone mad? Was he going to ravish the woman before their eyes? Who was she, anyway?

"Breathe," Sir Anthony commanded, taking off his emerald green coat and throwing it round the maid's shoulders.

Released from her restrictive clothing, she took several deep breaths, leaning against him.

"Beth," she croaked again after a few seconds. "He's taken her."

"Who has?"

"Lord Daniel. He threw me out of the coach."

The room was silent. Everyone was listening avidly.

"Did you see which way they went?" Sir Anthony asked. His voice was harsh and commanding, quite unlike his normal effeminate trill.

Sarah nodded, her chest still heaving, and seeing the eyes of several gentlemen fixed on her breasts, she drew the coat tighter around her.

"They went up the Strand. I think he's taking her to the Fleet prison," she said.

"Why would he take her to the Fleet? That's ridiculous!" said Lord Edward; but Sir Anthony was already out of the room, heading for the stables.

* * *

In the Fleet chapel the minister was waiting as they entered, the Book of Common Prayer open before him on the lectern.

"I will not agree to this!" Beth cried as they came to a stop at the altar. "I do not want to marry this man. I have been taken by force!" She addressed the minister, who looked down at her, his expression resigned and indifferent.

"I think the lady needs a little persuasion before we begin, my lord," he said. "But pray be quick about it. Time is money, as they say."

Lord Daniel took Beth by the shoulders gently.

"Beth, come on, see reason. I love you, truly I do. Once we are married I will turn over a new leaf, I promise."

"You think I will believe anything you say?" she cried. "No man of honour would behave as you have this night! I would not marry you if you were the king himself!" She pulled backward suddenly, tearing herself from his grip and would have run, but the coachman moved forward, blocking her escape. She turned back to Lord Daniel, and bringing her hand up hit him with all her strength across the face. His head snapped to one side, but before she could raise her arm again, he caught her by the wrist.

"By God, you will regret that!" he roared. His face was white, her handprint standing out livid across his cheek.

The minister tapped his fingers impatiently on the prayer book.

"My lord," he said, "if this is going to take time, might I suggest you return another day?"

"It will take no time at all, I assure you," Lord Daniel replied. "Hold her," he said, pushing her backwards to the coachman, who gripped her arms. In one smooth move, he drew his sword and pointed it at her chest. Her pupils widened, but she looked at him without flinching.

"I do not think that even *this* minister will marry you to a corpse. And my solicitor will certainly not release my dowry to you. You are wasting your time."

"I think not, my love. I have no intention of killing you. Hold out her hand," he commanded the coachman.

"What are you going to do?" the man asked. His voice was uncertain.

"I am going to cut her fingers off, one by one, until she agrees to marry me," Lord Daniel said coldly.

Tom felt Beth cringe instinctively backward into him. He did not like this. He had been promised ten guineas for allowing Lord Daniel to board the coach and had thought Beth would be persuaded to marry him en route.

"I don't want nothing to do with no bloodshed, my lord," Tom said, his voice shaking slightly.

"Don't worry, man, you'll be well recompensed," Lord Daniel said dismissively, gripping hold of Beth's wrist himself and holding it out horizontally.

"I will not marry you, whatever you do," Beth said, her voice trembling.

"You are very brave, my love, but also very stupid. Just how many fingers do you think I will have to cut off before you see sense and change your mind?"

"Oh, just the one, I would think," came a pleasant voice from the corner. "It is an excruciatingly painful operation, after all."

Lord Daniel spun round, dragging Beth in front of him. Sir Anthony was standing nonchalantly in the doorway. His wig was slightly askew, and he was missing his coat, but otherwise he looked exactly as he had an hour earlier when he had wished Beth a pleasant evening as she stepped into the coach. Except, of course, for the pistol in his hand, which was levelled at Lord Daniel's head.

Lord Daniel raised his sword, pressing the blade to Beth's throat.

"I will kill her," he threatened.

"Be my guest, my dear boy," Sir Anthony said. "Although I would beg you first to think about the consequences if you do." Behind him, Lord Edward appeared. Apparently on the point of barging past Sir Anthony into the chapel, he was restrained by another figure, who materialised a moment later from the shadows. Beth saw Richard, sword drawn, face white. A second later Edwin came into view. Sir Anthony showed no sign of being aware of the three men waiting tensely a few feet behind him. He continued chatting amiably.

"Firstly, of course, if you carry out your threat I would then be in the tiresome position of having to seek another bride. Secondly, I assume you have been driven to this desperate act because you wish to avoid imprisonment for debt. If you kill her, you will certainly avoid that, but then I shall be forced to shoot you, which I could really do without the bother of."

Lord Daniel snorted with laughter.

"You?" He said derisively. "You haven't got the skill or the balls to shoot me."

"I assure you, my lord, I am possessed of all the necessary male appurtenances," Sir Anthony replied, unfazed by this insult to his masculinity. "I also do have the technical skill to discharge my weapon. And even though I am terribly nervous at the thought of drawing blood – the sight of gore renders me quite nauseous and dizzy, my dear," he said, smiling affectionately at Beth, whose eyes were blazing with rage and fear, "- at this distance skill hardly comes into it, does it? I couldn't possibly miss." He took one step into the room, and seeing Daniel tense, stopped.

"I will confess to you," he continued evenly. "I am most terribly upset at the thought of taking a life, and although I shall do my best to aim for the heart and make a quick end of you, I am trembling so, that in spite of my best endeavours I fear I shall miss and shoot you in the stomach instead. I am assured that is a most lingering and agonising way to die." In spite of his words, the hand holding the pistol was as steady as a rock, the facial expression pleasant, friendly even, the dark blue eyes glittering, cold and hard.

Lord Daniel swallowed, and the sword blade faltered slightly. Beth pulled forward, but his arm round her waist stopped her from escaping. Sir Anthony held one hand up to her.

"Please stay still, my dear," he said. "I should hate for Lord Daniel to kill you by accident."

"I cannot go to prison," the young man said falteringly. "I could not survive it."

"Oh I do not think it need come to that," Sir Anthony replied.

In the shadows behind him Beth saw Lord Edward's mouth open, and Edwin's hand close over it to stifle his protest.

"What do you mean? If I don't go to prison for debt, I will surely go for what I have done tonight. I couldn't bear that."

"I cannot stop you going to prison for your gambling debts, Lord Daniel. Although I would be willing to make a small donation in order to secure you decent accommodation until your father sees fit to pay your debt and release you."

"He won't," Daniel said. "He has said so."

"Oh, I know your father well, dear boy. He will not let the future earl of Highbury languish in a debtors' prison for more than a week or two. As for tonight, well, you are amongst friends. I am sure that we can consider this little escapade as high spirits, a wedding-eve joke that was carried a little too far. If you let Elizabeth go now, you may leave, no harm done. No one need know any more about it."

"You can't be serious," he gasped. "Why would you do that?"

"Oh, dear boy, you may not believe it to look at me, but I have done many reckless things in my time, some of which I have lived to regret. I would not see a promising young man be disgraced for something that I might have considered doing myself, when a little younger and more impulsive. Of course if you go through with your intention to murder the young lady, then I am afraid I will be powerless to help you."

Lord Daniel thought for a moment. Beth's legs were starting to shake, and she put all her effort into steadying them. If she fainted now, she would cut her own throat.

"I have your word," the young man said after a moment, "that you will all allow me to leave unmolested?"

The three men behind Sir Anthony nodded reluctantly, although Richard's knuckles were white, he was gripping his sword so tightly, and his cousin's face was puce with rage.

"You have my word as a gentleman," Sir Anthony said.

In one quick motion Lord Daniel took the sword from Beth's throat and thrust her roughly forward, before turning and running out of the side door the minister had escaped from when he had first caught sight of Beth's rescuer.

Sir Anthony caught her as she staggered forward, and she leaned gratefully into him as his arms encircled her.

"Are you hurt?" he asked.

"No," she said, somewhat shakily. "But I would have been, if you hadn't arrived when you did. How did you know where I was?"

He didn't answer, looking instead over Beth's shoulder. Lord Edward and Richard had seized the hapless coachman, who instead of taking the opportunity to escape with the minister, had frozen, afraid Sir Anthony would shoot him if he made a sudden move. As she turned to look, Richard punched him hard in the face, although the man had made no attempt to resist arrest. Blood spurted from his nose.

"Stop it!" she said. "What are you doing?"

Lord Edward and Richard both looked at her in astonishment.

"I thought it would be obvious," Richard said. "This man abducted you."

"Lord Daniel abducted me," she pointed out. "This man was merely stupid enough to allow himself to be bribed." She knew the wages Lord Edward paid, and felt sympathy for him, in spite of the ordeal she had just suffered.

Edwin now moved forward to stand in front of the man. He took out his handkerchief and gave it to the coachman, who held it gratefully to his nose. He was shaking so violently he could hardly stand.

"What did he pay you to do, exactly?" Edwin said. Tom looked nervously over the MP's shoulder at Richard, who clearly intended the blow he had inflicted to be only one of many.

"He told me he would give me ten guineas if I stopped the coach at the corner of the Strand. He said that I would be doing the lady a favour, as she didn't really want to marry that homo…Sir Anthony, and that she'd be thankful to me for rescuing her."

In spite of the gravity of the situation, both Edwin and Beth smiled at the man's slip of the tongue.

"Did he actually give you the money?" Edwin asked.

"No. And I wouldn't take it now, sir, honest I wouldn't. If I'd known the lady was so against the match, I never would have agreed, I swear it."

"You're a damned liar!" said Richard, reaching past Edwin and hitting the man neatly in the stomach. "You'll hang for this, you bastard."

Beth made a move forward, sickened by the gleeful look on her brother's face, but Sir Anthony gently restrained her.

"Lord Edward, I assume you intend to dismiss the man?" he asked.

Edward looked at him.

"Good God, man, you think I would employ a man who aids and abets my cousin's abduction?"

"No, of course not. And some people would say that being dismissed without a character is a punishment in itself. May I suggest that as Elizabeth, and myself as her husband-to-be are the wronged parties here, that we may be the ones to determine what else is to be done with this scoundrel?"

That seemed fair enough, Lord Edward thought. You couldn't expect a woman to think rationally in these circumstances. They were far too soft. But Sir Anthony had just admitted the man was a scoundrel. He would certainly insist on the full weight of the law being brought to bear on this piece of scum.

"Of course, Sir Anthony," he said, ignoring Beth. "I leave the matter entirely in your hands." He actually stepped back out of the way, to emphasise the fact that he was washing his hands of the situation.

Richard, now in sole custody of the man, twisted his arm viciously up his back. Beth looked up at Sir Anthony, waiting to see what he would do before she raised any objections. The sight of her brother's obvious enjoyment at the pain he was inflicting had made her angry again, lending her new strength. Her legs no longer shook.

Sir Anthony looked down fondly at his fiancée.

"Well, my dear, I think I will leave it to you to determine the fate of this wretch. Call it an early wedding present." His eyes scrutinised her face. "Use it well."

She had no idea what he expected her to do, nor did she care.

"Let him go," she said, looking straight at Richard, who stared back at her incredulously. Tom was standing on tiptoe in an effort to stop his shoulder dislocating, and she saw her brother tighten his grip, forcing his captive's arm even higher.

"You're not thinking rationally, Elizabeth," he said.

"Let him go, Richard," she repeated.

The siblings locked gazes, the squalid surroundings and spectators fading into the background, eclipsed by their hatred for each other.

"I will do no such thing," her brother replied. "He deserves to hang for what he's done to you."

"Which is nothing compared to what *you* have done to me, *brother*," she replied, her eyes flashing, her voice ice-cold.

Richard flushed instantly scarlet and he let go of the coachman as though he had the plague. The man sank to his knees, clutching his injured shoulder. Richard raised his foot to kick him, but Beth held her hand up imperiously and he lowered it again. His eyes were blazing with hatred.

"Thank you," she said, looking up at her fiancé.

"My pleasure, my dear," he replied, twinkling down at her. "Are you hurt, Tom?" he called. "If not, I would suggest that you vacate these premises as quickly as possible."

The coachman needed no second telling. He got to his feet and stumbled out, still holding his shoulder, stopping briefly as he passed his saviour.

"Thank you," he said. "I won't forget this, Miss." Then he moved on into the shadows and was gone.

Edwin rubbed his hand across his face.

"Well, it's not what I would have done, Beth," he said. "But it was very Christian of you."

"Christian?!" snorted Lord Edward. "Insane, that's what it was." He looked at Sir Anthony with derision. "I pity you, sir, if you are going to allow your wife to make all your decisions for you."

"Oh, I don't intend to do that, my lord," Sir Anthony replied affably. "Only the ones which affect her personally."

"Did you mean what you said?" Beth asked on the way back to the house. She was riding in the coach with Sir Anthony, who had declared that he was so shocked and weakened by his experience that he was on the point of swooning, and could not possibly ride home. Edwin had stated that he would find it amusing to play the part of coachman, and Lord Edward and Richard had ridden off together, still grumbling about the softness of women, and the stupidity of men who allowed them too much leeway.

He did not appear in any immediate danger of swooning at her feet, so after a minute or two she had ventured the question.

"I said a great many things," he replied. "To which particular words are you referring?"

"When you said you didn't want Lord Daniel to kill me because it would be tiresome to have to find a new bride."

"Ah, you misquote me, my dear. What I actually said was that it would be tiresome to have to *seek* a new bride. But in fact I would not seek very far."

"Why not?" Did he have a stand-in ready, waiting in the wings?

"Because it is you that I want for my wife. If I cannot have you, I will take no other."

She stared at him, shocked, trying to ascertain his expression, but his face was in shadow, turned away from her as he looked out of the window.

"May I ask you a question?" he asked politely, lowering the blind.

"Of course," she said.

"What has your brother done to you to make you hate him so much?"

He turned to face her just in time to see the blood suffuse her face, and her eyes take on a hunted look. And then she had mastered herself and her voice when she answered was calm, her expression blank.

"Why, Sir Anthony, he has sold me to you, for a cornet's commission and some ready cash."

She expected flowery expressions of denial, a declaration of love perhaps, maybe the threatened swoon.

"And I have bought you, and your dowry, for the price of a cornet's commission, and some cash," he replied.

"Yes."

"Do you then hate me, also?" he asked.

"No," she answered immediately. "But I hate being part of a society that treats women as commodities, to be sold to the highest bidder. I know that is how it is, and I know all the arguments in favour of it. God knows, I've heard them often enough. I accept it. But I do not have to like it."

"And yet I think…I hope our union will be advantageous to you as well," he said. She did not reply, but looked away from him. "Do you wish to call off the wedding?" he asked unexpectedly. Her eyes widened with surprise, and she stared at him disbelievingly.

"I am no Lord Daniel," he said softly, leaning forward and taking her hands in his. "I will not force you to marry me, Elizabeth, neither at swordpoint, nor by any other means."

Her forehead creased. He was serious, she could tell that. There had been no flowery phrases, no 'my dear' at the end of every sentence. She had agreed to marry him because she thought he was blackmailing her into doing so. Now, for the first time, she wondered if she had misjudged him. She felt suddenly exhausted, drained by the evening's events. She could not make such an important decision now. She *had* to make her decision now. There was no more time. She stared at him, agonised.

"If you wish to avoid the censure of your family," he continued. "I will tell everyone that I could not possibly face the ordeal of marrying anyone after such a traumatic evening. I will declare that I am quite overcome, and swoon, and suchlike, and take to my bed for a few days, or a week, or however long it takes for you to decide whether you want to marry me or not. If you don't, you can say it is because you feel only contempt for such a weak specimen of masculinity. No one will blame you, I will make sure of that."

"You would do that, for me?" she asked.

"Yes, if you wish it. No one will be surprised. Do you wish it?"

She looked down at her hands, engulfed by his much larger ones. He still wore his formal cream calfskin gloves, now scuffed and dirtied by his headlong ride to save her. She considered seriously. Physically he repelled her. His primping and preening, his perfume and make-up were sickening. He was a gossip, and indiscreet. And in spite of his declarations of neutrality, he was a friend of the king she wanted to dethrone.

But he was also kind, considerate, educated and humorous. And he had never offered her violence. Would that change when they were married, and she became his property? She had no way of knowing for sure, but she did not think so. She took her hands from his, and sat back in the seat, as the coach drew to a halt outside the house.

"No, I do not wish it," she said. He let out the breath he hadn't realised he was holding until that moment. "I will marry you tomorrow morning, Sir Anthony."

"Are you sure? I want you to be certain you have made the right choice of husband."

"Few things are certain in this life, Sir Anthony," she smiled, feeling strangely light-hearted now the decision was made. "But one thing I am sure of."

"And what is that, my dear?" he said, handing her down from the coach.

"You are a far better man than my brother will ever be, sir, and that will suffice, for now," she replied.

Her light-heartedness was contagious. He tucked her arm in his, and they began to walk towards the house, Edwin bringing up the rear.

"I am glad to hear it, my dear, although I think you may change your mind when I tell you what I fear everyone in the house is now aching to be the first to say."

"And what is that, sir?" she said, laughingly.

He leaned down and whispered in her ear.

"You did what?!" she said, incredulous.

"Well, it was the fastest way to allow her to draw enough breath to tell me what had happened to you. Although now I fear that my action may have been misinterpreted. Poor Sarah. I cannot imagine what she must think of me."

Judging by the women now rushing to the door, Beth was certain his fears were justified.

"I would not waste your pity on Sarah. She will dine out on this for weeks. I think we need to save all our sympathy for ourselves."

They sighed in unison. The night had been long, and was far from over yet.

"May I make one more request of you, Sir Anthony?" Beth asked.

"Of course, my dear Elizabeth."

"My parents only ever called me Elizabeth when I was in trouble. I hate it. Please, will you call me Beth from now on?"

His lips curved in a smile, unseen by her in the darkness.

"I thought you would never ask," he replied, and they walked forward as one to face the onslaught.

About the Author

Julia has been a voracious reader since childhood, using books to escape the miseries of a turbulent adolescence. After leaving university with a degree in English Language and Literature, she spent her twenties trying to be a sensible and responsible person, even going so far as to work for the Civil Service. The book escape came in very useful there too.

And then she gave up trying to conform and resolved to spend the rest of her life living as she wanted to, not as others would like her to. She has since had a variety of jobs, including telesales, teaching and gilding and is currently a transcriber, copy editor and proofreader. In her spare time she is still a voracious reader, and enjoys keeping fit and travelling the world. Life hasn't always been good, but it has rarely been boring. She lives in rural Wales with her cat Constantine, and her wonderful partner sensibly lives four miles away in the next village.

Now she has decided that rather than just escape into other people's books, she would actually quite like to create some of her own, in the hopes that people will enjoy reading them as much as she does writing them.

Follow her on:

Facebook:
www.facebook.com/pages/Julia-Brannan/727743920650760

Twitter:
https://twitter.com/BrannanJulia

Pinterest:
http://www.pinterest.com/juliabrannan